A
Reluctant
Christmas Novel

By
J C Williams

Cover design by Drew Clark

Interior formatting and proofreading & editing by Dave Scott

ISBN: 9798327670037

First printing June 2024

You can subscribe to J C Williams' mailing list and view all his other books at:

www.authorjcwilliams.com

Books by JC Williams

The Flip of a Coin

The Lonely Heart Attack Club

The Lonely Heart Attack Club: Wrinkly Olympics

The Lonely Heart Attack Club: Project VIP

The Seaside Detective Agency

The Seaside Detective Agency: The Case of the Brazen Burglar

Frank 'n' Stan's Bucket List #1: TT Races

Frank 'n' Stan's Bucket List #2: TT Races

Frank 'n' Stan's Bucket List #3: Isle 'Le Mans' TT

Frank 'n' Stan's Bucket List #4: Bride of Frank 'n' Stan

Frank 'n' Stan's Bucket List #5: Isle of Man TT Aces

Frank 'n' Stan's Bucket List #6: Las Vegas

The Bookshop by the Beach

The Crafternoon Sewcial Club

The Crafternoon Sewcial Club: Sewing Bee

The Crafternoon Sewcial Club: Showdown

Life's a Pitch

Life's a Pitch: Rock the Rock

A Reluctant Christmas Novel

―――

Cabbage Von Dagel

Hamish McScabbard

Deputy Gabe Rashford: Showdown at Buzzards Creek

Luke 'n' Conor's Hundred-to-One Club

Chapter One

Last month, I wanted to jump off a cliff. It was on a Tuesday, I think. Or was it on Wednesday…? I dunno. The days often blend into each other. It was raining, that much I do recall. Although living on an island in the middle of the Irish Sea it does tend to have a significantly higher proportion of wet days, so that doesn't necessarily narrow things down.

No, in fact, it was *definitely* a Tuesday. I know this because I always take out Carol's (my neighbour across the road) bin for her on a Wednesday morning. And I remembered panicking that if I did jump off the cliff that day, I hadn't arranged for anybody else to take Carol's bin out for her the following day. Ever since her hip operation last summer, muggins here had assumed the role of her unofficial handyman, which generally involved helping her with anything a seventy-something widow with a dodgy hip struggled with, including, but not limited to bin removal, getting Christmas decorations down from the loft, grass cutting, and changing lightbulbs and such. I don't know how or why, but Carol seems to go through more lightbulbs than Blackpool in illumination season.

Still, I don't mind doing these things too much, and if I didn't step up and lend a hand then none of the other miserable buggers in the neighbourhood were likely to. Plus, my sporadic assistance wasn't an entirely selfless act. You see, Carol was, and is, a miracle worker around the kitchen. There are only seven houses in our modest development out in the middle of the Isle of Man countryside, and from the day I moved in, she's been feeding me homemade cake and biscuits, as well as the occasional lasagne. And, wow, Carol's lasagne is like a gift from the gods! Plenty of meat, loads of cheese, and the garlic and seasonings? Just *perfecto*. Hmm, I reckon I'll need to mention lasagne the next time I see her, as that might encourage her to get busy once more with the sheets of pasta and the lovely Bolognese sauce.

So, back to the reason that I'd originally settled on the 'clifftop swan-dive' option, was that I naïvely thought it would be a quick and efficient method. Just drive up, take in the view for a minute or two… and then jump. Easy-peasy. Well, that's what I had felt after another glass of Merlot when I was plotting the dramatic exit of me, Adam Catchpole, novelist.

However, the next morning, following my successful planning session, I'd woken up with a certain cynicism, plus a throbbing head like you wouldn't believe, as two bottles of wine on an empty stomach can do that to a man. Lounging on the sofa nursing my hangover, I started to doubt the wisdom of my 'glorious exit,' as it were. There was that issue of Carol's bins, of course. But also, I've never been particularly fond of pain. And ever since I got stuck up a gargantuan oak tree in my youth, I've never been too keen on heights either. So the thought of plummeting like a stone from a three-hundred-foot drop was starting to lose its appeal.

See, I couldn't help reflecting that everything I've touched of late has turned to shit (the very reason for my exit plan to begin with, as it should happen). So, as I had considered further—whilst eating a bacon sandwich, because a fellow's got to eat, after all— what if my master plan also went the shape of a pear? As in, what if I simply bounced off the rock face and came to rest on a jagged outcrop with multiple, severe lacerations and numerous broken bones for company? Realistically, there was every chance I could then fester on that outcrop for several days before eventually succumbing to my injuries, which wouldn't be ideal. Well, I suppose it would be from the point of view that it was a mission accomplished. But it wouldn't be a pleasant way to go, I shouldn't think.

Then, I allowed my mind to wander, imagining the hungry sea birds had started circling above, sensing the opportunity for an easy meal from a slightly overweight human who couldn't defend himself due to his snapped, useless limbs. And I've seen first-hand how those seagulls can demolish a portion of chips in short order. So they'd have had a field day plucking out my eyeballs and gorging themselves on my broken carcass.

Also, if I had driven up there by myself, then who would drive my car back? I always hate it when somebody else drives my car, mucking with the rear-view mirror's angle, adjusting the seat's position, and playing with the radio settings. And I couldn't have any of that, obviously. No, the more I reflected on it, jumping off a cliff wasn't for me. It simply wasn't the way to go. I'd need to go back to the drawing board and see what other end-of-life options were better suited to someone disliking heights. Or pain, for that matter.

But that was a few weeks ago, and this was now. And until an altogether more painless and efficient method presented itself to me, I would need to continue life's journey regardless…

Presently, after my morning shower and standing now at the top of my staircase, for the first time in weeks I didn't feel the over-whelming urge to throw myself down it. Some may have viewed this as a largely negative mindset, but I optimistically considered this a 'glass half full' scenario. I didn't even let the abandoned cob-web hanging agonisingly out of reach in the far corner of the stair-well ceiling for what felt like months dampen my spirits. Indeed, I took a mental note to attack it with a tea towel wrapped around the tip of a broom handle once I'd finished my bowl of Alpen break-fast cereal down in the kitchen.

I just hoped that this positive start to my day wouldn't be de-stroyed by the arrival of 'Pisa' Paddy, my postman around these parts ever since I'd moved in three years ago. He was nicknamed *Pisa* like the famous wonky tower, as Paddy, after thirty years of humping about a heavy mailbag, had unfortunately developed an issue with his spine, causing him to lean at a lopsided angle.

But Paddy was never without a jolly wave and a cheery smile whenever he called. I therefore sometimes felt guilty for wanting to punch him squarely on the jaw. Of course, I knew the content of the correspondence he was tasked with distributing wasn't in any way his fault. He was just the messenger, quite literally. It was just that whenever I received a letter telling me I was in arrears with my electricity bills or demanding that I urgently contact my mort-gage lender about overdue payments, it was always 'Pisa' Paddy, all happy and chirpy, who had just handed them over to me. And as I couldn't punch a utility provider or a mortgage lender in the face, Paddy unfortunately filled that void as a potential outlet for my frustrations.

Still, today would be better, I thought, while cautiously checking every inch of my tiled kitchen floor to look for evidence that Barriemore, my tortoiseshell cat, still had a gippy tummy from the day before. An unfortunate issue I had discovered while walking barefoot through the kitchen the previous morning. Luckily, the little guy appeared to have regained control of himself through the night, which was something of a result to start the morning.

Also, today was the first Monday in June. As such, Paddy's imminent arrival took on a different significance than his usual daily appearance. And the reason for this was that I was expecting the delivery of my quarterly royalty statement from my publisher. Why they didn't email it first and *then* stick a copy in the post was beyond me. Or, to save trees, simply email it to me and leave it at that. But my protestations fell on deaf ears, and the powers that be insisted on posting a hard copy, while emailing it through a week or so after that as well.

As a novelist/author/writer—or whatever you wanted to call yourself—that very first Monday of March, June, September, and December were undoubtedly the four most important days of the year. Why? Because that was when you discovered just how many copies of your books had been shifted during the previous quarter and, crucially, just how much cash would then be deposited into your bank account as a result of your endeavours.

Sadly, the last few royalty statements had confirmed that my overall book sales were much like my forty-something hairline—receding. But I wasn't alone in my pain, however, which at least afforded me some degree of comfort. Because while I was struggling, at least I knew my mortgage company and utility providers were also suffering alongside me. A point they were eager to stress each and every time they had the courtesy of writing letters to me with red ink notices stamped all over them.

But this hadn't always been the case. Indeed, for a period of about seven years or thereabouts, the arrival of my royalty statements was a cause for joy and much celebration, a time when the spondulicks were rolling into my bank account faster than I could spend them. That was a period in my life when the bank was more than happy to loan me the money to buy a much larger house than I ever needed. But now, on reflection, what did a single bloke need with a four-bedroom house in the countryside? After all, I'd rarely stepped foot inside any of the other three bedrooms in the last six months. I suppose that's what happens when an idiot with an ego starts to earn some decent money. It's also why the Porsche is currently parked in the garage much of the time, as I can barely afford to fill it with fuel these days.

Like many things in life, the popularity of certain stuff can start to wane over time, like shell suits, 3D TVs, and Noel Edmonds. As I had discovered over the last year, and as my bank account would happily attest, books were not immune from the changing tastes of the paying public. At first, I put the depressing numbers down to a seasonal variance and remained confident that things would pick up the following quarter. But that didn't happen. And after several months of banging my head against the side of my expensive 3D TV, I realised I wasn't a 'seasonal variance.' Instead, I was a "dwindling trend" according to my agent, who was knowledgeable on such things. Well, more so than I was.

Dwindling trend, I suspected, was a polite way of saying that my career was well and truly on the skids. A painful realisation that had shifted my attention away from the written word to thoughts of clifftop views and getting up close and personal with the island's population of hungry seabirds circling overhead.

But today, after breakfast and standing in my living room a bit later on this morning, I heard Paddy's van chugging up the winding country road at least thirty seconds before its arrival. "Yessir. Ten o'clock on the dot," I said, clapping eyes on my hallway clock, and then shifting my position to stand in the front doorway, ready to greet the postman like a doting parent waiting for their child to return home from school.

As I was often still in bed when Paddy would show up, I could already see him chuckling as he drew his van to a halt at the bottom of my driveway, like he knew something was afoot.

"You're up and dressed at *this* ungodly hour, Adam...?" Paddy joked, as he disembarked from his vehicle. "It must be that time again?" he hinted. "Hmm, is it *royalty* day or summat...?" he added, reaching into his mailbag to see what it might have in store for me. "Well, lemme just see what we have here..."

Walking up my driveway now, Paddy didn't seem to realise the significance of what was hopefully contained within the small wad of envelopes at his fingertips. I found myself unconsciously curling my right hand into a fist as I watched him ever so slowly making his way up my driveway—taking a step or two back periodically, and then hesitantly resuming—like a drunk staggering home from the pub. He clearly enjoyed teasing (or torturing) his client base.

It wasn't Paddy's fault that my blood pressure was approaching critical levels, I suppose, but he genuinely didn't appear to realise how close he was to perhaps being rugby-tackled. "Yep, it's that time of the quarter again, Paddy, sure enough," I replied casually, trying to make light of the situation, as he was generally a stand-up sort of guy. "So, you know... if you wanted to pick up the pace, buddy? It'd be..."

But he didn't pick up the pace, sadly. Instead, he stopped in his tracks, spun round, and pointed in the general direction of Bruce and Sheila's house at the top end of our little cul-de-sac. "You know what? I reckon I might mix things up a bit and do my deliveries in an *anti-clockwise* direction this morning, Adam...?" he announced cheerfully, and strictly for my benefit. "It's best to adjust one's routine on occasion, don't you think? Try something different once in a while...?" he suggested.

I could see he had a daft grin, but I just wasn't in the right frame of mind for it. And I felt guilty for my following sentence before the words had even exited my lips:

"For the love of God, Paddy! Just give me my bloody post, will you? Seriously, I'm not in the mood for any shenanigans today!"

Immediately, I could see his shoulders drop. It looked like he was about to try and apologise for his somewhat ill-timed attempt at humour, but I wasn't for listening to him just yet. I jogged down the driveway to meet him halfway there, as best I could manage for a forty-one-year-old wearing a pair of loose, floppy slippers, and snatched up the pile of envelopes secured with an elastic band that he kindly held out for me in his hand.

"I'm sorry, mate..." Paddy began. "You've been a bit down in the dumps, and I was just trying to perhaps make you..."

But I was already gone, having turned my back on the poor man so that I could retreat indoors without so much as a by-your-leave on my part.

The first three envelopes were rapidly launched in short order right in the direction of my giant frog-shaped bin in the corner of my kitchen, straight into the bin's laughing, open mouth. It's impressive, I liked to think, that I could now identify the companies I owed money to simply by the typeface they used for my printed address. A talent that saves me from quite a bit of additional administrative work in opening their correspondence.

And finally... there it was. The letter I was indeed waiting for. My agent, Millicent (also known as Milly) Maclean, had a habit of getting one of her team members to handwrite the address on all their external correspondence. It was a nice touch, I supposed, if not a tad labour-intensive. But it meant their letters were instantly recognisable, above all others.

I peeled open the envelope, warily removing the royalty statement like a student who'd just received their exam results. I'd long since lost interest in the details that made up the grand total appearing in the 'payment summary' portion of the statement, so I tentatively skipped that section, sucking in air through my teeth as I turned the page, saying a silent prayer that I'd soon be able to settle my mortgage arrears, catch up on my utility bills, and maybe fill up the fuel tank on my Porsche.

Barriemore, my cat, appeared to have a sixth sense about impending danger. Indeed, I could always tell when we were in for particularly nasty weather, as he would flat-out refuse to leave the house and would take up a defensive position behind the sofa until it passed. Fortunate, then, that he promptly vanished a moment before I began attacking my frog-shaped bin with a series of unexpected karate kicks. "You have to be freakin' kidding me!" I yelled as one of the frog's plastic ears (I wasn't even sure frogs had ears?)

was sent flying across the length of the kitchen, eventually coming to rest up next to the microwave, spinning to a gradual halt on the countertop. "Why are you doing this to me...?" I asked of no one specifically, screwing my royalty statement into a ball before pitching another determined assault towards the grinning, one-eared frog.

However, rarely in the history of mankind has a battle with an inanimate object had a positive outcome, especially when you're still wearing your fluffy slippers with the bottoms worn smooth. And that proved to be the case for me. With my right leg swinging towards the frog's head like I was about to score the winning goal in an FA Cup Final, the minimal grip on the worn-out sole of my left slipper was insufficient to keep me standing upright and I took flight, coming back to earth with a lung-busting slap against my tiled floor.

I don't think I lost consciousness. However, I can't be too sure, as the next thing I was aware of was the sandpaper-like caress of Barriemore's tongue licking my cheek.

It's fair to say my royalty statement wasn't quite the joyful news I'd desperately hoped for. Indeed, lying there supine on the cold floor, with blood possibly pooling around the base of my skull, my mind wandered, my thoughts turning to the critical question: *Just how many final reminders does a mortgage lender provide you with before the removal van arrives?*

But that was a question for another day. Because right now, I had more pressing matters to contend with. And with those pressing matters being me worrying about whether the damage to my frog-shaped bin was terminal, and also about how many vertebrae I may have just ruptured during my fall.

"Barry...?" I whispered softly, as my trusty sidekick continued licking my cheek. Although for a brief, chilling moment, I wondered if Barry thought I had died during the fall and was simply enjoying Adam Catchpole-flavoured hors d'oeuvres before getting stuck into the main course.

"Barry...?" I whispered again, struggling to raise my head from the floor. "Baz, go and raise the alarm, yeah? If that dog Lassie can do it without too much fuss, so can you..."

Chapter Two

The problem with agents, from my experience anyway, is that they can occasionally be somewhat fickle, unreliable creatures. I certainly don't say that to be unkind, as it's just a simple fact of life. As a writer—or I'd imagine within any creative industry—when you're flying high at the top of the bestseller's list, it's incredible how easy it is to contact your agent and how quickly they respond when required.

But the moment your book sales aren't quite hitting the same dizzy highs, or your last novel was, in the words of one particular 'esteemed' literary critic in my case, "the indolent ramblings of a scrivener who has long since lost respect for both himself and his readership," then your agent is busy, more often than not, each time you attempt to connect with them.

I laughed at the time, when that Sherman Buttress review had first landed. After all, my successful series of space opera books, *Intergalactic Zombie Wars* (think of *Star Wars* meets *Shaun of the Dead,* and you'll get the idea), were flying off the shelves, with talk of a television adaptation in the works. "And what does that toss-pot know about anything at all?" I casually remarked to the lads while having a pint or six at the time, shrugging off the criticism.

Well, quite a lot as it should happen, because it turns out that Sherman had his finger firmly on the publishing pulse and could see the writing on the wall a good few months before I could. An opinion that his two million or so followers on social media were now also privy to.

But I couldn't hate Sherman too much. After all, it was primarily due to his glowing praise of my early work that ultimately resulted in me securing a lucrative seven-book publishing deal that enabled me to buy the house I could no longer afford and a car that hadn't moved out of my garage in weeks.

In any event, given the current rate of my book sales, when I called my agent's office requesting a convenient time to speak with her about my most recent royalty statement, I was half expecting a brush-off from the person who answered the phone, with assurances that Millicent would phone me back at the earliest available opportunity (meaning pretty much the twelfth of never).

You can imagine my surprise when I was fitted in for a video chat later that same day. Grateful as I was, I then spent most of the morning worrying about why she was suddenly being so accommodating. And, already in a fragile mental state, it didn't take me too long to convince myself the reason she wanted to speak to me was so that she could promptly chuck me from her agency, what with my sales figures in a state of freefall as they were. It's funny, I reflected, that when your chips are down, it's ridiculously easy to be pessimistic about any potential outcome.

Of course if I lived in the UK where my agent was located, making contact with her would be much easier, as I would simply drive myself over to Milly's office. But living on an island in the middle of the Irish Sea, spontaneous meetings to assuage my spiralling depression weren't quite as effortless to arrange.

Now don't get me wrong, the Isle of Man is a tremendous place to reside—quiet, glorious scenery, and with the beach usually no more than ten minutes away in any direction. It's just that you can feel somewhat isolated at times. And even more so when your girlfriend decides that Giles, the estate agent who sold us my current house, is a better catch than I am. Which, to be fair, he probably was, on reflection—he had a cracking personality, and a marvellous set of teeth that I once threatened to shove my fist through. However, I was never a fighter. I always talked a good game, but I wasn't much of a physical threat when push came to shove.

Although in hindsight, Giles the estate agent may have done me a massive favour because Stacey, my ex-girlfriend, was one of *the* most self-centred, materialistic of persons I've ever met in my entire life. It was her idea, for instance, for me to buy the Porsche. One challenge, however, of living on an island only thirteen miles wide by thirty-three miles long was that you tended to bump into people quite often. Granted, that can be quite pleasant if it's an old friend from school or a mate looking for somebody to go for a pint with. Sadly, it's not so nice if it means that you keep meeting your former lover out gallivanting with her estate agent boyfriend with his impeccable teeth and his perfectly resilient hairline. (The absolute bastard!)

I've considered moving away, over to England, perhaps, for a fresh start and all that. But there was still something charming about living in a place where the risk of being mugged was always so negligible. For now, assuming I managed to avoid eviction from my house, the Isle of Man would remain home for a while longer.

By two thirty-eight in the afternoon, I was already on my sixth cup of strong coffee to help me stay alert and to fight fatigue. With the ever-present concern of my decreasing book sales and the prospect of becoming homeless, a good night's sleep was a luxury I'd not enjoyed for some time. The doctor prescribed some tablets to help the situation, but I'd so far resisted in taking them. After all, there were enough problems in my life without throwing chemical dependency into the mix as well (apart from the caffeine).

Sitting there, watching the screen on my laptop, I wondered how soon before a Zoom meeting you were meant to dial in. I was always early and ended up sitting there like a numpty for a fair bit as I waited for Milly or whoever to make their appearance.

In the past, I once tried to play it casual on a call she'd arranged with a production company when talk of a TV adaptation was first bandied about. I desperately wanted the deal to happen, although my confused logic told me to play it cool and dial into the video call at only the last minute, not wanting to seem too terribly over-eager. However, that meeting had also been my first introduction to Zoom, and by the time I figured out what access codes I needed to insert, I managed to disconnect myself and ultimately ended up being twelve minutes *late* for the meeting. The production team had insisted it "wasn't a problem," and we all had a jolly good laugh about my obvious struggles in making simple use of modern technology. That was two years ago, and I'm still waiting to hear how the TV adaptation is progressing, if in fact it's progressing at all.

So, yeah. Now I always dial in early, and I sit and wait.

"Hi, Milly!" I said brightly, once her familiar face popped onto my screen. I'd like to say it was a *friendly* face, but that was rarely displayed in my experience. It wasn't that she was unpleasant or anything like that. But she always appeared to approach any interaction with me in a strictly 'time is money' sort of manner, dispensing with the small talk and skipping straight over any idle chit-chat. As far as age, she was a difficult person to put a number on. Early to mid-forties, maybe? I'd never been brave enough to ask. Anyway, it's funny, I never really get intimidated by people, but there was just something about Milly that made me feel like a naughty schoolboy who was sent to see the headteacher. Perhaps it was her ruthlessly efficient manner or impeccable, no-nonsense dress sense.

Milly didn't look up from the stack of papers before her. "Hey, Adam. You're querying your royalties again?" she asked, getting fairly straight to the point as usual.

I cleared my throat, still anxious that she might look up at me at any moment and tell me we were parting ways. Although, from my experience of working with her over the years, she didn't come across as the sort who'd find it a challenge to just come out and say what was on her mind, no matter how difficult the subject.

"Uhm... yeah. That's right," I said tentatively. "Sorry to bother you. But I couldn't help noticing the figure in the payment column is once again smaller than what it was the previous quarter...?"

An uncomfortable silence ensued as Milly continued to examine what I could only assume were my sales figures detailed on the papers in front of her. I'm useless at awkward silences, and I always attempt to fill them with what I'm informed are nonsensical ramblings. I've also been known to break into song on at least a few occasions. But as Milly appeared busy studying the information on her desk—and did *not* seem to be building up to dismissing me as a client, or at least not yet—I remained silent for the moment, not wishing to break her train of thought.

I waited patiently for a response, conscious that Barriemore was currently circling my feet and being unusually affectionate— something he usually only does when he's hungry. He'd recently developed the frustrating habit of biting down on any exposed, available area of flesh when being ignored and his demands not immediately met. Which was the case now, in fact.

"Oi, bugger off, you!" I admonished as he started nibbling on my ankle, after which Milly finally looked up at me.

"I'm sorry, Milly, not *you*," I immediately stressed, pointing a finger downward, below the writing desk where I'd positioned my laptop. "Barriemore gets a bit physical when he's not paid attention to, so he's nibbling on me at present," I attempted to clarify.

Then, conscious that she had no idea who I was talking about and with it not being a typical animal's name, I panicked, worried she might think I'd got a new fellow in my life called Barriemore, who was currently doing something he probably ought not to be doing just now. So I reached down and picked the little guy up, dangling him before my laptop's camera like an angler showing off his latest catch. "This here's Barry…" I said proudly, as he rewarded me by lashing out with one of his paws towards my nose. As I was pretty fond of my sniffer, I promptly returned my pet cat to proper feline ground level. "I named him Barriemore," I explained. "You know, like the drummer from Jethro Tull? But I mostly just call him Barry, or sometimes Baz, for short."

"Very cute," Milly said, looking directly down her camera lens in my direction. "Now, about these sales numbers…"

"Not the best, are they," I answered, as more of a statement than a question. Because I already knew the answer—they were bloody awful!

Milly offered me a faint smile as she ran a hand through a portion of her shoulder-length hair, tucking some errant strands of it behind her ear. "Reader saturation, Adam," she said.

"Reader flatulation?" I answered, mishearing her.

Milly pressed the paperwork relating to my career to one side. "Saturation, yes," she said, resting her elbows on her desk and leaning forward a bit, while being gracious enough to ignore my obvious error. "You write in a niche genre, with only a finite number of potential readers available," she went on. "And you seem to have reached that maximum readership. At this point, you're unlikely to expand your customer base any further, and those who do enjoy your books appear to have pretty much devoured each volume already. It would explain why your book sales have steadily declined quarter on quarter."

I smiled politely. What she said certainly made sense, but I can't have exhausted *every* possible reader of the space opera genre on the entire planet Earth, surely...?

"Look," Milly continued, when I didn't reply right away, "Adam, you're a talented writer, as evidenced by the level of your previous success. But you desperately need to release a new novel in your series to appease your existing fanbase. Or, *instead* of that..."

There were already sixteen titles in my existing space opera series. And on the basis that I'd tried for months, with little progress, to expand that to seventeen, I was intrigued by Milly indicating a potential alternative. "Or...?" I said, happy to entertain any workable solution to the problem of my imploding career.

Milly waved to somebody outside of camera range, which I interpreted as me having roughly two more minutes or less of this meeting. Although, again, she didn't appear to be building up to dismissing me from her agency, at least. Which was a positive.

"Adam, you either churn out another book in your series, or, with a hungry readership desperate to consume something fresh, consider shifting focus to a different genre," she advised.

"But I have a passion for space opera!" I insisted. "And if I sell out to write something else, simply for a quick buck, then I'll only be cheating both myself and my readership," I told her.

If this were the answer to a question in an interview, I reckon I'd have definitely got the job. However, this *wasn't* a job interview, and Milly didn't appear overly impressed, and I saw her reaching for her computer mousepad.

"In that case, you stick to your guns, Adam," she responded coolly. "You must follow your dream and write what inspires you. However, we'll probably have the same conversation about your diminishing royalty payments in another three months."

She had a point I had to concede. Principles were one thing, but paying the mortgage was another more pressing matter. "Erm... what *other* genres had you been thinking about, Milly...?" I added quickly, before she could end the call.

"Romance is always popular. Even more so with a good smattering of titillation thrown into the mix. Everyone is drawn to some good titillation," she said.

"This is true," I answered, misunderstanding her once more. "People always love a good pair of—"

"Adam, apologies. But I've got another meeting to get to," she said abruptly, fortunately cutting me off before I could say something else stupid.

I'm not particularly good in the romance department (as my ex-girlfriend Stacey would be only too quick to attest), with my love life being presently non-existent, and a typical romantic gesture on my part consisting of little more than a bottle of wine and some kind of take-away food. In other words, not especially creative in that regard. As such, I couldn't say I much fancied my chances of penning a best-selling 'bodice-ripping' romance novel. "Sorry, before you go, Milly. Any other genres that sell particularly well…?" I enquired, desperately hoping for an alternate solution.

"Christmas," she replied, with her index finger hovering over her keyboard, ready to disconnect our call at any second. "Feel-good Christmas novels always sell well."

For me, this was an even *less* appealing prospect than catering for a bookshop full of horny housewives looking for a cheap thrill because, unlike most people, I hated Christmas.

"Yeah… I'm not too on board with either of those options, Milly. If I'm being entirely honest."

Milly shrugged. "If you want to make money, Adam, I've just given you two genres that are hot right now," she said. "Christmas books especially so."

Before I could respond one way or another, the video call came to its sudden conclusion. "Well, cheerio," I said to a blank screen, waving to nobody in particular. "Speak to you soon, yeah…?"

Leaning back in my chair with Barry the cat once again chewing on my ankle, I thought about Milly's suggestions. I could always press on with yet another episode of my (once) successful space opera series, I considered, looking at all sixteen titles lined up on my bookshelf by the window. But as I'd already been putting off doing that for at least several terribly frustrating, creatively unfruitful months, perhaps now was the time for a change of plan. However, I was possibly the most un-romantic person you would ever meet, so the prospect of attempting to write about that given subject sounded ludicrous in my mind. And that lack of a romantic bone in my body was also likely the reason I was still single, I further considered.

So, with a *Fifty Shades*-inspired smut fest on the backburner for now, that left me with the distinctly unpalatable option of writing a Christmas-themed novel instead.

"Oh, I bloody hate Christmas!" I whinged to Barry at my feet, before politely shooing him away with a flourish of my hand.

But that's when the miracle of Christmas, so to speak, presented itself before me, advising me of this option as the road to a resurgence in my overall fortunes. However, this wasn't the vision of three blokes on camels advancing towards a manger that convinced me I should write a Christmas novel. Nothing like that.

Rather, there was no shimmering Star of Bethlehem to guide my path forward, and my sign simply came in the form of three unopened mortgage statements distracting me from over on the edge of my desk. So, unless I wanted to live in a stable decorated in donkey manure rather than my comfortable countryside pile, I reckoned I'd best get busy writing some sort of Christmas novel. Only there was still one major problem...

"I bloody hate Christmas!"

Chapter Three

It was December, 1984. For weeks, there'd been a magical sense of anticipation wafting through the air. When it started, exactly, I don't recall. But it was the same thing every year, and it usually coincided around the time I would see the festive edition catalogue of my very favourite retailer, Toymaster, land on our Isle of Man doorstep. And even though I'd already put the big jolly guy in the red suit firmly on notice that year about what I was hoping to receive on Christmas morning, it still hadn't stopped me from poring over virtually every word and every image on every page, same as always (skimming straight past the Barbie doll section, of course). Indeed, in short order, I was so well versed in every detail of their product range that I could comfortably have worked in one of their showrooms—a possible career path I mulled over plenty of times during my youth.

And I wasn't alone. Because all of my fellow students at Onchan Primary School were equally invested in what was the most critical piece of literature produced each year, in our humble opinion. Far more valuable than maths or English textbooks. Mrs Corkhill, our teacher, would disagree with our festive priorities. But as an instructor of primary school children, I've no doubt she could appreciate that our loyalties might slip away from our education at that time of year. And I dare say that some of the giddy excitement in the air must have rubbed off on the faculty to some extent. After all, how could you be surrounded by hundreds of kids all drunk on copious amounts of festive cheer and not get caught up in the occasion yourself?

At home, from around the beginning of December, an influx of Christmas cards started to arrive, soon hanging from sections of string stretched out above the fireplace, like glittery little monkeys dangling from a tree branch. It wasn't long before the lengths of string started to bow under the weight of all the cards, forming a semi-circle display of Christmas wishes, with my mum's constant fear that one of the drawing pins might give way at any moment, sending them all crashing towards the open coal fire below.

Soon enough, as the days went by, more sections of string were being cut and pinned to the wall as the exhibition of cards multiplied exponentially. As such, the floral-print wallpaper was all but concealed until the first week in January at the earliest. However, this popularity came with its own problems, with mum and dad spending hours writing cards themselves, making sure to return the favour to everyone who took the time to send us one. And God forbid you received one and couldn't make out the sender's name. Such was the fear of being labelled a Scrooge that Mum would end up phoning through every contact number of *every* person written in her contact list to track the person down so she could be absolutely certain to reciprocate the gesture. It was a stressful time, that's for sure.

Also, there would always be a ready population of pre-written emergency cards and wrapped boxes of chocolates hidden away in the drawers of the hallway console table, only to be opened in case an unannounced visitor arrived on our doorstep bearing gifts (as was not unusual). Further, my sister and I were told in no uncertain terms what was likely to happen to us if that stash of emergency chocolates were interfered with at any point!

Being a mere slip of a lad at the age of eight, I didn't really have much comprehension of money other than the fact that it was pretty helpful in buying toys and sweets and such. I knew we lived in a council house—as did most of my mates—so I suspected we weren't rich by any stretch of the imagination. But with that being said, food was always on the table, and a new pair of trainers was available whenever I should need them.

We were often in and out of each other's houses around the estate, and it wasn't uncommon to have your tea in whichever house you happened to have ended up in after school. It was just the way it was. And in the run-up to Christmas, most parents went overboard trying to turn their houses into something the elves would be proud of. Corner-to-corner foil garlands would dominate the entire ceiling's available space, paperchains were draped around every lampshade, and shimmering foil stars would be distributed around every wall. I'll never understand how there wasn't a seasonal outbreak of house fires on the estate, as most of those decorations should have gone up in flames with the merest hint of a wayward ember from the coal fire. And that was without factoring in the danger posed by all the fairy lights, from which several plugs would often overburden every open electrical socket.

Against the backdrop of festive extremes, there was one house on the estate that never had any fairy lights, however, or any other type of decorations as far as I could tell. A boy the same age as me, Robert Bentham, had only recently moved in and lived three doors down from us. While we had an illuminated, flashing Santa Claus proudly positioned just inside our front window, only yellowing, nicotine-stained net curtains could be seen at Robert's home. Not to sound unkind or anything, but it seemed like you could always tell how poor a family was by how yellow their curtains were and how much they dipped down in the middle on the curtain wire.

Soon after he started school with us, he became the subject of constant ridicule because he always wore trousers at least three inches too short and he usually smelt of various types of cabbage. But I liked him anyway. He was always nice to me, so I was always nice to him. I had no reason not to be. It wasn't his fault his family was poor, for instance, and also, I actually didn't mind the smell of cabbages so much.

After classes one day, Robert came home to play Lego with me. He appeared totally mesmerised by all the fire-hazard Christmas decorations hanging from every inch of available wall space. And I had to drag him away from our tree, whose branches sagged under the weight of fairy lights and various red, green, pink, and blue glass baubles, accompanied by the first influx of wrapped presents already positioned at the base of the tree as well, teasing me daily. At that time, there were only a few more school days before breaking up for two weeks. TWO WHOLE WEEKS! The countdown to the big day was getting shorter.

And I couldn't help but notice another thing getting shorter—the length of Robert's trouser legs. His ill-fitting trousers were a regular feature of the school term, with the gap between his hem and the top of his scuffed shoes about the width of my hand at last estimation. And now, he wasn't wearing any pair of socks, either. This struck me as rather remarkable, considering it was wintertime and flipping freezing, with frosty mornings a common characteristic of the island's landscape.

"Uhm, you know you haven't got socks on…?" I felt the need to point out at the time, checking in case they were flesh-coloured or something and I was just missing them the first time I looked.

But Robert offered a distracted shrug in response, consumed as he was by the sparkling lights on our tree. I watched him staring without blinking for at least thirty seconds, as he was captivated like a caveman watching fire being made for the first time. I could see the flickering lights reflecting off his eyeballs, eyeballs which must have started to dry out by this stage.

Eventually, I dragged him away, as those Lego pieces wouldn't play with themselves. For the next hour or so, until Mum gave me the ten-minute warning that tea was nearly ready, we created a Lego fort that my plastic toy soldiers could claim as their temporary and well-constructed barracks. During that hour, I eagerly waffled about the main gift Santa was hopefully getting ready to dispatch. The most highly anticipated present it was possible to get was a Commodore 64 computer, along with several carefully selected games and a joystick. But I wasn't the first child in school to spend every waking minute daydreaming about plugging that magnificent piece of technological machinery in for the first time, as it'd been the conversation on *everyone's* lips since about July.

Once I'd finished talking about which game I would play first, I stopped for air, taking a moment to apply the final brick of Lego to our fort's watchtower. "So…" I asked Robert, kneeling across from me on the other side of our construction project, "What are you getting for Christmas?"

Robert looked up to his left, appearing to give the question a moment or two of thought. But then he looked straight at me, and with a shrug said, "I'm not really bothered about Christmas."

It took a moment to register what he had just said to me.

"*What?* You're not bothered about Christmas...?" I responded, replaying his words aloud, scarcely able to believe what I was hearing. Horrified, I asked, "There must be *something* you want...?"

"Hmm. I suppose I'd quite like a sparkly Christmas tree just like you've got. That was nice. I'd quite like that," he said.

I didn't know if he was being serious, because what eight-year-old could want a *tree* for Christmas—which, surely, everyone has got one of those anyway already—when there were Commodore 64 computers and BMX bikes up for grabs. But I didn't get to further quiz him on the matter because Mum's voice calling out from the other room advising that food was on the table told me that playtime was over for now.

"Do you want to stay for tea?" I asked.

"Nah, I don't think so," Robert replied. "I'd better get home and turn the chip pan on to heat up the oil."

Children didn't go near the chip pan in our house, so I assumed this to be an example of his quirky brand of humour. "Okay, see you tomorrow," I said, soon waving him off from the doorstep, unable to break my eyes away from his exposed, bare set of ankles.

❋ ❋ ❋

The final two school days were the best before we broke up for the Christmas holiday. Not only because we were rarely made to open a textbook, but in between carol services and an impromptu visit from Santa Claus, we were allowed to watch films in class as well. This particular year, my teacher even brought us homemade cakes and a tin of Quality Street sweets that was so big you could almost fit your head inside of it. It was bliss.

But even with all those lovely distractions, there was still time to discuss—at great length—each and every gift that was soon to arrive courtesy of the big guy in the red suit. By my reckoning, out of twenty-four kids in my classroom, at least thirteen of us had put a Commodore 64 on our Christmas lists. So not only did we have a shared interest and something to talk about, but with so many of us possibly owning the same device, there was every chance that between us all we'd probably own most of the games available—which we could then swap between us as we finished each one.

With so much to eat and to talk about, it didn't strike me that Robert Bentham wasn't in class. Indeed, it was partway through the last day before I noticed his seat was empty.

"Uhm, where's Robert…?" I asked of no one in particular, curious, and looking around the classroom for answers.

"He's probably rolling around in a bushel of Brussels sprouts," came the quip from one of my unconcerned classmates, who was also pinching his nostrils from the imagined smell as he said it.

I don't know why I did it, but I laughed along with the rest of them at poor Robert's expense. I immediately felt awful for doing so, even though he wasn't present to witness it. But any feelings of guilt on my part were soon set aside when Mrs Corkhill reappeared in the classroom, dragging the TV trolley behind her. "Who wants to watch *Mickey's Christmas Carol*?" she asked, before receiving the class's rapturous and enthusiastic response.

Later in the afternoon, the moment the school bell rang, there was an immediate mass exodus. In the panic to escape for the festive holiday, I nearly forgot to hand in the box of biscuits that Mum had made me bring along as a present for my teacher. "Have a good Christmas, Mrs Corkhill," I said, placing the box on her desk before I was swept into the corridor by an avalanche of excitable kids. Ordinarily, a few of us would typically hang around for a kick about on the school playground, but it was freezing, and plus I'd heard Mum mention that morning a hot chocolate would be waiting to welcome us home. I didn't even wait for my sister, who was in a class three years above me and in her final year of primary school.

The walk home was less than a quarter of a mile. Maybe a ten-minute walk on a good day and a good while longer if something took your interest on the way, like a rope swing or a potential location to build a new fort. But with the promise of hot chocolate on the table, I aimed for a personal best time of about six minutes.

The sun was already starting to get a bit low in the sky at that early time of the day, with a wicked chill in the air. Jogging up our street, I was drawn to the flashing fairy lights many houses had running along the length of their guttering. With any thoughts of school now a distant, fading memory, I felt like I was about ready to burst with a severe case of festive fever. Then, as I approached Robert Bentham's house, I was hit by an overwhelming sense of guilt once more for being part of the group who was laughing at him in the classroom. He considered me his friend, and yet for some reason I had been one of those giggling the loudest.

I slowed, wondering why he was absent from school. Not only were there no flashing lights fixed to the guttering of his house like the others, but I couldn't see any lights on a tree through the front window either. In fact, Robert's house appeared to be in complete darkness, with no sign of anybody at home at the moment. Perhaps he'd gone away for Christmas, I thought, walking past his house with the allure of Mum's hot chocolate still propelling me firmly onward.

I don't know why, precisely, but I then came to a halt, doubling back on myself until I was stood at Robert's gate. I walked up the concrete path to his front door, wondering if the worn-out fridge dumped in the front garden was now a permanent feature, as it had been left there for some time by now. Once at the door, I only knocked once, and not very loudly. Because the last time I called, Robert's dad had stuck his head out from an upstairs window and shouted down to "sling your hook before I set the dog on you." I never did ask Robert if his dad had purchased a dog at some point. If he did, I don't recall ever hearing it bark.

I pressed my nose against the frosted glass of the front door and spotted the shadowy outline of a figure moving slowly my way. Fortunately, it looked like a kid-sized person like me, rather than a larger adult-sized figure like Robert's dad. The silhouette of his dad would've been instantly recognisable as well, at least when viewed from a certain angle, as he had a belly like a pregnant woman.

The front door opened, but only a bit, and part of Robert's head tilted into view in the partial gap.

"Hiya. You weren't in school, mate," I said, although he was certain to be already aware of today's absence. "We watched *Mickey's Christmas Carol*," I told him. "And Mrs Corkhill brought this tin of sweets in that was so big that I could practically fit my whole…"

Maybe it was the guilt still simmering away, but I wanted to fill Robert in on everything he'd missed and hopefully convey the excitement we'd all experienced in class. However, I didn't finish my sentence as Robert emerged from behind the door, appearing only in his school gym clothes. But more importantly, I could see he had a massive gash above his eye, and a dark semi-circle underneath it, as if he'd smeared himself with coal dust. One side of his upper lip was swollen, and it looked split, with dried blood forming a scab over the crack. I stood there staring, not knowing what to say.

"Ttthounds good," Robert attempted to say, the damage to his lip apparently making it difficult for him to speak correctly. He sounded a bit like Daffy Duck when he talked, which ordinarily I would have found funny. But definitely not this time.

I couldn't look at Robert's face, so my attention wandered over his shoulder towards the living room, which had the same layout as ours. It was murky inside, as there were no lights on. But I could see no foil decorations hanging from the ceiling, no Christmas tree covered in fairy lights, and from where I was standing, I couldn't see any evidence of any Christmas cards hanging on string either. The room appeared cold, uninviting, and gloomy.

"Get away from that door!" screamed a furious voice, abruptly, from somewhere inside. "Robert! Get inside now!"

Robert didn't need to be asked twice, I reckon, and slammed the door shut, leaving me in the chilly, drizzling rain, which had just started. I didn't hang about for long, only long enough to hear the raised voice from behind the door getting decidedly louder. I spun around, moved out to the street again, and then sprinted the short distance to my house, at which point I was sure I could still hear yelling coming from inside of Robert's home.

I didn't say anything to my mum about what I'd just seen. I'm not sure why. I suppose, when you're the age I was, it's not so easy to put things into words as well as you'd like. Plus, if something's troubling you, it's easier sometimes just not to talk about it.

But as I enjoyed the mug of hot chocolate that was soon warming my hands, all I could think about was when Robert had said he wanted a sparkly Christmas tree from Santa. At the time, I thought he was mad. After all, again, what eight-year-old boy only wants a Christmas tree? Or would even have to ask for one to begin with?

But from my brief glimpse into his unwelcoming home, bereft of any kind of love, or decorations, or anything else, it started to make more sense. I could understand why having a sparkly tree was the only thing Robert Bentham might wish for Christmas that year. And that realisation made me sad. Desperately so.

Chapter Four

I had no intention of telling anybody, least of all my contingent of followers on social media, that I was going to start writing a Christmas novel. They were a loyal, engaging sort who regularly reached out if they wanted to talk about a character in my novels, quiz me on a particular plot point, or even pitch me ideas for future books. But my readers were, generally speaking, the sort who might turn up to a comic book convention dressed as an oversized Ewok, for instance, and who knew the details of every alien who'd ever made an appearance on any of the various iterations of *Star Trek*. And I certainly don't say that as a derogatory statement, as that community *is* somewhat unconventional. They're real salt-of-the-earth individuals who are fiercely committed to any franchise they're keen on.

Indeed, I'd often post messages to my social media fan base if I wanted to run an idea by them or ask for input into a new character's name. But while this enthusiastic group were subject matter experts on intergalactic exploration and warfare and the like, they probably weren't quite so knowledgeable about the plotline for a wholesome, family-oriented Christmas-themed novel.

So rather than just diving in cold, headfirst into the subject, I first needed to do some research. As a writer, I'd gathered the hard way that what I think is a popular, sure-fire winner of an idea isn't necessarily what the great reading public might believe. This is a harsh reality I first became aware of when sales of my debut attempt at writing came to about fourteen copies in total, if I recall correctly. Thirteen of them were snapped up between my mum, my sister, and myself. I still have three paperback copies kicking around somewhere that might possibly be worth a fortune one day, like an early version of the Apple computer. That first novel—

a story about an unscrupulous pirate (aren't they all?) who picked on the wrong ship, packed full of ninjas—was imaginatively called *Pirates vs. Seasick Ninjas.* In my naïve opinion, it was a quirky but guaranteed best-seller and sure to pave my way as a true force in the literary world. It wasn't, and it didn't.

My fledgling effort is still a source of embarrassment for me twenty years later. But as I consoled myself at the time while being mercilessly teased by my mates in the pub when the book didn't quite make it onto the bestseller's lists, I'd still managed to write a full-length novel (which is more than most could, I reckon), and I was immensely proud. Proud and skint.

The problem for a writer, however, is the time it takes to determine if you might've made a monumental error of judgement. If you were, for instance, a tree surgeon and a giant larch ended up crashing through the roof of your paying customer's home, then you would rapidly know you'd made a huge mistake the very moment you witnessed the tree falling in the wrong direction on its way earthward. And then a very short moment *after* that as well, as the furious property owner came storming out of their house, demanding to know why a tree had suddenly taken up unscheduled residence in their living room.

But if you're writing a book, on the other hand, it might take you a solid six months, maybe longer, to pen your masterpiece. All the while, you convince yourself that your novel will be a sensation, and that you'll have people camping outside bookshops the night before in order to secure a copy. Because of this, it's vitally important (as I found out with my group of seasick ninjas, though still a masterpiece, as far as I'm concerned) to do a bit of research and ensure that what you're planning on creating has a hope in hell of selling. Otherwise, without such previous exploration, you may end up frittering away the better part of a year—which includes editing time and so forth—of your life with no money ultimately coming in the door to compensate you for your troubles and all that time invested.

My present issue was that I, not being a big fan of the day myself, wasn't particularly clued up about Christmas. Or to be more specific, what aspects of Christmas might resonate with potential buyers so that they might part with their hard-earned cash to read about it. Even though the subject matter was quite specific, it can still be a bit tricky. To put things in context, both *Die Hard* and the British TV film *The Snowman* are considered to be Crimbo-themed movies. But for content, both are poles apart, so to speak, attracting wildly differing audiences.

For my own particular story, I imagined a cosy, heart-warming type of cheese-fest novel, one in which good overcomes bad, being my best chance of commercial success. But even considering this idea as a possibility made me gag. It wasn't really my kind of thing. Plus, hadn't this sort of tale been beaten into the ground already? Was there genuinely a market for yet *another* one of these stories like this, as my agent Milly suggested? Or in adding to the heaping pile, would I simply be flogging a dead wombat?

I figured I needed to pose these questions to somebody more of an authority on the genre than I was. A voracious reader who consumed mushy novels by the shedload. Someone unabashedly addicted to stories that were far sweeter than Lyle's Golden Syrup. Yes, my older sister Helen was the perfect person to opine on such matters.

As such, a meeting with Helen was duly arranged to discuss the situation in one of the plethora of coffee shops that seemed to have sprung up from nowhere in the island's capital city, Douglas.

Waiting patiently for my order at a café called It's a Mug's Life, I was reeling from the fact that two very thin slices of carrot cake and two small lattes had cost me nearly twenty quid. Granted, it had been a while since I'd last ventured into town, but seriously...? Also playing on my mind was the name of this establishment. I'm all for quirky wordplay, and I love a pun as much as the next fellow, but I couldn't figure out if it worked or was merely suggesting its client base was a bunch of mugs.

"Adam Catchpole!" the cheery young lady called out, holding a tray over the countertop in my direction. But I was evidently too consumed with trying to come up with an alternative witty name for the coffee shop, because I just stood there like a silly muppet, not responding. "Adam Catchpole!" she said again, and as only two people were currently stood there waiting for their orders, me and an older lady cradling a white handbag-sized dog in her arms, it was a fair assumption that I was the only Adam Catchpole present.

"I think that's you…?" the dog-holding lady said, freeing up one of her hands to tap me on the elbow, likely eager to get me out of the way so her own order could progress.

I snapped back to reality, still wondering if IT'S A MUG'S GAME would have been an improvement on the name of the place. I was tempted to ask the dog lady for her opinion on the matter, but the shop assistant's arms looked like they were beginning to wobble from holding out my tray of goods for longer than expected, so I thought better of it.

"Sorry, I was miles away," I apologised, unburdening the young woman behind the counter so she could move her attention to her other waiting customer.

My sister Helen had secured a table next to the window so she could no doubt observe the shoppers going about their business. She always was a nosey bugger.

"I brought over some carrot cake for us," I said, placing the tray down while noticing she'd already started in on a slice of lemon drizzle while waiting for me. I collapsed into one of the soft, black leather chairs, the sort that looked like it was once part of a living room sofa suite. It was the type of chair that swallowed you up whole when you sat down in it, leaving you to wonder how you were meant to get up again.

"What's with you and carrot cake?" Helen asked.

"What do you mean?" I said.

"You never get anything else," she remarked.

"I like carrot cake," I said with a shrug.

My sister, with a chunk of lemon drizzle on her fork, stopped to consider me with a quizzical eye, looking at me funny and not saying anything for a moment.

"What? I just like carrot cake!" I protested.

"No, not that. You're not ill, are you…?" she asked, pointing her fork at me.

Now, admittedly, I wasn't getting much sleep, what with all the financial worries. But still, I didn't think I looked *that* bad when I checked in the mirror before leaving the house.

"Ill? I don't think so," I said.

Helen popped the forkful of cake into her mouth, staring at me intently. "That's good. But what's with the invite for coffee, then? Not that I'm complaining, of course. Just pleasantly surprised."

"How are the kids?" I asked, figuring I'd better exchange some pleasantries before jumping straight into why I'd invited my sister along for an unexpected, overpriced coffee.

"They both want to see more of their Uncle Adam," Helen immediately replied. "You know how much the boys treasure spending time with you."

I lowered my head like a naughty canine pet who'd been told off for chewing its master's shoes. My first instinct was to suggest I'd been too busy to visit, but that was a barefaced lie as I hadn't written anything to speak of for several months now.

"I know. I'm bloody useless," I had to admit. "How about I come over at the weekend and take them both out for the afternoon? Maybe take them for a kick around on the beach, and then an ice cream after?"

True to form, Helen was enjoying a good nosey through the window. "They'd like that," she said, as she waved to a shopping-bag-laden woman walking by. Then, returning her attention to me and reaching for the carrot cake I'd provided, she asked, "So how are you, then? What is it that's brought you out here today?"

"I need your advice on something," I confessed.

"It's not about women, is it?" asked Helen. "Because I once told you what I thought about that Stacey, and you didn't listen to me then," she said, although she didn't sound like she was having a go at me, I don't think.

"You did. And you were correct," I was willing to concede. "No, but what I actually wanted to ask you about was work."

"Work? As in books?"

I nodded, taking a sip of my latte. I very much wanted to tuck into my carrot cake as well, but the chair that'd swallowed me whole made it difficult for me to manoeuvre as such. "Yeah. You see, my agent Milly suggested a change of genre might make some commercial sense."

"What, so you're not going to be writing about little green men shooting each other in oversized rocket ships anymore?"

I smiled, taking no offence from her distinct lack of knowledge about the subject matter of my books. Because besides my mum, Helen was my biggest supporter, telling anybody she came across that I wrote books, often thrusting my business card in their hand regardless of whether they wanted it or not. And a lesson I learned early in my career as a writer was that not everybody will appreciate your writing. Indeed, a friend of mine was an expert angler and wrote an exceptionally concise book about that subject. Now, I don't like fishing, so there was no point in me buying his book because it would've simply sat unread on my bookshelf. But what I did instead was to make sure that if I ever spoke to anybody even remotely interested in any variety of fishing, I made certain, and took great pleasure, in introducing them to the work of my friend Alan. Any writer wants their books in the hands of people who will read them, and who will, hopefully, also recommend them to their friends if they enjoy it. So, my sister's confession that she didn't really 'get' space opera was completely fine because her being my biggest advocate was significantly more important than selling one of my books to her, which would only sit and collect dust.

"No, I'm thinking of taking a break from little green men and trying something different this time," I told her.

"Oh. Such as?"

I might have winced at this point because I knew precisely what reaction I would receive to my following statement.

"Well, I'm thinking of writing a Christmas-themed book, actually, and..."

Helen didn't disappoint. And if she wasn't enjoying her carrot cake as much as she was, I suspect she'd have spat it right out. She laughed, and then finished chewing what was in her mouth so she could properly respond.

"But you hate Christmas!" she said, wiping a few crumbs away from her chin.

"I don't *hate* Christmas," I said in protest, though perhaps not so convincingly.

"You don't? Really? So when was the last time you bothered to put up decorations?"

This I had to think about. I'd been in my newish house for four years or so, and then before that, there was that flat in...

"Okay, so I don't decorate," I admitted.

"Trying to convince you to come for Christmas dinner is like pulling teeth. And I've invited you to the boys' carol service every year, and very rarely do you ever—"

"Okay," I said, holding up my hand in apology. "It's fair to say I'm unlikely to become one of Santa's elves any time soon. That's precisely why I need your help, though. Because it was either writing a Christmas-themed book, or..."

"Or?"

"Or one of those saucy, or maybe cheesy..."

"Cheesy sauce? What, like a cookbook or something?"

"No, not that," I said with a laugh, although I did sort of like that idea. "No, I meant one of those saucy, cheesy romance novels. You know, that frustrated housewives binge-read?"

This appeared to amuse Helen, if her mirthful grin was anything to go by. "So your present options are to write a Christmas story, or some kind of predictable, clichéd romance novel?"

"That's about the size of it," I said, before taking another sip of my latte, and realising it was about ninety percent froth and ten percent actual coffee. "Apparently, they both sell extremely well."

"Yes, I can see your problem," Helen advised, nodding sagely.

"You can?"

"Sure. You're rubbish with women, possessing no knowledge at all about them, and you don't like Christmas. No offence."

"I wouldn't say I'm *rubbish* with..." I started to reply. But there was little point in protesting again because Helen was only confirming what I already knew myself to be true.

"Right. Guilty on both counts," I conceded. "But I reckon I've got a fighting chance with a Christmas novel, because I at least understand the general concept. Whereas women? Well, that's another kettle of fish altogether."

It was getting noisy in the packed coffee shop, which appeared to be doing a roaring trade. I attempted to lean forward in my seat, which was a challenge. Each time I tried to move, it was as if the soft leather didn't want me to escape, like the furniture equivalent of quicksand whenever I attempted to adjust my position. Eventually, and to Helen's amusement, I perched on the edge of my seat, leaning over the table between us to be heard without shouting. "As somebody such as yourself, Helen, who both fully embraces Christmas and loves reading," I said, "I hoped to gain your insight into what might make for a compelling Christmas novel."

Helen considered this question momentarily, tilting her head one way and then the other. "How does Christmas make you feel?" she eventually asked. "Deep inside. In *here*," she added, placing her hand over her heart.

I resisted the urge to roll my eyes, because I knew she was genuinely trying to help me. "Well, if you're asking me how I honestly feel about it… then I'd say it was an expensive waste of time where people generally tend to overeat, drink too much, and cause themselves a harmful amount of unwarranted stress to live up to an unrealistic vision of festive perfection designed by marketing executives in large corporations."

Helen swatted a hand towards me like she was batting away a bothersome wasp. "Okay, just for a moment, let's try and cast the cynical, bah-humbug version of Adam aside, shall we?" she suggested. She then swept the same wasp-swatting hand out in front of her, slowly and illustratively. "Now, close your eyes and imagine you were getting into the mind of your potential target audience, yeah?" she said. "The sort of person who's just bought your book is about to curl up on the sofa in front of a roaring fire with a mug of steaming hot chocolate, or maybe even better, perhaps a mulled cider or hot toddy."

"Okay, well I do like that last bit," I offered. "Is there snow falling against the glass…?" I asked, doing my part in attempting to picture the scene as instructed.

"Ooh, yes. There *has* to be snow!" replied my sister. "*Now* you're getting in the spirit!" she said.

My eyes were closed, but if I knew Helen, she was nodding enthusiastically right about now. But I *wasn't* getting in the spirit. Not really. "So you're saying people want to feel wrapped up and cosy on a cold day with a roaring fire?" I asked, taking her scenario a bit too literally and perhaps missing the forest for the trees.

"No," said Helen. "Well, yes, they do," she added. "But it's more than only that."

Helen then elaborated on the subject, long enough for me to finally tuck into my meagre slice of cake. And what the portion may have lacked in size, it more than made up for in taste. So much so that I was tempted to revisit the serving counter for a second helping, regardless of the exorbitant price.

"So…" Helen said eventually, in summary of her explanation. "People want to escape to a world full of festive, feel-good cheer, to a place where decency always comes out on top, and where peace and good fortune ultimately triumph over adversity."

I desperately wanted to repeat my previous theory about large corporations trying to sell a vision of a world that didn't exist, but I resisted. I resisted because I could see from the twinkle in Helen's eyes that she was sold on the idea, which was important to her. Plus, as the type of reader completely invested in the genre I was about to embark upon, if this is how Helen felt, I thought I should listen to her.

"Thank you," I instead settled on as a response.

And I could certainly understand where she was coming from. After all, it was the age-old foundation of good against evil—like Luke Skywalker versus Darth Vader from *Star Wars*, or like Daniel LaRusso versus Johnny Lawrence from the *Karate Kid* films. But I suppose what I was hoping for from this coffee chat, besides some quality time with my sister, was for her to maybe give me a killer plot idea for a kickass Christmas novel. But, on reflection, life was never that easy, and I reckon I'd just need to consider the matter further myself.

Helen was still imagining herself curled up on a sofa in front of a roaring fireplace if her vacant, happy expression—like she'd just smoked something she shouldn't have—was any yardstick. Then, she was staring directly at me, with her schmaltzy look hardening now into something more serious. "Adam…" she said earnestly. "Adam, I completely understand why you don't particularly like Christmas. But for your sake, you must realise that what happened when we were kids was not in any way your fault. You *know* that, right…?"

The question caught me off-guard. I wanted to relax into my chair but didn't want to face the battle of trying to get back out of it again, plus risk losing the coins in my pockets falling down into the sides of the thing.

"I know," I said softly.

Helen leaned over and took my hand in hers. "Adam. It *wasn't* your fault. You have to know that!"

I forced through a smile, not saying anything for a moment or two, knowing I might begin to lose my composure in the packed coffee shop if I did, my emotions spilling out into the open.

"You know what you need to do?" Helen said, shifting the direction of the conversation and getting it back on track, thank goodness. "What you need to do if you want to get into the Christmas spirit, that is, and see what sort of thing sells…?"

I raised one eyebrow, as my positive response that I wanted to hear more from her.

"There's a TV channel with cheesy Christmas films on twenty-four-seven in the run-up to the season."

"It's only June!" I managed to say.

"They're also available online," Helen pointed out to me. "You can even download them and save them for later if you want," she added helpfully. "You see, some folks, including myself, occasionally need some cheer during the summer months," she explained.

Bloody hell, I thought to myself, although of course I didn't say it out loud. Instead, I cleared my throat. "So you're saying I should watch a few treacly, insufferable, gag-inducing Christmas films?" I asked. "To get a feel for things?"

"Yes. That's absolutely what I'm saying to you, Adam," my sister responded. "Once you've done that, report back, and we can possibly thrash out a few feel-good, uplifting plot lines for you."

"Helen? Helen, you're imagining yourself on the sofa before the roaring fire again, am I right?" I asked, noticing that her same contented, faraway look had returned yet again.

"Yes, Adam. Yes, I am…"

Chapter Five

I'd like to say I completely cleared my schedule in order to do as my sister Helen suggested, but as there wasn't anything on my schedule to begin with, there was nothing to clear. Although I did have a mental note to apologise to 'Pisa' Paddy, the postman, as I was a bit short with him when he'd dropped around to deliver my royalty statement the other day.

I was still unhappy about the dwindling book sales, but armed with a plan of attack, such as it was, I had a semblance of positivity about my current situation. I took solace in knowing that my existing books *were* still selling, at least (though granted, not in the numbers I would have liked), so it wasn't as if there was *no* money coming in the door. And on the subject of money, I'd even arranged a meeting with my bank, conscious that I'd soon suffocate if I continued to bury my head in the sand for too much longer.

For now, I needed to get some general idea of a plot formed in my head. I was one of those writers known as a *pantser*—as in "fly by the seat of your pants." Essentially meaning that you just jump in without too much planning and forethought other than a rough outline and a curious mind for where this thing was going to take you. On the other end of the creative spectrum were those writers labelled *plotters*—those who generally mapped out each and every chapter before even putting pen to paper or setting fingertips to keyboard. They ordinarily had a very clear idea of how the story would progress before they started. I sometimes admired those writers who knew precisely what they were doing before they began. Although there was also the danger, that way, that you could drown under a sea of yellow Post-it notes on which thousands of minor plot points were detailed and never actually get round to the writing. Indeed, some of my most significant plot elements might arrive to me when I was several chapters in, something that was unlikely to happen if I was organised enough to chart out the story in advance.

I had no intention of spending weeks in development for my new project. All I needed was a general feeling of which direction I wanted to go. And this would primarily be driven by what I felt would be commercially popular. After all, I was unashamedly doing this genre shift to pay the bills. I needed to figure out if I was going down the humour route, perhaps a rom-com sort of thing, some type of feel-good, uplifting adventure. But I wasn't averse to tackling a more serious, tear-jerking sort of plotline if I thought that would sell.

And, taking my sister's advice, I'd placed several Christmas film offerings in my queue, put my comfortable pants on, and prepared myself for an entire day of watching the TV (no real change to my recent routine, to be fair, except for the selected viewing choices).

However, it hadn't even started snowing in my first film of the day when my front doorbell interrupted my important research. And I'd only just got the sofa cushions as I liked them.

Since most of my usual visitors were at work at this time of the morning, between breakfast and noon, I thought this would likely be the postman, or possibly the nice woman who comes by to read my electric meter periodically. But it was neither. Because I soon caught sight of a particular silver-haired lady of about five foot in height through the window.

"Morning, Carol," I said to my neighbour once I'd opened up my front door. "If you need me to change a lightbulb, might I do it later...?" But I soon noticed Carol was currently wearing an apron, which set my taste buds to tingling in a sort of Pavlovian response.

"No, I'm all good on the lightbulb front, Adam," she said. "I was going to start assembling a lasagne today, and I wondered if—"

"Carol, I would crawl over a bed of jagged broken glass on my bare knees for one of your lasagnas," I instantly replied, leaving my guest in no doubt as to my response.

But rather than heading back to her house to commence work in her kitchen, Carol remained on my doorstep, looking up like she was expecting something of me.

"Erm... do you need something else, Carol?" I asked, although not in an impolite, *get-off-my-property* sort of way. "Does the grass need a trim or something? Because you know you just need to ask."

"That's very kind, Adam. But that's not what I was waiting for."

"It's not...?"

"No. I need my lasagne dish back."

I ran a hand through my thinning, dishevelled hair, suddenly conscious I'd not yet even brushed my teeth this morning either, worrying as to how presentable I might appear. "Oh, sorry, Carol. Have I still got your dish...?"

Carol offered a polite sort of laugh. "Yes. By my calculations, you should have *three* of them," she said.

I immediately panicked, wondering how I'd managed to accumulate that many of her lasagne dishes, and if they were dirty or clean, or heaven forbid lost. "I'm sorry about that. Do you want to come in while I have a look for them?"

Carol indicated a finger towards her apron, fully covered in a heavy dusting of a white, powdery substance that made her look like she had the world's worst cocaine habit. "No, I've been baking bread this morning, and I don't want to shed flour all over your nice carpet."

"Right-ho, Carol. Give me a tick, and I'll root around the kitchen cupboards."

It didn't take me long to put my hands on one of the glass baking dishes in question. I found it to be perfectly clean as well, surprising and impressing myself. But a further rummage of the surrounding cupboards bore no fruit. I cast my mind back to the last time I'd enjoyed one of Carol's lasagnas. And I recall her saying at the time that it should last me a week or more, as it was enormous. She was wrong. I distinctly remember eating nearly half of it for lunch and polishing off much of what was left at about two in the morning after a particular late-night, rather extended visit to the local pub. Something I don't ordinarily do too often.

I then had a glimmer of recollection that directed me towards my rarely used dishwasher, which I still hadn't completely figured out how to operate, as it was a fancy model which came with the house that featured too many bloody buttons to choose from and select. So why I'd stash the used dish in there was anyone's guess. But as I soon discovered, that was precisely where it was. And the fact that it remained unwashed was confirmed by the unpleasant odour that arrived a moment before the vision appeared of petrified sauce and cheese and such adhered to the inside of the glass. Conscious that I'd need either a blow torch or a diamond-tipped drill bit to remove the rock-solid remnants, I figured it was a job for another day, so I closed the door on my appliance.

"Sorry to keep you, Carol," I said, presenting myself before her once again. "I've found one of the dishes, but the other two remain a mystery for the moment."

Carol took possession of the single dish without bothering to look directly at me. For a moment, it seemed to me like she was thoroughly annoyed.

"Are you watching a Christmas film...?" Carol asked, still looking off to the side somewhere.

How she knew this was beyond me. So I glanced over my shoulder to see what she might be observing. "Ah," I said with a nod, spotting the partial reflection of the movie I'd paused, which was currently visible in the hallway mirror. "Yes, a keen eye you've got. I am indeed," I advised, looking at the image of an oversized tree consumed by far too many fairy lights and assorted glass baubles.

Carol offered a sympathetic sort of smile. "You do know it's only June, yes?" she added, in the same kind of manner you might ask somebody coming around from a concussion to check and see if there wasn't lasting head trauma. "Also, by your own admission, you don't particularly like Christmas, Adam. A fact you mentioned to me last year when I dropped your card around when there were, once again, no decorations or a tree present in your house."

"It's research. Research for a new book," I explained.

"Oh? Well, I do *love* a good Christmas movie, Adam," she said, giving the impression she was happy to stand around chatting all day if I let her. But I had some serious studying I needed to do if I was to keep a roof over my head. "Anyway," she said eventually. "I think I've left my oven on, so..."

"Cheerio, Carol. And thank you in advance of what I'm sure will be another lovely, magnificent lasagne."

I headed back to my sofa via a short detour to the kitchen, confident that a packet of Maryland Choc Chip Cookies would assist in my creative juices flowing freely (as well as my salivary glands). And although this first movie I'd selected wasn't giving the early impression of being a timeless classic, I remained optimistic nonetheless.

However, I'd just sat down with a cookie barely pressed to my lips when another chiming of my doorbell prevented any viewing pleasure. "I'm not in just now!" I shouted. But that announcement didn't work, and a gentle knock on my door soon followed. "For the love of…" I muttered under my breath.

The moment I walked back into my hallway, I could see Carol's head again through the window. I got worried, wondering if her glass dish wasn't as immaculately cleaned as I'd thought. "Heya, Carol, long time no see," I said, as I greeted her for a second time.

She offered an awkward half-smile, half-grimace that made her look like she could have a nasty bout of trapped wind. That's when I glanced down, noticing that she had changed out of her apron, which suggested to me that the lasagne was sadly on hold for the time being. "Uhm… Carol?" I said, admiring her bright red jumper with a giant reindeer design in the middle. "You weren't wearing a Christmas jumper a moment ago." She also had a large plastic bag along with her, stuffed full of something I couldn't see, and holding the bag out in front of her to keep it level and safe.

"Did I happen to tell you I absolutely *adore* Christmas movies, Adam?" she answered, reiterating her earlier remark, whilst brandishing the bundle in her hands, bobbing it and its unknown contents up and down in the air. "Don't they just make you feel all warm and fuzzy inside?"

"Even in June?"

"Oh, especially in June."

I wasn't entirely stupid, easily interpreting the somewhat less-than-subtle hints Carol was throwing in my direction. "Carol, how would you like to come inside and spend the day watching some Christmas movies with me…?" I offered.

Carol didn't need asking twice. "I've brought mince pies and a bottle of Baileys Irish Cream to enhance the seasonal cheer," she informed me, all but barging me out of the way as she bustled her way inside.

❊ ❊ ❊

Two films and three mince pies later, Carol was already half-cut on account of polishing off a good portion of the bottle of Baileys she brought along with her. I had abstained, so far, as it was still before noon, but I felt the alcohol might have perhaps numbed the pain of what we had been watching. Plus, it wasn't only a Tupperware container of mince pies that Carol had been concealing in her large plastic bag, as I soon discovered to my chagrin.

"You know that suits you," Carol remarked, as the opening credits on film number three introduced our next visual delight.

I smiled, looking down at what Carol was referring to. That being an exceptionally warm snowman jumper that once belonged to her late husband Frank, which I had dutifully slipped on, as instructed. "This is making me feel a little inadequate by comparison," I confessed, fiddling with the prominent knitted orange carrot protruding from the general area of my belly button. "Can I put a request in for a smaller carrot next year?"

Carol allowed the slightly off-colour innuendo to wash over her. "Well, I couldn't very well wear a Christmas jumper and not also bring one over for *you*, could I?" she said. "Another mince pie…?"

"No, I've already… Ah, go on. It's Christmas in June, after all!"

Sitting there with my notepad at hand, my intention had been to make extensive notes about character arcs and plot twists and the like, what I felt worked and what didn't, plus premise, background, and a plethora of other details that would help me to write my perfect Christmas offering.

The way I figured it, these movies were a free education—I just needed to endure watching a number of them to graduate. However, what was becoming increasingly apparent to me, based on the mostly blank pages in my notepad, was that television Christmas films were generally devoid of any substantial plot to speak of, and character development was pretty limited as well. But that didn't stop me from jotting down a cursory list of the general, oft-recurring plot outlines I'd observed thus far, for later review:

1. A girl (more often than not) runs some sort of small business (bakery/florist/coffee shop) but isn't especially good at it. Facing the risk of financial ruin, the community (along with a buff potential love interest who looks like he could easily handle an axe and chop down a large tree) step in to save the day. Plenty of snow, and everybody knows each other. They've always got great teeth.

2. A girl (more often than not) runs some kind of small business (bakery/florist/coffee shop) but isn't particularly good at it. An evil corporate fat cat type of company wants to buy the land it sits on to build something the community doesn't approve of. They club together at the last minute to fend off the evil capitalist pigs. Lots of snow, and everybody knows each other. And everyone's always got great teeth.

3. Female corporate lawyer works 400 hours a week, it seems like. Returns to her small American hometown for a family crisis (usually the funeral of a distant relative). As a kicker, she finds out she's been left a small business (bakery/florist/coffee shop) in their will. Does she go back to her hectic life in the city or stay in the modest hometown where there's another hunky recently divorced (or lost his wife in tragic circumstances and left with a young child) man hoping to fill the romantic void in her life. Plenty of snow and sparkly lights, everybody knows each other, and they've always got perfect teeth.

By mid-afternoon, my interest was starting to seriously wane. And even before the first snowman had appeared in this latest of offerings currently on view, I'd already had a rough idea about how everything would all turn out in the end.

Hell, the acting wasn't even that good, and I couldn't help but wonder if this genre of film was a place where only aspiring, inexperienced actors or those seriously past their sell-by date might ever turn up to audition. I was also sure one of the actors had been in *every* film we'd watched so far. Naïvely, at the start of the day, I'd wanted to feel what Carol referred to as "all warm and fuzzy." And it wasn't that I didn't wish to experience that same sense of magic that others enjoyed, because I did. Absolutely I did. Indeed, I rather envied those who took such immense pleasure from it and craved that sense of childlike wonderment. However, I started to suspect that none of these movies would ever instil in me that sense of Christmas cheer that had long since left me. Because, by now, I only found myself wanting to drop-kick an elf or destroy a poxy snowman with either a shovel or a big bucket of salt.

I glanced over at Carol, who somehow remained transfixed by the onscreen shenanigans I had primarily zoned out of. She was leaning forward in her seat, eyes glued to the telly, nibbling down on her bottom lip and giving the impression she was about to start sobbing at any moment. I wasn't sure if her glistening eyeballs were on account of too many Baileys Irish Cream refills or simply down to the fact she'd been transported to a world of crisp white snow underfoot, a seemingly never-ending supply of fairy lights, and a place where good always overcame evil (usually in a coffee shop, florists, or bakery).

The answer to my uncertainty came when I spotted a tear of happiness slowly working its way down Carol's cheek. "Are you okay over there?" I asked rhetorically.

Carol flashed me a kindly smile, wiping away her escaped tear. "Oh, I just knew the two of them would get together in the end," she said, before giving the television an approving look, happy it would appear that the good-looking couple with perfect teeth had found love in the face of overwhelming adversity (once again).

I couldn't help but laugh. But it wasn't a mocking sort of laugh. Not at all. Rather, it was more of a slight chuckle, with me laughing mostly at myself in an *I-just-don't-really-get-it* kind of way.

But as Carol released a contented sigh, a moment of clarity presented itself to me: Did I *really* have to be invested in the subject to write about it? After all, I was only writing the thing, and was not the target audience. Carol, and perhaps millions of readers like her, were my target audience. And hopefully, a target audience chock full of eager, voracious readers if my agent's words were anything to go by. A ravenous bunch who would hopefully help me climb out of the significant financial hole I'd been wallowing in.

"One more for the road...?" Carol asked, snapping me out of my literary musings.

I was starting to suspect that my lasagne delivery might be on hold for at least a day or two. "Baileys or movie?" I enquired.

Carol considered these two options for a brief moment. "Could I possibly go for both?"

"Sure," I said. "You choose the movie, and I'll be the barman."

Carol drained the creamy brown contents of her glass, to make room for more. "Are you enjoying them so far?" she asked. "The movies, I mean."

I could see an optimistic glint in her eye, and I didn't want to dampen Carol's overall exuberance. "I think I might be," I fibbed, figuring a wee untruth to be in order. But while I might be very unlikely to *ever* tune into this channel again, watching these particular films did help me to have a deeper understanding of the type of plotlines my potential readership might warm to. So, for that, I was mildly grateful, and it had been a somewhat helpful exercise as I knew a little bit more about the genre now than I did at the start of the day.

I wandered into the kitchen to top up Carol's glass and refresh her ice cubes, which had all but melted. And that's when I realised I was humming the tune to the seasonal classic "Jingle Bells" as I reached into the freezer to retrieve my ice cube tray. Gadzooks, I sure appeared to be entering the spirit of things for somebody who doesn't do Christmas. A fact supported by the vision of the oversized snowman's carrot on my borrowed jumper jiggling around my bellybutton, bouncing up and down as I laughed to myself.

"Ooh, I found us a brilliant one!" Carol then called out from the living room, with delight in her voice about her latest selection. "This one is about a single dad who helps organise his son's school panto!" she shouted, accompanied by the sound of her hands clapping. "I may have already watched it, but I'm willing to give it another go in the name of your research!"

I rolled my eyes, bracing myself for another hour and a half or so of treacly nonsense.

"Gosh, that sounds wonderful!" I said, doing what I hoped was an effective job at sounding completely sincere. "And don't you dare press play without me!"

Chapter Six

We ended up watching four and a half Christmas-related movies over the course of the day (with the half being only because Carol had perhaps had a bit too much to drink), and I never want to watch another one as long as I'm above ground and still breathing. On reflection, I didn't take *any* seasonal cheer from watching them. Still, I did experience some degree of enjoyment from appreciating the impact they had on my viewing companion. I suppose, I considered, it was like a parent watching the thrill in their kid's faces while they ripped open their presents on Christmas morning.

But I couldn't say it was an entirely unfruitful exercise for my creative juices because it wasn't. I had a handful of helpful notes written down and a few seeds of a story already taking root inside my head. Plus, it'd been pleasant spending time with Carol, who was lovely company even if she went into 'Mum' mode once she was nearing the bottom of that bottle of Baileys, asking several times why I hadn't found somebody else yet after Stacey and I had split up. God only knows what the other neighbours may have thought when I eventually escorted a very tipsy Carol across the road to her house—especially when she started belting out Mariah Carey's seasonal offering "All I Want for Christmas Is You" in the middle of June.

But Carol was quite astute, even in her cheerfully inebriated state. As she lifted her front door mat to retrieve her key lying beneath it (an apparent breach of ideal security protocol that I made a mental note to address with her when she was sober), she began to say something that hit the nail on the head about how I was feeling at that moment.

"I noticed you looking somewhat flat after watching Christmas movies," she remarked as she rose up and pushed the key into the lock. "Are you frustrated because you don't like it?" she asked, now looking over her shoulder at me. "Christmas, I mean. Because it's okay not to, you know."

She paused for a moment before turning to face me completely.

"Is there any particular reason you don't like Christmas, Adam? Because it's fairly unusual," she said. "By all means, tell me to mind my own beeswax if I'm sticking my beak into your business, but…"

I nodded, impressed by Carol's ability to read my mood, especially given her current condition. "Ah," I said. "Well, let's just say that a couple of my childhood experiences didn't quite live up to expectations."

Carol offered me the sort of consoling smile a doting mother might if I'd come home from the school playground with a grazed knee. Her caring nature made it tempting to open up to her. I don't know what she did before she retired, but I reckon she'd have made for a brilliant counsellor. Or perhaps an efficient interrogator.

"Maybe it's just too late for me to get a proper case of the warm and fuzzies," I said. "I don't know, perhaps my uncaring soul is beyond redemption…?" I proposed, partially in jest, but partly not. "Maybe I need to move to a town with a coffee shop on each corner, an overdose of fairy lights, and hunky lumberjacks just waiting for the pretty corporate lawyer to return to town for the holiday season," I added with a laugh.

Carol regarded me with a sterner expression than I was used to from her. "Adam, it's not about the location, however cheesy you think it might be. It's about the sentiment."

"The sentiment?"

"Yes, the sentiment," she continued, staring directly into the depths of my uncaring soul. "It's the feeling of good overcoming bad…" she said. "The appreciation of people helping each other out… The feeling of communities coming together to help one of their own…"

I thought about what Carol was describing to me. "So that's what makes you all 'warm and fuzzy' inside?" I asked. "Not the snow, the red-breasted robins, and all that?"

"Well, the fluff around the edges helps the story along. As does the appearance of a hunky fireman, for instance, or a buff lumberjack in a tight-fitting checked shirt over his bulging muscles," she advised. "But the *sentiment* is what it's all about. And if you don't get that feeling from watching Christmas films, perhaps you need to immerse yourself in the real world."

By this point, still standing on Carol's doorstep, I was starting to wonder if the copious amount of Baileys we'd both enjoyed was beginning to take hold. And I don't think I was doing a convincing job of disguising my quizzical frown, judging by the friendly slap on the arm that she administered.

"I know you're thinking what's this old thing, daft as a brush, wittering on about. But your problem, well, *one* of your problems, is that you're always holed up in that little office of yours, on your own, with next to no social interaction with your fellow humans."

Carol did have a point I had to concede. Still, "And that's a bad thing, is it…?" I asked her. After all, my fellow human beings often tend to irritate me. Them, along with yappy, barking dogs. Which is why I have a cat.

Carol appeared somewhat exasperated, placing a hand on each of her hips. "Adam," she said, effortlessly transitioning into 'Mum mode' again. "If you want to experience the *sentiment,* then I think you need to come out and smell the fresh air occasionally," she said, sounding like it was an instruction rather than a suggestion. "Perhaps do something selfless."

"Like what, exactly…?"

"Like I said a moment ago, it's the feeling of good overcoming bad. The appreciation of people helping each other out. The feeling of communities coming together to help one of their own," she had to remind me. "So…" she added, sounding like she was drawing to her conclusion. "Why don't you get off your arse occasionally, step out of your office, and venture out into the real world? Because I reckon you won't find what you're looking for hunched over your computer all the time."

Despite being chastised, I smiled because I appreciated Carol looking out for me. It was nice to have someone taking the time to do so. "I might just do that, neighbour," I said, giving her a quick peck on the cheek. "And thank you for your company today."

"Don't give up on Christmas!" Carol said as I walked along her garden path. "Oh, and Adam?" she called out, once I'd reached the middle of the street.

I turned around to find her pointing at me. "Yeah, Carol?"

"That thing you've got dangling down *there...*?" she said, with mischief evident in her voice. She then spread her first two fingers apart so they resembled a pair of scissors. "If you don't find my remaining lasagne dishes soon, then I'll cut that thing clean off of you!" she insisted, implementing her fingers in a quick, snipping motion. Repeatedly. So that I got the message.

I glanced down, hoping she was referring to the protruding carrot on my borrowed Christmas jumper, rather than something a bit further southward and significantly more painful should it happen to get trimmed off.

"You can lower your finger weapon! I swear I'll get right on it, Carol!" I promised.

❋ ❋ ❋

I tend to do much of my shopping online, at least whenever possible. This means I don't need to venture into town, find a parking spot, and then wander aimlessly around the shops in the hope of locating what I'm looking for with hordes of people getting in my way. However, one of the problems of living on an island out in the middle of the water is the cost to ship certain items over here from elsewhere. For instance, I was once taken in by one of those sofa companies promising "New Year Unbeatable Offers!!!" in their rather enthusiastic, high-energy television advertising campaigns. It turns out that these special, exclusive, "New Year" offers tended to last about 363 days of the calendar, however, and as I later discovered, the cost to deliver my new big, bulky purchase was nearly as much as the sofa itself. This was a fact I failed to notice when inputting my credit card details at the website's checkout.

A similar logistical issue proved to be the case when it came to replacing Carol's missing lasagne dishes. (The one I'd found in the dishwasher stank to high heaven, was covered in mould, and was now in the bin, while the other one, meanwhile, appears to have vanished into thin air.) With Carol's scissor-based threat still fresh in my anxious mind the day after our movie fest, I had managed to source replacements for the two items in question online. However, when I typed in my location in the Isle of Man, its quoted "free delivery" surged to over twenty quid! I might have swallowed it for an easy life if it was ten pounds or thereabouts. But *twenty*? Nossir. I figured I'd have to take a trip into town instead, using the opportunity to also get a long overdue trim of my hair.

Eager to avoid Carol's wrath, I jumped into the Porsche, hoping the gods of the fuel gauge would be kind enough to grant me a round-trip journey to Douglas—about a six-mile drive each way—without the need to take a wallet-draining pit stop at the petrol station. For a man with only six-hundred and eighty-three pounds to his name (I'd checked my bank balance just before leaving the house) and at least five weeks until my next royalty cheque would arrive, I was delighted to see the fuel indicator remain gloriously clear of the red section on the gauge. I was, however, acutely aware that such a throaty engine was as thirsty as a punter downing their first pint on a hot summer's day.

It was easy to forget how sublimely pretty the island I call home is when you're lurking in your shell like a hermit crab for most of the day. Indeed, as I was driving along the narrow, winding, tree-lined country roads, I'd even managed to forget about the stack of outstanding bills waiting for me to return and ignore them for yet another day. But it wasn't just the island's natural beauty offering me a pleasant distraction as my right foot got a little bit heavy on the accelerator pedal, because after a fitful night's sleep, I had the skeletal framework for several plot ideas for my new book bouncing around my head.

Ordinarily, when writing my typical space opera fare, I would be consumed in devising the names of different planets, creating new cultures, and crafting the backstory for dozens, if not hundreds, of new species. All of which was something of a migraine-inducing logistical nightmare. Christmas books, however, proved to be an entirely different animal, with the plotlines—to my narrow experience—being a bit thin. As such, the main difficulty now was that I had *too* much potential material forming in my mind. At this rate, I expect I'd soon have enough source material to fill an entire *library* with glittery literary tat. As such, attempting to weed out the evolving plotlines that might prove commercial and popular with the reading public was my main challenge at present if I didn't want to be evicted and wished to have food in the house.

When turning into the car park after arriving in Douglas, I felt pleasantly optimistic about my new writing project. For the first time in ages, in fact, I felt a long-forgotten desire to get home and bash a few chapters out on the laptop. Sadly, my buoyant manner was dealt a hammer blow by the sight of at least a dozen vehicles in front of me, all vying for what as far as I could see were no available parking spaces. Then, like a procession of mechanical ants, the convoy of frustrated drivers slowly proceeded in a series of loops around the area, waiting to pounce as soon as any individual currently on foot gave the impression they might be about to return to their vehicle and vacate their slot. It felt like a motorised version of musical chairs. And I'd hated that game as a child, ever since Carol Smollen fractured my nose in her haste to knock me out of the way to reach the last remaining seat to secure victory.

"Why are you packed out an hour before noon on a *Tuesday*?" I shouted to nobody except myself, wondering what this stop/start activity would do for my already atrocious fuel consumption. Usually, the town centre would be like a ghost town on weekday mornings because everybody would be at work, providing me with my choice of places to park. And that's when my eyes were drawn to a mum emerging from a nearby Range Rover with several tadpoles climbing out of her vehicle. Then, over on the pavement, I noticed more kids skipping merrily along, seemingly without a care in the world or any worries about where their car might be parked.

And then it hit me. "Oh," I said with a frustrated moan, slapping the top of my steering wheel. "It's the bloody *school* holidays."

I didn't mind children per se. Not necessarily. It's just that when they weren't held inside the school building on weekdays, they tended to clog up the easy movement around the island. This was proving to be the case today in this car park, which would ordinarily have plenty of available space when families didn't descend on the area in their droves. It was the reason I wouldn't knowingly dream of going shopping at the weekends when happy families often insisted on venturing outside to spend quality time together and make memories, all at the expense of my ability to transport myself around the island freely and unhindered.

With my blood pressure slowly rising, steam would likely soon be coming out of my ears if I were a cartoon character. Indeed, the extra ten pounds postage cost I'd been quoted for Carol's lasagne dishes was starting to feel like the bargain of a lifetime. I was also acutely aware of what a grumpy old sod I was turning into when I'd briefly considered stealing a parking spot from an elderly lady who was taking entirely too long lining up her reversing manoeuvre. As the old dear slowly, eventually, started turning her wheel, she took the opportunity to flash me a kindly smile, presumably as a reward for being so patient—in her eyes, at least—while she prepared herself to reverse into her space.

"God, I'm such a miserable shit," I said to myself, offering a friendly wave in return which hopefully disguised my unsavoury intent from only a moment earlier. "Don't worry, it's fine..." I then added, mouthing the words as the elderly driver raised her hands in a *what-am-I-like* manner.

Fortunately, an available spot soon appeared between an abandoned Tesco shopping trolley and a black Toyota Yaris that, sadly, looked like it had seen far better days. Once parked up, I struggled to peel myself out of the car without my door making contact with the battered Toyota in the adjacent space—no easy feat when the parking bays were designed to cram together as many vehicles as possible. I then eyed the Tesco shopping trolley that some lazy sod had left there, which was hovering perilously close to my passenger door such that a stiff breeze would most likely send it careering into my expensive paintwork. That being the case, I strolled over and repositioned the discarded trolley so that it was pressed up against the perimeter wall, at least out of harm's way, rather than menacingly occupying a valuable space where it could possibly bash into one of the surrounding vehicles.

My sense of achievement of doing the right thing lasted all of about six seconds, when a stern, shaven-headed bloke climbed out of his white builder's van and shouted, "Oi, don't just dump your trolley there! It could roll away and damage somebody's motor!"

Before I could respond, the old dear who I'd so patiently waited to reverse park was now out of her car, a few slots away, and starting to approach the irate bloke, appearing as if she might be about to leap to my defence and hopefully clarify that I'd only moved the trolley someplace safe (assuming, of course, she had been close enough to witness my gallant act of altruism).

However, she instead took up a position of solidarity, standing next to the overly muscled fellow with her arms folded across her chest. There, she shook her head in dismay. "Honestly!" she called over, in addition to a very audible tut-tut. "It's inconsiderate sluggards like you that ruin it for the rest of us!" she said, looking up to her new builder friend to back her up.

Either the old dear didn't recognise me now that I was out of my car, or she did, and knew precisely what my original intentions had been a couple of minutes earlier when I'd had designs on her parking space. For a moment, I wondered if I maybe should shout something back, or if it was perhaps best to simply walk away, as the rough-looking chap with a boxer's nose and rugby player's ears was almost as wide at the shoulders as he was tall, and the old girl beside him appeared to be spoiling for a fight.

"Fine!" I ultimately said, grabbing the trolley I'd only just selflessly removed from harm's way, while looking around, this way and that, for where I might return it to its companions.

"The trolley return is over there!" the elderly lady instructed, smugly extending a finger towards the far corner of the car park—the exact *opposite* way of where I was going.

I flashed an insincere smile. "That's very kind, thank you!" I replied, picking up the pace with the trolley as I started rolling along, and only just noticing that one of the wheels was distinctly stubborn, insisting on trying to guide me in one direction while I was attempting to steer in the other (and probably why its previous user had abandoned it in frustration). "Flippin' thing," I muttered to myself, now regretting that I hadn't nicked the old bird's parking spot when I'd had the opportunity.

Half an hour later and I'd secured the two replacement lasagne dishes, cheaper than the ones I'd initially sourced online, with sufficient time to still get that quick trim of my hair, as I'd planned to do, before my parking ticket expired. And even though the town centre shopping area was jam-packed with happy families, I was managing to navigate a route through the hordes with relative enough ease. However, an obstacle appeared ahead of me at a certain point in the form of a mass of people congregated in a rough semi-circle about ten or twelve deep, like they were all trying to get the bar staff's attention in a busy pub. They were evidently looking at some type of performance, judging by the fact that many of them were clapping along and generally giving the impression of having a good time.

Must be a small group of buskers, I thought to myself, as a melodic beat, accompanied by a feminine voice emanating from the general direction of where everybody was looking, wafted on the breeze in my direction. Eager to get my haircut and return to my car before my time ran out, I smartly switched trajectory, heading towards the rear of the crowd where a gap remained for me to proceed without further delay.

Well, that was the plan, at least, until my path was blocked by somebody very short who suddenly presented themselves before me, holding out a yellow bucket.

"Spare some change to rebuild Munchkinland?" the wee person said, talking in an odd, gruff voice, like he'd been smoking sixty fags a day for some extended period of time.

I came to an unscheduled halt, because otherwise I'd have likely ploughed over the individual who appeared intent on obstructing my way.

"Eh…?" I said, looking down at the little fellow wearing green felt shorts, a white and red patterned shirt that looked like it once belonged in a picnic basket, and alarmingly, a rubber skullcap that made the person appear bald apart from the two moulded, golden plastic curls of hair protruding from the temples at either side.

"Spare some change to rebuild Munchkinland?" he repeated in the same gravelly voice, giving his yellow bucket a shake this time, along with the coins rattling inside of it.

By this point, my ears had fully tuned in to the song that had so captivated the attention of the other passing shoppers. It became clear that it was "Somewhere Over the Rainbow," and whoever was belting it out was doing a pretty decent job of it, to be fair. Further, using my finest detective skills, I deduced that the vertically challenged person standing before me was somehow connected to the nearby performance.

"Ah, so you're a Munchkin," I confidently put forth, although I remained uncertain if this was a young lad I was speaking to or a small adult, on account of the heavy application of face makeup.

"We're collecting to rebuild Munchkinland," came the reply, followed by a further shake of the yellow bucket.

Now, even though I was practically skint, with bills landing inside my door at a most alarming rate, I've never been tight with spare change. But the truth of the matter was that I knew for a fact I didn't have any this time, because earlier I'd used every coin in my possession to cover the three-pound-twenty parking charge. (And why the machine didn't take a card payment, in this present day and age, I couldn't bloody say.)

"I'm sorry, mate," I replied, still uncertain if it was an adult or a child I was talking to. "But, honestly, I'm all out of pocket change," I said, offering him a disappointed sort of shrug.

However, as I attempted to recommence my journey with two glass lasagne dishes that were, by this point, starting to feel quite heavy in my hand, with the bag's handles digging into my fingers, the Munchkin skilfully countered my evasive movements. "We're collecting to rebuild Munchkinland," he reiterated, holding up his bucket closer to me.

"Yes, you told me that before," I said. I didn't know whether to laugh or simply barge past him at this stage. But that's when another one of the little devils appeared, similarly dressed in an old picnic basket tablecloth and green velvet shorts. So I now had two Munchkins blocking my path.

"Spare a bit of change to buy Dorothy some new shoes?" the current arrival asked in an equally gruff voice, although choosing to shake up the dialogue of his sales pitch, at least.

Surely Dorothy only ever wore the one special pair, the famous ruby slippers, I thought to myself, but didn't voice this out loud. "Guys, I *promise* you, I don't have *any* change on me at all," I told them. But the persistent little buggers wouldn't shift.

Sensing this extremely unprofessional (in my opinion) stand-off could continue into the next song, I used my free, non-carrier-bag-laden hand to pull out one pocket of my jeans to demonstrate to them that I really and truly had no coins on me with which to bolster the contents of their collection buckets. Sadly, I'd forgotten that was the pocket where I'd stashed a twenty-pound note to buy myself fish and chips on the way home.

I tried to grab the money as it floated towards the ground, but I was far from agile with the lasagne dishes in my other hand. "No, that's not for..." I started to say. But the two Munchkins were already on it like hungry flies on a lovely pile of dung.

"Thanks, mister!" the one on the left said, breaking character by speaking in his normal, regular voice, the higher vocal pitch confirming that I was dealing with children here rather than a pair of persistent, short-statured adults.

"Oi, that's for my lunch!" I protested, but they didn't seem interested in what I had to say. Instead, the two of them scampered away, forcing a route through the assembled crowd who'd just unleashed a generous round of applause, presumably for the benefit of the female singer.

"Come here, you lot!" I shouted, setting off in hot pursuit with a smile across my face, trying to make light of the fact I was chasing down two children who were making off with the last twenty-pound note I had on me, cash which was now being earmarked to *"rebuild Munchkinland,"* or to *"buy Dorothy new shoes,"* as it were. Either they were ignoring me, or the noise of the gathered crowd's applause simply drowned out my words.

"Excuse me... So sorry... My apologies... Sorry again... Coming through..." I offered politely, as I weaved my way through the assembled rabble.

About two or three rows from the front, I could finally see the source of the pleasant singing—an attractive young woman of indeterminate age wearing a blue and white gingham dress and a pair of sparkly ruby-red slippers, while clutching a wireless microphone in her hand. Standing either side of her like Secret Service agents flanking the American president were Tin Man and Scarecrow, with a timid-looking Cowardly Lion shadowboxing in front of them as well in his signature "put up your dukes" fashion.

I had no idea what kind of surreal world I'd inadvertently wandered into or what weird and wacky style of brick road I was heading towards. Furthermore, I was also quickly running out of time, if I wished to accomplish getting my hair cut before my parking ticket ran out.

Through multiple sets of limbs, I could see the two wee blighters who'd nabbed my cash. "Lads, hang on, there's been a mistake…" I pleaded, easing my way through to the front of the semi-circle of spectators, receiving a few audible grumbles in the process from those who must have thought I was merely attempting to snag myself a better view.

"Lads, I need to…" I attempted to reiterate. But that's when my right foot caught through the leather loop of a woman's handbag sitting on the ground next to a pair of feet, presumably hers. I stumbled forward, trying desperately to hang onto the bag of lasagne dishes in my left hand, aware they wouldn't be of much use to me or Carol if they became chipped or broken. Fortunately, the closest Munchkin spotted me just in time to step to the side as I staggered past him, dragging the handbag along with me for the ride with my toes. I tried to correct myself, but gravity had other ideas, with me hurtling towards the earth like a mighty tree felled during a terrific storm. In a panic, I stretched out my right hand to cushion my fall, catching a glimpse of a collection of green painted cardboard boxes and plywood positioned before me, directly in front of the shadowboxing Cowardly Lion.

"Argh!" I shouted moments before I careered towards the solid ground, in front of several dozen people watching on. On landing, I winced, awaiting a wave of pain that I was sure would arrive a split-second later. But nothing. Thankfully, the cardboard boxes had apparently absorbed the force of my weight, and I was fairly confident I'd not heard the sound of breaking bones, or for that matter, smashing glass lasagne dishes.

I rolled over onto my back, greeted by the vision of a furious-looking Dorothy glaring down at me with hands firmly pressed against her hips. "What in blazes are you doing?" she demanded, shaking her head in disbelief as the Tin Man tried to help me up, though the restrictive nature of his costume hindered his efforts.

"I was just trying to get the money out of the charity bucket…" I feebly offered, before checking myself over, now conscious that the gathered crowd were in hushed silence, likely uncertain if my arrival was somehow part of the performance.

My explanation did nothing to appease good Dorothy Gale. Just the opposite, in fact, as she looked like she was about to insert one of her ruby slippers into a place where it didn't at all belong.

"I don't believe this!" shouted Dorothy, looking skyward, perhaps thinking back to her former time in Kansas. "Not only is this *hooligan* trying to rob our charity bucket…" she said, stirring up the crowd as she did so. "But he's also flattened and destroyed the Emerald City that the kids have worked so hard on building!"

Dorothy was soon joined by the Cowardly Lion, looking down on me with uncharacteristic anger in his eyes and with padded paws folded across his furry chest. "Right. Way to *go*, there, buddy," he said with a growl. "Thank you for ruining two entire weeks of preparation work, you fantastic idiot!"

I raised my hand towards who I clearly recognised to be the Scarecrow, based on the tufts of straw protruding from his collar and such. "You couldn't help me up, could you…?" I asked, somewhat worried that if he didn't, I was about to have my own pieces of stuffing kicked out of me by his nearby colleague, the now not-so-Cowardly Lion.

Chapter Seven

T he day of Christmas Eve didn't really get off to a great start. My dad had promised to take me to the BMX track all week, which was a bit too far for me to pedal to alone. Then, about an hour before we were meant to leave, he received a call offering him another shift at the factory for "double time," whatever that meant. He had been working every single day for weeks, so *surely* he could have spent Christmas Eve of *all* days with his only son, I felt. But no. So I pestered Mum to take me for at least an hour, but she said she was too busy preparing for Christmas tomorrow.

As there was a very real danger that I'd soon get dragged into peeling potatoes, I opted to take my bicycle around the neighbourhood to see if any of my mates were out and about. I first rode my way down to the school playing field, then to the park, and finally to the shops. But there was nobody to be found.

I'll bet all their dads have taken them to the BMX track, I thought, sulking as I pedalled up our street, wondering how to fill the hours because Christmas Day still felt like a lifetime away. Slowly progressing up the hill towards my house, I spotted Robert Bentham's dad appear outside their front door, dressed in a suit like he was going to a wedding or something. But the only time I've ever seen him leave the house for anything was when he was heading to the pub, so I had to assume that's where he was going just now as well. Why he was wearing a suit, I hadn't a clue. Looking at him walking over his front steps, I couldn't understand how he could look so smart and yet live in such a shabby, miserable home where everything was filthy and grimy and stained with nicotine.

I slowed my pace, waiting for him to disappear from view be-fore completing a U-turn, and then popping an impressive wheelie as I pulled up outside of Robert's house, where I could already see him standing at the window. I liked to think it was from excite-ment in spotting me arrive, but I suspect he was just making cer-tain his dad had left for the afternoon.

Robert appeared at the front door a moment later, still wearing his gym kit like before, and with the injuries on his face showing not an awful lot of improvement. "Heya, Adam..." he said warily, looking nervous, like he wasn't sure his dad was genuinely gone. "What you up to?"

In answer, I pointed down to my bike, which I was still astride. "You coming out?" I asked, eager to kill as much time as possible before I could finally switch on my new Commodore 64, which I very much hoped to unwrap the next day.

Robert shook his head. "I haven't got a bike," he replied.

"What...?!" I asked, utterly gobsmacked by this revelation, as I thought *every* boy owned a bicycle.

Robert glanced down to his feet and seemed embarrassed, so I thought for a moment. "I reckon you could borrow my sister's bike if you like?" I offered. "I don't think she'd mind. But you should be aware that it's bright pink and has a basket on the front."

Robert didn't appear especially put out by either the girly col-our of my sister's bike or its accoutrements, so I thought perhaps I'd succeeded in finding myself a bicycling partner for the after-noon. "So we going, then?"

"Nah, I'd better not," Robert replied, after considering the mat-ter for a tick. "My father told me not to go anywhere."

"But I've just seen him heading out," I remarked, pointing a fin-ger in the general direction of the pub. "So he won't know?"

"Nah, I'd better not. I don't know when he's due back, and he'll go absolutely mental if I disobey him."

On the basis Robert already had several cuts and a massive, ugly bruise on his face, I didn't really want to see him get into any more trouble. "Okay, see you soon," I told him.

"All right, Merry Christmas. And I hope you get that computer you want," Robert said, before disappearing behind his front door.

Back at my house, I annoyed my sister for a bit while she was trying to record music from the radio. But, if I'm being honest, the pestering job wasn't my finest effort, and I soon got bored with it and even offered my services to Mum to help stuff the turkey. And that's when it hit me. I knew what I needed to do.

"Oi, I thought you were helping me out with this bird...?" Mum called after me as I bolted out of the kitchen and sprinted up the stairs towards my bedroom. Once in my room, I emptied the contents of my piggybank, which was pretty slim pickings on account of me buying a bunch of football stickers earlier in the week. Still, there was a handful of loose change in there, plus a few notes as well, that I hoped would be sufficient for what I wanted to buy.

❋ ❋ ❋

Scatty Newbold's is a large shop in the village that sells *everything*. Stretched out over multiple floors, it was the sort of place a young person could easily disappear in—something I discovered for myself a few years back when Mum, in a sheer state of panic, eventually found me hiding in a cupboard during a game of hide and seek that she didn't even know she was involved in. It was the type of shop where you could as easily buy something to decorate your living room walls, maybe purchase a new saddle for your horse, or choose, as I would occasionally admire, something from their extensive selection of petrol-powered chainsaws. If you weren't sure where to go to pick up some particular thing, chances are that you could find it somewhere on the three floors of Scatty Newbold's.

The friendly but unusual owner, Scatty, had an unruly mop of wayward white hair and always wore thin, wire-rimmed glasses. I've never seen him without his customary ankle-length white apron, either, making him look like a mad scientist. I was always mesmerised by the excessive hair growth coming out of his nostrils, which I usually had a perfect view of whenever he loomed over me when I was in the shop. He must have also lived on the premises, I reckoned, because the shop was *always* open or so it seemed. Fortunately, as I cycled towards his shop in the village on this fine day, I could see the lights on through one of the massive front windows, which meant he was still open for business.

Considering it was Christmas Eve today, I was surprised to see so many people milling about outside, all with the intent of making their way through the entrance. Most of them appeared to be men, which made me wonder if blokes tended to leave buying presents until the last minute. I made sure to park my bike away from Scatty's front windows, as he'd cautioned me about doing that on several previous occasions, saying he didn't wish for the view of any of his goods to be blocked. Inside, the shop always had an interesting mixture of smells, most notably of saddle soap and fresh wood, with the scent of the wood naturally making me think of the chainsaw section. But I couldn't examine them today, as I only had limited time, so I needed to remain focused.

I walked past the cashier's desk, where an orderly queue of people were stood waiting to be rung up for their purchases.

"Good day to you, young Master Catchpole," Scatty the owner said from behind the dark wooden counter, peering down at me through glasses with lenses so small in diameter I was surprised he could see through them, as each lens must have been no bigger than the size of a ten pence coin.

"Hiya, Mr Newbold," I replied, offering him a wave as I made my way towards a towering display case with dozens of plastic drawers offering quite possibly every variety of screw, bolt, and nail known to mankind. In the far corner of the shop, where I eventually reached, was a set of doors leading to a massive outside courtyard, where you could buy plants, soil, garden furniture, and other items you'd typically use outside your house. And I knew precisely where I was headed, as I'd walked through that doorway with my mum only a couple of weeks earlier.

The courtyard was surrounded by tall brick walls with a bit of barbed wire fixed to the top that always made me feel like I was in jail—I suppose it was to deter any shoppers sneaking in or out who didn't fancy paying for their purchases. But the moment I placed my foot on the cobbles of the courtyard, I felt a wave of panic because I could see what I was looking for was no longer where they were the last time I was here, with that space now home to a display of outdoor gardening tools.

I wandered aimlessly around, hoping against hope that they'd simply been moved to a different spot. But they weren't exactly small, what I was looking for, so if they were anywhere outside then I'm pretty sure I would be able to see them.

"Flippin' heck," I muttered to myself, making my way back inside, where I figured I'd ask Mr Newbold if perhaps, by some miracle, I might have managed to walk straight past what I was searching for, as unlikely as that seemed in my mind.

Fortunately, the queue had thinned out for the moment, and seizing advantage of this temporary lull, it looked like Mr Newbold and his staff were taking this opportunity to get into the festive spirit, each with a glass of something fizzy in their hand.

"Ah! Now then, Master Catchpole!" Mr Newbold said when he clapped his eyes on me once more. "What's your lovely mum sent you down for, eh...?"

"She doesn't know I'm here," I revealed. "Out in the courtyard, Mr Newbold, you had lots of Christmas trees on display earlier in the month?" I asked, hooking a thumb over my shoulder towards the area in question.

Mr Newbold laughed, but not in an unkind manner. "Master Catchpole, what sort of a salesman would I be if I still had loads of Christmas trees for sale by Christmas Eve, hmm?" he said, resting his elbows on the countertop and leaning down closer to address me. "Besides, I clearly recall you coming here with your mum and your sister earlier this month to purchase one...?"

"It's not for me, Mr Newbold," I clarified. "I'd hoped to buy one for my friend, Robert Bentham, because he hasn't got one."

Scatty held up his hands in a *not-much-I-can-do-about-that* sort of way. "Sorry, lad. We've sold the last one a few days ago," he informed me. "Would you like a glass of something to drink before you go? I'm sure we've got some orange juice," he offered.

"No. No thank you, Mr Newbold. I reckon I ought to get back home," I answered, feeling fed up with myself for leaving it so late. "Have a nice Christmas," I added, reaching the heavy front door that activated a little brass bell secured to a metal spring each and every time a customer came through the entrance either coming or going.

I headed over to my bike, giving brief consideration to maybe trying someplace else. But as Mr Newbold had just pointed out, it was unlikely that anyone would still have trees for sale this late before Christmas. So I figured I'd have to write it off as a nice idea and leave it at that. However, I'd only just slung a leg over my bike when I heard the shop's brass bell ring out with a jangle.

"Hey, lad. Before you go," said Mr Newbold, tapping me on the shoulder to get my attention before I could set off. "What was your mate's name again…?"

"Robert Bentham," I said.

Mr Newbold moved around to the front of my bike to talk to me more easily, and my attention was once again immediately drawn to the large, walrus-like tufts of hair jutting out from each of his nostrils. I don't know why, but they were like magnets to my eyes.

"Why, do you know my friend Robert?" I asked.

Mr Newbold caressed the underside of his chin, as if considering this question carefully. "Is that John Bentham's son? Lives up by you?" he offered.

"Erm, I wouldn't know his father's first name, Mr Newbold. But they live three doors down from us, and all I know is Mum says he goes to the pub an awful lot," I replied. "That is, Mr Bentham goes to the pub an awful lot. Not my mate Robert," I clarified.

Mr Newbold's ordinarily cheerful face hardened in an instant. "Yes, that sounds like John Bentham," he said, gravely shaking his head. "And you say he hasn't even bought a Christmas tree…?"

I started to panic at this point, worried I would get someone in trouble, especially it being an adult. But Mr Newbold was asking me a direct question, and I felt I ought to answer him. "Uhm, no, I don't think he has," I said. "There are no lights, no decorations, or anything like that at all."

Mr Newbold didn't say anything about the matter specifically, but I suspected he either knew Robert's dad or at least knew *about* Robert's dad, given the nature of his reaction.

"Right," he said, placing a firm but friendly hand on my shoulder. "Follow me."

The front door's brass bell jingle-jangled again as Mr Newbold escorted me back inside, leading me straight towards one of his impressive window displays. "You can take that one, lad," he said, as a warm smile returned to his face.

I followed the direction of his pointing finger and could only assume he was talking about the decorated tree he'd arranged front and centre there in the window. Now, as this tree was a fairly good size, plus drowning in tinsel, baubles, and a set of fairy lights to boot, I was concerned that the meagre amount extracted from my piggybank would never cover the purchase price. "Are you sure, Mr Newbold? Will you not need to use it again next year?"

"Nah, lad. It's a real tree and not likely to last more than a week, maybe two, beyond Christmas," he told me. "And if that miserable maggot..." he started to say. "Erm, I meant that if Robert's *dad*," he said, correcting himself. "If Robert's dad hasn't bought a tree, I'm guessing he has nothing to decorate it with, either. So I figure you can take this one as is."

I immediately reached into my pocket to scoop out my available cash (which, again, wasn't much), so we could quickly seal the deal before Mr Newbold might change his mind.

"Put your money away, Adam. You'll be doing me a favour in taking this thing off my hands," he insisted. Even though I knew full well he was doing *me* the favour rather than vice versa.

Mr Newbold then narrowed his eyes, looking my small frame up and down. "Hang on," he said. "How on earth will you get that tree home if you're on your bicycle?"

He had a point. When I initially headed out, I hadn't much considered the practicalities of transporting a tree.

"Gareth?" Mr Newbold said with a wry smile, speaking to one of his assistants near the cash desk. "Gareth, you haven't enjoyed too much of that champagne, have you?"

"Not with the measures *you* pour, Scatty," came the immediate, cheeky response.

"I'll ignore that, Gareth," Mr Newbold said with a laugh. "Right, then. Can you put this tree, along with the stand, in the back of the van? Young Master Catchpole here will give you instructions as to where it should be delivered."

I didn't know what to say for a moment, just thinking as I was about what Robert's face would look like when the tree was shortly dropped off at his front doorstep.

"Thank you, Mr Newbold," I managed to say, finding my voice again as I watched Gareth, the delivery driver, fetch his coat. "My friend will be *so* excited when he sees that. In fact, he told me all he wanted for Christmas was a sparkly tree. And now, he'll actually be getting one!"

Chapter Eight

The return journey home after my unsettling incident with the cast of *Wizard of Oz* street performers took a bit longer than originally expected, thanks to taking an unscheduled detour on my part to the dealership where I'd purchased my car.

Earlier, by the time I'd eventually finished apologising for having ravaged the new Emerald City, there'd been no opportunity left for a haircut and I ended up ten minutes late in getting back to the car park. As a consequence, I was met by the sight of an officious-looking fellow in a high-viz jacket slipping a ticket underneath my windscreen wiper. Not for a moment did I feel ill will towards the chap, as he was only doing his job as parking attendant. Indeed, it was my fault I was late in returning to my vehicle, not his. But as I didn't exactly have heaps of dosh right now, the last thing I needed was to have to set aside forty quid for a parking ticket.

I'd tried to appeal to the man's compassionate side, but it soon became apparent that the cold, dispassionate eyes staring back at me belonged to a gentleman who didn't offer tardy motorists a second chance.

"Look, mate," I had said, with all traces of my charm offensive nearly spent. "If you could see your way clear to letting me off, just this once, regarding that forty quid fine, I'd be ever so—"

"It's eighty," he immediately cut in.

"What is?"

"The penalty charge is *eighty* pounds, sir. Not forty."

It may seem like an overreaction, but I could have fallen to the ground just then and curled up into the foetal position upon hearing this devastating news. It didn't seem to be so very long ago that I had more cash than I knew what to do with. And here I was now, about to have an emotional breakdown over a parking ticket.

"I'm sure that amount won't be an issue for somebody owning such a prestigious vehicle as *this*," the parking attendant remarked unsympathetically, with a mixture of what sounded very much to me like scorn combined with a touch of envy in relation to my expensive Porsche coupe.

But because I could barely afford petrol at this stage, let alone anything else, this unexpected 'idiot tax' was the final nail in my supercar coffin. With my mind immediately made up that the vehicle was going back, I felt a warm sense of ease during my drive to the dealership. I had no idea how much money I still owed on the finance arrangement, but if I could hand the keys back and perhaps walk away with just a cheap little runabout to get me from A to B, I'd be absolutely delighted. I'd never really wanted a flash motorcar to begin with and shouldn't have listened to my ex, Stacey, when she suggested it would be a grand idea for me to get into so much debt for one.

The good news, as I subsequently discovered, was that the car dealer was confident they could broker an arrangement where I'd walk away without owing a penny to the finance company (I suspect he could smell the desperation dripping from my pores) and was able to offer me a vehicle that they'd recently taken in trade. So rather than delay the inevitable, I decided there and then that I'd just leave the Porsche with him and told him to give me a ring when I needed to call back and sign the final paperwork. Plus, leaving the old car with them meant I didn't need to put any more fuel in it—money I could then put towards that bloody parking ticket.

Driving back to my house in a boringly beige Nissan Micra felt briefly like something of a comedown from the vehicle I'd driven earlier that day. But I didn't mind in the least, really, as I soon felt a massive weight lifted from my shoulders. For some people, such a drastic change in their choice of automobile might feel like a sign of failure. But the way I looked at it, by not having to pay extortionate amounts for my car insurance, plus eye-watering finance repayments, road tax, and the constant threat of crippling maintenance and repair bills, I might now be able to make some headway in the arrears owed to the mortgage company.

Furthermore, I also had Carol's two replacement lasagne dishes in my possession, which meant I no longer needed to fear the dear lady's wrath (and I did hope she might offer to fill one of them back up for me soon). In addition, on the creative front, I felt my literary juices flowing for the first time in ages and was looking forward to getting some words typed up on my new novel. It was a *reluctant* Christmas novel, true, but it was a start.

Yes, despite the parking ticket and everything else today, Adam Catchpole was feeling pretty darned optimistic about things.

Once back home, I'd not stepped more than a foot inside my front door and Barry, my cat, was on me, nuzzling his head into my ankles as he does when he's hungry. "Heya, buddy. At least *some-one's* pleased to see me," I said, while resisting examining the en-velopes on my doormat for fear of dampening my bullish outlook.

But, as I was about to find out, it wasn't the contents of those envelopes on my doormat that I should have been worried about because other matters were about to come along and serve a ham-mer blow to my upbeat disposition.

Barry was soon tucking into his lunch when my phone vibrated in my pocket. I thought about ignoring it, as I really wanted to get several pages typed on the new novel while the emerging plot was fresh in my mind. But I could see from the caller ID display that it was my sister, attempting a video chat, and I knew from experi-ence she'd just keep ringing if I tried to ignore her.

"Hey, it's my favourite sister!" I said, sitting on one of the stools surrounding my marble-topped kitchen island. Of course, we both knew that Helen was my *only* sister. "What's new?" I asked.

It took me less than a second to realise that all was not well in the world. My sister Helen has always had the most expressive eye-brows. When we were kids, I likened them to either caterpillars or millipedes residing on her forehead, for which I'm sure she was al-ways eternally grateful. And right now, those caterpillars or milli-pedes were angled in an accusing manner.

"Have you been in town this morning?" Helen asked without introduction or pleasantries, moving her face closer to the screen so I could feel her steely gaze burning directly into my retinas.

This random question was delivered in a tone suggesting that my lovely sister already knew the answer. I was desperately trying to work out what the reason behind it could be. Had she somehow heard about me trading in the Porsche? Or, had somebody perhaps witnessed me having a near mental breakdown with the parking attendant? Both seemed very unlikely scenarios, but they were all I could come up with in the absence of anything else.

"Erm… yeah, I have been in town," I cautiously replied, fearful of opening up some potential can of worms, based on the odd look she was currently giving me. "Why do you ask…?" I said, suspecting that I may not like the explanation she was about to deliver.

"Because some rampaging nincompoop is becoming famous on social media! And that person, *Adam*, looks suspiciously like *you*!" she informed me.

Helen has always been known for her quirky sense of humour, but this one washed right over me. "Helen, have you perhaps been drinking…?"

"No, I've not been drinking!" Helen shot back, making a point to reach beside her and move the empty bottle of wine on the dining room table well out of camera range. "That was from last night!" she insisted.

Then, I saw a text message notification flash up at the top of my phone's screen. As I was on an active video call, I could only catch the first line of the message from one of my mates:

"Dude, seriously, WTF!!!"

Having just read this grave snippet at the same time as I was about to receive an apparent bollocking from my sister, I was starting to harbour a sense of impending doom.

"Help me out here, Helen, yeah?" I suggested, accompanied by a friendly laugh, hoping that what I'd allegedly done wasn't nearly as severe as the expression on Helen's face.

"You've no idea what I'm talking about?" Helen asked, moving her face menacingly towards the phone's screen again.

By now, I could feel my literary creative juices starting to dry up as we spoke. "Helen, I have absolutely no idea what you're talking about, I can assure you."

She stared at me again like she was trying to figure out if I was being serious or not. *"Adam,"* she said, like she was speaking with a three-year-old. *"Adam,* there's a video circulating on Facebook of a man trying to steal money out of a child's charity bucket!"

I raised a finger in the air like I was perhaps testing which way the wind was blowing. "Ah. Well. About that," I replied. "You see, I didn't technically know it was a child at the time," I offered as my defence. "His face was covered in gobs and gobs of makeup, right? And further compounding the issue, he was dressed as an Oompa Loompa as well, making a clear identification near impossible."

"An Oompa Loompa?"

"Yes. You know, from The Wizard of Oz."

Helen rolled her eyes, and she never was any good at hiding her feelings on account of those expressive eyebrows of hers. "Do you not mean a *Munchkin?*"

"Do I?" I asked, more to myself than to her. I think I was getting confused about my cherished childhood films the more I thought about them. "Hmm. Yeah, you could be right."

"So you don't deny robbing a child's charity collection bucket?!" Helen pressed. "God in heaven, there's a question I never imagined I'd ever need to ask you."

"Well, basically, yes, I did try to take money out of his collection bucket," I admitted. "But it was my money in the first place, Helen, and I didn't intend to give it to him to begin with, so..."

"Oh, well that makes it *perfectly* all right, then," Helen said, laying the sarcasm on so thick she probably could have used a trowel. "And at least you didn't make matters any worse by ruining what must have been weeks and weeks of work from the children and destroying their carefully designed stage set. Oh, *wait.*"

"Ah, did they catch that bit on the video, then...?" I asked, suddenly aware of a knot forming in my stomach. Helen simply nodded in return, confirming my fears.

After processing that my fellow island residents must now believe I was prone to stealing from children's charity buckets, I took the time to explain to Helen what had genuinely happened earlier. Although replaying the actual chain of events—both in my mind and spoken out loud—I didn't see how I was going to come out of this situation steeped in any kind of glory. After all, I had not only stolen from a Munchkin, but I'd deprived the group of wee ones of their beloved Emerald City as well.

At least by the end of the call, my sister could sort of see things from my perspective and didn't feel the immediate need to disown me. I hoped.

"Oh, Adam. What are you like?" she said, shaking her head, and clearly struggling to suppress a smile, as the corners of her lips curled slowly up. "Well, you've convinced me you're not the most wretched of all human beings, at least, as one of the Facebook commenters had suggested," she added in closing. "All you need to do just now is somehow convince the other twenty thousand people who've viewed the video of that fact…"

Chapter Nine

The good news, at least in one particular respect, was that it didn't take me too terribly long to track down the video my sister and a few of my mates had tipped me off about, each in quick succession. And why didn't it take me too terribly long? Because it was bloody *everywhere*, that's why. In the short time it took me to locate after Helen mentioned it initially, the video had amassed nearly thirty thousand views and counting!

In the shaky, handheld footage, as I soon discovered for myself, the person capturing the event is focused on a lovely afternoon of children enjoying themselves when things take a decidedly sinister turn. And for pity's sake, the person who posted it to the internet had even taken the opportunity to edit it with some ominous-sounding music added in, which made me look like even *more* of a despicable sewer-dweller. And to be fair, watching onscreen what I was watching, I could understand why the comments being left about it were so abrasive. Heck, I was tempted to leave a scathing remark myself! Until, of course, I remembered the cartoon villain featured in the video clip was me.

Oh, this wasn't good. This wasn't good at all. As far as I could tell, the only saving grace was that those commenting didn't seem to know who I was. Although living on a small island as I do with a fairly modest population, I knew it was only a matter of time before somebody managed to put a name to my face, figuring it out.

I looked at the coffee I'd just made, seriously considering swapping it out for maybe a large whisky, or perhaps adding the whisky right in. Being viewed as a callous, child-robbing ne'er-do-well was terrible enough. Awful, even. But I couldn't help but suffer a rather sinking feeling, as well, about what this video could potentially do to my already struggling publishing career. Don't get me wrong, I wasn't fantastically famous or anything like that. But to those in the know—and to those who enjoyed my certain category of writing—I was a somewhat recognisable name. As such, being vilified for what was nothing more than a harmless mistake and a touch of clumsiness on my part would likely do little to counteract my lacklustre book sales.

After watching the clip twice more and observing the number of times it was being 'shared' blow up considerably, I placed the phone down on the shiny marble in my kitchen, lowering my face to the cold countertop as well, and groaned. "I've been reduced to driving a little beige Nissan Micra, and now I'm also public enemy number one," I said.

And that's when Barry leapt up, briefly sliding on the polished surface before coming to a controlled stop just in time to cuddle into me. "Thanks, Baz," I responded, scratching the back of his ear, to which he purred softly. "I needed that, mate. I really did."

I resisted my urge to down a large whisky, realising I needed to act before this situation spiralled out of all control. My only saving grace, at least as far as I could tell, was that you couldn't clearly see my face in the video. I was identifiable to those who knew me best, of course. Otherwise, my sister and my friends wouldn't have been able to reach out to me in varying stages of disgust. But if I didn't take any action, it was highly likely that someone else would soon work it out on their own and let the entire world know. So I threw on my jacket and I picked up the keys to my Nissan, with every intention of heading out the door to, ehm...

Well, that was just the problem, wasn't it? Because by the time I got to the front door I realised I had absolutely no idea what to do next. It wasn't like I was planning on driving over to Silicon Valley to confront Mark Zuckerberg and insist he remove the video from Facebook, or anything like that.

But some semblance of a plan, no matter how minute, would have been helpful, considering the timescale to nip this potent situation in the bud was dwindling each time that video was shared. And that's when I spotted the bag with Carol's lasagne dishes in it, which I'd placed next to my coatstand in the hall.

"Ah!" I said to myself.

I may not have had the faintest idea about what to do next. Still, I knew of a shrewd old captain, so to speak, who would hopefully be able to help guide my troubled ship away from choppy waters before it capsized and sank to the briny depths of the ocean floor. So that's when I decided to head across the road to return Carol's lasagne dishes and, hopefully, seek some pearls of wisdom about how I might make my way out of the spot of bother I'd suddenly found myself in. While Carol may not be any sort of expert about anything related to the internet, necessarily, she's still one of the wisest people I know, having given me most excellent counsel in the past, and only just recently, in fact.

By the time I reached Carol's garden path, she had already appeared in her doorway, having seen me approaching, apparently, and was giving me the look of a teacher who'd caught me cheating on a maths exam.

"From your grim expression, I take it you've enjoyed the video of me online?" I surmised.

Carol accepted the carrier bag I placed in her hand, shaking her head disapprovingly.

"Doris, who goes to my church, has forwarded it over, Adam!" she informed me. "Doris is eighty-nine years old and included the message, *They should string this bloody wazzock up by his balls*," Carol advised. "So if you've managed to elicit that kind of language from a devout octogenarian churchgoer, then I think you're in a fair bit of trouble. Fortunately, from the impression I get, our Doris doesn't seem to know that it's you in that video. So there's that one small favour, anyway."

I lowered my head in shame. "Can I come in...?" I asked, hopeful of receiving some positive words of advice or encouragement.

"No. No, you can't," she said.

Dear God in heaven, I thought. *Even Carol doesn't want anything to do with me now.*

"I thought you might be able to..." I attempted to say.

"You're not coming in, Adam. And that's because we're going out," she told me.

"We? As in the two of us...? Where are we going?" I enquired, slightly confused. Well, more than slightly, really.

Carol set the lasagne dishes on her hallway table before grabbing her handbag and joining me outside on the steps, closing her front door behind her. "Right. We're going to the Union Mills dance studio before a baying mob descends on our neighbourhood with pitchforks and blazing torches," she announced.

I had no idea why any Union Mills dance studio should be our destination of choice, but I thought it best to follow orders as Carol appeared to have some solid idea in mind, which was better than I had right now. "Shall we take my car?" I proposed.

Carol looked at the beige Nissan Micra parked on my driveway with an uncertain expression. "Hmm, no," she decided. "No, how about we take mine instead," she said, sounding as if I didn't have an awful lot of say in the matter.

* * *

Union Mills was a village not too far away, and also home to my closest pub. During the drive there, as I'd done on the call with my sister earlier, I thoroughly explained to Carol the adverse chain of events which resulted in me being viewed on social media as the most dangerous current threat to society. Carol, to my relief, soon saw the funny side and felt some degree of sympathy for the slight sticky wicket I presently found myself in.

"Well," Carol said, as she soon turned off the main road and into the dance studio car park. "Here we are."

The 'here' that Carol referenced was, as it turned out, the HQ of a children's musical theatre group called TAPPIN' FEET. Further, as she'd revealed during the drive over, she immediately recognised the young lady dressed up as Dorothy Gale as Chloe Tappin—the granddaughter of Gladys Tappin, who'd founded the well-known and established musical dance group in the mid-1950s. According to Carol's quick research, TAPPIN' FEET had rehearsals from four to eight p.m. on Mondays, Wednesdays, and Fridays.

Carol applied the handbrake and was, it would appear, unable to resist a faint smile. "Honestly, Adam, what are you like?" she remarked, before shifting her attention to the vital matter of how I might get myself out of this mess. "Right. Today is Wednesday," she said. "That means Chloe should hopefully be here for rehearsals."

I gave a quick nod, eager to hear more. "Noted. And…?"

"And, you go in there, find Chloe, and beg for forgiveness as if your life depended on it. Maybe you could convince her to give you something tangible to get you off the hook. You know, something like a letter? An official statement where she confirms you weren't stealing from her charity bucket and *didn't* then set out to destroy their stage set either?"

I liked Carol's thinking. Because if I didn't do anything, there was every likelihood that the semi-viral video of me presently circulating would become a *fully* viral video. This unsavoury result had the potential to damage what reputation I've enjoyed up until now, and in turn, seriously hamper book sales.

I unfastened my seatbelt, hastily rehearsing in my mind what I might say, wanting to appeal to Chloe Tappin/Dorothy Gale's compassionate side. But I was rubbish at this sort of thing, and often when I needed my verbal capacities to make things better, I usually cocked things up royally. Give me a keyboard and the time to think about and consider what words I might best employ, on the other hand, and that became a horse of a different colour.

"Ready? It's all up to you now," Carol encouraged. "Well? Go on, then, get to it," she advised, when she noticed I had my hand on the doorhandle but was failing to exit her car.

"Wait, hang on. You mean you're not coming *in* with me…?" I said, starting to panic.

"Not a chance, dear. Have you heard of being guilty by association?" she replied. "Nossir. You need to pull up your big boy pants and go in there and use that charm of yours," she said with a wink.

"But Carol. You know how you're just a really, *really* nice person, and *everybody* you meet tends to like you a lot…?" I pleaded. "That would be a *very* useful thing to have at my disposal right now."

I utilised my most giant puppy dog eyes as I'd said this, yet Carol remained unconvinced and seemingly immune to the so-called charms of mine that she'd just touted.

"Fine. I'll go on my own," I said in response to her silent grin. "But if you hear emergency sirens in the next five minutes or so, you can take it as indication that Dorothy wasn't too keen on receiving me."

Once outside the car, I noticed there were no other vehicles in the car park. I glanced at my watch, observing that it was still only half past three, perhaps a bit too early for anyone else to arrive for rehearsals just yet. I resisted the urge to climb back into the passenger seat, and as Carol, with another placid grin, had just activated her car's central locking on me, I couldn't have retreated to the safety of the car if I wanted to.

"Fine! I'm going, I'm going!" I said in response to Carol's various nodding and pointing. And I did. Go, that is.

The dance studio building, I could now see, was a fairly decent size, and how I managed to drive by it in the past without noticing it struck me as odd, considering it was so clearly visible from the main road. A generous outdoor veranda and contrasting green and white painted woodwork reminded me of a lovely cricket pavilion. Indeed, I could quite easily see myself sitting on the veranda or the manicured lawn out in front with a glass of something fizzy and refreshing on a warm summer afternoon. But it wasn't really time to admire the location, as I was on a damage-control mission.

A set of double patio doors with dance shoes etched into each pane of glass suggested I was in the correct area. I pressed my nose up against one of the glass doors, hoping to see some movement within. But nothing. I tried one of the doors, and thinking it might be locked, pressed down on the handle, too bloody hard, like a fool. Fortunately, it remained perfectly intact. Fortunate, as I was there to apologise for the wilful destruction of property, amongst other offences, and I didn't think having to hand over a demolished door handle would've got our meeting off to a very good start.

"Hello...?" I said once inside, as I allowed my eyes to adjust from the sunlight outside to the somewhat darker interior. "Jesus!" I exclaimed, catching a glimpse of somebody in the shadows, before realising it was just my reflection in one of the full-length mirrors that spanned the length of the opposite wall.

"Hello?" I said again. "Is there anybody—"

"I'm in the kitchen area!" a response came, from what, if I had to hazard a guess, was the confines of the kitchen area. "If you're dropping off the ice creams, would you mind just bringing them through?"

As I didn't have ice cream, I didn't know if that invite was still extended to me. And I don't know why, but seeing all of the mirrors, feeling the sprung wooden floor under my feet, and running a hand over the nearest handrail that ran horizontally around the hall perimeter, I felt a sudden impulse to perform a lovely pirouette, or perhaps one of those fancy leaps. I resisted that urge, and instead wandered across the dimly lit hall, passing several rows of seats laid out in front of a slightly raised stage towards the back of the room, from where the voice was roughly emanating.

"Hi there, it's not the ice cream man!" I announced ahead of my arrival, as friendly as you like. "It's, erm... it's— well, that is... my name is Adam!"

I peered behind a door in the rear of the room, spotting a figure kneeling in the middle of the floor behind it, attending to a thin section of plywood with what I could see was the depiction of a green castle skilfully painted on its front. I grimaced, recognising this as part of the stage set that I'd tumbled into and destroyed earlier in the day, which was now apparently having to be redone.

"Are you after tickets for the nearest performance?" the young lady—who I could now recognise as Chloe Tappin/Dorothy Gale— asked without turning around, busy as she was at the moment with putting the finishing touches on her painted scenery.

I took a step closer, though was suddenly conscious I may startle her once she became aware that the maniac from before was now standing directly behind her. "I... I just came to apologise," I said softly, holding out my hands, palms raised, to demonstrate I wasn't a crazed psychopath with ill intent.

Chloe looked over her shoulder at me. "Ah. You're the bloke who stole from the charity bucket and broke our stage set, which we'll need to use again in less than three hours, and then ran away," she coolly observed.

At least she knew who I was, which meant an even more awkward introduction wasn't required.

"I know it looks bad, Chloe," I said, preparing to present the case for the defence. "But the charity bucket was a simple misunderstanding, I can promise you, and I only stumbled *accidentally* into your stage set while trying to catch up with the Munchkins."

This explanation had all sounded perfectly reasonable in my head, but I was acutely aware of how terribly lame it could come across when actually spoken out loud, as I was now doing.

"…And the only reason I scarpered was that I was in real danger of receiving a parking ticket," I added. "Which, as it turned out, I actually still did end up getting."

I laughed an ironic laugh, hoping this last detail I'd provided might somehow garner some sympathy. It didn't.

Chloe reached up, using a nearby worktop to pull herself to her feet. She had blonde hair tied on either side of her head in bunches. And while she was also petite—only about five foot tall at best—I can say she was somehow still pretty adept at radiating menace when she wanted to.

"Look, Chloe. I just wanted you to know that I'm so sorry about what happened, and I'll do *anything* to make up for the damage I've caused," I pleaded.

After giving both of her hands a quick rinse in the sink, Chloe returned to look me up and down like a sculptor might review a piece of marble, which brought to mind the repeated use of both a hammer and a chisel, thus placing me in a slight state of unease. Then, she began circling me, looking me up and down again as she considered me carefully. "Anything, you say…?" she asked eventually, once she'd completed a full circumnavigation and was standing directly in front of me.

"Erm, yeah. Anything," I replied.

"Hmm, marvellous," she said, along with a sudden glint in her eye, sounding a bit sinister. "That's just marvellous. Yes."

…

And about ten minutes later, I emerged from the TAPPIN' FEET dance studio, wiping some moisture from my forehead and aware that I could also feel a patch of sweat increase in size on my back, with my shirt sticking to it.

"I was about to send a search party out for you!" Carol said the moment I opened her car door and deposited myself onto the passenger seat. "Everything okay, Adam? You look a bit peaky."

I didn't reply straight away. Instead, I was still busy processing what had just happened.

"Adam?" Carol pressed, coaxing me back to the present. "Adam, did she refrain from accepting your apology? Is that why you look so anxious? Adam...?"

I sucked in a lungful of air, before releasing it in a steady stream. "Oh, Chloe *did* accept my apology, all right," I said.

"So... what's the problem?"

"Well," I said, scarcely believing what I was about to say. "It's the price I had to pay in *order* for her to accept that apology, Carol."

Carol placed a hand to her mouth, looking worried. "What did you have to do?" she asked.

"Well, it turns out the stage set for the Emerald City wasn't the only thing ruined during my clumsiness earlier today," I revealed. "You see, during the incident, it turns out that the actor who plays the Scarecrow somehow sprained his ankle when trying to haul my ridiculous carcass off the ground."

Carol wasn't stupid. Far from it, in fact. As such, her shoulders started to heave as she quickly put two and two together, followed by a poorly stifled laugh. "Oh, Adam. Oh, dear. Has Chloe gone and signed you up?" she said with a snort.

I clapped my hands smartly together, giving the impression I was entirely enthused by what I was about to admit.

"She sure has, Carol," I was thrilled to confirm, through gritted teeth. "You'll be honoured to know that you're sitting next to none other than the Scarecrow himself, one of the lead performers in the upcoming Tappin' Feet dance school's summer interpretation of *The Wizard of Oz*..."

Chapter Ten

The problem with social media was that it was ruthlessly efficient at distributing information to a broad audience—fantastic if for instance you were a small business promoting your products or services. It's not so awesome, however, if the content shared features you, a particular individual, when you're not at your finest hour. As I found out to my peril.

Fortunately, Chloe Tappin, whose dance troupe was on the receiving end of a steady stream of rallying remarks and messages of support and solidarity—mainly slagging me off to high heaven in the process—came to my rescue as she had graciously agreed, based on the arrangement we'd made. Chloe, the benevolent soul she is, kindly shared a post on her official Facebook page explaining how the video wasn't quite as awful as it appeared, as it simply featured the actions of "sadly, a clumsy, uncoordinated oaf with perhaps a diminished mental capacity," as she so eloquently put it.

Further, she took the opportunity to announce to her followers how I had courteously agreed to step in for the recuperating Scarecrow. (A role she assured me would require minimal acting experience on my part to perform, by the way, as all I would need to do for the role was to act a bit dim at times, something I was "already quite good at," according to her.) As Chloe revealed to her followers, I was to join the cast for their summertime performance of *The Wizard of Oz*, based of course on the absolute corker of a film of the same name that everyone was surely all familiar with. Aside from a handful of adults (one of which would now be me), the cast was mainly comprised of the local children who attended her popular dance group.

According to Chloe, the shows were scheduled to commence the following week and occur over several evenings, with a couple of matinee performances thrown in for good measure. In addition to allowing the youngsters to perform in front of a decent-sized audience, seasonal shows such as this provided a vital source of funds. Those funds were invested back in to subsidise the dance school so it could continue to offer its services to the island's children without charge. And the high street performance I had unintentionally gate-crashed was designed to drum up interest in their upcoming production and hopefully encourage ticket sales.

However, I couldn't help but wonder if Chloe also had hidden designs about taking me from a "clumsy, uncoordinated oaf" and turning me into some sort of polished end product—not unlike the plot of *My Fair Lady*, the old Audrey Hepburn film classic, I thought. After all, if she might guide a talentless twit with the acting skill of a stale loaf of bread into delivering a credible, convincing performance, then she could confidently state in future marketing efforts to be able to help virtually *anybody* develop their talent.

But whatever Chloe's true intentions, be they good or bad or somewhere in the middle, they were a small price to pay if Chloe saved me from being strung up and drawn and quartered by a baying mob, as would hopefully be the case. Hopeful in the *saving* me part, that is. Not the drawing and quartering part.

Still, at least my upcoming debut stage performance served to temporarily take my mind away from the arrival of various 'Final Reminder' letters that were an ever-present threat.

❋ ❋ ❋

My sister Helen paid me a house call periodically, usually armed with a small white box stuffed with treats from the local bakery. She'd make out as if they were purely social visits. Although I suspect the motive was more about ensuring I wasn't sitting around in my undergarments surrounded by a vast array of empty beer cans and discarded takeaway food containers, in light of my fragile mental state of late. But whatever the case may be, I appreciated her taking the time to check in on me and see that I wasn't swinging from the rafters, as she was doing this Wednesday, presently.

"Don't touch that custard doughnut!" Helen insisted, swatting my inquisitive hand away from the white cardboard box. "There's only one, and it's mine!" she advised. "Now, make yourself useful and go get the kettle on," she added, grabbing something from the kitchen cabinet to lay the selection of doughnuts on so that they would form an appealing display.

"Eating straight from the box was good enough for me," I said with a shrug, doing as instructed and filling the kettle. "Now that's just another plate I'll need to wash," I complained.

Through the corner of my eye, I could see my sister conducting a visual sweep of my kitchen, like a health inspector examining a restaurant's hygiene standards. She continued with her small talk, fetching the milk from the fridge and having a good nosey at the other contents while she was in there, making sure I wasn't living on purely bread and water alone. Then, bottle of milk still in hand, she moved over to the door to my utility room, looking inside and casting her eye over where I usually stored my dirty laundry.

"Jesus, Helen. I know what you're doing!" I protested.

Helen appeared unconcerned, continuing with her inspection of my life. "I'm looking out for my brother," she explained, shifting her attention to the shopping bag she'd also arrived with and then advancing towards my fruit bowl armed with a collection of apples and a net full of oranges. There at the bowl, she examined a pair of existing nectarines, which, to be fair, did have more fluff on them at this point than a teenage boy's chin. "You need to eat fruit more regularly," she admonished, building a pyramid out of the fresh apples and oranges she'd brought along after first pitching the dodgy, out-of-date nectarines. Fortunately, she avoided any additional discussion about housekeeping and such, which I could only interpret as glowing endorsement of my recent efforts about the place. "So. This video doing the rounds of you trying to steal from a child's bucket, and then you bashing things to smithereens when you couldn't get your way…" she said, changing subject.

"Oh? What video is this you speak of?" I replied, with a thinly disguised smile.

"What I mean is, I don't need to be worried, do I?" she asked.

"Worried?"

"Yes, *worried,* Adam! I know you've had a bit of bad luck lately, both on the relationship front and also with your book sales, as you've mentioned. So I was worried this video might be evidence of you spiralling downward, just when I thought you may be starting to return to your old, jolly self."

"Jolly?" I teased. "I don't think I've ever been—"

"Adam!" Helen scolded me. She then lowered her head, looking down at my kitchen tiles for a second or two before returning her eyes to mine with a softer expression visible. "Adam, I just... I'm concerned about you. And when I hear you just sold your beloved Porsche, and replaced it with that very much less remarkable object parked on your—"

"Helen, I'm fine!" I chirped, offering up my sunniest of dispositions. "And that Nissan Micra out there isn't all that bad. Honestly, it's really loads more practical, actually."

But she tilted her head, looking me up and down like she wasn't sure if I was just putting on a brave face for the critics.

"I promise," I insisted. "I'm *glad* to see the tail end of that four-wheeled financial drain. Plus, I can nearly fill the fuel tank on the Micra for twenty quid, whereas in the Porsche, I'd have been lucky to get to the end of the street on that amount of petrol. Aside from that, I've also written two entire chapters, so far, of my reluctant Christmas novel."

Helen's eyes lit up in response to this revelation. She knew, like me, that if I was actually getting words written, it would be a good indication that I was sailing on at least a moderately even keel and exhibiting an overall positive mental health. On the other hand, if I *wasn't* writing anything, then it was a sure sign that something was amiss, like a dog with a dry nose.

Helen handed me the plate she'd arranged. "Here. You take the custard doughnut, I insist," she said, looking at me with pride. "I'll make the tea, and you can tell me all about your new book."

I started to protest about her giving up the lone custard doughnut, as she seemed to have her heart set so firmly on it before. But I gave in to temptation once I caught a whiff of its heavenly scent. "Well, only if you're *sure*...?" I offered feebly, as by now it was already pressed to my lips.

"So this new book of yours," Helen said, waiting for me to chew and swallow. "Tell me more, yeah?"

I shrugged as always when asked about my work in progress. It wasn't that I didn't like talking about my writing because I did. But I'd learned from past experience that discussing a partially written book was counterproductive, as no matter how you described it, an incomplete plotline always sounded a bit crap. I often imagined a young J K Rowling, for instance, relating with enthusiasm her idea for a new book long before it was completed:

"Yeah, it's about a boy who gets a ride on a special train to magician school with two other kids who end up being his friends, eventually. He's also got some kind of unusual pet... Maybe a vole, or a pine marten...? I haven't decided on what. Oh, and he's got a funny-shaped scar on his elbow, or perhaps the back of his knee...? Again, I haven't decided on the particulars just yet," J K might say.

"Oh. Ehm... okay...? That sounds like it's going to be... erm... Well, anyway, keep up the good work, Joanne...?" could very well be someone's response.

And this is something I've suffered over the years. As a writer, people are generally interested in your efforts, and asking about what I'm working on is usually the most common question. However, as the person asking the question isn't yet privy to the entire plot—often because I've still not formulated it—then little snippets of the plotline in isolation are usually received with a look of *"What the hell are you talking about?"* by the recipient. I know this isn't malicious or in any way deliberate on their part, but it doesn't stop writers from then questioning themselves and wondering if their work in progress is a bucketload of slop. As such, I had long since given up on offering up any details of my current project until such time as it was finalised and I could provide a synopsis that did the thing justice.

Helen reached for the doughnut in my hand, which now had a large, half-moon-shaped section bitten out of it, as if it had got attacked by a shark. "If you don't tell me, I'm taking this back," she threatened. But then, after a moment, "You're not going to tell me, are you...?" she said, asking and answering her own question.

"No, ma'am. Because it'll be like a comedian telling you only a part of his new joke, with the most important bit, the punchline, not entirely worked out yet, and then getting demotivated when you're not curled up on the floor pissing yourself at his creative genius," I said. "But I can share a separate development in my life, if you're interested?" I proposed.

Knowing my sister liked a bit of hot gossip, she was naturally all ears, with any concerns about my latest plotline apparently a distant memory already. "Ooh, *go* on. Spill it," she encouraged.

So spill it, I did. With 'it' being the details about how I signed up to make my debut stage appearance as the Scarecrow because I'd inadvertently incapacitated the previous actor playing the role. I could tell from Helen's uncertain expression that she wasn't sure whether I was yanking her chain or if I was serious. But when I produced a wad of advance tickets I'd committed myself to selling, she started to believe what I was telling her.

"Right," Helen said, after enjoying a few mouthfuls of tea, plus several bites of her own doughnut she had chosen, that being one filled with lovely strawberry jam. "So in the space of a week, you've appeared in an embarrassing viral video on social media, got rid of your expensive, petrol-hungry Porsche, started in on writing your 'reluctant' Christmas novel, as you call it, and now you're sched-uled to appear as the Scarecrow in a children's dance group's ren-dition of The Wizard of Oz. I haven't missed anything, have I?"

"Nope. At least, I don't think you have. Anyway, how many tick-ets shall I put you down for…?"

Helen looked at the stack, about an inch thick. "Why don't you give me half of them, and I'll sell them to the other parents at your nephews' school?"

In my mind's eye, I could see Chloe Tappin's face beaming as I arrived into rehearsals, tufts of straw protruding from my collar, and handing her a respectable pile of cash for the tickets I'd man-aged to sell. "Helen, that'd be amazing. Thank you."

"It's fine," she said. "In fact, I'm quite looking forward to seeing my big brother treading the boards in a sold-out performance."

I didn't want to temper my sister's hopes by admitting it was more of a church hall-sized affair, as opposed to something at the magnificent Frank Matcham-designed Gaiety Theatre in the heart of Douglas. Although one day perhaps it might be, if I took to this acting thing.

Helen returned her attention to her cup of tea, but I could tell by the devilish twinkle in her eye that her mind was whirring.

"What are you thinking about?" I asked.

She looked over the top of her mug. "What? *Me...*?"

"Out with it."

"I was just thinking about Chloe. I've met her a couple of times, and she's pretty."

"Is she? Oh, I'm sure I hadn't noticed," I offered weakly. "Anyway, what about..." I said, attempting to change the subject.

But Helen wasn't exactly stupid. "You hadn't noticed? *Pfft*, I'm calling bollocks on that one," she replied.

I felt my cheeks flush like a ten-year-old boy who'd just been accused of 'fancying' the new girl in school. "Okay, she's not without her charms," I admitted. "But surely she's too young for me anyway?" I protested.

"She looks much younger than she actually is," Helen informed me. "She's younger than you, yes, but not by nearly as much as you might expect."

"Still, the whole reason I'm getting involved is to put something back into the community," I said further. "My intention is *not* to put something into—"

"Into the community? A community that, thanks to that video, probably thinks you're the biggest scallywag on the island," Helen felt the need to point out, along with a chuckle.

I wouldn't have put it quite like that, I don't think, but my sister did have a point. "Well, yes. That was also a small consideration. To try and modify that opinion."

Helen then stared at me, wide-eyed, like she was about to grab the unused rolling pin out of my kitchen drawer and club me to death with it.

"Err, why are you looking at me like that...?" I asked, wondering if I should suddenly be concerned for my health.

"Oh my God!" Helen said, placing her cup down. "This is unbelievable," she added, holding her hands out like she'd just received a dose of divine inspiration from the good Lord himself. "Adam, you're becoming the plotline you've been looking for in your new book," she insisted.

I waited a moment or two, expecting further clarification to help me understand what she might be talking about. "Eh? What are you on about...?" I asked, when she didn't immediately resume speaking.

My sister jumped up from her chair, pacing back and forth on the floor like she was about to pitch a script to a Hollywood film producer. "No, I'm being serious, Adam," she insisted, holding out her hand and waving it slowly through the air in a manner presumably designed to help me visualise what, as I'd asked, she was on about.

"You were looking for a cheesy, feel-good sort of plotline for your Christmas book, yes?"

"Well... yes."

"So don't you see it? Sheesh, man, *you're* the bloody writer here in this kitchen."

I had no idea where Helen was going with this, which only inspired her animated hand gestures further. "Adam," she said eventually, when it became clear I had nothing meaningful to contribute. "Adam, you've got a miserable writer who's just been dumped by his girlfriend, yeah? He's antisocial, with only his one pet cat for company, wiling away the afternoons by himself, sitting in his tighty-whities eating Pot Noodles—"

"I don't *actually* eat them anymore," I cut in with a raised finger, taking no offence to the undergarment reference as, to be fair, that portion of her scenario was not entirely inaccurate.

Helen largely ignored me. She was in the creative zone.

"Then," Helen continued, carrying on just where she'd left off. "Then you eventually leave the house, only to make a public nuisance of yourself, destroying the hopes and dreams of a boatload of children—"

"I wouldn't say *destroy*, necessarily. And surely there wasn't any *boat* involved...?"

Again, Helen ignored me.

"...And to regain some dignity and dig yourself out of the giant hole you've dug for yourself, you end up starring in their show to help them raise funds, and..."

"Well I wouldn't say *starring*, really, as that's perhaps a bit of a stretch."

"... And you end up playing a major part in their show to help them raise funds, and..."

"And?" I asked, somewhat intrigued now, despite myself, as to where she might be leading.

"... And you end up falling head over heels in love with the absolutely gorgeous dance teacher before you turn your life around by releasing your best-selling Christmas novel based on your recent exploits."

I took a moment to digest what my sister had presented to me, slightly amused by how much fire and energy she'd thrown into her pitch. "Erm..."

"Yeah?" Helen said, moving close again, eager to hear my initial feedback.

"I don't even think that horrible Christmas movie channel you put me on to would commission that script, if I'm being honest. After all, there's no buff lumberjacks, no cutesy coffee shops, and from what you've said, there's no big-city lawyer returning home for the reading of a distant uncle's will anywhere to be seen in this synopsis."

Of course, I was only being slightly sarcastic, more of a distraction tactic to help steer the conversation clear from the idea of me falling head over heels in love with the dance teacher.

Helen threw me a fierce but playful scowl. "You're only mocking because you know it's gold dust, dear brother. And if you don't see that, maybe I'll head home and write it myself. This time next year, *I'll* be a global literary megastar!"

"Make sure you give me a signed copy?"

Helen pulled a face. "I'm starting to regret offering you that custard doughnut."

"Which was delicious, by the way," I informed her. "Just so you know, though, I *do* appreciate the doughnut. I also appreciate that you dig around my laundry... and my fridge... and my kitchen... to make sure I'm looking after myself. And thank you for the plot suggestions. Again, I'm not ungrateful."

"Don't bloody know when a literary masterpiece is wafting right under your nose," Helen remarked with a playful sniff. "Anyway, on the basis you don't seem to mind me sticking my beak in if the intentions are honourable…" she began to add.

I groaned. I don't know if it was audible, or purely in my head. "Oh, blimey, what have you done, Helen?" I asked.

"You previously mentioned that money was a bit tight," Helen said, trying not to look too awkward. "And I might have noticed a few envelopes with red ink lettering stamped in bold on the front while I was having a look around previously…"

"It's a temporary cashflow situation," I interjected, making excuses for my dire royalty statements. "Hopefully things will get back on track shortly, especially if I can make serious headway on my new book."

"Okay. But just so you know, I've spoken with your brother-in-law Paul, and we've got some savings tucked away, sitting there in the bank doing nothing, and we—"

"No!" I immediately shot back.

I don't know why I was so forceful in my reply. Perhaps it was a sense of embarrassment or just feeling like a bit of a failure. After all, here I was, living in an oversized country pile on my own while my sister, her husband and two kids were squeezed into a modest, two-bedroom terraced house. And the thought of taking money they'd worked so hard for was something I couldn't do.

"Helen, that's one of the nicest things anybody has offered to do for me. Thank you, but no."

Helen didn't press the point, which I was grateful for, as I felt a little bit emotionally fragile from such a generous offer. I drained the remaining contents of my mug of tea, using the brief time to compose myself.

"I know you're worried about me," I eventually offered, once I'd removed my lips from my mug. "But I'll be fine, I promise. You see, I've got this gold-plated plot for a new book where this loser of an author and his dopey sister come up with a Christmas number one best-seller, and are soon swimming in cash."

"Cheeky bugger!"

Chapter Eleven

It was torture. I'd been awake for what felt like forever, though I couldn't be sure for exactly how long, as I'd purposely turned my bedside clock around and moved it out of reach so that I couldn't spend the whole entire night staring at it. *Have I even gone to sleep yet?* I wondered, leaning over and peeking outside through my bedroom curtain. It sure didn't feel like it. *How the flippin' heck is it still pitch-black out there?* I thought. *Surely it must be morning by now, after this many hours…?*

I laid my head back onto my pillow, wondering when this pain would end. At one point, I even considered downing some of the awful-tasting cough syrup placed near my bed, because I knew it had the warning 'May cause drowsiness' written on the label of the bottle. My annoying cough was gone by now, having disappeared a few weeks earlier, but the prospect of drowsiness was tempting considering I couldn't get to sleep. All I could think about, over and over, was loading the first game on my new computer.

I squeezed my eyelids closed as tightly as possible, hoping this would allow me to drift off to sleep. But just as I started to relax, my mind wandered from reflections on computers to thoughts of my friend Robert. I wasn't there when Gareth, the delivery driver, had dropped the tree off, but Mum had taken me and my sister out for a walk today just after it got dark so that we could appreciate the Christmas lights one more time before the big day arrived.

"Oh, well isn't that lovely," Mum had remarked, as we came up on Robert's house.

I couldn't see what she was talking about right away, as I trailed behind with my face buried into my Toymaster brochure despite the sun having already gone down. But when I glanced up, I saw sparkling lights behind the ugly, nicotine-stained curtains of the Bentham house. I stopped, amazed at how the lights could transform the residence so thoroughly, making the home appear warm and inviting. I squinted, attempting to get a glimpse inside, wondering if Robert was currently sitting next to the tree, mesmerised by it just as he had been at ours. But I couldn't get a clear view from where we were, and Mum didn't allow us to stand and gawp.

"It's nice that Robert's dad has finally bought them a tree," Mum commented as we walked past. I didn't correct her to let her know it was me that got it for them. I'm not sure why. But either way, I was happy. Happy for Robert.

At this point, lying in bed and recalling our earlier walk, I must have dozed off, because the next thing I knew I was hearing footsteps on the landing just outside my door. In my half-asleep state, I wondered if it might be the jolly guy dressed in red, searching for cookies and milk he knew we must've left out for him somewhere. However, my dad's whispering voice indicated otherwise.

"Dad, is it time to get up...?" I asked, raising my head from the pillow with sudden hope that it wasn't two o'clock in the morning with my father simply getting out of bed for a wee.

"Get up?" Dad replied, like he was a bit annoyed. "Get *up*...?" he repeated, this time sounding like he was ready to give me a good telling-off, like that bloke in Oliver Twist when young Oliver asks him for more porridge, or gruel, or whatever it was.

But then, "Of *course* you can get up, Adam!" Dad said, throwing open my door and turning my light on, nearly blinding me.

"It's Christmas morning?!" I shouted in delight, struggling to throw my duvet aside quick enough.

"It sure is," Dad said, before heading towards my sister's room, in case she hadn't heard the hullabaloo. "And remember, you know the Christmas morning drill, okay? Don't forget!"

I was halfway down the stairs when Dad's comment registered. The "morning drill" he was referring to was his insistence that we all congregate around the kitchen table to enjoy a cup of tea before any opening of presents was permitted. We weren't even allowed to stick our noses into the living room to see if Santa had visited, or even confirm if there were any presents under the tree.

It was infuriating, especially as I didn't usually drink tea at *any* time of the year, much less this very special day. And when you're a kid on Christmas morning, it's unbelievable just how slowly that darned kettle comes to a boil and then how difficult it is to try to rapidly gulp down a cup of scalding hot liquid. How I never ended up in hospital because of a burnt oesophagus is beyond me.

Sitting around the kitchen table in our pyjamas, my dad drank his tea very slowly, taking small sips, savouring it, making it last, knowing precisely what effect this sort of delaying tactic was having on my poor sister and me. It drove me mad, but the more I protested, of course, the slower he went. And I've seen my dad down a pint or two of beer before, so I know he can drink faster when he wants to.

I resisted the urge to say anything more, knowing from previous experience that it would only result in him placing his mug on the kitchen table for long periods between his tiny sips. I couldn't help but notice the twinkle in Mum's eye, which told me she was enjoying this annual performance but didn't want to get involved too much for fear of being on the receiving end of a tirade of desperate pleading from her two frenzied children.

Finally, Dad took his last sip, jokingly asking Mum if more tea was in the pot for a refill. But Mum knew we'd suffered enough and nodded towards the other room, as the next stage in the morning's drama, as always, was that dad would disappear from the kitchen to stick his head around the living room door, ready to come back and report whether Santa Claus had visited us overnight.

A few moments later, he reappeared with a glum expression, slowly shaking his head as if he was the bearer of awful, devastating news. But I'd seen this exact performance in the past. And even though I knew he would break into a smile at any moment, it still didn't stop me from having that momentary feeling of dread.

Gradually, Dad's gloomy face gave way to an emerging grin, as fully expected. He raised his hands and started doing this awful dance that he was always so good at, it being somehow wonderful and awful both at the same time. "Santa's been!" he yelled, while pulling Mum into his arms as well to include her into his happy, awkward jig. "Santa's been!"

The sense of excitement from hearing those two words was like nothing I'd ever felt aside from that of other Christmas mornings. The second Dad stepped to one side, allowing us access to the living room, was the most tremendous feeling in the world. I shifted so fast that the grip on the soles of my slippers nearly gave way on the tiled floor.

"Slow down!" Mum cautioned, fearing either me or my sister would run ourselves headfirst into the doorframe, but we didn't heed her warning because obviously there were presents waiting to be opened.

I gasped with delight because two piles of gifts were on either side of the tree, the tree's lights already having been switched on. "Which one's which, Mum?" I asked without looking around, desperate to dive straight in and start ripping paper.

"How would I know?" Mum replied, feigning ignorance. "You'd need to ask Santa, of course. But if I had to guess, I would say yours are the ones wrapped in the blueish paper, and your sister has the ones wrapped in pink."

I fell to my knees before the pile indicated, overwhelmed and unsure as to which gift to start with. From experience, I knew the soft, floppy-looking ones tended to be things like pyjamas, t-shirts, or socks. Those could probably wait, I reckoned. So the first present I selected was rectangular in shape, about as long as my arm, half of that as wide, and about one of my hands in thickness. I couldn't be certain, but I had a sneaking suspicion this was the board game Mouse Trap, which I had played at my friend Tommy's house and desperately wanted.

"Yes!" I yelled, punching the air in delight after I tore a strip of wrapping paper away, revealing the partial image of a red basket trap. "It's Mouse Trap!" I announced, just in case my mum and dad were curious. I ripped the rest of the paper clear of the box, casting it behind me where Mum was poised with a black bin bag to collect what my sister and I discarded.

I continued on, occasionally coming up for air, looking over at my sister, who appeared equally thrilled with the stack of gifts in front of her. But selfishly, I was more interested in my own pile of presents than hers. Before too long, I'd made my way through the wrapped solid boxes and progressed to the softer, floppier ones. It was difficult pretending to be pleased about receiving some new jumper or a pair of trousers, but I felt I was convincing. What concerned me, however, was that the pile of opened gifts was larger than that of my unopened pile. And so far, there was no sign of a computer, joystick, or any related games. I paused, checking what boxes were still left to tear open, and even without handling any of them, I was sceptical that there was anything even remotely resembling the shape of a computer to be found under or around the tree. I was starting to panic.

As I suspected, the last few presents opened were indeed clothing items, along with a couple of chocolate selection boxes, which was a welcome bonus. On the other side of the tree, my sister appeared to be at a similar stage in her unwrapping process and was currently explaining the various merits of a case of makeup to my dad. Although Dad didn't seem overly keen on the prospect of his daughter wearing too much makeup, or her practicing on his face as she'd just suggested.

"Is that you finished?" Mum asked me, once I'd ripped open my final gift.

I looked behind our long set of window curtains flowing down beside the tree, in case more boxes might somehow be concealed there. But much to my abject horror, there weren't.

Mum quickly moved in to collect any balls of wrapping paper that'd accumulated by my feet. "Right, you two. How about some breakfast? I've got Spam, sausage, egg, Spam, bacon and Spam," she said playfully. Then… "Adam, are you okay? You look sad?"

"Was that t-shirt not the colour you were hoping for?" my dad chipped in innocently, directing his Polaroid camera to point and capture a shot of my sister and me. "Smile, you two!" he cheerfully added, a brief moment before a flashbulb rendered me temporarily sightless.

I didn't want to go for breakfast. Because if I did, it would mean that all the presents had been opened, with nothing left. I couldn't believe it. There was no computer, joystick, or accessories. All I could think of was my mates, who would right about now happily be loading their first game without a care in the world.

For me, even the thought of having a go at Mouse Trap, a gift I'd truly wanted, was no longer appealing to me. I just wanted to head to my bedroom, pull the covers over me, and scream in frustration. I'd been hoping and dreaming about my new Commodore computer for months, and that dream was now shattered.

"Adam?" Mum said. "Adam, pass me that ball of used wrapping paper, please, would you?"

"Your mum's talking to you," Dad entered in, when I didn't respond. I was just staring blankly at the carpet, unsure how to face my mates again when they had a computer, and I didn't.

"What...?" I asked, looking up at Dad standing there.

"Pass your mum that paper," he said, indicating with one hand towards the sofa.

I followed the direction of Dad's pointing finger, unable to see what I was meant to be fetching. "What paper? I don't..."

"There," Dad said with a laugh, momentarily looking up from his camera's viewfinder. "That ball of wrapping paper you threw over your shoulder. It's gone behind the sofa."

"What? But I never..." I began to protest, as I didn't recall doing any such thing. But Mum and Dad seemed rather insistent.

I shuffled on my knees before shifting to all fours, crawling towards the sofa. "Where...?" I asked, making my way around to the rear. "There's nothing here that..."

And that's when I saw the glorious, heart-arresting vision of one remaining gift hiding behind there. I immediately looked back to see Mum and Dad smiling down at me.

"Oh, my. Is that another present?" Mum asked casually, as if she hadn't known the answer.

"So you know, kiddo," my dad added in. "Old Saint Nick needed financial help with this particular present. So it's a joint gift from him, your mum, and me."

I wanted to jump up and hug them, but I'd been on my knees and such for so long that the blood had probably stopped flowing, providing a struggle for me to rise up. "Is it a computer?" I asked, daring to dream, returning my attention to the unopened present.

"You'll need to unwrap it and find out," Mum suggested.

Please be a computer, I thought, putting a quivering hand on the box. I slipped a finger under a section of folded paper, and slowly pulled it away from the box. My mouth was dry, perhaps because of the strong cup of tea, or probably in heightened anticipation, as my ability to show my face in the school playground was about to be restored. I continued tearing paper, although it was neater and cleaner than the previous presents I'd attacked with messy abandon, I reckon out of sheer reverence this time.

Mum, Dad, and my sister were now all standing over me, watching and waiting. "Well?" my sister asked.

"Oh, my *God*," I squeaked out in an overly excited, high-pitched voice, having just clapped eyes on the Commodore logo that was as well-known to me as Toymasters. "It's a computer!" I shouted, along with some additional jumbled, garbled words that probably made no sense to anyone, including me.

All thoughts of precision unwrapping were quickly jettisoned, the rest of the paper removed quicker than Mum tearing away a plaster from a skinned knee. I briefly looked up to my audience, offering them a raised thumb as I simply didn't know what else to say. I'd been dreaming about this exact moment for ages.

With the paper completely torn off, back to a kneeling position now, I rested my bum on my heels, taking the opportunity to appreciate the large image of a computer illustrating the front of the box. I was in heaven. And I'd now noticed two smaller presents to open as well, which I assumed must be the accompanying joystick and some games.

Mum leaned over and gave my shoulder a gentle squeeze. "So, you're a happy boy…?" she enquired.

I was. And even though my legs were still bent up like a folding lawn chair just now, with bloodflow to my lower extremities questionable, I figured I had best give Mum and Dad the biggest hug I'd ever administered.

But before I could shove myself into a standing position, I had a moment of realisation. The keyboard in the cover image was a different colour than the one I'd seen in the Toymaster brochure. And as I was an expert on every intricate detail of this particular computer, it didn't take me too terribly long to notice this.

That's when it struck me. In my initial excitement, my eyes had only been focussed on the picture of a boy playing with his computer and having the best time. I hadn't noticed the description of the box's contents, clearly printed above the image, though I was noticing it now.

"Commodore *Sixteen*...?" I said, looking up to Mum and Dad for possible answers.

Mum could interpret the expression on my face, and her warm smile faltered somewhat. "Yes, that's right. Commodore," she said.

I thought this was possibly another joke at my expense, like when they'd first hidden the gift behind the sofa. So I laughed.

"Mum, this is the box for a Commodore *Sixteen*. Not a box for a Commodore *Sixty-Four*," I replied.

Mum stared at me blankly, before turning to my dad for help. "It's a Commodore," he offered, raising a hand, as if that would explain everything. "It's what the man in the shop sold us when we were assisting Santa," he added, shrugging helplessly.

"Please tell me you've got the real one hidden elsewhere? Or this one maybe just has a false box...?" I asked. But I could tell by their confused faces that this wasn't the case. "Oh, no... oh, *no*..." I said, putting my hands to my face as I felt my eyes quickly welling up.

"Adam, it's still a Commodore!" my sister snapped at me.

"But it's not a Commodore Sixty-Four!" I screamed back as the tears started to flow. "It's not the computer I wanted! It's a rubbish model, and everybody in school will laugh at me!"

"Adam!" Dad responded. "Nobody is going to—"

"What do you know, you've not been here for weeks!" I wailed. "Always working so you don't have to take me to the BMX track!"

I barged past him and sprinted over to the stairs. I was devastated. The gift I'd been dreaming about for months had been replaced by a hunk of junk that was about as powerful as a bloody solar calculator.

"Adam Catchpole, get back here!" Dad shouted after me. But I was halfway up the stairs at this point in a flood of tears. "Come back here, Adam! It's Christmas morning!"

"I hate Christmas!" was all I could say before slamming my bedroom door shut behind me.

Chapter Twelve

Despite Helen's suggestion that I could be the subject of my own novel, or at least that my current life could provide the basis for the book's subject matter, I resisted. Instead, I pressed on with the book I'd already started. I admit I briefly considered my sister's idea, however. For instance, as Christmas tales tended to have a positive outcome, perhaps I might be prompting the universe to deliver me a slice of good fortune if I was to serve as the lead character in my own novel...? But I didn't feel I had the luxury of time to ponder such a decision and waffle about, deliberating as to whether or not I should implement my sister's proposition. After all, my existing story, as it stood, was already three complete chapters and growing, and was my best chance at revitalising my sales numbers and thus rescuing my income.

On the subject of money, I'd received confirmation of a meeting at my local bank to discuss solutions to my current cash flow situation. On the drive to Douglas in my new beige-coloured chariot, though, I didn't know if I was more nervous about seeing the bank manager with my cap in hand or the fact I had my first rehearsal at the dance studio later that afternoon. But the way I figured it, by at least speaking with the bank, I'd finally pulled my head out of the sand and would soon have a feel for just how patient and accommodating they might be with me that I'd been a bit tardy on my mortgage repayments of late.

Fortunately, the kids had all gone back to school, resulting in plenty of available spaces in the town centre's car park, as fewer mums and dads were currently out and about. And this time, I'd brought additional change to ensure that I didn't end up with another excess parking charge. Though I couldn't help noticing that *another* Tesco trolley had filled the void occupied by its predecessor, right there in the middle of a parking space, and *it* didn't have an eighty quid fine affixed to it.

My plan was that I wanted to show the bank manager I wasn't some scruffy layabout. As such, I'd first arranged a hair appointment to smarten myself up, considering I'd missed my opportunity the previous week because of the unfortunate Munchkin kerfuffle. Granted, there wasn't too much hair to trim as I'd like these days, but what was still there tended to curl out conspicuously from the sides of my head, making me look a bit like the Grandpa character from the television show *The Munsters* when I was overdue a cut.

So, soon looking more presentable, I found myself in the waiting area of my bank with clammy hands and a sense of foreboding. Sitting there, watching the hustle and bustle of a busy branch, I couldn't help but feel like I was at the doctors waiting for the test results about an embarrassing rash. It didn't help matters any that I was also scratching like crazy on account of the hairs shaved off from the back of my neck which, although I couldn't see them behind there, had worked their way under the collar of my polo shirt and were now successfully making themselves known.

"Mr Catchpole?" a well-dressed young woman said, presenting herself before me a short while later. When I smiled and nodded, she thrust a hand in my direction. "Nice to meet you. I'm Bethany Aitken, your small business manager."

I jumped up from my chair, holding out my meat hook as well. But before our two palms had a chance to connect, skin to skin, Bethany retracted her hand like a gunslinger quickly reholstering their pistol. Confused, and with my own paw dangling midair, I glanced down, spotting the previously unnoticed clumps of neck hair that had somehow stuck themselves to the back of my overly moist knuckles whilst I'd been digging away under my collar, now giving me the appearance of a pubescent Sasquatch.

"Oh, sorry about that, Bethany. I've just been for a haircut, and a good portion of it ended up in difficult-to-reach places," I said as explanation, wiping my hand on my trousers. "It's very itchy, too," I added, offering a nervous laugh that only made me sound, I'm sure, like a muppet.

"I see. Would you like to come through to my office?"

Following Bethany to her workspace, I couldn't help but notice how young she looked. Not that it contributed to how efficient she may be at her job in one way or another, of course. Rather, it simply made me feel even more awkward than I already did about baring my financial soul to her.

After some brief pleasantries and the offering to me of either a coffee or a tea, which I politely declined, I explained how I'd made the appointment in response to a 'few' letters I'd received concerning my overdue mortgage payments.

Bethany listened intently, and her friendly manner quickly put me at ease. Once I'd finished my short speech, she turned her attention to the screen of her computer, which was just out of view to me from where I was sitting. I tried to arch my neck for a sneaky peek, but she clearly knew the optimum angle in which to position her monitor to prevent such an outcome from happening.

Once she'd finished reviewing what I assumed were my financial case notes, she straightened up in her chair again and directed her attention to me once more. "So, then, Mr Catchpole, our records—"

"Please. Call me Adam," I interrupted.

"Okay, Adam," she said, pressing the frame of her glasses up the bridge of her nose. "Adam, our records indicate you've been in arrears for six months on your mortgage payments."

"Six…?" I immediately replied in a state of disbelief. Bizarrely, I thought it was more, so this was actually positive news.

"We've written to you on *eleven* separate occasions," Bethany said, keen to stress the specific number. "Mr— erm, sorry… Adam. Adam, is there any chance there's been an issue with receiving our correspondence?

For a moment, I considered throwing Paddy, my postman, under the bus and blaming him for my supposedly 'missing' mail. But that wasn't fair. This financial mess was all on me, and I knew I had to take the blame and face this like a man. "Eleven notices…?" I asked, incredulous. "Ehm… maybe we should double-check the correspondence file you have on file there?" I suggested, not completely ready to own up to my cowardice, despite what I'd just convinced myself.

Bethany was great, however. Not once did she talk down at me, and she was eager to find solutions to my dire financial situation. As she did feel compelled to point out, though: "Adam, you need to maintain open dialogue with us because it's not in anyone's best interests if your mortgage ends up in default."

She went on to explain that I needed to outline a strategy where I could not only catch up on the arrears but detail how I intended to cover my future mortgage payments as well, which, thanks to a rising interest rate environment were now several hundred more pounds a month than I realised. Apparently, the interest rate increase was fully explained in one of the letters that I didn't bother opening. But as pleasant as she was, Bethany made it abundantly clear that if I didn't devise a plan, there was every likelihood that I'd end up forcing the hands of the banking powers that be, leaving them with little option but to commence recovery proceedings. Which, translated to plain, uncomplicated English, meant kicking my broke arse out of my home.

"Before we finish up here, Adam," Bethany said, with her attention on her computer screen again. "I've got your occupation listed as a novelist. Is that still the case?"

"It is, yes. I write space opera novels if you're interested." I said, using the opportunity to promote my books to any potential new customer.

"Space opera? No," Bethany said politely, waving away the suggestion. "No, I only tend to read romance novels. But thanks."

"Ah, the saucy genre where you end up in a billionaire's dungeon, chained to some kind of crazy torture device?" I responded. "You know, my agent recommended I try writing one of those," I told her. "Perhaps you could give me a few suggestions? A couple of potential plot points?" I added with a laugh.

But when I looked up, I could see the expression of horror on Bethany's face. "The type of romantic novels I tend to enjoy do not end up in anyone's dungeon, Mr Catchpole," she informed me.

I'd clearly misread the room and forgot that there were also plenty of other styles of romantic literature which didn't involve clothes being ripped off by kinky billionaire tech entrepreneurs in their well-appointed bondage dungeons.

"Please forgive me," I offered feebly, feeling both of my cheeks turn warm. I then hurriedly collected the eleven letters of unread correspondence that Bethany had been so kind as to print off for my convenience.

"If there's nothing else..." I said, pushing my chair back, "then I sincerely thank you for your time." I resisted the urge to extend my hand, however, worried there might still be some residual hair left on it. "Could I ask you a question before I leave, Bethany...?" I added.

Now also standing, Bethany regarded me uncertainly. "Yes, of course," she answered, although she appeared wary of what other stupid thing might exit my mouth just now.

"From your experience, how long do you think the bank would continue to put up with my current financial situation? You know, before the removal folks turned up with a large empty van at my house?"

"Ah. Well, every case is based on its own merits and discussed in length by our credit committee, and—"

"Bethany, I won't hold you to it, but please... could you give me some rough idea?"

Bethany momentarily considered my question, seeming reluctant to go on record with any definitive answer. "I can't be sure, Mr Catchpole. But I've seen other cases in which recovery proceedings start around the six-month timescale," she eventually said.

This wasn't good. This wasn't good at all. I was *already* at the six-month mark, so this didn't give me much time at all. Plus, the interest rate hike meant I was now needing to somehow find even more money than I would've ever foreseen previously. "Oh. Oh, I see," I replied, with the wind blown well and truly out of my sails. "Blimey, I suppose it's good that I've just got an additional job as an actor," I considered out loud.

"Should I make a note of that on your file?"

"No. Best not to, Bethany. Because I'm unsure how long this acting gig will last before I get dragged off stage by either the audience or my fellow cast members," I advised. "Plus, this particular gig isn't a paying job anyway."

It wasn't the news I'd hoped for. Indeed, I was in a worse financial situation than I thought. But at least now I knew what I was up against and a general idea about how long I may have to rectify it. I didn't know, however, if I'd have a snowball in hell's chance of clearing the arrears before I had to pack up my things and move them into a cardboard box.

At least there were positives, I thought to myself on the walk back to my car: First, I was feeling a bit more groomed after my haircut. Second, my new novel was progressing nicely, I felt. And third, thankfully not one soul during my morning out and about appeared to recognise me as the unsavoury scoundrel from the worrying online video. So it wasn't unwelcome news entirely.

* * *

I didn't think I was too nervous about my first rehearsal at TAPPIN' FEET. But since I'd come home from my visit to the bank, all I could think about was making a complete tit of myself. Other than a few school plays, I'd never been on any type of stage. Plus, as most people who knew me would attest, I was also an undeniable introvert who was much more comfortable holed up on my own, hunched over my laptop typing away and doing my own thing, rather than parading around on the floorboards of a stage.

But never let it be said that I'm not prepared. Since Chloe was kind enough to email me a copy of the script in advance, I'd solidly rehearsed my lines (and thankfully I'd only seven lines to worry about), to the point where the words were firmly etched into my brain. I'd briefly drafted my neighbour Carol in to offer her critical opinion to ensure my performance wasn't too wooden. And after three flawless run-throughs, I was delighted to receive glowing reviews for my acting prowess. There was even talk of a Tony award bandied around my living room. But I still think I had more to give.

By taking this seriously, I reasoned, I was less likely to make a fool out of myself. But, even more importantly, I genuinely didn't want to let Chloe or the rest of the cast down. After all, the performances they staged were the result of months of organising and countless hours of practice. Plus, the proceeds from ticket sales were crucial for their studio's upkeep and paying their bills. I had already sabotaged one of their performances—albeit unintention-ally—and I wasn't keen on doing so again by this time turning up unprepared. Sadly, as I'd been drafted in at the last minute, I would only have a few rehearsals with the rest of the gang before curtains up on our first performance in front of the paying public. I was, as they might say in the acting game, "bricking it."

Having parked up and begun walking towards the TAPPIN' FEET entrance, I was conscious of my racing heart bashing against my sternum. The lines of dialogue I had so diligently rehearsed were melting in my brain like hot paraffin with each step, and my knees felt like they were about to buckle at any minute. I wanted to be sick. I turned back towards my car, seriously considering hiding in the boot or driving off, I didn't know which.

However, my uncertainty was interrupted by a firm gripping sensation on my right hand, which initially made me panic, leav-ing me wondering if I wasn't perhaps having some sort of anxiety-related episode. Fortunately, I wasn't. Because I glanced to my side, surprised by the presence of a young girl, aged five or six, who had crept up on me and wrapped her tiny fingers around my hand.

She looked up at me with a pair of adorable sparkling blue eyes, smiling to reveal the absence of her two front teeth. For a moment, I wondered if she'd lost her bearings on the way to rehearsal and needed some help. "Hiya," I said, lowering myself so I wasn't quite as intimidating by towering over the wee thing. I wasn't that great with kids, however, and never knew how to speak to them. "Hello there, are you okay...?" I asked, for some reason altering the pitch of my voice so it sounded like I was talking to my pet cat Barry. She stared back at me like I was a patronising idiot.

"Are you that man that broke our Emerald City to pieces?" she asked, letting go of my hand.

Sadly, I couldn't deny it. "I'm afraid I am," I replied, resting my right knee on the tarmac. "And I'm very sorry for making such a mess of things."

She looked me up and down. "And now you're thinking of run-ning away because you're scared about acting?" she surmised.

How this young lass talked to me made her sound wise beyond her years. I immediately felt embarrassed because she was spot-on in her assessment. I fumbled about for an excuse. "Uhm, well, I was just heading back to my car to, erm…"

Leaning in close, so that our foreheads were almost bumping, the girl gave the impression I was in for a severe dressing down. "Right," she said instead. "Without thinking, tell me the names of seven animals you'd find in a zoo," she instructed, just as her mum wandered over, wondering who this stranger she'd accosted in the car park was.

"The names of…?"

"Do it!" the girl insisted, stamping her little foot with impressive authority.

"Erm… well…" I stumbled, suddenly unable to remember my name, let alone seven animal varieties.

"Hurry up!"

"Okay, em… hippo, lion, zebra, goose, otter… oh, uhm… snake, I guess, and…"

"Think of a long neck," my new car park friend prompted.

"Ooh, ooh, a giraffe!" I said, pleased I'd passed an IQ test issued by a five-year-old. "What do I win?"

"You don't win anything, you big silly. But I bet you're not nervous anymore about coming inside to rehearse, are you?"

Wow. She was right. This was like some sort of Jedi-esque mind control technique at work right now. "I'm Adam, by the way," I said before returning to full height.

"And I'm Evie, by the way," Evie said in return, flashing me a gummy smile and, I couldn't help noticing, appearing well chuffed and distinctly pleased with herself.

"So," she added, turning round to start heading into the building. "Are you coming inside or what? If we're not careful, we'll be late for rehearsals."

"Yes, Evie, I'm right behind you," I said. And then, looking at her mum, "Now that's an impressive kid you've got there," I remarked.

Mum nodded, casting a doting glance in her daughter's direction. "She's one in a million, all right. Although I often wonder, in this relationship of ours, who the child is and who's the parent," Mum admitted.

Standing with her hand on the dance studio's front door, Evie looked at me with her left hand placed firmly on her hip. "Adam, will you *please* hurry up. Stop dawdling," she said, with that same impressive air of authority again.

"And you should know," Mum whispered to me out of the corner of her mouth. "Evie doesn't like to be kept waiting for her rehearsals!"

"I'm starting to get that impression," I said with a laugh, before breaking into a gentle jog. "And it was nice to meet you," I added, waving over my shoulder to Mum. "I'm hurrying, Evie! And can I double-check that a goose is an animal you'd find in a zoo? Because I'm not sure now that I think about it!"

Chapter Thirteen

As far as first rehearsals went—not that I had much experience to compare with—I suppose I couldn't have too many complaints. However, my initial arrival in the dance studio was a smidge awkward, with a few of the smaller children reacting to me as if the Grinch had just arrived to steal Christmas from them, on account of the unfortunate prior incident in town.

But even before Chloe could leap to my defence and defuse the situation, my new best mate, Evie, calmed things down, assuring her fellow cast members that I wasn't there to nick their presents or destroy their happiness or anything like that. And even though Evie was tiny (about waist-high) and one of the younger kids in the group, it was obvious her opinion carried a fair bit of weight amongst the others. Given this, and despite some suspicious looks at first, I seemed to have been ultimately accepted into their fold— albeit on the proviso that I didn't muck things up.

But it wasn't just the kids (of which there were plenty) I needed to win over. Because a few of the adults in attendance didn't appear too thrilled by my being there, if their frosty reception was any measure. One chap in particular was shooting me daggers, giving a death stare that was slightly unnerving. Although when I spotted the crutches resting next to his seat, I went out on a limb and had a guess at his identity without makeup.

"Hello, mate," I said, sitting beside him. "Are you, by any chance, the Scarecrow…?"

"Not anymore I'm not," came the curt response. But I couldn't really blame him. After all, he was the one with a pair of crutches for company. But we exchanged some small talk before I explained things from my perspective. Fortunately, he did see the funny side, and as it should happen, turned out to be something of a science fiction fan as well. Sadly, he'd never heard of my work, but I offered him a signed book by way of apology for damaging the ligaments in his ankle.

I subsequently discovered that Steve, the injured ex-Scarecrow, was Chloe's brother, and often lent a hand when required. Along with his cousins, Jason and Trevor, they were all drafted into the ensemble whenever characters might require male adults to portray them. In this particular production, Jason and Trevor were cast as Tin Man and the Cowardly Lion. However, I couldn't tell the two apart because the both of them are identical twins (Jason and Trevor, that is, not the Tin Man and the Cowardly Lion, obviously), which caused me some confusion early on. But after a few days and a couple of pleasant rehearsals, I could finally differentiate one from the other. Trevor, as it turned out, had a rather distinctive laugh, and he also loved talking just like the Cowardly Lion character even when not in costume.

After a while, I started to feel like I wasn't the new kid at school anymore. Above all, I was bowled over by the talent on display. I mean, these kids were like nothing I'd ever seen before. One minute they were mucking about and being, well, kids. And yet when Chloe called them to order and brought them to attention, they switched into their roles with aplomb. For an acting novice like me, it was both inspiring and intimidating to witness. I thought I'd been walking into a glorified school play. But, as I'd soon discovered, their collective singing, acting, and dancing abilities wouldn't have looked out of place in a professional West End theatre. They were terrific.

The only slight fly in the ointment was the Scarecrow costume I'd inherited from Steve. The large, floppy black hat fit fine, as did the baggy green shirt made from what felt like an old potato sack. However, with Steve being an avid cyclist—rather than a middle-aged slob like myself sporting a bit of excess timber—the trouser portion of the outfit that was intended to be loose-fitting stuck to my legs like a wetsuit. So, besides being uncomfortable, there was the real danger they might split, providing the audience a bit more than they bargained for.

Fortunately, as Chloe explained, all the costumes were made in-house by her best friend. Meaning there wouldn't be a need for me to brave another shopping trip into town to purchase a new pair. The dance group's volunteer seamstress, as it should happen, was none other than Evie's mum, Julia, whom I'd met briefly in the car park. As she already had the material in stock from the previous Scarecrow outfit she'd constructed, the plan was to arrange a convenient time to grab a pair of trousers to be fitted before the first performance.

Soon, then, with that convenient time thus having been dutifully arranged, I found myself making my way through a maze of a busy housing estate called Farmhill, easing along in my Nissan Micra at the sort of sedentary speed befitting an experienced kerb crawler. Julia had provided me with the address beforehand, but I was having trouble reading the house numbers from behind the wheel. As luck would have it, I spotted two Flying Monkeys walking towards a corner property in the tree-lined cul-de-sac, so I suspected I was heading in the appropriate direction. Further confidence arrived from the ominous form of a Wicked Witch costume hanging from a washing line in the front garden.

Once parked, I spotted several of my fellow cast members, who I assumed must also be booked in for some last-minute costume adjustment. And as I pushed open the garden gate, I could hear the sound of children laughing through the opened window, with perhaps some of my fellow cast members already inside. Ordinarily, the thought of a load of kids getting underfoot may have resulted in some eye-rolling, as well as some tut-tutting, and mumbling and grumbling under my breath. But now, after having spent a few rehearsals with them, I was starting to warm to the little blighters' company. Something about them made being in a bad mood nigh on impossible.

Bloody hell, I thought to myself, is Adam Catchpole no longer a grumpy old sod?

With the front door already opened, I popped a cautious head slightly inside. "Knock-knock, it's just Adam," I said, announcing my arrival.

Julia appeared briefly. "Come on in, Adam. I'm hemming a few skirts, and then I'll be right with you. Take a seat in the living room for ten minutes."

I did as was instructed, but suddenly felt a sense of impending doom as soon as I'd entered the living room. Because there, sitting on the floor in the shape of a neat circle, was Evie surrounded by a group of her mates, engaged in what looked very much like an impromptu tea party.

"Hiya, guys," I said, offering a friendly wave. But the way Evie was looking at me, I knew what was coming next. "Ehm... I'll just leave you to your tea party and wait in the..." I attempted to say.

Evie stopped pouring the imaginary liquid from her sparkly pink teapot for a tick. "There's always room for one more, Adam," she promptly suggested, patting the carpet beside her and shifting her position to open up a spot for me. "You can have a nice cup of tea while you wait for Mummy."

Seven sets of expectant eyes were on me, and I sensed that any hopes of a strategic retreat were hopeless. "Erm... okay?" I said, having no choice but to give in. I settled on the floor, struggling to sit cross-legged like my fellow tea party members, wondering at what age you stop being so flexible as them. A small plastic teacup was thrust into my hand a moment later, having already been graciously filled with invisible tea by Evie's magic teapot.

"Thanks. Is there any cake?" I asked, playing right along, as by now, resistance appeared to be very much futile.

Evie reached for an empty plate. "Chocolate or sponge?" she offered, sounding like she'd spent the afternoon baking.

"Chocolate sponge sounds lovely," I said.

"*No*, mister silly. Chocolate *or* sponge. There's *two* of them," she explained, clarifying the situation.

"Ah, sorry," I answered. Though in my defence, the cake was imaginary, after all, and thus difficult to see. "In that case, what do you recommend?" I asked.

"Why don't you have both?" Evie insisted, starting to cut into one of the invisible cakes with her equally invisible and imaginary knife.

"A wise choice," I replied. "But not too much. Only a slither of each, yeah? You see, I'm carrying a bit of excess padding and I've got a new pair of trousers to fit into."

And soon enough, after pretending to eat and enjoy my imaginary slices of cake and drink my tea, I was out of one torture session, so to speak, and straight into another...

Oh, why did I have to wear my Star Trek underpants? I had just assumed Julia would do what she needed to do over the protective layer of my jeans. However, she needed to get more precise measurements, which required removal of the jeans, if only briefly. Of course she was entirely professional and discreet, but it must have been a bit challenging to ignore the fact that I was wearing a pair of bright red Y-fronts with the Star Trek logo placed squarely on the location of my space rocket, or space shuttle, or what have you. Plus, the image of Captain James Tiberius Kirk emblazoned across the rear was probably an extraordinary sight as well. It didn't help matters, either, when Evie and a couple of the others from the tea party popped their head around the door to see what was happening. And they weren't as professional or discreet!

A gift from my sister, I had a full set of these particular undergarments, all in assorted colours and each featuring the image of a different key crew member of the USS *Enterprise* NCC-1701. Not that Evie or her friends probably understood what I was on about as I tried to explain, of course, especially when I launched into an explanation about why the colour red was a strange choice to pair with Captain Kirk, given what always happened to members of the away team who sported red uniforms in TOS (The Original Series). To put it plainly, the "red shirts," as they are affectionately referred to by fans, were always the ones who ended up dying.

Anyway, Evie and her mates probably didn't care about all this information. Instead, just the sight of me standing there in silly coloured underpants was enough to set them into a fit of giggles, getting them eventually shooed away as a result.

Once I was mostly dressed and fairly decent, Evie reappeared after assurances by me and her mum that it was safe to do so, with Evie enquiring if I were, as she'd heard, an author.

"Yep, I sure am," I advised proudly, as I put my shoes back on. "I write science fiction books."

"Is that about microscopes, and people having long white coats and wearing funny goggles?" Evie asked, trying her best to sound interested, although perhaps not entirely succeeding.

I looked at her mum and smiled. "No, not that sort of science, Evie," I said, while turning to address her again. "I write about different types of aliens all battling for supremacy in strange, unexplored galaxies."

This explanation seemed to pique her interest a little bit. "Oh. Like Star Wars...?" Evie asked.

"Exactly! Or Star Trek, like we were just talking about."

"Will you come to our school to read some of your books?" she enquired. "Because me and my friends watch that Star Wars show and love Grogu."

I was also a fan of Grogu, the cute little green dude with big ears. But reading in front of a class of real-life little dudes (and dudettes) didn't appeal. "I couldn't," I said, receiving a disappointed frown in response. "My books are for grown-ups," I explained. "Plus, getting permission to come into your school to read books would be difficult," I added, hoping that would bring that subject to a close.

But Evie was nothing if not persistent. "But you could write a space story especially for our class," she suggested, looking to her friends for support. "And *Mummy* is a teacher in our school. So she could let you come in," Evie also pointed out.

I groaned internally. Julia, who'd now begun setting to work at her sewing machine on my Scarecrow trousers, glanced back up at me. She gave me a sheepish look that I translated as, *I could make that happen if you wanted me to.*

My gut reaction was to offer Evie some kind of further waffling excuse as to why I couldn't come to her school to do a reading. But then I couldn't help recalling my neighbour Carol's sage words of advice about "getting off my arse" and "getting out into the outside world" on occasion. Because ever since I did just that, as she'd suggested, some good things had started happening in my life. And, as I further reflected, what harm could come from standing up in front of a class of schoolkids?

"All right, fine," I said, willing to wander out of the limiting confines of my darkened office/comfort zone again. "But there are two conditions for me to do this, young Evie..."

"Yay!"

"Firstly, you'll help me write the children-friendly space story we'll read. And do you know what the second thing is?"

Evie shook her head. "No. What?"

I lowered myself down so I could look her in the eye. Once there, I extended an unfurled finger towards her.

"The second thing, Evie, is that you can't tell *anybody* about my silly Captain James T Kirk spaceman underpants. Deal?"

Evie eagerly agreed, shaking the hand I presented to her to seal the deal. "I won't tell anybody about your silly spaceman underpants, mister silly," she then promised, locking an imaginary lock over her mouth and throwing the key away for good measure.

Chapter Fourteen

Christmas Day 1984

I was absolutely devastated. I slammed my bedroom door shut behind me and was immediately greeted by a Commodore 64 poster I'd stuck on my wardrobe. With tears streaming, I ripped it off and tossed it to the floor. All I could think about was each of my mates sitting in front of their new computers, eagerly loading a game. But when they heard about what I'd got, I knew I was going to end up the butt of their jokes for years to come. They'd most likely give me a nickname like "Sixteen Boy," or similar. I knew this because that's what I'd probably do if the roles were reversed. It was Christmas morning, and it was the worst day of my life.

I lay on my bed for a few minutes, expecting Dad to come bursting through the door. But nothing. At least not yet. I didn't know what to do next, other than I needed to get out of the house while I formulated some excuse for my rubbish present. I could tell my friends that I'd be getting the Commodore 64 for my birthday and that this older model was just to get me started on, I considered, as I pushed open my bedroom window. With some manoeuvring, I knew I could climb down onto the roof of the small porch below, as I'd done previously when leaving the house without being noticed. Or in this case, escaping before Dad decided to make an appearance to give me a severe bollocking.

I jumped carefully from the porch roof, making it down, and across the front steps without anybody in pursuit. The street was empty. Usually, the area would be packed on Christmas morning with us young people playing on their new bikes, despite the winter cold. But not today. And it was probably just my mind playing tricks on me, but I convinced myself I could hear people laughing at my misfortune from inside their homes.

"Useless Christmas," I moaned, kicking out in frustration at a discarded Coke can. But my foot hadn't yet returned to the pavement when I heard the voice of someone loudly shouting, scaring the heck out of me. I spun around, panicking that Dad was tearing down the street looking for me. But nothing there. The neighbourhood was still like a ghost town. And then, again, even louder this time, the same booming voice as before, sounding like it was echoing off each house in the street. But this time, I recognised it and knew precisely where it was coming from. I glanced further down the pavement towards Robert Bentham's house, where the volley of shouting and bad language was originating.

To run away from home, even briefly, I needed to proceed forward, but I was worried about getting too close to Robert's house. I cautiously proceeded, keeping one eye on his front door in case his father appeared and somehow found a reason to have a go at me. There was an unnerving silence as I approached, and I considered breaking into a sprint. But getting a little closer, I could see into their garden, and that's when I realised I could no longer spot the abandoned fridge that was dumped there and left on the grass for months. And the reason I couldn't immediately see it was because it was obscured behind a tree placed in front of it.

It took me a second or two to register what I was looking at. I tilted my head, recognising the green and red baubles poking out from the branches, with the tree partially squashed under its own weight. *That's the one from Scatty Newbold's*, I thought, standing there with my mouth wide open. At first, I wondered if Gareth, the deliveryman, had perhaps left it in the garden. But that tree previously took pride of place in Mr Newbold's shop window, so surely Gareth wouldn't have just pitched it over the garden wall and left it to rot? Plus, I remembered seeing it lit up behind Robert's living room window the previous evening, now I thought back on it.

I continued closer to my friend's house, where a trail of tinsel, broken coloured glass, and crushed fairy lights were visible on the weed-infested garden path. I couldn't be a hundred percent sure, but from where I stood it looked very much like the lovely tree had been unceremoniously chucked from the front door, baubles and all, before coming to rest in front of the abandoned fridge.

I felt sick, seeing it so heartlessly cast aside like that. It was like I'd just been kicked in the stomach. I couldn't understand why the Christmas tree had been tossed outside. It's not as if they were Jewish or anything, as Robert surely would have informed me of that. And they had no Andorra as well, or whatever that special thing with the candles is called that Jewish people displayed.

I hadn't noticed it at first, but their natty, yellowed front window curtains were open enough so I could see into the living room. With the morning sun interfering, it took a moment to adjust my view, using my hand to shield the sun's early rays. *Is that Robert?* I thought, able to make him out in the middle of the living room. It was. He was just standing there, scrunched down, not moving a muscle. And I could also see he was still wearing that same white sleeveless t-shirt he always wore to PE class, as if he had nothing else to possibly wear around the house, even on Christmas.

Instinctively, I was about to wave hello to him. But then his father appeared into view, with the raised voice I'd heard a few moments ago starting up again in spades, sounding just like the devil. I don't know what Robert could ever have done to deserve it, but the shouting continued, with his dad shaking his hands in the air, one of them grasping a can of beer, even at this early hour, and looking like he was about to hit Robert with it. I didn't know what to do. I wanted to run away, but my legs wouldn't move.

Then, as if my arm had a will of its own, I reached down to collect a small stone I located at the base of their garden wall. Without thinking, I launched the pebble at their front window, where it soon bounced off with a sharp, louder-than-expected noise. So loud, in fact, that for a moment I thought I'd smashed the glass.

Robert's father appeared briefly shocked. I looked at his overly tight shirt struggling to contain his big fat beer belly, and I desperately wanted to throw another rock, only a bigger one, and throw it harder. He was in front of the window now, yelling and cursing, his hands waving around like mad. He reminded me of a crazed gorilla, the only thing missing being him thumping his chest.

Just before I started running, Robert looked across his shoulder at me. He had a haunted expression on his face that sent chills up my spine. He looked petrified.

I was clear of our street and nearly at the park before I stopped sprinting. I was sure I could still hear the yelling, even from a distance. I sat on one of the swings, swaying back and forth, trying to calm down, but unable to get the horrible look on Robert's face out of my mind. I thought about how excited he must have been when Gareth, the driver, had turned up on his doorstep with the tree he'd so desperately wanted. And I thought about how gutted he must have been when his dad had dumped it outside, like trash.

I made sure I was alone before I started to cry. I don't know if it was because of Robert that I was crying, or because I hated myself as well. After all, I'd just ruined Christmas for my entire family. And why? Because I hadn't been satisfied with the certain, *specific* model of computer I received. By contrast, I knew Robert would've given his right arm to be in my position, surrounded by gifts in a nice, clean, tidy home, along with a family who truly loved him.

I sobbed, unable to control my trembling lip, thinking of the life I enjoyed and how good I had it, and how awful my friend Robert's was by comparison.

"You stupid muttonhead," I said, slapping one of my hands on the swing set's metal frame in frustration. I was thinking of some additional choice things to call myself, but I knew I wasn't really permitted to say those kinds of words out loud.

"You're simply a stupid, greedy, selfish idiot, Adam Catchpole, aren't you?"

❊ ❊ ❊

There was only so long I could linger in the park alone, and it's not as if I felt like playing at this point anyway. I trudged back home, taking the extended, alternate route so I didn't need to walk past Robert's house and risk another interaction of some type with his father.

Once back at my house, to say the atmosphere was frosty there would be an understatement. Even Mum could barely look at me when I walked through our front door, so I knew I'd messed up. I apologised. I tried to explain why I was upset about receiving the wrong computer, but all I got were shakes of the head and looks of disappointment. And I deserved them.

But I wasn't concerned about the computer now. Instead, I was more worried about Robert. Eventually, Mum instructed me to go into the kitchen because she wanted to discuss my behaviour. So we sat down, and I swear it wasn't distraction tactics, but I needed to fill her in about everything that was going on with my friend. I started by revealing the time I'd found Robert with an injured face, and how his dad had yelled at me. I then conveyed the whole situation about the Christmas tree, which Scatty Newbold had been so kind to provide at low cost and have delivered.

Mum listened intently, calling my dad into the room when I began talking about the events of today, in which I observed Robert's father screaming at him for no discernible reason, the can of beer in his hand this early in the morning, on Christmas of all days, and threatening to hit my friend over the head with it. I'm not sure I could accurately describe the intensity of Mr Bentham's anger, the look of utter despair on my friend Robert's face, or how upset it all made me as I decided to throw a rock at the window.

When my dad's face turned a furious shade of red, I thought I was in even more trouble for admitting about the stone. But rather than shouting, Dad walked towards the door, with Mum trying to hold him back. But it was useless, because Dad is a unit of a man with hands the size of coal shovels, so it was like trying to stop a freight train once it got set in motion and started hurtling down the tracks.

"I'm sorry, Mum," I said, a little concerned as my father left the house. "I didn't mean for— I mean, I didn't know Dad would…"

"It's okay," Mum offered. "John Bentham is a horrible bully who needs to be brought down a peg or two. It'll be fine."

Time felt like it was standing still. I desperately wanted to run to Robert's house and be a witness to whatever might happen, but Mum told me to stay put. And as I was already in so much trouble, this time I thought I should listen.

I heard the first siren about five minutes later, followed by another very quickly after that, the sound of both getting closer and louder. I could only imagine Dad punching Robert's father right in the face and that big stupid jerk falling right on his big dumb arse. Mum threw on her coat and bolted out of the house, telling my sister and me to stay where we were. I'd never seen my mum look so worried about what Dad might have gone and done.

I sat staring at the fairy lights on our tree, which appeared to melt into each other after a short period of time, blending together like I was dreaming. More sirens sounded. I don't know how many, exactly. Then, through the front window, I could spot some of our neighbours peering through their curtains, trying to see what was going on down the street.

It was maybe fifteen or twenty minutes after Mum left when I heard the front door open. While she was gone, I'd spent the time thinking about what to say and how to apologise for being such a selfish pig earlier. But I felt I should offer more than simply words. I knew from past occasions that Mum didn't look forward to the mountain of dishes after we'd had our Christmas dinner. As such, I reckoned it might be a pleasant surprise if I offered to wash them for her, put them away, and then clean the sink once I'd finished. I wasn't sure how to get back into Dad's good books, though. I knew he liked beer and football. So perhaps we could watch a match together on the telly, with him sitting all nice and cosy in his favourite chair and me fetching him a beer whenever he asked?

Upon hearing the door, I cautiously walked into the hallway, ready to begin offering my grovelling apology. However, it wasn't Mum and Dad standing there, as I'd expected. Instead, it was our next-door neighbour, Mrs Cannell.

"What's going on?" I asked, without even saying hello, forgetting my manners. I was worried that my dad might've got carried away, based on all the sirens I'd heard, and that Mr Bentham was in a terrible state and on his way to the hospital. I just hoped Dad wasn't in desperate trouble with the police for it.

Mrs Cannell was the oldest person I knew, with a face lined with deep wrinkles and a head of thin white hair that reminded me of candyfloss. She always had a happy expression whenever I spoke to her over the hedge. But not today. Not now.

Mrs Cannell shuffled fully into our hallway, wetting her top lip with her tongue, looking like she was trying to say something but didn't know how. My sister joined us there.

"Mrs Cannell, what's wrong?" my sister asked.

"Your mum asked me to call in and sit with you," Mrs Cannell explained. "Children, I'm afraid Mum has had to go off to the hospital."

"Did my dad injure Mr Bentham very badly? Has he been sent to the hospital?" I asked. "Is that why Mum's gone there? To look after him?" I asked. But that didn't make any sense to me, as why would she do that? Mum was simply a very compassionate person, I had to suppose, and cared about everybody, even a miserable so-and-so like Robert's father.

Mrs Cannell suddenly appeared even more frail than she usually did. She shook her head, her bonce of white hair jiggling like a blancmange.

"No, Adam. I'm afraid your dad's been taken to hospital as well. That's why she's gone."

"Our dad? But why, what's happened to him?" my sister Helen asked, just as confused as I was. "Mrs Cannell?" she said a moment later, when no reply was immediately offered. *"Mrs Cannell?"*

"I don't quite know how to tell you this, dears," Mrs Cannell answered. "But your dad, well, he's been stabbed. They've taken him away in an ambulance…"

Chapter Fifteen

My first adult onstage performance was in front of a packed house of, according to what I was informed, one hundred and forty-six people. When I'd first walked into the place, I had no idea the modest hall could cram so many people into it. But it did, with all available seats occupied and several rows of people squashed in at the rear.

Standing in the wings I was a bag of nerves, unlike the kids, who were fuelled by a mixture of sugar and adrenaline and were eager to have the curtain raised to strut their stuff. They were an impressive bunch, to be sure, and I was pleased that so many people had turned out for their initial performance. And it wasn't only today's show that sold out, because there were no tickets available for the rest of the week's performances either.

There were, however, slightly mixed emotions on my part. And that was because Steve's ankle had healed up much quicker than he'd anticipated. And despite the pre-performance jitters I was experiencing, I truly *wanted* to go on stage. I'd put in a lot of rehearsal time by now and was genuinely looking forward to it.

Of course I certainly didn't want Steve's injury to be worse than he'd originally thought. But his remarkable recovery skills meant he'd be available for the rest of the show's run. In fact, I suspected he was fighting fit for tonight's performance as well, but he magnanimously suggested I take the stage for him this time, for which I was grateful. I think he was gracious enough to know how much work I'd put in, and that it would've been a disappointment for me if I hadn't the opportunity to get out there at least once. I couldn't harbour any ill will going forward if he took my place on future shows, however, as Steve had taken part in rehearsals for several weeks in the lead-up to me rendering him temporarily incapacitated, and it was nice to see him up on his feet now.

Fortunately, this was also the night my sister Helen (along with those she'd sold her stack of tickets to), my Mum, a few other family members, and even Carol had purchased a seat for, all so they could appreciate my efforts. And I refused to let them down. Well, at least I hoped I wouldn't...

In reality, my fellow cast members were so talented that any small mistake on my part was likely overlooked. And when I managed to trip and fall off the edge of the stage at one point, I liked to think it was done with such comedic effect that the audience imagined it was all part of the act. It certainly raised a laugh.

As for Chloe Tappin, starring as Dorothy, just wow! I was blown away. I knew she was special when I heard her singing in the shopping street that day. But watching her performance in front of an audience was mesmerising. Indeed, it was her stunning rendition of the famous rainbow song again that distracted me to the point I tripped off the side of the stage. I was additionally impressed with her ability to motivate the children and give them a gentle helping hand during the show if they'd forgotten a line or weren't certain where they ought to be standing and such. The kids adored her, as did everyone in attendance.

As my first proper show in front of an audience reached the end of its final scene, I couldn't help but hold a somewhat heavy heart, as I knew my turn at this would soon come to an end. Even though I'd only been drafted in at the eleventh hour, I'd ended up, much to my surprise, having a blast and loving each and every minute of it. I would genuinely miss it. Acting—and even dancing!—on stage as the audience continued to show their enthusiastic appreciation, I have to admit I was considering ways in which I might put Steve out of action again without causing him any lasting damage. But I wasn't serious about it, of course. Or not *too* serious, at least. Being on stage was addictive. I'd experienced an exhilarating buzz and was keen for more, like any junkie would be. Curse that Steve and his healing ankle!

Regardless of my feelings, the main thing was that the kids had fun, the audience appeared to enjoy themselves immensely, and some much-needed ticket revenue had successfully found its way into the dance club's coffers. Plus, it wasn't like I was utterly surplus to requirements either, as henceforth, my services had been secured as the meeter/greeter tasked with selling raffle tickets and manning the stall selling programmes and light refreshments for the rest of the show's run.

"Oh, you were *brilliant*," my mum declared, presenting herself before me after the conclusion of the show, bursting with pride. She looked me up and down, admiring the costume, fussing over me, and instinctively straightening any stray pieces of straw protruding out of my collar. "You have such a talent, Adam! The way you fell off that stage was so realistic, we all thought you'd genuinely tripped. Very convincing!" she declared. "Right, Helen?"

"It was thoroughly enjoyable," Helen replied, nodding in agreement. "And the children were adorable," she said. "But what about that *Dorothy*...?" she quickly added. "Wasn't she *superb*?"

I could feel myself blushing, and I was worried my sister would follow up her statement with some foolish jibe about me having a crush on Chloe. And sure enough...

"Hmm, your cheeks are getting red," my sister was kind enough to point out to me. "I wonder why that is?" she said with a smirk.

"Just stop it, you," I said, pursing my lips. "But thank you again for selling all of those tickets!" I offered brightly, swiftly altering the conversation's course to a different heading.

Afterwards, I hung around long enough to help the others tidy up, and I officially turned over my costume to Steve, who was kind enough to tell me I'd done the role proud. I knew I would miss the smell of straw from now on.

As I was leaving, Evie tapped me on the elbow and gave me a reminder about my upcoming reading at her school. She said it was all sorted, and I was to liaise (my word, of course, not hers) with her mum to arrange the specific date and time. And as for the story we'd agreed to co-create, she was pleased to inform me that she'd jotted a few initial ideas down for us to discuss. I listened intently, giving the impression that I was enthused. But honestly, I'd hoped she might have forgotten about our plan, as the thought of giving a talk in front of a classful of children, despite my positive experience performing with the kids in the play just now, was still a bit daunting.

"You probably thought she'd forget about it, didn't you?" Evie's mum Julia whispered, somehow reading my mind. "But once that girl gets her tentacles on something, she doesn't let go."

I offered a resigned laugh. "Yes, I'm starting to get that impression," I admitted. "How about I call around once the show ends its run, when you both have a bit more free time?" I suggested.

"Sounds good. Maybe next week?" Julia asked.

"It's a date," I replied. "Well, not a *date*, obviously. It's business, I mean. Nothing more. Erhm… yeah," I said, staring at her blankly, wondering when I got to be such a clutz when it came to speaking with members of the fairer sex. "I, ehm… I look forward to seeing you next week," I concluded, before bolting for the exit.

❋ ❋ ❋

I pulled into my driveway, concerned about a slight rattling noise emanating from the underbelly of my Nissan Micra. I expect the downside of owning a car old enough to vote was that it was more prone to things failing or having bits of it fall off. After parking, I gently patted the top of the steering wheel like I was bidding the car good night and wishing it to get well soon.

Once inside the house, I was greeted by Barry, my cat, who was probably annoyed that I'd been out gallivanting for a good part of the day without so much as a moment's concern about who would scratch under his chin or tickle his furry tummy as required.

Sadly, it wasn't just good ol' Baz waiting to greet me, as a familiar-looking letter was *also* vying for my attention.

I could immediately tell by the distinctive typeface (along with the return address on the envelope) that it was from my mortgage provider. But even more concerning was the absence of either a stamp or a franking mark, suggesting this particular correspondence had been delivered by hand. In my limited experience, banks didn't often hand-deliver letters unless they needed to ensure the recipient received them.

"This isn't good, Baz," I said to my feline companion, feeling all the stage performance positivity I'd gathered dipping faster than the oil level on my Nissan Micra's dipstick. "This doesn't look like a love letter from them, does it?"

And I was right. Sitting on my sofa with a large whisky to help numb the pain I fully anticipated, I read through the contents of the eight-page document. Much of it was technical babble, citing breaches of terms and conditions and whatnot. But the long and the short of it, as I understood it, was that the bank had reached the end of its tether and was formally notifying me that unless my arrears were cleared, or significantly reduced, then they had few alternatives but to boot my broke arse out of my house, or words more polite to that effect. There were options provided, none especially useful when I had no extra money coming in each month. With a decreased income, I didn't see any of their suggested options as viable, with the forced sale looking the most likely alternative. In fact, rather like my Porsche situation, I was reaching the stage where simply handing back the keys to clear what I owed sounded like a not entirely unattractive proposition. And if a few quid were left over, that would be even better still. However, with the interest rate increase Bethany from the bank had cautioned me about, I knew there was a chance I might actually end up still *owing* them money, plus have no home to show for my troubles.

Using a glass-half-full approach, the positive side was that they were giving me a few months to sort things out, which would take me towards the end of the year. Hopefully, sufficient time for my book sales to pick up, maybe win the lottery, or to perhaps find a wealthy widow with a penchant for helping to support languishing, middle-aged authors. In the meantime, inconveniently, I still needed to feed both myself and the little bundle of fur at my feet.

"Baz, I think I need to find more work," I reluctantly advised to my whiskered sidekick, while loading up the Job Centre website on my phone. The concern I had as I started flicking through the positions listed, however, was that I wasn't necessarily employable. Yes, I was probably one of the most commercially successful writers living on the Isle of Man, but that didn't necessarily translate into skills that any potential employer might want or need. Sure, I can write books. But can I rewire a bathroom? Or troubleshoot a clogged fuel injector, for instance? No, I cannot.

I had previously worked in the office environment, which was presently making up about ninety percent of the current positions I was seeing available. But all I tended to do back in those days was fax, shred, file, and post things. Oh, and if anyone in the office had a birthday, I was usually dispatched to pick up cake, trays of lovely Cornish pasty and such, or sometimes both. From the job descriptions I was reading now, I began to get the sinking feeling that any career I was capable of or qualified for would involve flipping burgers or packing groceries into a paper bag. Not that there was anything innately wrong with those things, of course. Because we all had to do what we needed to keep a roof over our heads. But as an experienced novelist with over a million book sales collectively to my name, I couldn't help but wonder if there was something better suited to my particular skill set.

However, the answer to that question was answered (or *not* answered, as the case may be) when I reached the very bottom of the alphabetical page listing of jobs. "Hmm, do you reckon I could be a zoning officer or a Zumba instructor…?" I asked, looking to Barry for answers. But he was too busy licking his unmentionable areas to be concerned about my employment status. And it wasn't like I was looking to be chairman of the board or anything quite so grandiose. I just needed something to bring in a few extra quid to supplement the money from my lacklustre book sales and allow Barry and me to keep ourselves warm and fed.

"Bloody hell, I'm not qualified for anything other than churning out novels no one's going to read much anymore," I moaned, spilling over the contents of my glass-half-full, so to speak.

But then it occurred to me. There was indeed a potential career opportunity I was qualified to do. Not only that, but I was authorised to do this task by the Isle of Man's government itself. In fact, they had even given me a special license to prove the point!

"I can *drive*, Barry!" I announced, then scrolling back to the 'D' section of the alphabetised list. There, I read a job description that I'd initially flicked past, previously overlooking:

Driver wanted to transport members of a popular social club between various initiatives. Must have a cracking personality, patience, and desire to make a difference in the community.

"Hmm," I said. It seemed promising. After all, I knew I did have a personality. Some might argue that it wasn't *cracking*, really. But I *did* have one. And, granted, I wasn't the most patient person you were likely to come across. But I did have a desire to make a difference in the community, I reckoned. In fact, the more I reflected on it, all I could think about was Carol's theory about "sentiment," and how you needed to get out and help those around you in order to begin receiving that "warm and fuzzy" feeling she was so keen on advising about.

I liked the sound of this job. It meant I wouldn't be stuck behind a desk all day, and it would serve to generate some essential extra income. And also, if I could discover some of Carol's "sentiment" while I was at it, well, that was an added bonus.

Yes, I believe I quite liked the idea of becoming the driver for the Lonely Heart Attack Club.

Chapter Sixteen

Christmas Day 1984

One of the problems of being a kid was that grown-ups often didn't feel like they needed to tell you an awful lot. I wasn't blaming Mrs Cannell, really, as she didn't appear to know all that much more than she'd already told us. Despite our repeated requests, however, the police officers who remained in our street revealed worryingly little, speaking to us as if we were being nuisances when we asked about our parents. At one point, I even conspired with my sister Helen to make our own way to the hospital. The problem with that, of course, was that neither of us knew the way, plus there were no buses operating on Christmas Day. Also, when Mrs Cannell heard me talking about it, she told us it was best to stay put for the time being, as she'd promised Mum that she'd look after us, and we were to just sit tight.

So the three of us sat in our living room, staring at the television for what felt like ages, even though the telly wasn't even turned on at first and we were all initially just looking at a blank screen. The pile of presents that had caused many a sleepless night leading up to the day remained untouched, as neither me nor Helen had the desire to play with any of them.

Despite the awful anxiety of not knowing what condition my dad was in, my mind began to wander as we waited, and I couldn't help thinking about my friend Robert. I again imagined his face lighting up when he opened the door to see Gareth, Mr Newbold's delivery driver, carrying the beautiful Christmas tree already covered in decorations, and how he must've felt as the sparkling fairy lights brightened up his drab living room, bringing him joy. And that's when I also pictured his father in my mind's eye, staggering home from the pub, furious when he saw the tree. And if that was what had happened and why he was screaming at his son, as I'd witnessed, then I just couldn't comprehend why he would do that. Why would his father be that mean to him? And at Christmas, too.

I eventually heard the front door open just as the evening news came on—a time I'd usually be told to soon start getting prepared for bed. We all stared at the living room door, unsure who was going to appear through it. Would it just be my mum? Or would my dad be with her as well?

I leaned forward from my spot on the sofa, unwilling or unable to blink, as the living room door slowly opened. It was Mum. She'd clearly been upset, and continued to be upset, if the look on her face just now was any indication.

"Mum?" I said, once it was obvious that my father wasn't in the hallway behind her.

"Where's my dad?" Helen asked, her voice breaking with emotion. "Mummy? Where's *dad*…?"

Mum removed her coat and thanked Mrs Cannell for tending to us, especially for so much longer than expected. Then, she walked over to us, first looking at me, and then at my sister. "Your father got into an altercation with—" she started to say.

"Altercation?" I interrupted, not quite understanding the word she was using. "Like mending clothes…?" I asked, confused.

"No, dear. Altercation is just a nice way of saying a fight," Mum patiently explained. "Dad got into a fight with Robert's father," she said. "And during that incident, Mr Bentham suffered several serious injuries."

I don't know if I should have felt guilty for thinking it, but hearing Mum say this made me immensely proud of my father for giving that rotten bully a taste of his own medicine. "But what about Dad? Mrs Cannell told us he got hurt as well…?"

"Yes, it seems that during the fight, Mr Bentham attacked your father with a knife, stabbing him in the thigh. Your dad's lost a lot of blood, but he's in a stable condition and the doctors are entirely confident he'll make a full recovery."

I could have leapt up and punched the air, because having to sit chained to the sofa all day, waiting for any possible news to arrive, had been awful.

"When's he coming home, then?" I asked, looking at Mum and wondering why she still had this very odd expression on her face, considering she knew Dad would be perfectly okay.

My sister wasn't totally clueless, either. Like me, she could tell something was off. "Mum? What are you not telling us…?"

Mum removed a well-used tissue from her pocket, dabbing underneath each of her eyes. "Your dad won't be coming home from the hospital, children, because—"

"But you said he was going to be okay!" I cut in. "Mum, you said he was in a stable!" I insisted, uncertain what that could mean in this circumstance, but having been reassured by it nonetheless.

Mum stepped in close, pulling my sister and me in for a cuddle. "Your dad is going to recover fully, just like I said," she assured us, giving us a firm squeeze. "But…"

"*But?*" Helen and I both asked at once.

"But due to the condition of Robert's father, I'm afraid your dad is going to be arrested. Once the doctors verify that he can be discharged, it's likely that officers will be waiting to take him directly to the police station…"

I didn't see Robert Bentham again. The first sign of any movement at his house was when two men in bright yellow jackets parked a van outside of it at the beginning of January. As they started emptying the home's contents, I went over to ask if they possibly knew where my friend Robert had gone. But one of the fellows shrugged, saying to me, "Sorry, mate, I really couldn't say. I don't know the people who used to live here. We're only meant to empty the place out before the next tenants arrive."

I don't think Robert's dad must've owned too much stuff, because emptying the home wasn't taking that long. I sat on the garden wall watching, feeling an irrational anger towards the house, wishing I could go inside and rip down the filthy net curtains that were still up, plus anything else that was gross and stained by Mr Bentham's constant smoking of cigarettes. The workmen probably wondered what was so interesting that I should be watching them so intently for close to an hour.

They made light work moving the abandoned fridge, which revealed a perfect imprint left behind, the grass underneath it having been killed. But when they grabbed hold of the Christmas tree to clear that out as well, I hopped down from my perch on the wall. "Wait!" I said, dashing over. I'd already been down while they were working to collect all the baubles and ornaments that Scatty Newbold had included on the tree, so I could return them to him. But I could see I'd missed one painted ceramic angel hiding in one of the underside branches. "I need to get that," I advised.

One of the workmen agreed, tilting the tree obligingly so that I could easily retrieve the item I wanted. "Thank you," I said.

"Anything else before we throw it in the back of the lorry?"

I scanned the remaining branches for something else I might have missed, but the tree was clear. "No," I said. "Thank you."

Later in the day, well after the workmen had gone, we were going to visit Dad again. Unfortunately, it wasn't in the hospital, as he'd already been booked in and charged for the assault by now. So this time we were heading to the police station, where he was being held while the police continued to investigate and then decide what to do next, I reckoned. Apparently, Mr Bentham had a broken jaw, and would also require an additional operation of some kind to fix some sort of internal bleeding somewhere. (Yes, *that's* how powerfully my dad could hit, when he felt someone—like Robert's father—very much needed hitting.)

I asked Mum why he was like that. Mr Bentham, I meant. Mum was reluctant to talk about him at first, but I persisted. Eventually, my mum gave in and told me Mr Bentham had been an absolutely horrid person ever since she'd known him. In and out of trouble for one thing after another, his wife eventually had enough of his drinking and his constant abuse, and she left him. His wife was a lovely woman, by all accounts, and my mum explained to me that things must have been very terrible indeed for her to have to leave without Robert, but that she was also fighting to try and regain custody of her son.

Apparently, my dad had a number of unfortunate run-ins with Mr Bentham over the years. Then, when I'd told Dad about Robert having been beaten up (as evidenced by his bruised and injured face), plus Mr Bentham shouting at me as well, I reckon that was enough to send my father over the edge. I do know on some level, I guess, that it was wrong of Dad to hurt Robert's father. But again, it didn't stop me from being proud he'd stood up to him.

I then asked my mum about Robert, but she wasn't exactly sure what would happen to him now. She said he would probably end up in the care system, where a new, loving family would hopefully be found for him, at least temporarily.

"Can we look after him, Mum?" I asked. "Robert could share my bedroom, and I'd happily split my pocket money with him."

Mum knew this was important to me. After all, Robert was my mate. "Adam, we would if we could. But your friend will probably be moved to a family far away from here where his dad won't be able to hurt him anymore. Assuming his dad doesn't end up in jail for the stabbing, of course, which is entirely possible as well."

It made sense, I supposed, even if I didn't like the idea of Robert moving away. But even though I might not see him again and I'd miss him, I was pleased his father wouldn't be able to shout at him anymore, and especially that his father would no longer be able to hit him. It made me smile, imagining my friend with a family who cared about him, and hopefully even getting back together with his mum. Either way, he should be surrounded by kind people in a warm, inviting house next Christmas, where he'd have his own sparkly tree, jam-packed with presents underneath.

I hadn't played with my Commodore 16 yet, though it wasn't because I didn't want to. Mum did suggest trying to swap it when the shop reopened at the beginning of January. But as she'd soon found out, they were rather uncooperative in this regard.

However, I wasn't disappointed about that. Not really. Because, as I discovered while out playing with my mates, I wasn't the only one to receive a computer they weren't expecting. Apparently, the shop in town had been overwhelmed before Christmas and quickly sold out of all of the Commodore 64s they'd had in stock, with no time to obtain more. Rather than turning away customers, they'd convinced many parents (who were *also* helping Santa Claus fund a more expensive gift, from what I was told) that the Commodore

16 was "as good as, if not better than the Commodore 64." As such, there was now no shortage of my friends to swap games with.

But while I did come around to the idea of owning a Commodore 16, I couldn't shake the guilt for ruining Christmas for the others in my family. To make matters worse and make me feel even more awful, my sister told me she'd overheard Mum and Dad talking before Christmas arrived. According to what Helen revealed, the extra shifts my dad had taken at work were in large part to help Santa with the cost of the computer I so desperately wanted. So, the fact that I then accused Dad of rather being at work than spending time with his son made me feel even more rotten than I already did.

And what if I never mentioned anything to Dad about Robert? If I'd said nothing, Dad wouldn't have gone around to sort out Mr Bentham. Dad wouldn't have got stabbed in the thigh, and then he wouldn't have spent days locked up in a police cell, with the threat of being locked up for an even longer period once he went to court to face charges for the assault.

It's fair to say that Christmas of 1984 was by far the worst of my young life, made worse by the fact I'd been a selfish idiot. Although I was pleased to discover, at least, as one small saving grace, that three of the emergency chocolate gift selection boxes had still remained in the hallway console table drawer. We sat on the sofa and divided the spoils, with Mum's permission.

"Mum…" I said, midway through demolishing a Mars Bar. "Do you think it would somehow get to him if I should write a letter to my friend Robert?"

"Maybe, Adam," Mum replied. "How about if I speak with somebody at the school? They might have a contact who could arrange something."

"Thanks. Oh, and one more thing I was thinking…"

Mum glanced across at me. "You're not having *another* bar of chocolate, young man. You're already on your third."

I could easily have eaten a fourth, but that wasn't what was on my mind. "No, it's not that," I said. "Do you think we could take all the decorations down today…?" I asked. "I think I'd like to put this Christmas behind me, if that's okay."

Chapter Seventeen

It's remarkable how the days blend into each other when you're engrossed in writing a book. You become consumed with the plot, characters, locations, and more—though sometimes you do spend an inordinate amount of time staring at a blank screen on your laptop or other device. I never consider writing a book as one project in its entirety. Instead, it's like every chapter is its own little book of sorts, and the feeling of coming to the end of each of them feels like a significant milestone. The challenge, on occasion, can be starting to write the next chapter when you're once again faced with the daunting sight of a blank page, often without a clue as to what to type next.

This time, at least, I was determined not to fall into my previous trap of becoming a hermit during the creative process. As those who knew me would likely attest, I could go missing for weeks on end, sitting alone in my underpants, living on an unhealthy fast-food diet, with only one of Carol's lasagnas hopefully arriving now and again as a source of some proper nourishment. Especially after Stacey left, I avoided natural sunlight or fresh air for extended periods. Indeed, my mates remarked that they could tell how far I'd progressed with a book by how pale my skin had become.

But now I had other things going on in my life to provide pleasant distraction. Aside from penning my current novel—destined to be a global sensation, netting me millions, if not billions of dollars in revenue and attracting a new legion of adoring fans (I dared to dream)—I had other things to coax me away from my computer. Though the successful production of *The Wizard of Oz* had completed its run, I had enjoyed it while it lasted. Although I was only required to wear my straw-lined boots just the once, I did fully embrace my role on the refreshment stand, and not one patron, as well, escaped without buying a raffle ticket on my watch. I relished every moment I spent helping, and I'd since volunteered my time to Chloe, meaning I was now a part of the ensemble cast, as and when required, a set designer and painter, as and when required, and a general dogsbody who was happy to pick up any of the other ancillary tasks, again as and when required. Which may sound like a lot of work, but there wasn't much to do when no productions were scheduled. So I ensured the grass outside remained immaculately trimmed, for instance, and inside, the refreshment cupboard was stocked for the various dance classes and such. And I love doing it. Being a novelist is often a solitary affair, so feeling like you're part of a team is something I didn't know was missing in my life until I'd experienced it.

A further unexpected development in my life was in receiving a positive reply to my job application to be a driver for the Lonely Heart Attack Club. Not only would it bring in an extra bit of dosh, which was desperately required, but it also meant I needed to put some trousers on and leave the house for a decent number of hours each week.

As for the Lonely Heart Attack Club, Jack Tate and his girlfriend Emma run a busy coffee shop café in Douglas called JAVA THE HUTT, I learned—an establishment I must have walked past many times but never noticed for some reason. But in addition to their normal jobs, the pair of them were instrumental in setting up an island-wide charity—with branches further afield also—intended to give those suffering from loneliness the opportunity to both meet and socialise with people in the same boat as they were. And thus *The Lonely Heart Attack Club* was born.

For someone impressed by clever wordplay like me, I was immediately drawn to both the Lonely Heart Attack Club and JAVA THE HUTT the moment I walked into the café to meet the proprietors for my job interview. Though calling it a 'job interview' may sound too formal for what ended up being a friendly, genial coffee chat in which Jack outlined the charity's vision (and afterwards quizzed me about writing science fiction books). The primary aim of the role as driver was to be available to shuttle around the club members between their various activities. One day, for example, a party might be heading for a pottery class and another for some type of drawing class. According to Jack, the members were primarily, but not exclusively, older folk for whom mobility was often an issue. As such, the club's minibus formed a vital function in service of their community, as did their driver.

Jack offered some advice before I put pen to paper and accepted the job offer. "Don't turn your back on them for a second, Adam," he cautioned. "One minute, you'll think they're all sweetness and light, but that's usually when they're plotting! Honestly, they're like a bunch of hyped-up, giddy schoolkids who've just eaten their own weight in sweets."

I couldn't tell precisely how serious Jack was being, but the very faint flicker of a grin suggested that there was a fair amount of affection for his club members at play, mixed in with his dire warnings to me about them.

Jack looked over his shoulder, as if checking the coast was clear, before leaning in a mite closer. "Especially watch out for Geoffrey, my grandad," Jack advised, wide-eyed, as if speaking from previous, traumatic experience. "And also his best mate Ray as well. If there's any mischief afoot, you can be absolutely sure those two hooligans will be smack bang in the middle of it."

Sitting with my pen poised over the one-page job contract in preparation to sign, I could imagine most rational people might've walked out at this point, or at the very least pressed for additional details before committing. Not me, however. Spending my mornings with this boisterous mob sounded like a right laugh and just what I needed. I couldn't wait.

❋ ❋ ❋

It was nearing the end of August and the final few days of the island's summer school holiday. Ordinarily, I wouldn't pay much attention to whenever the kids might be sent kicking and screaming back to the classroom, but this year was different. And it was different because, thanks to a wilful little sprite called Evie, I'd soon be standing amongst them, giving them a talk on what an author's life was all about and then reading them a story.

The initial suggestion was one I'd hoped was simply a passing comment on Evie's part, something quickly forgotten. Regrettably, that didn't prove to be the case. With her mum's help, Evie had made all the arrangements with her school, and I was thus scheduled to appear in the first week of the new term. But as I had soon learned, authors brave enough to put in a personal appearance before a set of miniature-sized critics with absolutely no social filter were apparently as rare as hen's teeth. In fact, when word got out about my future commitment at Evie's location, I was asked to go on the road and visit several *more* of the island's schools!

Ah well, in for a penny, in for a pound, as the saying goes. The only thing I had to do now was write a brand-new children's story to entertain the wee creatures. At least I was getting a fair bit of assistance from my present co-author on the project...

"Right," I said, sitting in the living room of Evie and her mum's house, armed with a pen and notepad and jotting down our latest brainstorming results—our third such session this week. "So, this alien by the name of Victor is the one with four arms who—"

Evie shook her head. "No, you've got it wrong," she said. "You need to pay attention. *Victor* doesn't have four arms, Adam. You're thinking of *Ibrahim*. Victor has got three ears."

I glanced at my set of notes, which were becoming more extensive with each of our meetings. Not for one moment did I want to curb Evie's infectious enthusiasm. But the way things were going so far, I reckon I'd need to write another sixteen-book epic saga if I wished to mention all of the characters proposed to date.

Fortunately, my brain was allowed a brief hiatus when Evie's mum Julia appeared with a strong coffee in hand, in addition to an American-style thick milkshake for my trusty sidekick, made with chocolate ice cream and milk blended together, and replete with a little whipped cream added over the top. Looking at that luscious creation, I have to say I had beverage envy, immediately regretting choosing the caffeine over the much more decadent option.

"Would you like one?" Julia offered, spotting me staring.

I desperately wanted to say yes, but on the other hand I didn't wish to be a bother. "No, coffee is good to keep the old grey matter ticking along," I insisted. "But thanks."

"In that case, I'll leave you two creative persons to your work," Julia replied, blowing her daughter Evie a kiss before closing the door and retreating.

I then watched in wonderment, mesmerised that a creature as small as Evie could drain the contents of her glass so quickly. "You must have been thirsty?" I asked.

"Adam, you big silly, you don't drink one of these beauties because you're *thirsty*. You drink it because it's made out of *ice cream*," she advised, shaking her head at me for being so daft.

"Fair enough. I stand corrected," I replied.

Evie wiped a frothy ice cream moustache away from her upper lip with the back of her hand, and then glanced down at the well-used notepad I'd been filling up. "Hmm, do you think we have too many characters in our book…?" she considered.

Absolutely we did, and I was relieved to hear her say that. With only three brainstorming sessions so far, we'd produced enough material by this point to write perhaps the longest book in history, something to rival Tolstoy's *War and Peace*.

"I suppose you might be right, Evie," I replied. "Could we maybe aim for something simpler for this project if you wanted to?"

Evie nodded. "We could always bring Victor and Ibrahim back for another book when we have more time," she agreed.

"If you insist, Evie. Yes, we could do that. So, what type of story do you think we should write to impress your school friends?"

Evie thought about this for a minute, while taking a moment to see if she had any milkshake in her glass remaining. She did not. "Dunno," she said. "What are the most popular kinds of stories?"

"Ah. That I know the answer to, at least according to a certain someone I work with," I was happy to report, recalling my conversation with that one particular someone. "According to my agent Millicent, I was advised I should write either Christmas books or spicy romance novels," I informed my young friend.

"Spicy? Like pepper and chilli powder?" Evie asked.

I realised what I'd just let slip, and was thankful Evie remained clueless as to the precise implications. "Yeah. Yeah, that's *exactly* what I meant," I said, fibbing, and praying the little mite wouldn't think about it too hard.

"I don't really like hot spices so much," Evie told me. "So, in that case, I think we should go for a…"

"Yes?" I said, groaning to myself, as I'd only proposed one alternative to her, so realised what was likely coming.

"… a Christmas book," she declared.

I groaned internally again, while simultaneously scolding myself for being careless enough to bring up the idea in the first place. For somebody who didn't like Christmas, it sure had a lamentable habit of following me around, even now, at the tail end of August. Still, writing about Christmas was the far, *far* better of the two options I'd mentioned, of course, while working with a five-year-old, regardless of how grown-up Evie may sometimes act.

"Okay, sure. Yeah, we can do that," I said. "Any ideas?"

I started drinking my coffee and had most of it already gone by the time Evie eventually stopped to draw breath. The girl had quite the imagination. From the extensive download she had provided, I was getting a clear Grinch-meets-Arthur Christmas sort of vibe. Fortunately, we had a couple of more weeks to thrash out an exact plotline. And I have to admit, I was always well fed and watered on these occasions I was visiting. So I didn't mind too much, even if I sometimes left with an Evie-related migraine.

I looked at my watch before finishing up the last of my coffee. "Okay, so how about we leave it there, keep our thinking caps on, and then start again in a few days?" I suggested.

Evie didn't respond right away, staring at me for that long that I thought I must have something caught between my teeth, or perhaps protruding from my nose. "Erm, everything okay?" I asked.

Then, she blurted out, without any sort of preamble at all: "Do you think my mummy is pretty…?"

"What?!"

"My daddy has a new girlfriend," Evie explained. "So I thought it would be a good idea if Mummy got a new boyfriend. And you seem nice, most of the time. So do you think she's pretty?"

I was happy to take the compliment, such as it was, but I was also mortified.

"Ehm… I think I should probably—"

"Can I get you two busy writers anything else?" Julia asked, as she popped her head around the door. But as I was half standing at this point, she rightly assumed I was packing up to leave.

"No, I'm all good, thank you," I replied, eager to get out of there before Evie could expand on her current thought process. I could almost hear the little cogs whirring inside her head.

"Adam was just wondering if you were pretty or not," Evie put forth, without any consideration for social graces.

I wanted a gap to open up in the middle of the carpet just then and swallow me whole. And probably Julia did as well.

Julia didn't really seem to know where to look, in fact. "Oh, I see…" was all she could say.

But not content to leave this particular itch unscratched, apparently, Evie felt the need to press the point. "So, Adam, what do you reckon? Do you think Mummy is pretty or what?"

I remained frozen in my crouched position, unsure whether to sit down, stand up, or hurl myself headfirst through the window, with the final option being the leading contender. "Uhm…" I eventually replied, my jaw hanging low like I was trying to catch flies. "That is, I mean…"

Julia filled the subsequent, awkward silence that followed by reminding Evie that it was time for her to start getting ready for bed. But Evie just stared at me, awaiting a proper response.

"I think… I think you're *both* very pretty," I offered, happy with this diplomatic solution, and hopeful that it might put an end to the current line of questioning.

However, a teensy part of me did want to tell Julia I thought she was lovely. Because she was. Sure, spending time brainstorming with Evie was invigorating (if a smidge mentally taxing on occasion), and something I genuinely looked forward to. But, I also relished the opportunity to be around Julia. She made me smile.

And that's when it struck me: *carpe diem*. Ever since Carol and my sister (and several others who'd said the same thing to me over the years) had finally convinced me to get my arse out of the house once in a while, good things have started to happen to me. I somehow managed to get myself involved in a musical theatre group, I ditched my stupid, costly, impractical Porsche, found a part-time job I knew I was going to love to bits, and I was scheduled to tour the island's schools reading from a story I was co-authoring with a charming five-year-old menace! Yes, good things were happening when I seized the day. It was now or never, I decided.

"Erm…" I said, looking down at my feet. "As it should happen, I do think you're pretty," I admitted. "And I wondered… I wondered if you'd like to go on a date with me? Pizza, perhaps? Or the cinema, if you like…?"

There was a pause. A long pause. I was still unsure if I should be standing or sitting, so my legs started to buckle under the strain of indecision.

"Adam, I'm only *five*. I don't think I'm old enough to go on a date with you," came the response. "Even though I really like pizza and going to the cinema. I like both those things."

I broke my gaze away from my shoes. "Not you, you cheeky little monkey!" I said, laughing. "Although, if your mum agreed to come on a date with me, I reckon I could book a third seat at the restaurant easily enough," I added.

"And the cinema?" Evie asked, filled with hope.

"Nah. You'll need to stay in the car when we go to the cinema," Julia entered in. But she was grinning when she said it, which was also a positive indication that she wasn't totally repulsed by the idea of an evening out with me, I hoped.

"Adam," Julia said, turning her attention my way. "Yes. I would love to go out on a date with you. And, Evie, thank you for sticking your cute button nose into our business."

Evie was flippin' clever for a wee one, I couldn't help but think. And when her mum wasn't looking, I mouthed the words *"Thank you!"* to the girl, accompanied by a raised thumb in appreciation. I don't know how Evie did it, but she was about the smartest five-year-old I'd ever encountered.

"Mummy. You like reading, don't you?"

"I do, Evie. Very much so."

"Well, Adam's writing a romance novel you might like. It's got lots of hot spices in it, he told me…?"

Chapter Eighteen

Jack Tate was right. When he'd warned me to be on my guard, I wondered just how troublesome a bunch of ageing pensioners could possibly be. Sure, the club members were model citizens for my first several shifts—polite, considerate, and mostly charming. But as they got to know me and I got to know them, the mood switched up, and the practical jokes started.

For example, 'Patch' is an older, retired plumber with only one eye (hence the descriptive nickname). While I was waiting to drive a party from the Castletown division of the Lonely Heart Attack Club to a session of crown green bowls, he asked me if I'd mind, as a strong young fella, stopping off at the ironmongers to pick up a "long stand" that he'd ordered, whatever that might be. I assumed he couldn't drive himself because of his age, or because of his lack of stereoscopic vision. So being helpful, I happily agreed, as it was simply a minor detour to pick up his order. Plus, I figured it would only help endear me to the group as well, showing them all what an amiable, obliging sort of chap I was. What I didn't realise was that Patch's mate owned the ironmongers (and was thus warned I was coming). And after waiting for well over twenty minutes in the establishment with no possible end in sight, it finally dawned on me that the so-called "long stand" in question was simply how long I'd be willing to stand there in the shop with my thumb up my bottom like a prat.

When I returned to the minibus, my passengers were in hysterics, even having placed bets on the precise amount of time I might wait in the shop before eventually catching on. To make matters worse, I soon discovered that 'Patch' was in possession of both eyeballs, even enjoying flawless eyesight with perfect 20/20 vision. As it turned out, the eye patch was just part of a pirate's costume he'd worn to the previous year's Lonely Heart Attack Club Hallow-een party.

Another time, my lunch tin went missing, and when I managed to recover it, I found my sandwiches had been replaced by a set of false teeth. It didn't take me long to locate the culprit. After all, I only needed to spot the first person who was flashing me a gummy smile without their bloody chompers in.

Additionally, as soon as word spread that I was an author, I was inundated with potential plotlines for my upcoming books. And they were imaginative, with some of their story ideas bordering on the ridiculous. But we had fun in discussing the various merits of each suggestion as we journeyed around the isle. Some of them had also taken to swapping out my actual name, always referring to me as whichever famous author popped into their heads at the time. On one trip, everyone was calling me Stephen King. As in, "Oi, Stephen King, watch out for that parked lorry!" for instance. Another time I got stuck with the name Agatha Christie, despite it being fairly obvious I was a male of the species. But I didn't mind the gentle teasing, as it was always in good fun. And I could even dish it out myself, occasionally, as well.

My duties usually entailed two or three pickups from amongst the club's various branches around the island, dropping the different groups off at whichever activity they'd booked that day to engage in. Sometimes, they'd ask/drag me along to join them in it. At other times, I sat in the minibus with a flask of tea, using the opportunity to hammer out some new content on my latest novel via my laptop, or giving the minibus a clean. Funny how I had no use for tea as a child but now I couldn't seem to get enough of the stuff.

Anyway, the whole gig was perfect. And to witness people 'of a certain age' living a carefree life with the ability to laugh at a moment's notice and never take themselves too seriously was both humbling and inspiring. Spending time with them all was a treat, and something I looked forward to. It was also why I was often willing to stay on beyond my allotted hours, without additional charge to the charity, if the group decided an unscheduled lunch was in order (or maybe an unplanned visit to a gin distillery, as had transpired on one recent excursion).

I still got down in the dumps periodically about money woes and dwindling book sales and such, or life in general on occasion. But spending time with my new pack of friends at the Lonely Heart Attack Club was like a tonic for the soul. A pick-me-up that should, in my honest opinion, be prescribed on the NHS if you ever needed your funny bone tickled or your personal load lightened. And here I was, getting paid to escort them around the delightful island I had the pleasure to call home. If things continued along like this, I reflected, there was a real danger that Adam—or more specifically, the miserable git version of me—would be no more.

Currently, parked up in front of Fenella Beach—a small, sheltered cove in the historic seaside town of Peel, with the ancient fortress of Peel Castle acting as a dramatic backdrop to the place—I'd just relaxed back into the driver's seat after having a tidy around the minibus to ensure no incendiary devices or booby traps had been left behind as a special surprise. Fortunately, a quick visual sweep revealed the coast was clear. Unlike the coast of the Irish Sea, that is, which was about to be invaded by thirteen club members who decided it should be loads of fun to all get dressed in wetsuits and go what's known as 'coasteering'—basically, exploring the rocky coastline with, in my view, the real potential to smash your head off the rocks at any given moment. As usual, members of the group had tried to tempt me. But as I was useless at swimming and didn't fancy willingly falling into the choppy waters, I politely declined.

Although, as I suspected, that hadn't stopped them from trying to coerce me: "Hey, Enid Blyton!" a voice had called out earlier from the back of the bus as I'd been carefully reversing into a parking space. "Don't you worry about the waves, yeah? Because Brian can swim like a dolphin to save you!"

"And even if you *did* start to drown, then I'm quite the expert at administering the kiss of life!" another voice had then called out, and even more worryingly, it came from one of the men.

My saviour had arrived in the form of Henry, the floppy-haired activity instructor who'd come to greet us and collect the participants. Henry successfully pulled my fat from the fire by informing us that he didn't have any spare wetsuits about to accommodate an "additional adventurer," as he had phrased it.

So now, with a steaming cup of tea poured from my flask at present, and filled with a sense of relief, I looked down towards the beach below. "Absolute crackpots, the lot of them," I remarked to myself, along with a fond smirk.

The coasteering lesson was scheduled for an hour, but I'd factored in an extra half hour as a buffer as they liked to talk and carry on a bit. Plenty of time, I imagined, for me to get busy on my handy portable laptop and extend the word count on my novel. "Getting there, Adam," I observed, upon opening my saved document. The previous evening, I'd finished writing chapter fourteen, and I was now at the lovely stage of the process where I knew, give or take some various details, in which direction the novel was heading, and crucially, how it was likely to end. Whether the story was any good was another matter, but after completing so many books, I tended to have a feeling about these things. And my gut told me that this one wasn't bad. Not too bad at all, I reckoned.

After half a cup of tea and two paragraphs written I panicked, suddenly hearing what I initially thought was a scream. I immediately turned my attention to the beach, worried I'd see a lifeboat deployed to rescue one of the gang from the briny depths. Fortunately, what I thought was a cry for help was actually the screeching of a nearby seagull attempting to wrestle a bag of chips from a startled child. I knew it was wrong, but witnessing this familiar seaside battle made me laugh, as it was something that happened on many an occasion over the years, even and especially to myself.

With my concentration broken for now, I closed over the laptop to unpack the towels for when the mermaids and selkies would eventually return to base camp. Like a mindful parent checking on their offspring, I cast a quick eye across the cove just in time to see one of the adventurers leaping from the rocks and into the choppy swell. "Rather you than me," I said with a chuckle, flicking on the radio to listen to some music. I walked into the rear of the bus, tapping my foot and gyrating my hips while I started unpacking the provisions in advance—sandwiches, towels, a selection of biscuits, and three flasks, the consumables likely being demolished in very short order once my charges returned.

At this moment, I felt content. And I hadn't thought about it till just then, but I couldn't recall grinding my teeth any time during the day lately. It was a frustrating habit for which my dentist had previously admonished me, and I suspect it was a physical manifestation of my financial anxiety. I'd been doing it for months, to the point where I didn't even realise anymore that I was doing it, although it did leave me with an aching jaw and a dull headache that was often present. But not now. My jaw moved freely like it'd just been oiled, and there was no pain in my head. No pain in my head, that is, until…

"Bloody hell!" I shrieked, flinging the bundle of towels into the air. In abject fear, I grabbed for the handle of the bus's sliding side door without success, trying desperately to distance myself from the horrible venomous beastie I'd just shockingly spotted on the floor. There was nowhere to run.

I furiously stamped my foot like I was trying to extinguish an imaginary fire, blindly, as it should happen, as I couldn't bring myself to face the hideous thing that I was doing my absolute frantic best to avoid. I also yelled incoherently and flailed my arms like a fledgling bird practising for its debut flight, as I felt that might be of help as well. When there was no crunching sound underfoot, however, I raised my shoe just enough to see if I'd squashed what I was sure I had seen, or if the little demon had somehow managed to escape. But it was still there.

I jumped back, shouting a stream of expletives, extending my foot like a kung fu action hero from the films I had enjoyed when I was younger. Sure enough, it was exactly what I thought it was—a scary scorpion. It just sat there, straddling the floor. Taunting me. Mocking me. Not making any movements. We had a stand-off for a second or two before I had a sudden realisation. Or two of them, actually. One, scorpions are not indigenous to the Isle of Man. And two, it wasn't moving at all. As in, not at *all*.

I gradually lowered my striking foot to the floor of the minibus, relaxing my leg.

"You devious buggers!" I said, seeing now that the thing was an obvious toy made of rubber. I was the victim of another practical joke, it would appear, with one of my passengers having left a fake scorpion concealed within the pile of towels as a surprise gift for me to discover.

With shaking legs and a racing heartbeat (along with an unquenchable thirst for revenge), I returned to the front of the bus and sat myself down before I fell down. "Ahh... brilliant," I said, slowly shaking my head in recognition of the skilful mischief. I'm glad it was me that discovered the rubber scorpion, at least (which I assume was the intention), because at least three of my passengers today were in their late eighties, and I hadn't had my CPR refresher course.

Half-listening to the radio at my spot in the driver's seat, I took my partially drunk tea from the cup holder, preparing to take another sip. However, my ears pricked up when the presenter on the radio reached the closing stages of her breaking news. All I caught was the end, with her saying, "...ance school in Union Mills. Police are asking witnesses to contact them."

Although I'd only heard a snippet, the tail end of the news item, a sinking feeling washed over me. Was she speaking about Chloe's dance school? And if it *was* the TAPPIN' FEET dance school, why was it being mentioned in the news? And more importantly, why were the police appealing for witnesses? Witnesses to *what*?

I was uncertain as to what I should do. My first instinct was to turn the key in the ignition and drive straight over to Union Mills. But abandoning a bus full of pensioners at this early stage of my new job probably wasn't a good idea. Instead, I tried to look up the radio station's Facebook page to see if they might've published any reference to the story online. However, surrounded by a towering headland, the mobile internet data reception wasn't ideal, and my phone's internet wouldn't load just now.

Fortunately, I still had sufficient phone signal to make a call. Granted, Chloe might think it was a bit odd that I was calling if the report ended up having nothing to do with her or her dance group, but there was only one way to find out, I reckoned.

"Hiya, Chloe, this is Adam," I said, once Chloe answered. "This might sound a bit..." I began, but then stopped, as it was obvious that something was amiss simply from the way she had answered the phone. "Chloe, what is it? Tell me what's going on."

As I listened to her respond, I became aware that my hand was clenching itself into a fist. "They *what*?! Oh, bloody hell, Chloe, I'm so sorry to hear that," I said, as she continued to disclose details to me. I was also aware that I was now clenching my teeth together as well because of what I was hearing.

"I'm driving a group of the club members this morning," I advised to her. "Yes, the ones I was telling you about before," I said. "But I should be finished by about one o'clock. How about I come right over, in my own vehicle, once I've completed dropping everybody off? Okay? Right, I'll see you then."

I ended the call, gripping my phone and wanting to hurl it out of the window. But I had to refrain myself, as after all, none of this was the phone's fault.

"Why would you *do* that?" I asked into the void, struggling to comprehend what I'd just learned. "You absolute *lowlifes*!"

Chapter Nineteen

Poor Billy and the rest. Apparently, my plucky band of water-based adventurers were looking forward to returning to the minibus to see if they'd succeeded in inducing an arachnid-related panic attack in me. But when they'd reappeared, exhausted yet cheerful, they didn't receive the lively reaction they likely hoped for. Indeed, Billy—the chief instigator, from what I gathered—was crestfallen when he clapped eyes on my sombre face, worried that he'd overstepped the mark and perhaps offended and upset me.

But I explained to Billy that my sour expression was not in any way related to his fine efforts, assuring him I was duly impressed with his creative tomfoolery. I then stressed that revenge was a dish best served cold, and that henceforth he should make a habit of sleeping with one eye open. (While making clear, of course, that I was only joking. For the most part, anyway.)

With my passengers, minibus, and rubber scorpion all returned safely to their respective origins, I jumped into my car, where my next stop was the dance studio in Union Mills.

By the time I arrived, I could see Chloe standing outside, talking to a police officer again. Or still talking to one, as the case may be. I wasn't sure which.

The damage was already apparent as I stepped out of my car. The pristine front lawn that I'd only just trimmed the day before had a number of very noticeable chunks taken out of it, like it had been attacked by a golf club, or struck by meteors or something. A garden statue of a couple dancing now lay smashed in pieces near the trampled remains of a once glorious rose garden. It was heart-breaking, as I knew how much time and attention Chloe and some of the parents had invested over the years in making the property beautiful.

But what concerned me more was that I'd only seen the damage to the outside area so far. I dreaded to think what additional vandalism had been perpetrated *inside* the dance studio as well. Chloe had apprised me over the phone, but not so much that I was aware of any of the specific details just yet.

I cautiously wandered over to the entrance, not wishing to disturb Chloe and the police officer, who were still deep in conversation. She looked over to me, shaking her head and holding out her hands in a why-on-earth-would-they-do-this manner. "Adam, just watch you don't cut yourself on the glass," she advised.

When Chloe cautioned me, I assumed she was referring to the broken glass pane I observed from one of the entrance doors. That would have been bad enough, but at least it would've been a relatively simple fix. If only that were the extent of the damage. However, that was not the case, as I learned when I stepped inside.

"Oh, *no*," I said, gutted to see that all of the floor-to-ceiling mirrors around the dance studio had been struck, presumably with the same heavy object that had devastated the front lawn. A substantial pile of shattered glass had been brushed into the far corner of the hall, left in front of a wall that I could see was covered in offensive graffiti. The swept-up glass was only the start of what would likely be a considerable clean-up operation, I imagined.

Sadly, it was the same story in the rear portion of the building. Many cabinet doors of the kitchen were kicked in, and the theme of offensive graffiti continued throughout the back room. Also, the locked cupboard in which the tuck shop supplies were stored had been forcibly opened, the wood frame being destroyed in the process. The shelves inside were left empty as well, with the vandals helping themselves to whatever food items had been on them.

It was mindless destruction.

Only when I thought it couldn't get any worse did I realise my shoes were making a strange squelching sound whenever I took a step. I lowered myself down to one knee, administering pressure to the laminate flooring with my fingertips. It was sodden underneath, a small puddle forming with even modest pressure applied from my fingers. I stood myself up, the knee on my trouser leg now soaked. Beyond the kitchen was a utility room, which also doubled as a storage space in which presently unused stage props and costumes were often kept. I opened the door but didn't even need to step inside, as I could already see Chloe's Dorothy costume hanging prominently from a clothes rail. It was covered in black spray paint, as were the others I could see beside it.

I slumped against the wall, rubbing my eyelids with my thumb and forefinger. I'd only been involved in helping the dance school for a few short weeks, but it was clear that it was a unique, selfless place that did so much for the youngsters in the local area over the years. Why anybody would want to cause this amount of damage to such a valuable community initiative was utterly beyond me. It was reprehensible. And if I was feeling this much outrage about it, I could only imagine how Chloe must feel. I also dreaded to think how the kids would react to seeing the mess. They'd be devastated. There were very clearly thousands of pounds in repairs that would need to be performed, and I couldn't imagine resolving the water damage was any kind of simple, easy task, as every issue or problem was rarely immediately apparent with that type of work.

What made everything more frustrating, and even more maddening, was that there wasn't any reason for any of it. Chloe had no enemies, and in fact was well-liked by absolutely everybody in the community. Plus, stuff like this just didn't ordinarily happen in our sleepy little isle. It seemed to be simply one of those things, something completely unfortunate and entirely random.

For now, I tried to make myself useful in soaking up as much water as I could by using a mop and bucket. But there wasn't much progress to be reasonably made.

"Do you need a hand?" Chloe asked a moment later, along with a deep sigh.

"I'm fine, don't worry about me," I said, setting the mop to one side as it wasn't doing much good anyway. "Do you need a hug…?"

Chloe nodded, walking into my outstretched arms.

"You'll recover from this, Chloe, I swear," I assured her. "This place will recover."

"I don't know how to tell the children," she replied. "I think the entire floor will need ripping out. Adam, we could be out of action for *weeks*, if not months."

I had nothing to offer in that respect because I knew, sadly, she was very likely correct. "Do you want me to start picking up the glass in the hall?" I suggested.

Chloe let me go, pulling back and shaking her head. "Thanks, but no. I started doing that, but the police told me to leave things as they were for now while they're still investigating. Plus, I'd better phone the insurance company and see if they need me to do anything before we properly begin the clean-up procedure."

"And the police don't know who did this?"

"They found empty cider bottles in the car park, and I noticed discarded cigarette butts in the hall. Make of that what you will, as I'm not sure that helps us much," she said with a shrug.

Chloe then placed a hand against her cheek to catch a tear spilling over. "What do I say to the kids, Adam? How am I supposed to tell them we'll have to close for who knows how long? They'll be absolutely gutted."

❋ ❋ ❋

Of course I'd offered my services to Chloe, but there wasn't much I could do at that stage. Reluctantly, I headed home with assurances provided that I was only a phone call away if she needed anything.

Trying to push that awful situation to the back of my mind and concentrate on something more positive, I turned my thoughts to the story that Evie and I had been working on together. The school term started the following week, and we still needed to finalise the tale I was scheduled to read from as part of my upcoming 'Meet the Author' roadshow. We'd made excellent progress, and I was confident one further push would get us to the finish line. I had one final planning session with Evie later that afternoon, to be followed by my first official date with Julia (with Evie acting as chaperone). And so, a few hours later…

"Ah," I said in Evie's living room, clapping my hands confidently in a *that-takes-care-of-that* fashion. "Can we finally write 'The End' on our festive creation…?"

To give Evie full credit, she was the only child I'd ever encountered who could sit still for more than twenty minutes to focus on a job at hand. And as for a creative writing partner, well, she was tremendous. Granted, I had to occasionally filter out an additional few whacky suggestions, like the idea where Santa enters one of his reindeer in a prominent horse race like the Grand National. But as I stressed to her, "No idea is a bad idea, necessarily," which she did seem to appreciate. "Perhaps we could consider including that in the sequel?" I proposed.

I had to admit that this was probably the most fun I'd ever had writing a story. Perhaps it was because I was doing it for the pure enjoyment of creating the written word, instead of trying desperately to pay the bills with my output. It reminded me of when I first started writing short stories, way before my first attempt at a full-length novel which involved pirates and seasick ninjas.

"And you're happy with the title?" I asked Evie, with my fingertips hovering above my laptop keyboard in case any last-minute changes should need to be made.

Evie held up a pair of enthusiastic thumbs and flashed me an adorable, two-front-teeth-missing smile. "Santa's Training School for Christmas Elves? I posilutely love it!" she exclaimed.

I didn't bother to correct her English, as I reckoned I 'posilutely' loved the title as well. And with our story completed and its finishing touches thus decided upon, I headed home to freshen up before my date with Evie's mum and ensure that Baz's food and water bowls were adequately topped up. I'd booked a table for three at a delightful little pizza restaurant in Douglas that offered the most fantastic chilli dipping sauce, and I agreed to meet the two ladies there.

While looking forward to a nice meal in pleasant company, I was also delighted that I was in a position to pay for it. Thanks to my new driving job, I had some money in my bank account for the first time in months. Granted, it's not like I was going to retire on how much I had, but it was an immense relief nonetheless, and it was bloody good fun earning it. Planning out my finances after the stark warnings from the bank, I figured that, so long as the royalty cheques from my book sales didn't plummet too much further, I *should* (I hoped), with the additional money coming in from my job, have enough to live on, pay the mortgage, and chip away at the arrears I owe the bank. Additionally, once I had finished my new book and submitted it to my agent, surely there would be a flurry of publishers all battling it out to secure my signature and chuck a significant advance payment in my direction. I didn't know precisely how likely this would be, but it didn't hurt to dream.

So, with a few quid on the hip, my writing mojo restored, owning a more practical car that I didn't owe a fortune on, and my first date in months, I felt pretty pleased with myself as I pulled up outside of La Piazza restaurant. I'd even ironed a shirt for the occasion beforehand. As an author, who didn't typically need to leave the house or see people, most of my ironing was usually done by wearing a garment until my natural body heat served to flatten out the wrinkles. But this was a special occasion, and my shirt deserved the special attention.

Walking towards the restaurant, my stomach was flipping. Was I nervous? I think so. I liked Julia. She was funny, smart, and great company. But our interactions had so far been casual and relaxed, whereas this was a date. Or was it? I wondered if Julia viewed this as merely a meal shared between friends, rather than something with romantic intent. And what if I mucked things up by offering her a peck on the cheek at the end of the night and ruining a great friendship by misreading the situation? *And this is precisely why you're single*, I said to myself, frustrated by the fact I was useless when it came to matters of the heart. Still, the enticing aroma of garlic and baking pizza dough that smacked me in the face when I opened the restaurant door snapped me back to the present.

I stood inside the entrance, suddenly conscious that my forehead felt a bit clammy from a mixture of nerves and, well, even more nerves, I suppose.

"Good evening, sir," a suave-looking chap in a tasteful dark suit greeted me. "May I ask if you have a reservation for this evening?"

I nodded, which may not have been a good idea as I could now feel a bead of sweat manoeuvring down my forehead. "I do, yes. It's under the name of Catchpole."

"Very good, sir," came the polished reply as he turned his attention to his iPad. "Ah, the rest of your party is already here, sir. If you'd like to follow me?"

I managed to get the fellow's attention just before we set off.

"I'm sorry, you wouldn't have a napkin, would you?" I asked, pointing to my moist forehead.

"Certainly, sir," came the polite response as he retreated behind the bar area for a moment. "There we are," he said shortly afterwards, handing me a black napkin. He then leaned in conspiratorially. "Is this perhaps a first date?" he asked, as I dabbed my forehead with the napkin.

"You've seen the look before?"

"Many times, sir. And might I be so bold as to offer you a piece of advice before you join your two lovely companions?"

"Yes. Please do," I said. I already liked this guy. I hoped he might have a snippet or two of information to impart on the subject of first dates, so I was all ears, anxious to hear more.

"One shouldn't meet a female companion with a postage-stamp-sized piece of paper napkin stuck to one's forehead," he whispered discreetly.

It was an odd bit of advice, I thought, and I wondered if this was some sort of cryptic, Mr Miyagi-style coaching method. "Go on. I'm listening," I said, hoping he'd tell me more.

"No, you really *do* have an actual piece of napkin adhered to your forehead, sir. It must have stuck fast when you were busy mopping your brow," he explained quietly, with the same degree of discretion as before. "If sir will allow me?" he added, reaching up and peeling off the unwelcome lodger.

Upon reaching the table, Julia and Evie were already seated, with Evie busying herself with a colouring book and an assortment of crayons. "Hiya. I hope I haven't kept you," I said, unsure if I was supposed to give Julia a hug or a kiss before taking a seat. So to be on the safe side, I did neither.

"Are you wearing some kind of vagrants, Adam?" Evie offered, looking up from her artwork.

"Do you mean fragrance?" I asked.

"Yes, that's what I said. Vagrants. Because you smell just like the toilets in school after they've been cleaned," she responded. "I like the smell of the toilets in school," she told me. "After they've been cleaned," Evie stressed, saying this again so I didn't think she was in any way peculiar, apparently.

"Well, I suppose they must call it *eau de toilette* for a reason," her mum offered with a smirk.

Evie held up the page she'd been working on. "I've started making illustrations for our story," she advised, showing me her progress. And it was surprisingly good for someone her age—a colour depiction of Santa Claus surrounded by elves lifting weights like they were in a North Pole gym. My prior experience of reviewing artwork from a five-year-old had been acting amazed about how good it was and promising to place it on the door of my fridge for eternity to marvel at it. That's what I'd done with my nephews when they went through the gifting artwork stage, only for it to go into a kitchen drawer, never to be seen again the moment they'd left. But this time I didn't have to merely pretend to like it, and I could actually tell what each of the individual figures was meant to be, astonishingly enough.

"The elves are in training to lift all the presents," Evie explained before getting busy with her red crayon again, sticking her tongue out the side of her mouth as if this would aid her artistic efforts.

The waiter soon arrived to take our food order. I briefly considered a small glass of red to settle my first-date nerves, but realised I didn't need it. Julia was so easy to talk to, as usual, that I felt immediately at ease. She had a similar sense of humour as me and a tendency to laugh at the same stupid things I did. The only downside was that she wasn't a sci-fi fan, but I would help her convert, as I'd promised her.

I found myself holding my gaze across the table, mesmerised as Julia's eyes sparkled in response to the candlelight as she twirled strands of her lovely chestnut-coloured hair around her finger as she spoke. *Gordon Bennett!* I said to myself, looking away, but then sneaking another quick glance. *I think I really* do *like her.*

During the wait for the pizzas—one pepperoni, and one ham & pineapple—Evie suggested a quick run-through for Mum's benefit of our story, "Santa's Training School for Christmas Elves," as Julia hadn't yet heard the thing in its entirety. I was reluctant, but as the girl pointed out, I only had a few days before I would be reading it in front of her class (and several other classes, for that matter), so it was the ideal opportunity to have a sort of dress rehearsal at present, in her learned opinion. But rather than a complete rendition, we settled on me trotting out only the first chapter for now, as after working on it for several days I had it more or less consigned to memory by this point.

Conscious that in school I'd be reading to a young audience that I suspected would have a tendency to drift off—or even fall asleep, bored—if the fires of their imagination went unstoked, I had spent some time in front of the mirror practising. I drew on the valuable experience I'd obtained during my brief stint as the Scarecrow onstage, I felt, and I'd invented voices for each of our new characters. I even rehearsed the animated hand gestures I'd utilise to keep my youthful audience captive (or so I hoped).

And as I started my performance, Evie watched on with an expression full of pride that the tale she'd help create was being read so impressively. Julia laughed at just the right moment whenever there was a funny bit, which only spurred me on. I even caught a glimpse of the couple on the adjacent table directing their listening holes towards us.

"Oh, but you can't leave it *there*," Julia said, once I'd concluded my recitation. "I have to know which elves get accepted to Santa's training school, and who won the gift-wrapping contest."

"Me too!" the earwigging chap at the nearby table said, craning his neck in hopes he'd hear more.

I laughed, offering Evie a high-five in celebration that our story appeared to have received critical approval on its first outing. And it wasn't long before we got stuck into the now-arriving pizza, and my mind drifted back to the dilemma I'd earlier considered—was I out on a date, or just a meal with a good friend? Whichever the case, I reckoned it didn't matter either way, really, because it was the first time during a social occasion in a long time where I genuinely didn't want it to end.

Evie was the only person in our group to avail themself of the desserts menu because of all we'd had for the main course. I genuinely didn't know where she put it all, and I suggested to her that she must have a hollow leg or two. But I didn't mind her enjoying her dessert because it only served to extend our enjoyable evening that much further.

"Now, Adam," Julia said, as Evie spooned the last of her vanilla ice cream into her mouth. "On the chance that you were going to turn all chivalrous on us, I would much prefer if we split the bill instead. Is that okay with you...?"

I nodded, offering a weak smile in return. I had no problem with whether I paid the bill in full or, as Julia requested, that we split it. I did take this as a sign, though, that this was just a friendly get-together we were having rather than a date. Whether I was correct in this assumption, I couldn't say, however, as I lacked experience in these matters and was not wise or well-versed in the ways of romance. But again, I was enjoying myself. So I didn't let it bother me too much.

Once we'd settled the bill and snatched up the complimentary foil-wrapped mint chocolates, I offered to escort my companions back to their car (not before slipping an extra tip into the hand of the helpful greeter who'd saved me in the earlier napkin situation), suggesting a slight detour first to stretch out legs.

I always enjoyed walking along Douglas Promenade on a pleasant evening, watching the waves gently lapping the shore along the length of the crescent-moon-shaped bay in Douglas Harbour. Plus, it was an ideal excuse to prolong the 'date' a little bit longer, if in fact that's what it was. Once safely across the road, I stepped to one side as a young lad on a bicycle came tearing towards us, his chin millimetres from the handlebars and his hindquarters in the air. His panicked dad chased after him, but the youngster looked like he definitely had the edge on him.

It was a familiar scene, because my dad often took me down on my bike here when I was a nipper. Just a smidge past a mile and a half in length, stretching from one end of the bay to the other, the promenade was flat, free of traffic (other than wary pedestrians), and an ideal place for parents to go tearing after their enthusiastic offspring who could pedal faster than they imagined.

Also watching the cyclist disappear up the promenade, Evie stood between Julia and me, taking our hands, deciding she'd like to use us to turn her into a human swing.

"Hey, with the amount you've just eaten, do you really think it's a good idea to…" Julia began to ask, but Evie was already airborne with her legs extended, offering a squeal of delight.

After several extended back and forths, Evie planted her feet once again on terra firma, after which she turned to face the both of us. "I overheard Mummy on the phone to Auntie Chloe before," she said casually, sounding as if this recollection had just popped into her head. "And Mummy has a problem," she revealed.

"*Evie…*" Julia cautioned, seeming worried like she wasn't sure where this was going, but having an inkling it wouldn't be good.

I didn't know when this specific conversation with Chloe may have taken place. But based on Evie's light-hearted manner, I felt it was safe to assume it wasn't about the horrible events of earlier in the day. I hoped neither of them knew about that just yet, and it wasn't my place to say anything about it, I felt, so I kept schtum in that regard.

But I was intrigued, as any nosey bugger worth his salt would be. "Oh? Anything I can help with?" I asked.

Evie giggled, avoiding her mum's attempt to scoop her up in her arms. "Mummy asked Auntie Chloe…" she said, squealing with delight again as she avoided her mum's grasp by swerving this way and then the other.

Julia gave up trying to grab her daughter. I suspected the recent bellyful of pizza might have hindered her mobility. "Evie!" she said instead, placing a firm finger against pursed lips.

However, Evie didn't appear especially interested in staying silent. "Mummy asked Auntie Chloe if she thought you and her were going on a date…?" Evie said. "But then when I was invited along, she reckoned it might be just as friends."

"Evie!"

"And Mummy asked if she should try and kiss you or not?"

I loved this kid. I was now indebted to her to the tune of an endless supply of ice cream, or any alternative treat of her choosing, for putting my restless mind at ease. I replied, as nonchalantly as you like, "Oh…? And what did Auntie Chloe suggest?"

Sadly, I didn't get a direct response to the question, as Julia then held up her phone, looking somewhat relieved to have received a well-timed distraction. "Funnily enough, that's Chloe calling," she said. "You don't mind, do you?"

"It's fine," I replied. "Why don't I take Evie down to the beach, and we can skim some stones into the sea?" I suggested, as it was still light enough out and the sea calm, so there was no chance of us getting soaked. And Evie didn't need to be asked twice, as she was already gone before I'd reached the end of my sentence. Even though I knew it was perfectly safe, like the dad chasing after his cycling son, I set off after her, picking up the pace to catch up. Not easy after eating too much pizza.

With soft, golden sand soon underfoot, I was about to pick up the perfect pebble and dazzle Evie with my stone-skimming skills, honed over a lifetime of living on an island. However, she grabbed a handful of stones without hesitation, rapidly filtering the selection down to one. "Watch this, Adam," she said, stretching her arm behind her head before snapping it forward like a striking snake.

I watched as her stone skimmed a total of seven times. *Seven*! My record was nine, and I'd been doing it for nearly forty years.

"Your turn, Adam," she instructed.

But I politely declined, feigning some sort of injury to my shoulder for fear of being shown up by a five-year-old girl. "No, go ahead and carry on, Evie, you're doing brilliantly," I said.

"I'm doing it the right way?" she asked, choosing her next projectile with a discerning eye.

"Yeah, I should say so," I offered. "You could teach me a thing or two, kiddo!"

And it wasn't a fluke, as her next effort was equally impressive, although falling slightly short of her previous attempt. As she prepared for a third go, I wondered if it would be terribly inappropriate to ask Evie if she'd overheard her mum saying anything else about me in previous phone conversations. Like, if she thought I was maybe... I don't even know what word Julia might use... *Fit*? *Hot...*? *Tidy...*? *Handsome...*? Something else?

Whatever way women referred to men they fancied these days, I hadn't a clue. But anyway, I immediately talked myself out of this idea, realising that had Evie heard anything in this regard, she no doubt would have just come straight out with it, most likely, with no coaxing, prodding, or encouragement required.

Through the corner of my eye, I caught a glimpse of Julia walking down the concrete steps leading to the beach. Even though the light was starting to fade and she was about fifteen metres away, I could still tell she didn't look overly impressed about something. I wondered how much she knew about the whole situation with the dance school, and what Chloe might've revealed.

"Did she fill you in about everything that's happened?" I asked, once Julia was standing next to me.

Julia sighed. "She told me earlier, but I was trying to keep it out of my mind," she explained. "But just now, Chloe has come out of her initial meeting with the insurance assessor."

I didn't need to ask if it was further bad news, as that answer seemed fairly obvious. "Please tell me the damage to the property is covered?"

Julia looked out to sea, observing Evie's latest attempt at skimming over the surface of the water. "It looks like the contents insurance will cover the cost of repairs in relation to the vandalism," Julia offered. "But the assessor has encountered *another* issue, unrelated and separate to the vandalism."

"And it's not good, I'm assuming?"

"Subsidence. The land the building rests upon is settling," Julia grimly advised. "It appears it's been going on for years, very gradually, apparently unnoticed until now. The assessor recommends the building remain unused until a full survey is carried out."

This wasn't great news, of course. I'd seen first-hand how much the dance studio meant to its members. But I felt the need to place a positive spin on things.

"Well, at least she can get the vandalism damage and the subsidence issue both sorted out at the same time. That's good, right? I mean, it was very fortunate that it was spotted before the hall fell down, yeah?"

Julia slowly shook her head. "The contents insurance covers the damage caused by the vandalism. However—"

"Chloe doesn't have buildings insurance…?" I surmised, putting two and two together, but almost afraid to hear the answer.

"No she doesn't," Julia responded. "And she was absolutely gutted over the phone, Adam. Without that type of insurance to handle the cost, she's looking at a repair bill in the tens of thousands, quite possibly. And the worst part is that she's not even allowed to reopen until the problem's taken care of."

Chapter Twenty

I awoke early, unable to stay asleep, which was unusual of late. Unusual because I'd recently been sleeping so well that I was worried Barry the cat might even be spiking my evening beverage, in fact. But it was remarkable, I'd considered, while looking at my bedroom ceiling, just how draining it had been to constantly worry about money. Granted, I wasn't earning a fortune from my part-time job now, but it did serve to relieve some of the constant pressure from being an author with diminishing book sales. And the restorative effect of a decent night's kip had been remarkable. I felt like I had more energy lately, my general mood lifted, and my face, when I looked at myself in the mirror, didn't appear like I'd just stumbled in from a three-day bender.

I didn't need the alarm clock today, however. I never did, really, on the third of September. Granted, I might have been a bit apprehensive about my reading at Evie's school later that morning. But that wasn't why I'd been tossing and turning for most of the night. No, my restlessness around and about this calendar date was because I knew I had the painful duty, each and every year, of doing something I dreaded.

The cemetery where my dad was buried was close to home, no more than a five-minute drive. Although I often travelled past it three or four times a week, the only time I parked up and paid a visit at his graveside was on his birthday. I felt it was better doing it then, as I had no desire to celebrate the date of his death.

He was constantly in my thoughts, so I didn't feel much guilt for not paying more frequent visits, but I could completely understand those that did take comfort from putting in an appearance on a more regular basis. My sister and my mum, for example, were regular visitors. But they never judged me, as far as I know, one way or the other, as it was a personal decision to make.

I did, however, always feel a touch guilty by the fact that I rarely turned up with flowers. But, as I reconciled in my head, my mum and sister routinely arrived with an armful of blooms. So if I did bring any, I always struggled to find anywhere to put them! This again proved to be the case as I walked through the quiet cemetery, spotting a splash of colour by my dad's headstone even from some distance away.

"Heya, Pop," I said awkwardly to the engraved black granite slab upon arrival. I paused, unsure what to say next, and also wondered whether I should use my internal voice, merely inside my head, or if I ought to speak out loud, talking as if we were catching up over a pint down at the pub. I opted for the internal voice, same as I ordinarily employed over the years.

I didn't go into detail about what had been going on in my life, as I tended to do that anyway at the time it was happening, rather than wait for my annual visit with him. This might occur when I was in the car waiting at a traffic light, taking a tea break while writing, sitting on the loo, or before I drifted off to sleep at night. Whenever it was, I'd always take comfort in speaking to my dad and feel confident that he was somehow, in some way, listening to me prattle on.

Whenever the inevitable tear would arrive while at the cemetery (which it always did), I was still unsure if it was because my father had died or because of the crippling guilt I felt due to my involvement in the events leading up to it.

As a kid, my dad was my hero. He still is. A big bear of a man, I remember my mates always being amazed that he could easily lift me clear over his head like I was little more than just a tiny sack of potatoes! Every Friday, without fail, he'd come through the front door with a bag full of treats. Me and my sister Helen would wait patiently for his car to drive up the street, but before he even got his coat off inside, we both pounced on him, desperate to see what he'd brought us this time. But he wouldn't let that bag go without a play fight, and the three of us would often end up rolling around the living room carpet like the wrestlers on the telly, with my mum acting as referee to break us up. God, I miss those days. I'd give up everything I've ever owned to be kneeling on our sofa again, peering through the front window to catch a first glimpse of him driving towards the house.

Despite the fond memories of my dad, I hated that my thoughts invariably turned to that awful Christmas of 1984. Since his death, I don't think there's a day gone by when I've not regretted what I said to him in a fit of selfish pique. He'd worked weeks of overtime to buy me that Commodore 16, yet all I could do was accuse him of preferring to work rather than take me to the BMX track. From his expression at the time, I knew I'd upset him. And in my immature rage, that was precisely what I was trying to do.

I never did get around to apologising for what I'd said to him. I like to think he never harboured any sort of ill feeling towards me. But to imagine, even for a second, that I'd caused him any amount of pain or made him sad about not spending time with me while he was busy working to buy me a computer, well, it's devastating. I'll never forgive myself for that. In moments of quiet reflection, I must have apologized in my head to him countless times over the years. More than anything, I dreamed about seeing him coming up our garden path again, the bag of treats hidden behind his back— as he did every week without fail—so he could see the delight on our faces when he eventually revealed it. But in these fantasies, I wouldn't make a grab for the bag of sweets as I usually did. Instead, I'd throw my arms around his waist and tell him he was the greatest dad in the world, the greatest that ever lived.

After the incident with Mr Bentham, my friend Robert's father, life would never be the same again, though. I hadn't appreciated it at the time—as I was so proud of my dad for beating up such a horrible bully—but you couldn't just go around and give somebody a bloody good thumping, even if you thought they deserved it.

My dad was charged by the police because of the severity of Mr Bentham's injuries. From what Mum remembers, they were gutted about having to arrest him, as they knew what a wretched excuse for a human being John Bentham was. But the law was still the law, and my dad had to answer for his actions. (As Robert's father did as well, which I suppose was some small consolation, at least.)

I wish I never mentioned anything about Robert's father shouting at us, or of seeing the evidence of beatings on a son he should have been there to protect and not abuse. If only I'd kept my mouth shut about it, then maybe my dad wouldn't have gone around and kicked lumps out of the man. If I'd said nothing, perhaps my dad wouldn't have been locked up.

I don't remember too much about that period of my life. Maybe I've blotted out a lot of it as a sort of self-defence mechanism. But I do recall my mum's utter despair when Dad was sentenced to six months in prison. This was a man who'd never even had a speeding ticket, yet there he was, incarcerated for stopping a helpless child being beaten by his own dad. Even the police tried putting a positive word in with the judge, which apparently helped reduce my father's sentence though didn't serve to prevent it entirely.

The first time we visited Dad in prison, I was shocked. Mum had warned us beforehand, but I still couldn't believe what I saw. That big, huge bear of a man appeared half his ordinary size, hunched over and losing too much weight. It seemed like his hair was even thinning, and his face was gaunt with dark patches under his eyes. His usual, cheery demeanour was a thing of the past. It was like he had been replaced by a much, much older, frailer version of himself. Of course, he tried putting up a brave front whenever we went to visit, but we could tell he was obviously struggling.

My dad never got to finish his sentence for dishing out revenge on a child-beating bully. He died three months into it from a massive stroke, likely triggered by the stress of the whole situation he found himself in. My life and my family would never be the same again without that wonderful, kind, and loving man in our lives.

Years later, whenever I wouldn't have Christmas cards hanging over my fireplace, a Christmas tree in my front window, or any sort of inclination for enjoying a plump turkey with all the trimmings, it wasn't because I was a miserable bugger, necessarily (although I reckon, at times, I could be). No, the reason I didn't celebrate Christmas was because it immediately transported me back to that horrendous time in 1984 when I wished I would have handled things so very, very differently.

I knelt in front of the gravestone, adjusting some kind of reddish flower (I wasn't good with knowing the names) tilted to one side in a vase no doubt left there by either my sister or my mum. The inevitable tears arrived as I placed a hand on the engraving of his name. "So that's me, then," I said quietly, forcing a smile. "I love you, Pop. And I think of you always."

I rose, offering a polite nod by way of goodbye. "Oh, and if you're free this afternoon, Dad, doing whatever it is you do up there…?" I added, pointing a finger heavenward. "You can stick your nose into Braddan Primary School, if you like. I'm doing a reading, and I've got a funny feeling I'm going to be eaten up by a classroom of ankle-biters that may just as well be piranhas!"

❋ ❋ ❋

After a spot of lunch, I jumped into the car, armed with the manuscript that Evie and I had diligently worked on. The thought of a large whisky to help settle down the butterflies fluttering away in my stomach briefly appealed, but the idea of potentially breathing alcohol fumes over the wee ones didn't.

During the short drive to Evie's school, I was again hit with the realisation that life was, to some extent, imitating art. If my current existence was turning into the plotline of a Christmas novel— as had been previously suggested by my sister—then the present issues at the dance hall were a perfect twist in the storyline she'd put forth. In Helen's 'best-selling book' synopsis, I was the failing author who found salvation by getting involved with a children's dance group. Then, according to my sister, I'd fall in love with the pretty dance instructor and be the lead character in my book based on my heart-warming journey of redemption.

In Helen's imaginary festive script, I'd no doubt finish my novel, it would surge to number one in the bookselling charts, and I would then use the shedloads of cash I acquire to repair all of the various damages to the dance studio. Everyone, subsequently, would live happily ever after (and would, of course, all have amazing teeth).

Sadly, things weren't going to happen like that in the real world. Not even as a result of the book I was writing in my genuine, actual life. While I was nearly finished with the creative portion of the process, it would be in editing for weeks thereafter, and then with my agent for goodness knows how long while she touted the manuscript around the various publishers, hoping they might take a nibble at it. You indeed needed some patience to write a book. But you *also* needed a boatload of patience in waiting to possibly make any *money* out of it.

I presented myself at the school's reception desk, after briefly inspecting myself in a wall-mounted mirror in the outer corridor. I didn't often 'smarten up,' so to speak, but I felt I appeared rather smashing in my light tweed blazer over a crisp white shirt, with a pair of fine trousers included as well. I'd thought of wearing my nice herringbone tweed cap also, but wasn't sure I'd be allowed to keep it on inside the school, so ended up leaving that at home.

"Can I help?" the school receptionist asked brightly, from her place behind the welcome desk.

"Hi, I'm here to see Julia?" I replied. "Erm, that is… I mean, Miss Monroe. She's agreed to meet me here and show me the way?"

"Certainly. And your name?"

"Oh, sorry. I'm Adam. Adam Catchpole."

The receptionist directed me to a clipboard secured to the desk by a length of string. "Well, Adam, if you'd care to sign the guest register, I'll be happy to locate Miss Monroe for you," she said. And then, "You're here for the affair…?"

"Wh–what?" I sputtered.

"The storytelling affair. The event that's been scheduled today," the receptionist answered. "You're the famous author, yes? You'll be reading for us?"

"Oh. Oh, yes," I replied, relieved that's all she meant, and trying to get my pulse back to normal rate.

"Splendid. We've been looking forward to having you," came the reply. "I've got you jotted down on the schedule here, but young Evie has also been telling us all about the Christmas story you've both been working on. Right. Bear with me for just a tick."

I waited in the reception area, admiring the children's artwork posted up on the giant corkboard there. At least, I hoped it was the children's work. Because if it was the handiwork of the school's teachers then they needed an awful lot more practice, I imagined with a laugh. Hanging next to the gallery of what I believed were depictions of farmyard animals by the students featured on the corkboard, was a framed display of the various faculty members.

My eye was immediately drawn to Julia's photo, a vision of loveliness that I could feel raise a smile on my part. "Ah," I said, noticing her job title identified below her image: *Julia Monroe – Music Teacher*. I knew that Julia was a teacher here, of course, but for some reason I'd only thought of the standard variety stood in front of a primary school classroom, instructing maths, English, handwriting, and so on. I suppose her involvement with TAPPIN' FEET made perfect sense if she was a melophile, I considered.

But before I could congratulate myself on finally being able to use the word *melophile* in a sentence, even if I'd only used it simply in my head, Julia walked up the corridor towards me, waving as she approached.

Upon her arrival, I stood at attention and moved my face closer, intending to give her a peck on the cheek. But remembering where I presently was, I immediately pulled back.

"Are you trying to smell me or something?" Julia asked with a laugh. And then, after looking me over, "So how are you feeling? Are you ready for this?"

"I feel a bit like a gladiator about to be let onto the floor of the Colosseum to fight against lions and they've only armed me with a soup spoon from the kitchen to defend myself, along with perhaps a cup and saucer."

"Hmm, I suppose in that scenario you could hurl the saucer like a discus? Or you might possibly use it as a tiny shield?" Julia proposed with a chuckle. "But seriously, Adam, you'll be just fine. The kids are all waiting for you in the assembly hall. I've agreed to lead things off, and then later, after you've finished, we can grab a coffee in the staff room, yeah?"

"Okay, sure," I said, following Julia through the corridors. Then, outside a pair of imposing hardwood doors with a porthole window on either side, she gave me a final look.

"Here we go, Adam. And don't worry, they don't bite."

"I'll be the judge of..." I started to say, as the doors were pressed open and a sea of tiny inquisitive and expectant faces turned my way. Julia led me through the assembly hall towards the stage at the opposite end, where a single orange plastic chair was waiting for me. *How can a roomful of children be so intimidating?* I thought, offering a timid wave to nobody in particular.

After I parked myself down on the little plastic throne I'd been appointed, Julia clapped her hands, bringing the restless hall to a hushed silence. "As you know, children, we've got with us a very special guest today," she declared. "And how do we greet our very special guests at Braddan Primary School...?"

Without further prompting all the kids, sitting cross-legged on the floor, responded accordingly. "Good afternoon, Mr Catchpole!" they shouted in unison. I could see Evie's face on the front row at that moment, her face beaming.

"Good luck," Julia whispered to me just before exiting stage left, leaving me alone in the middle of the floorboards with an ocean of heads staring back at me.

"Uhm, thank you for the warm reception," I said, conscious that my back was starting to feel a bit damp, and worried that my pores were about to spring a leak on me again, as they so often did. "Do you... erm, that is, does anybody have any questions for me before I start...?"

The room was quiet, apart from what sounded like one child's gentle snoring, a bit like Barry my cat. "No?" I said after an uncomfortable interim. But that's when I clapped eyes on Evie again, this time nudging the pigtailed girl beside her. *Yes, Evie, thank you*, I thought to myself, certain she was asking her mate to chip in with a question, getting me out of a tricky spot. And thankfully, the pigtailed girl did raise her hand—raising it so high, in fact, that she seemed in real danger of dislocating her shoulder.

"Yes? Over there," I gratefully said, pointing towards the front row. "Do you have a question for me?"

The little girl nodded, briefly glancing across to Evie, and then back to me. "I just wondered, Mister Catapult..." she began, before trailing off.

"It's Catchpole," I said, gently correcting her. But I wanted to put the little creature at ease. "It's okay, don't be shy. You can ask me anything," I reassured her.

This appeared to perk her up quite nicely, with the girl arching her spine and pressing her shoulders back. "Mister Catapult..." she said. "Mister Catapult, I just wondered what colour Star Trek underpants you wore today?"

I threw Evie an *I'll-get-you-for-this* look, a moment before the assembly hall burst into a fit of uncontrollable giggling. And to be fair, it wasn't long before I joined them.

Chapter Twenty-One

I was at that stage in any new relationship where everything was fresh, exciting, and filled with possibilities. It had only been a month or so since our first date, but each time I had to say goodbye after spending time in Julia's company was difficult. I don't know how she did it, but she made me a much better version of myself. For instance, things that would ordinarily have resulted in raised blood pressure—like traffic congestion, the sound of people loudly chewing their food, or people walking slowly in front of me on the pavement or at the supermarket—no longer resulted in an overwhelming urge to choke somebody. Put simply, Julia made me happy. And Evie was just a complete joy to spend time with as well, so there were certainly no issues there.

This uplifting change to my personality hadn't gone unnoticed by those closest to me. As a result, my sister's welfare check visits were now about spending some quality time together rather than her clumsily snooping around my house for signs that I was heading for some sort of mental catastrophe.

In these new and improved moments of feeling contented, I reflected on my neighbour Carol's speech about "the sentiment." She said if I didn't get that feeling from watching Christmas movies, I should venture outside the house occasionally and do something positive. She'd been right. Carol was absolutely spot on. By doing as she suggested, my life was enhanced exponentially, with good things happening routinely every time I decided to step out of my comfort zone.

Of course I'd be lying if I said I wasn't excreting buttons whenever I *did* leave my comfort zone, such as climbing onstage at Evie's school. But I would usually come through it unscathed. And in the specific case of Evie's school, I rather enjoyed the experience once everyone settled down and stopped having a jolly laugh at my expense (myself and the teachers included). Since that appearance, I had visited five more primary schools on the island, throughout September and the beginning of October, to read the story me and Evie wrote and to talk about the life of being an author, with several more appearances scheduled in the lead-up to Christmas.

Over the years, it never really occurred to me that people might be interested in what it is I do for a living. After all, I tended to sit hunched over a laptop for the better part of my day, while only occasionally surfacing for air. But for many, both children and adults alike, books were portals to lose yourself for a while, enabling you to escape to far-off lands and dip your toe into a sea of adventure that wouldn't be possible in the real world. As such, every school visit resulted in a barrage of questions about the process of creating a story. These were questions I was thrilled to receive and answer. But what was even more pleasing was the enthusiastic reaction received while reading the new tale me and Evie had written, "Santa's Training School for Christmas Elves."

Ordinarily, whenever one of my books were sold either online or at a brick-and-mortar location, for obvious reasons I was never on hand to observe the reader's eventual reaction to it. However, reading to my young school audience, I could glance up from the pages directly and see the children laughing where I hoped they would, or sitting open-mouthed, gripped by the unfolding action. It was rather exhilarating to witness this real-time response, and I don't mind admitting feeling quite proud when some of the kids asked for my autograph once I'd finished.

With this boost to my ego serving to buoy my sense of creativity, I was also able to make great strides with the novel I was working on. As I'd just started in on the final chapter, I'd already put my agent, Milly, on standby that I'd soon have the finished manuscript with her. I knew from experience that it would still take some time before anything of interest might happen afterwards, but it didn't hurt to keep her in the loop.

Sadly, I'd still not made all that much progress into the sizeable debt I owed to the bank. Yes, I was trying my very best. But with the increased interest rates at play and a limited (though admittedly improved) income, it still felt like I was attempting to empty the North Sea with a thimble. But I wasn't letting a minor detail like this dampen my spirits because I had a dinner date with Julia to look forward to and several items on my shopping list to make it an evening to remember.

And so, walking around the busy aisles of Marks & Spencer in Douglas, I was impressed that I hadn't growled at a single person for getting in my way or dawdling in front of me as they examined the biscuit selection. "It's fine. Don't worry about it," I even offered to one lady with thick-lensed glasses when she'd smashed her trolley into my knees. "You have a lovely day, dear," I added, surprising myself for being so courteous.

With several items soon ticked off my list, I stood before a large display of flowers, wondering which blooms indicated, *You mean a lot to me, but I don't want to possibly scare you off by appearing too overly eager*, when I heard a pleasant voice from behind me. "Adam, is that you?" the pleasant voice said.

"Harry," I said, upon turning around, pleased to see the familiar face of Harry Pickard smiling at me. Harry was the fine proprietor of BRIDGE BOOKSHOP, which had two branches on the isle and kindly held a stock of my assorted books for sale.

"Romantic date, or grovelling apology?" Harry enquired, looking first at the box of chocolates in my shopping basket and then the display of flowers I'd just been scanning.

I laughed. I liked Harry. He and his wife were ardent supporters of local writers, offering shelf space in their Port Erin and Ramsey stores to showcase the local talent. I remember how thrilled I was, seeing one of my books in their shop window all those years ago, for the very first time.

"Well," I said, addressing his question, "I'm hoping it's a romantic date, Harry. But after she's tasted my cooking, I might be offering her a grovelling apology after all. How's things?"

"I'm on a flying visit to buy a kid's birthday cake," Harry offered, holding the evidence out in front of him. "I'm glad I bumped into you, though, just now. Do you not read your emails?"

"My emails…?" I said.

I was notoriously bad for reading emails on account of most of them being offers of marriage from Nigerian fraudsters and such.

"I'm not the best with emails, no," I admitted.

With a Marks & Sparks special Colin the Caterpillar cake nestled safely in hand, Harry had one eye on the exit. "I emailed because I need to order some books from you," he explained.

Now, *that* was the sort of email I liked to receive. While selling most of my books by standard means via my publisher, I always made sure to retain my own stock for things like book signings, to fulfil direct orders on my website, and to supply a few local shops like Harry's. It was a good way to make extra money. Money I was grateful for. And as I had sixteen titles in my space opera series, a decent-sized order from Harry would always be most welcome.

"Sure thing," I said. "Is it the entire series you're looking to top up, as usual?"

"No, it's the new one I'm after, Adam. Do you have any in stock?"

"The new one…?" I asked.

Perhaps I'd been doing my agent a slight disservice by suggesting she was sometimes a bit tardy in selling and marketing my work. I'd only just told her I was nearly done with my new novel, yet apparently word had already successfully been spread within the bookseller retail world.

"Ah, not quite yet, Harry," I said apologetically. "I should be finished with it probably in the next week or so. And then, once I've edited it and—"

"But I've had at least twenty people in the shops trying to order it already," Harry cut in, thoroughly confused. "So if it's not even finished yet, how could they be asking for it?"

Twenty enquiries about a book I'd not yet finished were encouraging. However, I wasn't certain of the answer. "Dunno, Harry, I'm not sure. But as soon as I get my author copies, I'll be sure to get in touch, mate."

Harry turned to start walking towards the check-out registers. "Brilliant. I've kept their contact details so we don't lose the sales."

"Ehm, before you go…" I said, following after him, reluctant to lose any possible sale as well. "How are you for stock on my other books, Harry? Do you need any titles replenished?"

Harry considered this briefly, likely running through his inventory levels in his head. "Nope. I'm all good at present," he said after a moment. "It's only that current one about the Christmas elves I'm after for now. Perhaps you could drop a supply into one of the shops when you pass, as soon as it becomes available?"

I waved Harry goodbye, returning my attention to the glorious-smelling display of various flowers. "Now, should I go for..." I said, speaking to myself again. But I didn't progress past the shelf filled with pink blooms of some unknown variety when the particulars of Harry's recent remark suddenly registered. *"Christmas* elves...?" I said, replaying his words. And then, "Christmas *elves!*"

I bolted after Harry, who was by this time walking through the automatic exit doors. "Harry!" I shouted, but the sound of a passing bus outside drowned out my voice. "Harry, wait up!"

Fortunately, once he was outside, Harry came to a halt, waiting for a break in the traffic before crossing the road, by the looks of it. "Harry, just a sec!" I shouted after him, jogging through the automatic doors and catching up.

"Hey, Adam. Fancy meeting you here," Harry joked, as if seeing me for the very first time today.

"The book you just mentioned, yeah?" I responded. "You did say Christmas elves?"

"Uhm... yeah?" Harry answered, appearing unsure as to what I was getting at. "That'd be your new book, mate. In case you may have forgotten?"

"Just to be clear here, are you speaking about *Santa's Training School for Christmas Elves*?" I asked.

Harry looked at me quizzically, as if I were speaking some kind of odd alien dialect taken from one of my space opera collection of novels. "Well, unless you've written some *other* book about Christmas elves which I don't know about yet, then yep, that's the one," he said. "Now I'm sorry, but I do have to run. Otherwise, there'll be a child's birthday party without any cake. And that's a dangerous situation for anybody to be around."

I placed a gentle hand on Harry's arm, temporarily preventing his escape. "Just so I understand you, you've had multiple enquiries about Santa's Training School for Christmas Elves?"

"Bloody hell, what are you on about?" Harry said with a laugh. "*Yes*, I've had people asking me for it. Don't be so surprised, mate. You're a talented writer, after all, if a little peculiar sometimes."

Harry had a point. Maybe even several. "Ah," I said, catching up with what was going on. "A young friend and myself have drafted a brand-new tale, and I've done a few readings from it at some of the local schools," I explained. "Perhaps a few of the kids wanted to buy a proper version of it for themselves?"

"It's only a story, in draft form?" Harry asked. "So you *don't* have physical copies available?"

Never one to turn down any prospective sale, I reckoned I could wriggle my way out of this. "Of *course* we'll have copies for sale," I lied, not wishing to look a gift horse in the mouth. "Just keep on taking those orders, Harry, and I'll chase up the printers, yeah?"

"Jolly good, Adam. Now, I really have to go."

I stood on the pavement, smiling happily to myself and probably looking like a weirdo. Ordinarily, selling books was an uphill slog that usually required significant amounts of money spent on advertising before you were able to see any sort of return. But the story I wrote with Evie was already selling before I'd even considered turning it into an actual children's book and getting copies of it printed. I was astounded.

"Excuse me, sir," came a stern voice just then, along with a firm grip on my arm.

I adjusted my position slightly, worried I was perhaps blocking the pavement. "Sorry," I said, glancing over my shoulder. But the person standing there didn't move.

"Store security," the man said, thrusting an identification card towards me with his free hand. "Do you have a receipt for the contents of your shopping basket?"

I looked down at what I was holding, panic-stricken. I'd completely forgotten about the expensive box of chocolates I'd picked up, amongst other assorted items, before chasing after Harry.

"Oh, no. I'm so sorry. No, I don't have a receipt," I said.

"I didn't *think* so," said the security officer imperiously. "And that's precisely why I'm the most *accomplished* store detective in all of Douglas," he added. "Now, if you'd like to follow me back into the store, sir, we'll need to have a little chat, you and me. And this is not a request."

I held out an apologetic hand. "No, this isn't what you think," I offered, as the firm hand guided me towards the automatic doors I'd just jogged through from the opposite direction. "Honestly, this is an innocent mistake, and I can completely explain. You see, sir, I was just—"

"Don't bother, I've heard it all before," said the man. "In fact, I've heard so many excuses I could probably write a book about them."

"Ah, it's funny you should say that," I responded, being escorted back into the store and doing the walk of shame in front of a number of gawping shoppers. "You see, I'm an author. And funny story, actually, it's precisely because of books that I ran outside without paying for the box of chocolates. You see, as it should happen—"

"That's *terribly* interesting, sir. I'm *certain* the police will wish to hear *all* about it when they arrive shortly to speak with you."

❋ ❋ ❋

The corners of Julia's mouth curled slowly into a mischievous grin. She placed her hand over her mouth in an attempt to hide it, but I wasn't daft, as I could see what she was doing.

"I know what's going on there behind your hand, you know!" I protested, while clearing away the dessert plates at the conclusion of what, I felt hopeful, was a culinary work of art. I may not be at the same level as my neighbour Carol with her lovely lasagnas, but I'd given this cooking thing a go, watching YouTube videos for inspiration and ending up pleased with the results. And judging by the empty plates after each course, I trusted Julia had been equally impressed.

Julia made a half-hearted attempt to insist upon her innocence. "What? I would *never*," she said, before pursing her lips shut and reaching her hand over to her wine glass, which she briefly swirled before taking a dainty sip.

"You're still having a laugh at my expense," I put forth with a playful scowl.

"Oh, I would never do that," Julia reiterated, before lowering her glass. And then, "Did you get the rubber glove treatment from the security guy?" she asked, as I was approaching the kitchen. As I set the dishes in the sink, I could hear her breaking into another fit of giggles in my temporary absence.

I stuck my head around the kitchen door. "I'll have you know, Julia, there was no strip search or probing of body cavities during my brief detainment. All it took was a simple explanation, and I was soon on my way," I advised.

After filling the dishwasher, I reappeared with a new bottle of wine and the box of chocolates—one of the items that had nearly resulted in me being carted away by a constable. Fortunately, a review of the store's CCTV had revealed that I was just a distractable dimwit rather than any kind of master criminal, and the store security officer sent me away with a flea in my ear.

I placed the gold-coloured box on the table, just outside of Julia's reach. "So, I suppose you don't want any of these supposedly stolen goods, then...?" I asked.

"You slide that thing over here this instant, mister. Otherwise, I'll personally phone Marks and Spencer and tell them you're the Isle of Man's answer to Fagin," Julia replied.

Unlike me, who would simply grab any chocolate at random, I watched Julia studiously examining the contents of the box, occasionally referring to the printed leaflet offering an illustration of each chocolate along with a teasing description to whet one's appetite. "Hmm," she said, nibbling on her lower lip as the tip of her finger swirled above two potential targets. "I think... I think I'll go for *that* one..."

"Aww, but that's the one I wanted," I teased, while topping up the wine glasses.

It was one of our first date nights without Evie along (who frequently spent the weekends with her father), and things were, I suspected, going fairly well. The conversation flowed freely, as did the wine, nobody had choked on the meal I'd prepared, and even Barry appeared to like our human guest, nuzzling into her at every opportunity like a big furry flirt. I had to admire his tactics, even if I felt they were a little forward.

Despite feeling absolutely comfortable in Julia's company, we'd still not shared what I would consider a proper kiss yet. It wasn't that I didn't want to, because I absolutely did. I just wasn't especially good at instigating romantic gestures for fear of overstepping the mark and potentially receiving a slap across the face for my troubles. I probably worry far too much. But still.

Julia dipped her fingertips into the chocolate box for a second pass while I attended to the wine glasses once more. "So I was just thinking," she said, slightly distracted again by the available selection. "Getting the Santa's Training School story in book form and on bookshop shelves would be brilliant. Imagine Evie's little face when she sees it."

I'd been a busy fellow since running into Harry earlier. Encouraged by the talk of pre-orders, I had made a few calls to some of my local contacts. As a novelist, I routinely rubbed elbows with such folks as publishers, illustrators, editors, and other assorted people within the industry. As such, it was a relatively straightforward process for me to turn the manuscript I'd written with Evie into a physical book. However, when publishing a book yourself, you're responsible for the associated costs of doing so. This is why talk of pre-orders has always been appealing, because from the numbers involved you know you can offset some of the cost from the outset.

"I was thinking as well," I said, continuing on with the subject Julia had brought up. "You didn't keep any of the doodles Evie did, by any chance? The ones of the elves in the book?"

"You mean the collection of drawings still stuck to the front of my fridge?" Julia responded. "Yes, absolutely."

I handed Julia a topped-up wine glass before taking a seat. "Ah, excellent," I said. "I've spoken to this amazing illustrator I'm familiar with who reckons she can incorporate all of Evie's drawings in the book, plus create more based on Evie's style. I then spoke with a bloke I've worked with in the past who assures me he can print the book for us as soon as we like within the next couple of weeks."

Julia's eyes sparkled, which would've ordinarily made me feel weak at the knees if not for the simple fact that I was currently already sitting down.

"So that means you'll be able to start offering *Santa's Training School for Christmas Elves* in plenty of time for Christmas...?" she asked.

"Precisely!" I said.

"You know, Adam Catchpole, for a shoplifting hoodlam who also destroys children's stage sets, you're actually a very thoughtful person sometimes."

"Thanks. I think? Also…"

"Also?"

"Well, I thought if we managed to shift a few copies, we could donate any of the profits to Chloe. You know, help her out with the repair costs for the hall?"

Julia placed her glass on the table, pushed her chair back, and stared deep into my soul. It was unnerving, yet also kind of sexy. She got up and walked around the table, maintaining eye contact throughout, wrapped her hands around my face, and then administered a long, lingering kiss. "You…" she said, once she'd removed her lips from mine. "Are a wonderful human being, and I think I'd quite like it if I could tell people you were officially my boyfriend."

My lips were still in the pucker position for a few seconds, and my head felt warm and fuzzy like I'd just been administered a powerful anaesthetic before major surgery.

"I think I would quite like that, actually," I informed her. "But before you sit down again…"

"Yeah?"

"You couldn't kiss me again, could you? Because that first one was pretty epic."

Chapter Twenty-Two

The first week in November was special because I finally got to type an author's two favourite words in any novel they'd been working on: *The End.*

This was the new book I was sending off to my agent, which would hopefully be snapped up by a publisher in short order. I'd tried finishing it in October, but a pesky case of writer's block had reared its ugly head, delaying progress a bit. Still, I hadn't stressed over such matters as I used to, as I was positive the words would eventually start flowing again. And indeed they did.

However, it wasn't as simple as completing the novel and moving on to the next project, as there was the small matter of editing. It was an enjoyable time for some writers to give their manuscript a further spit 'n' polish treatment, tightening things up and improving the content and flow. For me, it was some measure of torture. I allocated myself two days for each chapter, where I'd need to pore over every word, picking up spelling mistakes, continuity errors, plot holes, and countless other things that always ended up presenting themselves. I usually, at the start, felt relatively confident about the standard of my work. Until I was required to re-read it with a fresh pair of eyes, that is, at which point I started to feel like the world's biggest loser, wracked with feelings of imposter syndrome as I wondered what kind of blithering idiot could have produced a product of such poor quality.

Slowly, however, as you fell back into proper editing mode and began to play about with your words, you could fine-tune punch lines, tinker with the dialogue, and generally restore faith that you somewhat knew what you were doing. And it was even better if you started believing that what you'd written was any good. If it wasn't, you could be sure your agent would be on the phone soon enough to let you know, of course. Over the years, I learned first-hand that Milly was never one to sugarcoat any feedback she had to offer, so I had to make sure any new book, including this latest one, was as good as possible before it landed on her desk.

So, having re-read and completed the editing of six of twenty-nine chapters so far, I was delighted to have a distraction to drag myself away from my computer for an hour or two so I could get a bit of fresh air and also stretch out and straighten up my spine, realigning my vertebrae into a proper, more appropriate configuration. And this specific distraction today was one I'd in fact been looking forward to all morning.

With the benefit of some impressive work by Hannah, my illustrator associate, I was finally able to reach the printing stage, now possessing a physical copy of the story Evie and I had created. Only Evie had no idea that, with her mum's kind assistance, we'd turned our manuscript into a beautifully illustrated hardback Christmas book that would soon be on sale both online and in several local bookshops around the island.

The venue for the grand, personal unveiling was after school in the nearby Kirby Garden Centre. A place it wasn't a challenge to get Evie to go to on account of the lovely café that just so happened to be there, and the delightful cakes to be found therein…

"So nothing exciting happened at school?" Julia pressed, eager to hear what her daughter had been up to all day, a daily task that a great many parents indulged in.

Evie shrugged, paying much more attention at the moment to the jammy sponge cake she was presently tucking into. Although to be fair, with the promise of an imminent sugar rush after a hard day at the office, so to speak, she wasn't especially listening to what was being said.

"Surely something of note must have happened today," Julia commented. "Evie…? Hello…?"

I raised a finger, seeking to contribute in some way. "Well, on the basis that you also work in the same school, Julia, *did* anything interesting happen?" I asked.

"No. I don't suppose there was," Julia conceded, pulling a face that told me I was *supposed* to be on her side. But then she grinned.

"Unless you don't count that Tyrannosaurus rex in roller skates who came crashing through the canteen window," she added.

But Evie didn't react to this, confirming that she wasn't, in fact, paying attention to whatever was being said.

We allowed Evie to finish her last mouthful of cake before feeling it safe to continue. Now confident there was no earwax build-up to contend with, I glanced at Julia, raising an eyebrow conspiratorially. "Evie, now you're done with your cake, why don't you go and get one of the colouring books you like…?" I suggested,

I was referring to the collection of books the owners left out for their younger clientele to enjoy. When we'd first arrived, I had run ahead for a moment, using the opportunity to plant our own book we'd created for Evie to discover. However, there were two minor problems with my plan just now. The first was that another young girl was presently approaching the modest library, getting worryingly close to spotting what I'd meant for *Evie* to spot. And the second problem was that Evie appeared more interested right now in rearranging a bowl of sugar cubes she'd laid out on the table first into the shape of Stonehenge, and then one of the Great Pyramids.

"Evie…" I tried again. "Evie, why don't you go and grab a book while me and your mum finish eating our own slices of…"

But I didn't get to complete my sentence, as the other little girl had beaten Evie to it, I noticed, proudly walking back to her place at the adjacent table with our book grasped firmly in hand. "Look, Grandad!" she said. "It's about a training school for Satan's elves!"

Grandad took a sip from his cup of tea before offering his granddaughter a gentle smile. "Sophie, my dearest, I think it's probably *Santa's* elves, rather than *Satan's*? But yes, I can see it, darling."

For the briefest moment, I considered snatching the book away. But given my recent viral video success, plus common human decency, I didn't think it wise to be wrestling a Christmas book away from a girl of maybe seven, or possibly eight years old at best. Instead, I watched as Evie raised her head. It was like the lights had just been flicked on as she suddenly reappeared from a deep sleep.

"Santa's Training School for Christmas Elves…?" Evie said, now looking over her shoulder to the table behind us. "That's *our* book," she declared, spinning around in her seat.

It certainly wasn't how I imagined things would go, but she was still discovering the book, and surely this was a good thing. She was up on her tiny feet, glancing over at the cover. However…

"Mummy, look, they've *stolen* our book!" she said. I could see her bottom lip start to quiver, and sadly, guessed that the waterworks weren't too far away. No, this was not going to plan at all, actually.

Grandad, the poor fellow, looked like he didn't understand what was going on and didn't know what to do. "Sophie, why don't you share the book with—" he began.

"But that's *our* book… Our book that *we* wrote…" Evie sobbed, while extending a trembling finger. "Mummy, somebody's stolen our idea! They've used the exact same title and everything!"

The other little girl looked down at the item in hand. "Wait, is your name Evie? Evie Monroe?" Sophie asked, reading out the co-author's name from the book's front cover.

Evie nodded, not having a clue what was happening. "That's… but that's… our book…" was all she could get out between sobs.

"I know it is, Evie. That *is* our book," I said. "It's *our* book, see?" I offered, placing a consoling arm around her. "Ehm… surprise?"

❋ ❋ ❋

With me and Evie's book now rolling off the printing presses, Julia had suggested a cunning plan to get the word out around the Isle of Man, hoping to drum up some further interest. Fortunate, then, that one of her oldest friends was a journalist with the local paper. And local newspapers loved nothing more than a feel-good story to fill a few column inches. Particularly when that news piece involved, in this case, a five-year-old author, plus a clumsy oaf trying to make amends for being an idiot, who were both trying to raise funds for a dance school in its direst hour of need. As a compelling news article, it pretty much wrote itself. If you also threw in a picture of a cute kid flashing a gummy smile, then you had all the ingredients to capture the attention of the local population.

As I suspected, this proved to be the case. Because not long after the island's complimentary newspaper landed on residents' doormats, I received a phone call from my pal Harry Pickard at BRIDGE BOOKSHOP.

"Oi, what's going on? Have you got those books for me?" he said. "Aside from the thirty-six pre-orders we've had so far, there's been at least another twenty this morning alone. What's the situation? We don't have any stock to give them?"

While I was obviously pleased by the numbers I was hearing, I couldn't help but ponder how to utilise a similar marketing tactic with my other assorted books going forward. After all, they were the ones that usually helped me to pay the mortgage.

"Don't worry, they're coming soon," I assured Harry. "Just you keep taking those orders, and I'll drop off a batch of books once I pick them up. They'll be hot off the printing press."

Once I'd spoken with Harry, I couldn't wait to phone Julia and update her that sales were starting to filter through, which I knew Evie would also be thrilled about. I didn't get a chance to call Julia to share the good news, however. But that was only because Julia phoned me first, talking so fast that trying to catch everything she was saying was a struggle.

"*How* many...?" I asked, able to squeeze in a few words. I walked around my kitchen, phone pressed to my ear, with Barry trailing after me as he often did when he thought food was on offer.

Julia, for her part, had some experience setting up a web page. Indeed, it was her efforts that had created TAPPIN' FEET's own website. So making a couple of pages specially dedicated to promoting and selling *Santa's Training School for Christmas Elves* wasn't too difficult for her. She detailed how the idea for the book came about, including several images of me and Evie's various brainstorming sessions, plus one picture of me reading the tale apprehensively to a group of captivated schoolchildren.

I wasn't sure how many sales the website would generate. However, as there was no actual financial outlay, it was certainly worth the effort on Julia's part. Further, unbeknownst to me, she had also emailed colleagues at all of the island's schools—including the ones I appeared at—asking if they'd mention the book to the parents. After all, the book had been positively received by the students already, and all the profits would be directly benefitting a dance studio that supported many of these same local children. So, the hope was that this would generate additional interest for what could be an ideal stocking-filler, what with Christmas fast approaching. But when Julia revealed just how many orders she'd received, I nearly tripped over Barry. "Did you say *four hundred…*?" I asked. And she did, which explained why she was so excited on the call.

The total amount of sales was four hundred and two orders, not including the pre-orders that BRIDGE BOOKSHOP had taken. Whilst this was fantastic news, it presented me with a minor problem— I'd only ordered three hundred and fifty copies from the printers, which had been their minimum print run.

Priced at £8.99, the profit margin from each book equated to a £4.00 donation to Chloe's dance group. So while the money earned from well over four hundred books (so far) wouldn't come close to fixing the dance studio, it would nevertheless still put a nice little dent in the total amount needed. And from what Julia told me on the phone, Chloe was over the moon when she found out.

Later that same afternoon, I was excited though a little nervous on the drive over to WORDS AND SPACES, the printing company on the outskirts of Douglas that I was working with. Because not only did I need to ask them to accommodate me in running more copies off the press with no notice, but it also occurred to me that the suspension on my ageing Nissan Micra might struggle with the weight of three hundred and fifty books piled into the boot and perhaps stacked onto the backseat as well…

"Oh, my!" I said a short while later, when introduced to the pile of boxes waiting for me in the reception area.

Mark, the friendly owner of WORDS AND SPACES, whom I knew well, laughed when he looked through the window at my current means of conveyance parked outside. "I can have one of the drivers drop them off for you instead, Adam, if you like?"

"Nah, I'll squeeze them all in," I said confidently, thinking about the comedy routine where a steady stream of clowns climb out of a car far smaller than mine having somehow through some miracle all fit inside. "Besides, I'm good at fitting puzzles together, so this lot should be no problem sorting out," I added.

Mark helped me load up the boot, which as it turned out had a deceptively generous amount of space. "So, do you think you could run off a few more copies for me?" I asked.

"Sure, if you need them, we can keep 'em coming. Shouldn't be a problem," he said. With all the boxes soon loaded, Mark stretched out his back. "Oh, I nearly forgot," he said, reaching into his pocket. "Here, this is for you."

I accepted the bank notes handed over, but was a bit confused. "Uhm, I thought it was *me* that paid *you* for the printing job…?"

"I've kept a few copies for the grandkids," Mark explained. "And a few of the guys in the print shop wanted one. I'll also leave a few for sale in the reception area if you like, going forward?"

"Yeah! Thanks, mate," I answered.

"It's for a good cause. One of my girls went to Tappin' Feet when she was younger," Mark informed me. "So what you're doing is a good thing. Absolutely a good thing."

"Mark, you're a legend," I replied. "Now, I'd better get this little lot dropped off," I advised, checking that my rear wheel arch wasn't pressed flat against the back tyres. "Oh, and I'll let you know how many more copies I need later today."

As I drove off, I tooted my horn, extending a hand through the opened window in a wave. "Cheers, buddy!"

Next up was a whistlestop tour, dropping books off at a few locations, leaving Julia's school until last, where she'd hopefully be free for me to whisk her off for a lunch date at the local chippy. The drive around the island also allowed me to think about the ending for my *other* book, which I'd assured my agent would be with her later that week. I'd nearly finished with the editing, but I always revisited the last few pages of every book I'd ever written to make sure it was perfect. I knew from experience just how vital a corker of an ending was to any story. Because no matter how good a book was, those final words could undo all your hard work if your readers weren't entirely satisfied that everything was wrapped up sufficiently, nice and neatly, with a shiny ribbon and a pretty bow.

Approaching the lovely seaside village of Port Erin in the south of the isle, I decided the existing ending to my book was mostly there, with only a few minor tweaks required. My mind then wandered to thoughts about whether a sequel might be in order, or if I should explore something entirely different next time. However, writing a sequel to a book that doesn't end up selling many copies would be a complete waste of time. So, without knowing in advance how well the title would perform, I couldn't really make a decision on that just yet.

I pulled up outside of BRIDGE BOOKSHOP's location in Port Erin, opposite the golden sands of the beach nearby, which was a mecca for tourists during the summer months. Now, in mid-November, though, a lone dog walker had the entire beach to himself, with a stiff sea breeze buffeting both him and his pooch by the looks of it.

Knowing this to be my first stop, I had already transferred four boxes onto my car's passenger seat, ready for quick dispatch. Seeing them there made me smile, as they provided a visual manifestation of my aim. In my head, I pictured Evie's little face beaming from ear to ear when we told her how many books we'd sold, and what that would mean for Chloe's dance studio.

I climbed out of the car, taking in a lungful of the invigorating, salty air whipping over the Irish Sea as I wandered over to the passenger side and opened the door. But before I placed my hands under the first of the cardboard boxes, I spotted an envelope with my name on it that'd fallen into the narrow gap on the floor between the seat and the door. My first thought, as I manoeuvred my hand to retrieve it, was that this was perhaps a note from Julia or Evie. However, once I'd snatched it up, I could see the WORDS AND SPACES logo printed on it. So, that meant it was either a love note from Mark or, as I suspected was much more likely to be the case, simply an invoice for the books provided.

I opened up the envelope, and sure enough, it was an invoice, accompanied by a message saying: "No rush on this, Adam. Good luck with sales."

I knew it'd take me a few days to collect the required cash, so it was grand that there was no immediate rush to settle the bill. But that's when my eyes dropped down the page to the invoice breakdown, and then to the 'Total' column. "Eh?" I said, quite surprised that the amount owed was over double what I'd been expecting. "This can't be right…?"

At first, I assumed—or desperately hoped—that Mark had billed me for the extra books I'd asked for today, in addition to those I'd already just received. But the answer to my confusion presented itself when I noted that I'd been charged an £8.99 printing cost for each book, when that was the same price we were *selling* them for. My heart raced, and I prayed this was just some kind of crazy error, as the eight pounds ninety-nine purchase price was something we had printed right on the book's cover, and maybe that amount became somehow stuck in someone's head...?

I pulled my mobile out of my pocket and called Mark straight away to let him know, and asked if he could perhaps email me an updated invoice to save me from having to stop back there. To my immense relief, he said he would investigate immediately and sort things out, assuring me that, as I had expressed, it was most likely just some kind of silly mistake. He was most apologetic, and asked if I would kindly excuse him for a few moments while he went to locate the party responsible for the mishap and "slap them repeatedly about the region of the face and neck with a trout, or perhaps a halibut," as he colourfully put it.

As I waited for him to return to the phone, I strolled across the road towards the beach, where I watched the solitary dog I'd spotted earlier chasing after a tennis ball its master had kindly thrown for its benefit. I took a mental note to bring Evie and Julia down for a drive at the weekend and grab an ice cream if it wasn't too terribly cold outside. Although upon reflection, I couldn't imagine the weather would put any child off an ice cream in either case.

"Yes, I'm still here, mate!" I responded cheerfully, when Mark came back on the line, asking if I was still there.

I listened to what Mark had to say, but what he had to say was not at all what I was expecting. The moment he told me there was in fact no discrepancy, and that my invoice had been genuinely correct, I could feel my legs start to buckle. I placed my left hand on my forehead, attempting to steady myself. "No, Mark, it's not your fault, I'm sure it must be mine," I told him, as he apologised again. "That fish you were going to use before, to beat the responsible party with? You'd better make that a large one, mate. Like a sturgeon, or maybe a tuna," I said glumly, before ending the call.

I headed back over the road towards my car, wondering how I could have been so bloody stupid. From the outset, I'd been given a variety of printing options: paperback, hardback, full-colour or black & white, laminated cover, and so on. I wanted to do the book justice, opting for the hardback, full-colour option with a glossy cover, so that it would be on par with those books from the major publishers. But with all the different quotes flying back and forth, it seems I'd stupidly confused the printing cost with the amount we were selling them for. In other words, it wasn't *their* mistake, it was *my* mistake. So, after printing up this large amount of books, we were already *losing* money, not making money, by the time I'd factored in what I also owed my illustrator.

"Oh, Adam Catchpole," I said to myself aloud. "You are a right, absolute dill-weed."

But Harry Pickard poked his head out through his shop's front door before I could commence striking myself in the face. "Heya, Adam! I thought that was you," he said to me in greeting. "Are you dropping those books off? I've got a customer in the shop looking to buy one. Maybe you could sign it for her?"

"Sure thing, Harry. Oh, and the books you've already sold. Have they already paid?" I asked.

"Yes, all of the pre-order customers have already paid," Harry answered, taking the first of the boxes I handed over to him. "Why, there's no problem, is there?"

"No..." I said, crying on the inside. "But we might need to consider amending the price for future sales..."

Chapter Twenty-Three

I was early for my present driving shift, waiting for the gang from the Lonely Heart Attack Club to finish a pottery class at the upper-floor studio located above JAVA THE HUTT, where I'd deposited them earlier. With some time to kill before shuttling the group home, I sat myself down at a table near the front window of the café with a cup of tea and a blueberry muffin. Having my driving HQ in a coffee shop was doing nothing to help my expanding waistline, I reckoned, but ah well.

"Oi, that sour expression of yours is in danger of scaring my customers away," came the familiar voice of Jack, my boss, before he took a seat at the same table.

I looked behind me for another table, somewhere perhaps a bit less conspicuous, where my dour mug wouldn't be on display for all the residents of the isle to see. "Sorry, Jack, I could…" I offered, hooking a thumb over my shoulder.

Jack laughed. "I was only pulling your chain, buddy. You didn't seem your usual self, so I thought I'd join you for a cuppa."

I liked Jack. He was just one of those guys that didn't have a malicious bone in his body. And what he and Emma had done in setting up the various branches of the Lonely Heart Attack Club was nothing short of inspiring. Particularly as I had the pleasure of witnessing the positive impact it had on their members first-hand when ferrying the group about the island.

Jack was also a perceptive fellow, successfully recognising that I wasn't my usual self at present. In typical fashion, my shiny optimism had been a case of one step forward and two steps back. For the first time in months, I'd finally had a few quid at the ready to help chip away at what I owed the bank. But this mistake with the book pricing was a massive financial blow.

And it wasn't like I could just come clean and admit I'd made a dog's dinner of things by selling the books for what they cost me. Because by the time I realised what I'd done, Chloe had already put a post on social media thanking Evie and me profusely for raising more than two thousand pounds towards the rebuild costs at the dance studio. And as I'd gone full circle from being the person who damaged their stage set to being a gracious benefactor, I'd look like a complete tit if I went back on my word now.

As such, the funds I had set aside for other purposes were now promptly handed over in lieu of profits from the book sales to date. I know I could have filled Chloe and Julia in about me being such a dunderhead. But I also knew that, if I did that, they never would've let me hand over the money as intended. With the total repair estimates coming in at over a hundred thousand pounds from what I'd heard, Chloe would need every penny she could possibly get her hands on. And I wasn't about to take back what I'd promised, even if it was an honest (albeit daft) mistake I'd made.

Fortunately, a little white lie on my part explained the subsequent price rise—from £8.99 to £12.99—by suggesting the lesser, original price was down to an initial discount I'd enjoyed from the printers (with a cover price which could now be easily changed). At least by correcting the RRP on the book, I wouldn't need to subsidise any future donations out of my own pocket going forward.

The money I'd handed over wasn't a huge sum. But it was a real kick in the family jewels at that precise moment—I no longer had any money to give to the bank, and knew I'd long since cashed in any remaining brownie points I had with them.

I'd had no intention of telling anybody about my misfortune with the books, or my current dire financial position. Not at first. But Jack was the type of person you felt you could unburden yourself on without any judgement in return. And God bless him because Jack listened to me prattle on and then immediately offered me more hours and even a small loan, which he said I could repay from deductions in my future earnings.

I was grateful for the additional hours, but I declined the generous offer of a loan, although I did appreciate it. And just by talking about my problems, I felt an immediate weight lifted.

"Well, I reckon I'd better go and help Emma behind the counter," Jack announced, upon finishing his cuppa. He stood up to go but then he paused, a funny, faraway expression on his face. "You know the dance club…?" he said.

"Yes. Tappin' Feet," I offered.

"Yeah. Where are they practising and performing and whatnot, if their hall is currently condemned?"

"They're not," I said, immediately thinking of young Evie. "And along with having to cancel a show they were working on, the kids don't as frequently get to spend quality time with their mates. So it's fair to say they're all a bit down in the dumps just now."

"And have too much time on their hands and probably getting in their parents' hair," Jack said with a laugh. But then he pointed his empty cup towards the café's ceiling. "Look, as long as it's not in conflict with the times my club members may be using it, why don't you offer use of the upstairs studio to Chloe and the nippers for as long as they need it? We've had loads of people up there with room to spare, so it should be plenty big enough. Plus, whenever the kids are here, I can make sure the smoothie machine and hot chocolate maker are always fired up for them."

I had to resist the urge to get up and throw my arms around the man. "Jack, that would be *fantastic*, mate. Thank you. And you're sure Emma won't mind…?"

Jack dismissed my concerns with a flourish of his tea towel, which he'd taken from his waist to wipe up a few remaining drops from his tea cup that had escaped while he'd been brandishing it in the air and using it to point. "*Pfft*, she'll be in her element with a bunch of singing and dancing kids on the property, I can promise you. But be forewarned, you may need to pull in a few favours to get her a role in their next performance, which she'll surely want."

"I'll see what I can do," I answered. "Maybe I can also put a word in for you as well?"

But unlike Emma would no doubt be, Jack, by contrast, didn't appear too keen on the suggestion.

"Erm… yeah, I *would*, Adam, honest," Jack said with a grin. "But, you know, I suspect I'll be far too busy manning the hot chocolate machine…"

❋ ❋ ❋

I've absolutely no idea why I agreed to it. I mean, up until a few months ago, I was a classic introvert, happy to spend my days in my study with only a computer and my pet cat for company. Yet here I was, walking up the steps to Manx Radio, about to speak live over the airwaves. Fortunately I wasn't alone in this, however, as Chloe was beside me. Which was just as well, I thought, considering this little outing was all her idea.

"You'll be fine," Chloe assured me as we made our way through the main entrance. "There's nothing to worry about."

But I didn't feel reassured. Instead, I felt like I was walking the green mile on my way to being fried like a slice of bacon. "I'm not quite as comfortable performing in front of an audience as you," I pointed out.

"Nonsense. Your turn as the Scarecrow was perfectly sublime," she said, before diverting her attention to the receptionist sitting behind the nearby desk.

I wasn't sure if Chloe was being serious with the compliment or not, but whatever the case, I assumed she was probably just trying to build my confidence.

"Good afternoon, it's Chloe Tappin and Adam Catchpole," Chloe announced for the both of us.

The receptionist gave a few taps on her computer's keyboard before flashing a welcoming smile. "Yes. Marvellous. If you'd care to take a seat? Matty will call you in when he's ready for you."

The modest reception area was partially surrounded by glass walls, behind which the entire studio was clearly visible. I was a regular listener to Manx Radio, so it was strange to see the person talking into his microphone in the studio and listening to the output being aired through a speaker in the reception area.

"So do you really think my performance was sublime?" I asked Chloe, in reference to her remark. However, there wasn't any time to receive a reply before Matty, the show's presenter, removed his earphones and gestured for us both to come into the room and join him there.

"Well, here we go," I said nervously. "Dead man walking…"

There wasn't too much time for a formal introduction, as we only had the remainder of the current musical track to quickly get comfortable, with microphones suspended directly in front of our faces as soon as we were seated and situated.

"Heya. Thanks for popping in," Matty said to us, fidgeting with several switches on the console before him. "Once the music comes to a stop, I'll introduce you, and then we'll just have a chat like old friends over a glass of wine," he advised. "And don't forget to speak actual words into the microphone. Remember, listeners at home can't see you nodding your head or gesturing with your hands," he added with a wink.

"I could do with a glass of wine about now," I commented. "A large one at that."

Unfortunately, the familiar sounds of "Mamma Mia" came to a conclusion before any drinks trolley could possibly be rolled out, imaginary or otherwise.

"There's the little bit of ABBA I promised you a bit earlier," Matty announced into his microphone. "And next up, I'm delighted to introduce Chloe Tappin from the Tappin' Feet dance school and local Manx author Adam Catchpole. Some listeners might know Adam from when he became the unsuspecting star of a viral video where he gate-crashed a Tappin' Feet performance earlier in the year."

I forced through a smile, suspecting that Matty wasn't quite as friendly as first assumed and briefly considered choking him with the cord on his headphones.

"But you turned all that around, Adam," Matty added, much to my instant relief. "So, tell us all about how you redeemed yourself and raised a fair bit of money to benefit the Tappin' Feet school after they'd been the victim of a horrible incident."

Chloe took the reins first, speaking eloquently about the dance group and what it meant to the community's younger members, whose confidence was bolstered by being given the opportunity to perform on stage. Of course, many of those listening would be well aware of the group from having their children attend the dance school over the years (or know someone else's child who did), or from watching one of the dance school's performances. Chloe then spoke about how shocked and disappointed she'd been about the vandalism, and then about the discovery of the subsidence issue. However, with a sunny disposition, she soon shifted away from the recent adversity she'd suffered, focussing instead on her plans for the dance club, including its temporary home above the JAVA THE HUTT café in Douglas and how the children were so excited that their regular sessions had been restored.

Following a short interlude during which Matty played the Bon Jovi song "Livin' on a Prayer," he invited me into the conversation. I started with a nervous, croaky voice, probably sounding to the listeners like a boy in his teens who was just reaching puberty. But following a sip of water, I soon got into my stride. I briefly talked about the kerfuffle that introduced me to Chloe and the group and which made me internet famous for all the wrong reasons.

"And I understand you've written a Christmas book to aid in raising money for the building works?" Matty asked.

I nodded in response, forgetting the earlier instructions I was given that listeners at home couldn't *see* me. "Yessir. Yes I have," I answered. "Well, I should mention the story was co-written with my good friend Evie," I added.

I went on to explain how the book had come about originally, and how I ultimately decided that all proceeds should go to help Chloe and her fine school in their hour of need.

"…And you can buy copies both online and in-store from Bridge Bookshop for only twelve pounds ninety-nine," I concluded, making sure to get the price correct this time.

"There you have it, folks," Matty said, while giving me a private thumbs-up. "With Christmas only several weeks away, what a perfect stocking filler for the big day," he added. Then, turning his attention back to Chloe, he said, "So when can we expect to see the next stage production, Miss Tappin?"

It was evident from her extended pause before answering and the look on her face that Chloe didn't know the answer. "Ooh, I'm not too sure, Matty," she offered after a moment. "But as soon as I know the answer, I'll come back to fill all of your listeners in on it."

"So there'll be no Christmas panto to look forward to?" Matty asked, sounding disappointed.

"Sadly not, no. At least not this year. But if we—"

"Actually, we *are* going to do a Christmas panto!" I cut in, interjecting before Chloe could properly finish.

I had absolutely no idea what I was doing right now, or what words were about to come out of my mouth next. Perhaps it was because good things appeared to happen every time I would step out of my comfort zone lately, and I sincerely hoped that somehow this trend would continue. Also, if I were in a Christmas movie, I couldn't help but think this was the sort of impulsive action the main character might do after giving precisely zero thought as to the practicalities and implications of such a thing.

Chloe gave me a *what-the-actual-hell-are-you-talking-about* sort of look before speaking into her microphone. "Are we...?"

"Yes! Yes we are," I said, laughing uncertainly, hoping Jack Tate's generous offer of a temporary home for the dance group extended as well to us hosting a run of festive shows in that location for the fine Manx public. "Tickets will be on sale soon!" I insisted. "With all proceeds going to benefit the Tappin' Feet dance group!"

"You heard it here first, good listeners, a Manx Radio exclusive," Matty announced. "Chloe and Adam, thank you for popping in to speak with us, and good luck with the fundraising efforts," he said.

"And coming up shortly will be 'Vienna' by Ultravox," Matty informed his audience. "But first, a lovely little gem from all the way back in the late seventies, a smashing number called 'Hit Me with Your Rhythm Stick,' by Ian Dury and the Blockheads..."

Chapter Twenty-Four

What I thought was a noble gesture to aid a good cause might not have turned out as expected. It was a bit like when you agreed to do something when you've had an excess number of pints, too sozzled to really think things through, and then wake up the next morning wracked with regret.

Chloe didn't seem cross with me, necessarily, following our interview over the radio. But driving her home, I did notice that she wasn't her usual, buoyant self.

"Sorry about that," I offered. "I stupidly thought that putting on a panto would be a perfect opportunity to generate some revenue for the cause. And because we had the ears of the many listeners, it seemed like the ideal occasion to mention it. I don't really know what came over me," I explained. "Should we just forget about the idea, and blame it on the witless ramblings of the village idiot?"

"You *are* the village idiot, Adam," Chloe replied. But she laughed as she said it, which put me at ease. "Though your heart was in the right place," she said. "The problem is this," she added, holding her phone out in front of her like a hand grenade about to explode—or more to the point, like she was expecting a flurry of calls to start commencing at any moment. "From past experience, I know the parents in any musical theatre or dance group are a competitive bunch. Some might say passionate. Others might even say ruthless. They always want only the best, starring roles for their children. And the issue now is that—"

"That you've got a group of excitable kids now champing at the bit to appear in a very spur-of-the-moment, *completely* unplanned Christmas panto?" I ventured. "Chloe, I apologise. If I had cared to think about it first, instead of just…"

"Honestly, Adam, it's fine. I'm genuinely touched that you're so concerned about us. I'll just need to get my thinking cap on and sort out what usually takes a fair few months to organise in, what, five weeks or so? If we want to be ready for the start of the panto season, that is."

I knew staging an amateur performance wasn't a case of simply giving the kids a script to take home, having one or two rehearsals before the show, and then pulling the curtain up on opening night to a packed house. But as Chloe explained to me, it was a logistical nightmare with so many moving parts to consider and people to organise. According to Chloe, the children, especially the younger ones, were notoriously challenging. "A bit like herding cats," she told me, although she did say these words with an obvious degree of affection.

Further, there were certain other issues/complications, like insurance, hiring musicians, and sorting out costumes and stage sets. And that was before even thinking about where the venue might be, of course, as they were currently bereft of one. Also, I'd naïvely failed to consider the content of the proposed panto. Because, as I was soon reminded, you couldn't just select one at your whim and merrily print off the scripts. Like in any creative industry, there was somebody somewhere who owned the intellectual property and would like to be paid for the use of their work. It was no different for stage plays and musicals—if you wanted to put on a show, you may be faced with a bill for doing so. And the more well-known the show, the heftier that bill could become.

I parked outside Chloe's house, feeling awful for dumping this problem on her. "Why don't I phone the radio station and ask them to say something?" I offered.

"Like what?"

"Like, I'm an idiot who shot his mouth off without the correct information…? And they should retract what I said…?"

Thankfully, Chloe's friendly demeanour was still at the ready. "Adam, don't worry about it," she insisted. "In fact, there's nothing like a challenge to get the ol' heart pumping," she declared.

"I'll speak with Jack," I said, when Chloe climbed out of the car. "Just to double-check if we can use the studio to stage the panto, as well as the rehearsals. Oh, and I'll also be there to offer you as much help as you need."

Chloe bent down, sticking her head back inside the open door. "Oh, you'll be *helping*, all right, Adam Catchpole," she made clear. "If we're to put on a Christmas pantomime, then believe you me, you're going to make yourself useful!"

❋ ❋ ❋

I read and re-read my email to Milly, my agent, so many times that the words started to lose meaning and began to blur onscreen. However, the content was important, as attached to the email was the final draft of my newly edited book. The very book that would hopefully liven up to a great degree my currently flagging royalty cheques. I'd worded the email to outline just how important this project was to me, with the hope that it would not sit in her 'to-do' pile for any number of weeks, as had happened in the past.

A huge weight lifted when I eventually clicked the send button. Leaning back in my chair, I enjoyed a moment of quiet reflection and satisfaction about finishing another novel. A serene moment that Barry the cat took as the perfect opportunity to jump up and land squarely on my crotch. Which took me a moment or two to recover from.

As I was already in emailing mode, though, I realised I couldn't continue to shirk around the subject of my ongoing mortgage arrears. Having depleted my modest savings account because of the book pricing error I'd made, things were about to get even worse for my laughable credit rating if I didn't take positive action. As such, I decided to be front-footed about the situation and contact Bethany, my account manager, to keep her updated.

And I had some real reason to be optimistic. After all, I'd been offered more hours driving for the Lonely Heart Attack Club, and I was about to release a new book. I'd also made regular repayments since my last meeting with Bethany, so I hoped this would demonstrate to the bank that I *was* trying. But other than updating them on my current situation, there was little else I could do other than offer them encouraging words.

With those emails taken care of, my financial destiny was out of my hands, at least for now. All I could do was wait patiently to hear some good news back from Milly (I hoped) and throw myself before the mercy of the banking gods.

Later that same afternoon, I sat in the minibus at the National Sports Centre car park, enjoying some quiet time to myself. The Lonely Heart Attack Club members had very kindly invited me to join them in their synchronised swimming class, but I'd politely declined. Despite living on an island, I don't think I've been swimming since I was a kid, and I didn't own a pair of trunks. I did have regular shorts, but they were somewhat loose-fitting, and I didn't reckon they'd be suitable for a swimming pool in case 'Little Adam' popped out during the water-based exertion. Although listening to the group on the outward journey, I had to admit the prospect of swimming again did sound fun in general. So I made a mental note to pick up the appropriate swimwear attire in the very near future so I'd be able to join them on their next lesson.

There was just something about spending time with this bunch of loonies that invigorated me. I still didn't know how many members there were around the island, exactly, but I'd yet to meet one of them who didn't have an enthusiastic zest for life.

When they finished their lesson, I could hear them before seeing them. They bounced giddily along towards the minibus like they'd been sitting in the pub all afternoon and were on their way to the kebab shop.

"C'mon, you lot," I said, jumping out of my seat to help those a little more unsteady on their feet to climb aboard. "Sheesh, I can smell the chlorine on you already."

I had to laugh at myself as I counted heads while they boarded. I was like a primary school teacher on a field trip, worried I might leave a child behind. And I didn't fancy calling Jack to say one of the bodies entrusted to my care had somehow gone missing.

"I meant to say earlier that I heard you on the radio, Adam," one of the ladies called out from the rear of the bus, once seated.

"I've always said Adam had a face for radio!" quipped one of the others, Frank. It was like the comedic duo had rehearsed their performance beforehand.

I looked in the rearview mirror, where I could see Louise lean across the aisle to give Frank a playful slap on the arm. "Nonsense," said Louise, looking in my direction now. "I thought you sounded very professional, and had a very sexy voice," she insisted, blowing me a kiss that floated through the cabin of the minibus. "Anyway, how about Suzy and me appear in that Christmas panto you mentioned during your interview?" Louise added, with a nudge to her mate beside her. "We've both had experience on the stage in our younger days."

"Yeah, experience *sweeping* it!" quipped another of the gang. I resisted the urge to laugh like the others, for fear of any potential repercussions. But neither Suzy nor Louise appeared to have taken any offence anyway.

"Adam, what panto is the group putting on? Have you decided on it yet?" Louise asked. "How about Dick Whittington?" she suggested. "Dick Whittington's a belter."

"I say Snow White," Suzy added to the list of potentials. "Or Jack and the Beanstalk."

And so began a debate regarding the virtues, and various pros and cons, of practically every Christmas panto that had ever been staged. But I didn't mind, as it helped to pleasantly pass the time during the drive. I was also encouraged by the enthusiasm on display, figuring that we might have a significant amount of ticket sales coming from club members alone.

"I'm not entirely sure which one they'll go for," I said eventually, talking to them over my shoulder while keeping my eyes fixed on the road. "You see, there's a fee you need to pay whenever using existing ideas that belong to somebody else. So I guess it will all depend on the costs when Chloe makes further enquiries."

"Well, you write one instead, then!" George's firm, raspy voice called out.

"Me?" I asked.

"Yeah. You're a writer, are you not?" George reminded me and the rest of the bus. "So you just write the Christmas panto *yourself*, you lazy bugger!"

Waiting for the current traffic light to change from red, I considered this. And George had a point, was the conclusion I reached by the time my light changed to green. Because I ordinarily write novels, I'd never even considered putting myself forward to write a pantomime. But it couldn't be *that* hard, could it? So... why not?

"What could it be about?" I asked my captive market research group, who were chatting amongst themselves behind me. "Any ideas, you lot?"

"I love a good musical!" came the first response.

"Ooh, with a Christmas theme!" came another.

"Well there you go, son. You need to write a Christmas musical," George summarised. "Here, what about that Christmas book you were chatting about on the radio? That one with the elves. Why don't you just use that?"

I appreciated the faith in me. But as many had told me over the years, I was utterly tone-deaf—as anybody who'd heard me singing in the shower would attest—so I didn't think I was really the right person to compose songs. I had to admit the idea of using the book Evie and I had written wasn't the daftest thing I'd heard recently, though. "Hmm, I do like the thought of that," I replied. "But turning it into a musical might be a step too..." I said, trailing off for just a second. "Wait, hang on. Oh, George, I could kiss you when we get off this bus!" I exclaimed. "In fact, I could kiss you all!"

"We don't mind if you do," Louise countered.

"Not in the slightest," added Suzy. "In fact, I'm already puckered up. My lips, I mean. Not my—"

"He knows what you mean!" George added.

I chuckled at the replies. "I might not have the required skill set to be able to convert the book into a proper musical," I advised the group as I steered the bus along the road. "But I flippin' well know someone who does!"

Chapter Twenty-Five

Jack had already offered the generous use of his spacious upper-floor studio to host TAPPIN' FEET rehearsals for as long as was needed. So I was delighted when he was agreeable to the dance school also using it for a run of Christmas panto musical performances. Although it wasn't an entirely selfless offer, as Jack was happy to admit that the prospect of having dozens of thirsty and hungry punters passing through his coffee shop before and after each performance was also quite appealing. So, it was a win-win for all concerned.

Now that an appropriate venue was secured and with the seed of an idea for a theme that wouldn't cost a penny, I just needed to put the concept to Chloe. She was the brains behind the outfit and the person with the experience to pull the whole thing together. As I figured it, me and Evie's children's Christmas book had already sold a few hundred copies, with additional sales continuing to accumulate. I liked to think that most who'd purchased one would be intrigued enough to also come along to a musical stage performance version of it. And it would be even more grand if they also encouraged and/or dragged along a few family members as well. All in all, if things went as I'd imagined, the musical idea had the potential to pull in some serious dosh for Chloe's dance group.

Rather than relaying everything to Chloe over the telephone, I decided to hop in the car and call around to sell the notion to her in person. I also wanted to stress, in person, that if I was possibly overstepping the mark in any way, all she had to do was say the word and I'd let go of the idea.

However, I needn't have worried because Chloe was over the moon and immediately sold on the proposal even though it meant a boatload of additional work for her. I didn't even need to sweeten things with talk of how much money could be raised towards the renovation costs, as the overwhelming desire to make the island's children happy was motivation enough for her—something that was readily apparent whenever you spoke to Chloe.

Unfortunately, neither of us had the ability to develop a book into a credible musical. A crucial stumbling block. For that, we'd need to convince our resident music teacher to drop everything to help us to make that happen! A task on which I volunteered to use my considerable charms.

As I wasn't awash with cash, a romantic meal for two whilst I also pitched Julia the idea simply wasn't viable at the moment. So I suggested sharing a big bag of freshly procured chips on Douglas Head, sitting on a wooden bench with a splendid view of the bay. And, yes, it turned out to be a bit breezy. Good kite-flying weather, as my dad used to say when I was a kid. But it was an al fresco dining spot I'd enjoyed many times over the years—as did a regular stream of tourists rewarded for their strenuous hike up the rocky point with sweeping views across both Manx countryside and out over Douglas Bay and the Irish Sea. The added bonus was the availability of plenty of green space up there, meaning plenty of room for Evie—wrapped up with more layers than an onion—to explore the headland to her heart's content while the firm breeze tousled her hair.

I couldn't help feeling a degree of sympathy for the fishing boat I spied chugging away from the safety of the harbour towards the rolling waves—where sea foam smashed against the rocks when making landfall. But as an islander, being buffeted by salty wind was heaven for me. Throw in a bag of chips drowning in lovely malt vinegar, and this was much better than any Michelin-starred restaurant in my opinion. Although with rosy-pink cheeks and a wind-induced tear or two, I'm not entirely sure if Julia would agree to my culinary review or my chosen venue.

"So… I was speaking to Chloe earlier about the idea of staging a fundraising pantomime," I casually slipped into the conversation, before spearing another chip on my small wooden fork.

"Mmm-hmm," Julia answered, along with a simple nod, as her mouth was presently full.

"To avoid paying a ridiculous fee to buy the rights to an existing production, I thought about adapting *Santa's Training School for Christmas Elves* instead," I told her. "Now that I've submitted my novel to my agent, I'll have time to jump straight into it."

"Ah!" said Julia, who was now able to speak properly once more. "That sounds like a good idea. I like it!"

I went quiet momentarily, watching the fishing boat pitching and rolling as it cleaved a path through the choppy waters. "The thing is," I added, picking up where I'd left off. "The thing is, we thought it'd be pretty special if we played about and adapted it into a Christmas musical. You know, with it already being a Christmas-themed story and everything. I reckon a musical would really pull in the crowds," I said.

I looked over, waiting for some reaction.

Julia was staring down the grassy hillside, waving back at Evie, who was about to press her eyes against a pair of tourist binoculars the local town council had recently installed, the device having been mounted on a sturdy metal base.

"Wait," said Julia, turning to face me now. "No offence, but how are you going to make it into a musical…?" she asked, though not unkindly, and sounding genuinely curious. And she had a minor point. Well, it was more of a humongous point, really.

I smiled broadly in response to her question, revealing my teeth and probably looking like an exaggerated, cartoon version of the Cheshire Cat.

"Wait, hang on," Julia said, along with a disbelieving laugh. "I'm busy at my day job, and I've already volunteered to make costumes on short notice for a Christmas panto of some variety that I wasn't expecting," Julia began. "And now, I'm guessing that you want me to drop everything to magically create a musical in just a few short weeks? Something that would usually take a number of months, if not the better part of a year to accomplish? Am I getting the idea?"

To be fair, not being musically minded myself, I wasn't entirely sure of the practical considerations of what we were hoping to achieve or how long it might take. I smiled again, although this time it was a kind of half smile and half grimace.

"Ehm… yes?" I said cautiously.

However, Julia wasn't quite finished yet. She gravely shook her head. "With what limited time I have available to me, I was hoping to repaint my living room before Christmas," she declared.

I raised my wooden fork so I could respond. "I'm quite good at painting," I was pleased to report. "I could do that for you."

"And *then* there was the regrouting of my bathroom tiles that I was desperate to get done in time for the big day," she added.

"Erm…" I said, with my fork still held aloft. "Well, I'm no expert at grouting. But I'd happily give it a go, if it means…"

"*And*," Julia advised, continuing on with her list of outstanding projects needed around the house, it would seem, "I was desperate to get Evie's bedroom wallpapered."

I was useless at wallpapering, as the peeling Anaglypta in my study would easily suggest. "Uhm… again, I'd be happy to take that task on board, if it meant you could…"

But the faintest hint of a smile suggested that Julia was presently yanking my chain.

"Wait," I said, pointing my fork accusingly. "You already *knew* I was going to ask you about the musical, *didn't* you?"

Julia placed a hand over her mouth, briefly feigning innocence. "Yeah, Chloe was so excited that she phoned me earlier and spilt the beans to me," she admitted.

"So, with all this DIY business you were on about… You don't really need any help wallpapering, then? Or the other tasks?"

"Are you serious? No, I've *seen* the peeling paper in your study," Julia joked. "Hmm, but I may just hold you to helping me repaint the living room in the new year, yeah?" she added, narrowing one eye as she considered this.

"Deal," I promptly replied. "So does that mean you'll do it, then? Getting involved with the adaptation?"

"Oh, I dunno, a primary school music teacher having to create an entire musical from scratch?" Julia said, initially turning up her nose at the idea. But then…

"Of *course* I'll do it! I'm terribly excited about this, and I've been thinking about a couple of tunes already since Chloe called. Not only that, but I've managed to rope in some of my musical friends to lend a hand as well."

To say I was buzzing about this news was an understatement. Raising money for a good cause was brilliant, of course, and was first and foremost the primary motivating factor. But the prospect of turning a book I'd worked on with my little friend Evie into a thing even more special than it already was, well, it was exhilarating. And the icing on the cake, for me at least, was the chance to work happily alongside a woman I both admired and deeply cared about. Even if she *had* blackmailed me into repainting her living room and criticised my wallpapering skills!

Noticing that Julia was shivering slightly, I slid closer, placing a warming arm around her. "Do you want to head back to the car and get the heating on?"

Julia rested her head on my shoulder. "Nah, I think I like it here fine, just as we are," she told me. "It's lovely sitting here with you, watching Evie running around like a loon."

Evie, who'd moved on from examining the landscape through the binoculars, was now tearing after a rubber ball she'd brought along, throwing it, and then sprinting after it. "Aww, she's like a dog with a lazy owner who can't be arsed to throw the thing for them," I observed, following her progress with my eyes.

"You have an unusual way with words, Mr Catchpole," Julia responded.

"That's why I'm a writer!" I insisted.

"And I'm guessing you're itching to run down the hill and play fetch with her?" Julia ventured.

"You know me so well. Coming?"

Julia removed her head from my shoulder so I could get up. "No. I reckon I'm still digesting those chips we've just eaten," she advised. "But if you want to go ahead and…"

Only I didn't need asking twice to throw a ball around, and I was already gone.

Chapter Twenty-Six

One of the many challenges of staging a seasonal Christmas production was that the window of opportunity to do so was around December or not at all. As such, we all wasted no time getting stuck in and setting the wheels in motion.

It'd been a week since Julia began working on the musical side of things. And I, with Evie's considerable input, had the bones of a working script for an hour-and-a-half-long show. You'd think that writing was writing. But hammering out a script was a different endeavour than producing a novel—like a watercolour artist turning their brush to oil painting, for example. It was similar, but not quite the same. However, it *was* enjoyable. Massively so. Of course, it also helped that the majority of the content already existed. It was just the small matter of adapting it so that the actors had clear instructions for what they should be doing at any given time during the performance.

On more than one occasion, in fact, I'd written a scene where a character arrived on stage but wasn't given any direction for what they were meant to be doing once they'd delivered their lines. As such, they'd just be standing idly twiddling their thumbs. But fortunately, this was where Chloe's expertise entered into the picture. As somebody involved in musical theatre all her life, she could instantly translate the words on a script and visualise the presentation in her mind's eye. It was an impressive skill that assisted me immensely during the creative process. And I didn't want to be responsible for anybody idly twiddling their thumbs—or any other bodily appendages—in front of a live audience.

A substantial benefit of running an established dance studio was the pool of acting talent and assortment of volunteers Chloe could mobilise on short notice. Indeed, she was like a military commander rounding up the troops before a skirmish. Before too long, Chloe had people working on plans for stage sets, costume designers pulling together ideas inspired by the book illustrations, and a large number of parents primed and ready for action as and when required.

It also looked like there would be no issue recruiting sufficient children from Chloe's impressive roster to cover the amount of shows we planned to schedule. With some of the kids being relatively young, like Evie, you obviously couldn't work the little critters into the ground, with regular rest periods required. As such, there was a need to have a generous pool of performers to dip into to accommodate this.

The abundance of young talent was fortunate. But as Chloe also pointed out, there were elements of the required cast where she couldn't draw solely on this resource. In the book, *Santa's Training School for Christmas Elves*, the story revolves around elves worldwide trying to secure a coveted spot working directly for the big man in red himself—the dream of any self-respecting elf. As such, those interested candidates sign up for Santa's training school, where the raw recruits show their worth. During a six-week intensive course, they're put through their paces with only the best of the best graduating to work at the North Pole. A bit like *Top Gun* for elves, for example.

Putting the wannabe Christmas elves through their paces was the training school's faculty—a small army of retired elves who'd served their time over decades of loyal and exemplary service. Their mission was to use all their experience to ensure only the elite would make the grade and graduate to become one of Santa's helpers. But as Chloe mentioned, she only had a handful of grown-up volunteer actors (like those who appeared in the *Wizard of Oz* recital) that she could call upon. To comfortably accommodate a dozen or so shows, we were ideally looking for at least twenty willing participants to put their names down to don plastic ears and perform as the older retired Christmas elf characters.

From the considerable list of outstanding action points, I was happy to assume responsibility for this last one. After all, I knew precisely where I could put my hands on a fair few fun-loving folks of a certain age who would find this prospect right up their alley. In fact, as I informed Chloe, I reckoned I could muster up an entire minibus full of willing volunteers!

And it turned out that the confidence in my recruitment abilities had been justified. Once word started to spread about an opportunity to appear in a Christmas musical, I was inundated with offers from the Lonely Heart Attack Club members. Indeed, some were so eager to strut their stuff on stage that baked goods, knitted items, and even financial incentives were offered to sweeten the pot and secure a coveted position on the cast list. However, they weren't entirely serious with these offers (I don't think...?), and I assured them that we would do our very best to accommodate anyone who was interested, with absolutely no need for bribes at all. Although, if they really, *really* wanted to provide me with baked goods, I wasn't going to sneeze at them.

❄ ❄ ❄

Walking through the town centre on my way to the first rehearsal session after depositing my car in the nearest car park, my attention was drawn by one of those discount pound shops that appear to spring up overnight. It wasn't the quality of the merchandise displayed in the window that drew my eye, but rather its adorable tackiness. "Oh, *yes*," I said, directing my nose closer to the glass. It was the last week in November, and the shop staff were busy preparing a festive window presentation to entice passersby to maybe come inside and spend a little bit of money. The shimmering gold tinsel framing the glass was complemented by snowman stencils along the bottom formed with fake snow. Foil decorations of all shapes and sizes dangled from the ceiling, while a young shop assistant was applying the final coloured baubles to a small artificial Christmas tree in the available space of the deep windowsill.

They weren't using high-end, quality decorations to advertise their goods, by any means, as it certainly wasn't the sort of window display that would look at home on Bond Street in London or Fifth Avenue in New York. But to me, it was absolutely perfect. In an instant, I was transported back to a time in my early childhood when the excitement building up to Christmas Day was nearly unbearable. A happy time in my life. A period when our family was still complete.

The young shop assistant looked up, likely wondering who the weirdo was who was gawping through the glass at her like she was an exhibit in a zoo. She briefly smiled before returning her attention to the tree, trying to manoeuvre one last bauble onto a slightly out-of-reach branch like she was threading a needle.

Ten minutes later and I emerged from the discount shop with two carrier bags stuffed full of tinsel, foil decorations, and four tins of fake snow. Yes, I could barely afford to buy my weekly food shopping right now, but I *needed* these decorations in my life, I'd decided. The tinsel even smelt the same as I remembered, and it still made the skin on my hands itch the moment I picked it up. For many, it was most likely cheap tat that I'd procured. But not for me. It was a priceless glimpse of my childhood.

I continued my journey along Strand Street, the central shopping district, and with festive music being piped through the overhead speakers, I suddenly noticed a peculiar tingling sensation in my fingers. At first I thought it was from whatever chemicals the tinsel had been coated in (or perhaps, more worrying, the onset of a mild stroke). But the sensation spread, feeling warm and cosy like a thick coat on a cold winter's day. It was many years since I'd experienced this particular type of phenomenon, so I didn't recognise it immediately. But eventually I did, successfully identifying it as "that Christmassy feeling." I quite liked it. And I was also relieved that I wouldn't need to phone an ambulance.

At 4 p.m., Jack and Emma's coffee shop, JAVA THE HUTT, was often relatively quiet whenever I popped in at this particular time. But not today. Nearly every table was filled, and a queue of eager faces waited patiently to be served. But as far as I could tell, Jack, working his magic on the coffee machine, didn't appear to mind one bit if his broad grin and ringing till were anything to go by.

"Heya, Jack!" I called over the counter between a row of heads. Jack turned slightly, offering me a friendly nod instead of waving, as his hands were currently engaged at the moment in filling his customer's various orders.

"Do you mind if I hang up a few Christmas decorations in the studio?" I asked him, holding up my two well-stuffed carrier bags. "I thought it'd help to get people in the festive mood?"

Jack nodded in agreement. "Go for it, mate," he said. "We've also got a couple of boxes full in the store cupboard," he added. "I'll dig them out when things quieten down."

"Cheers," I told him.

I climbed the staircase to the upper-floor studio, and before I'd even turned the corner, I could already hear the rehearsal in progress. I paused, just listening and enjoying. It was remarkable to hear the group of young people reading out words from a script I'd only finished writing a couple of days earlier. I then heard Julia's familiar voice calling out, "One… two… three…!" before the piano erupted into life, accompanied by the sound of a talented young person singing the opening musical number. This particular song, I knew, served to introduce the story's main character, Cornelius, an elf who passionately tries to convince his parents that he's old enough to attend Santa's coveted training school.

Given the limited organisational time, Julia had already managed to write and compose four songs—at least so far—to be performed during the musical. And if the other songs sounded even half as good as the one I was presently listening to, then I reckoned we were on to an absolute winner.

To avoid disturbing the proceedings, I waited until the present song's conclusion before walking through the door, at which point a wonderful vision greeted me. In front of the piano, roughly two dozen children sat cross-legged on the floor, looking up at Julia and Chloe standing over them with scripts in hand like they were reading a bedtime story. And then behind the kids, sitting on wooden benches, were three rows of additional actors with their backs currently to me, who I presumed must be the retired elves. From what I could see, they looked resplendent in their little green hats complemented by a cherry red headband, even though it wasn't an official dress rehearsal as far as I knew. Perhaps it was any excuse to get costumes on.

I crept towards the nearest available seat, taking care not to interrupt Julia, who offered me a quick wave. Looking around, it was definitely a 'pinch me' moment. Not for one instant would I ever think a miserable, introverted bugger like me would be thrilled to be surrounded by a musical theatre group, including three rows of senior citizens dressed as retired Christmas elves. I glanced down at my ten-pence plastic carrier bags, both of them bursting at the seams from being stuffed with garish decorations. And I couldn't wait to start getting the room looking all festive ahead of the first actual performance a week or so away. How times had changed, I reflected with an ironic smile.

"How do I look, son?" the elf beside me whispered, once Julia was done speaking.

Due to the hat and the oversized plastic ears, I hadn't immediately recognised him as George, the friendly, raspy-voiced chap from the minibus who'd originally suggested that I should write the Christmas musical in the first place.

"Oh. Hi there, George," I said, admiring the red makeup circles painted on his cheeks. "George, I think you look brilliant, actually. Absolutely, bloody brilliant!"

Chapter Twenty-Seven

Waiting to hear anything from your agent is, in my experience, a bit like waiting to hear back after you've had a difficult job interview—torturous! You don't want to do it but you find yourself checking your email every ten minutes, hoping for an update. It may have been wasted time, but I couldn't help myself.

Granted, I had only emailed the new novel to her a few days ago. But given my clearly articulated desperation in the covering note, I dared to dream that I might hear some early, encouraging feedback. With the hope that I could then share that information with my bank manager, who also has a vested interest in my success.

In my gut, I suspected that a quick response was doubtful. Especially as we'd now entered the start of December when I imagined Milly would likely have her hands full in the busy lead-up to Christmas. "Does she not know how critical this is to me?" I asked Barry the cat, as I refreshed my email page for the umpteenth time for no good reason.

Ordinarily, at this stage, I tended to drift into a slump if I didn't have something meaningful to do, such as jumping headfirst into my next book. I don't know why it happened, but if I had too much idle time on my hands, I usually went into a bit of a self-destruct mode. I'd find myself chronically unmotivated to the point where even getting into the shower became a chore. Worse still was when I'd enter 'imposter syndrome' mode, in which I questioned everything I'd ever written and convinced myself I was a joke who'd be found out at any moment as a fraud. I didn't like this side of myself. And I suppose it was the crippling fear of floundering about in these choppy seas that made me want to seek out validation of my work even more. Hence, the irrational need to receive this type of immediate response from my agent.

However, while I may not have had anything productive to do in the specific form of starting my next book just yet, fortunately, I *did* have on a figurative life vest to save me from drowning. And that was because working with the TAPPIN' FEET crew on our upcoming musical was, without a doubt, one of the most rewarding experiences of my life. It was exhilarating. Even though I wasn't a featured performer in this current endeavour, I'd still not missed a single rehearsal. As a result, I think I knew every actor's line word for word, and I was confident I could step in as an understudy for anybody in the extensive cast at a moment's notice if that should prove necessary. Indeed, I made a passing comment about somehow incapacitating one of the retired elf actors (same as I did with poor Steve, Chloe's brother) in order to have a shot at those plastic ears. But I was only joking, of course. Or at least, I think I was…?

When I wasn't at the various rehearsals, I spent my evenings wondering what we could perhaps do to enhance the show, particularly in the case of the script I had written. In fact, I wouldn't have blamed Chloe and Julia one bit if they'd considered blocking my phone number, owing to the number of "Just one more thing!" calls they received from me. But I knew they were equally invested in the project, and suspected they didn't mind—or at least tolerated—me poking my oversized beak into things.

I was also surprised that Jack hadn't given me a right bollocking about the sheer volume of Christmas decorations that had turned his studio space into something like a Santa's grotto from a 1970's department store. Yes, I had paid several more visits to the pound store—to the extent that they now knew me by name there.

And it wasn't only Jack's studio that'd benefited from the cheap festive inventory from the pound store, as my neighbour Carol had not failed to notice…

"Hey, Carol," I greeted her, after answering the knocking at my front door.

She thrust a bunch of flowers in my direction, which I accepted, but didn't quite know what to do with. After that, she didn't say anything just yet, looking me up and down instead like there was something wrong with me. Or like she wasn't sure it was actually me in there, underneath the outside of my skin.

"What?" I asked. "I've just never had a woman give me flowers before," I explained.

"The flowers are to wish you all good luck for the first performance this afternoon," Carol advised. "But it's not that. Are you feeling okay…?"

I wasn't sure what she was on about. Granted, I'd not slept too much, as I was full of nerves. But I didn't think I looked *that* bad. "I think so, Carol, yeah. Why do you ask?" I said.

Carol stepped back onto my garden path, directing an extended finger towards my living room window. "That!" she said.

I stepped outside, even though I was still wearing my slippers. "Ah, that," I said, catching up with what she was talking about. "Do you like my fairy lights?"

She nodded. "I do, Adam, yes. It's perhaps a bit early in the day to turn them on…?" she replied. "But, yes, you've made an effort," she observed, stepping closer to the glass to look inside and admire the decorations I had hanging from every single wall and across the ceiling. "Is that my Christmas card hanging above your fireplace?" she asked.

It was. I'd fixed a piece of string on the wall like my mum used to do when we were kids. Sadly, I only tend to receive maybe two or three Christmas cards these days. So the generous length of the string might have been a touch optimistic.

"It is indeed, Carol. And you'll be pleased to know that my card to you was posted yesterday."

"Posted? Your front door is only about eight metres from mine."

"I know. But I thought you'd like to receive it through the post rather than me dropping it through your letterbox. I've posted one to all the neighbours as well."

Carol held a hand to her forehead as if trying to prevent herself from passing out. "Let me get this right. You've hung up Christmas decorations, helped organise a Christmas musical, and now you're posting Christmas cards as well? Adam, for a man that *doesn't do Christmas*, according to you, you're certainly sending the universe mixed-up signals!"

I shrugged, fully aware I was on the receiving end of a gentle ribbing.

"Well, it's mostly your fault, Carol," I insisted. "After all, you're the one who brainwashed me with those schmaltzy Christmas movies and had me thinking about all that 'sentiment' business."

Carol rubbed her hands together. "My work here is done, then?"

"And in case I never said it, thank you," I told her.

"Oh? For what?" Carol asked, clearly fishing for compliments.

"For that— that 'sentiment' stuff, Carol. At the time, I thought you were mad as a box of frogs. But now, I kinda get what you're talking about," I said. "Oh, and get yourself to that pound shop in town," I advised. "They've got some great stuff in."

"I'm just pleased you're pleased, Adam," Carol said. "And I've got my ticket for the show, so I'll be there this afternoon to cheer you all on."

"Thank you, Carol," I said again. And I meant it. Probably more than I'd ever meant those words. "You might have, by some sort of miracle, made me a better iteration of myself."

"*Pfft*," she said, waving away my words. "Now, you make sure to get those flowers in a nice vase."

"Uhm… I'm not sure, but I don't think I actually own a vase?"

"I'll go and get you one," Carol answered, rolling her eyes. "It can keep all of my stolen lasagne dishes company," she joked, as she turned to leave.

"Break a leg!" I blurted out, calling after her.

Carol halted on her journey down my garden path and turned briefly as my words caught up with her. "Pardon me…?"

"When you wished us good luck earlier. I think you're supposed to say, *break a leg!*" I clarified.

"Oh. Well, in that case, Adam Catchpole, I sincerely hope that you all break a leg."

✱ ✱ ✱

I turned up earlier than required at Java the Hutt ahead of the inaugural performance of *Santa's Training School for Christmas Elves – The Musical*. Despite that, I wasn't surprised that ninety percent of the cast were already in attendance as well, either milling about in the café or getting some last-minute practice in upstairs before the curtain went up.

As well as volunteering to become the affair's official voiceover artist/narrator to provide the introduction to the show, I was also the person with the all-important job of running the refreshments station during the remaining portion of the performance (plus directly beforehand also). Some might say it was the most critical job of all. As such, I needed to set everything up before the paying customers arrived, ensuring for instance that the ice cream fridge was adequately stocked. Additionally—and surprising myself in the process—it turned out I was also a dab hand at preparing hair and makeup before the show, as a number of the Christmas elves would confirm. Fortunately, however, if more skill was preferred, plenty of other volunteers with much more expertise than myself were available upon simple request. And no offence was taken on my part.

Having such a large cast of actors, both young and old, was a wonderful thing. And having everyone willing to jump in on short notice was a godsend, raising the quality of the performance beyond our wildest dreams. Indeed, hearing the combination of vocals, all singing at full volume within the relatively intimate setting, produced a rather splendiferous racket, as I well knew from our rehearsals. Although the only downside to having such a large group was that, in adherence to fire regulations, there was a maximum limit on the number of people permitted in the venue at any one time. In practical terms, this meant that with a floating cast of twenty-seven people, the number of tickets we could then sell was seriously curtailed. I was disappointed, when I'd become aware of this, that this resulted in a reduction in the amount of money we could raise. But, as Chloe was happy to point out to me, "We'll *still* be raising money." And she was of course correct. I'd just need to ensure I got double-busy on the refreshments station to make up for the difference!

At half past one as we neared this early, weekend performance, Jack appeared in the studio doorway looking frantic. "The coffee shop is full, and there's a queue forming outside on the pavement waiting to get in," he revealed, once I walked over. "Should I start letting folks come upstairs?"

I glanced about the studio to the rows of empty seats we'd set up in front of our stage. Because of the time, and because of the update Jack had just given, Julia and Chloe were now desperately trying to corral some of the younger members of the cast—and a few wayward older elves as well—herding them along to make their way behind the stage curtain where the painted set awaited them, ready for its moment in the sun, so to speak.

"Ladies," I said when Chloe and Julia each passed with a child in tow. "Are you ready to greet your public?"

Chloe looked over her shoulder, checking behind her. "I think that's all of them? If there aren't any more hiding underneath the seats, then I believe we're good," she said, before disappearing behind the stage curtain.

"Break a leg," I offered, before turning back around to face Jack again. "I think we're good to go!"

After greeting everyone, dispensing as many refreshments as I could possibly manage to sell before the beginning of the show, and then making sure everybody was comfortably seated, I finally made my way behind the curtain myself. I peered a nervous eye through the slightest of gaps, watching as a few stragglers eventually took their seats. Even though it was only my voice appearing this time, my stomach was churning like a washing machine on a spin cycle. Behind me were the cast members required for the first scene—an upbeat opening where several elves were wrapping presents in a Christmas workshop, all doing their best to outdo each other and impress their boss. What was surreal to me was that the cast was perfectly still at the moment, frozen like statues and barely blinking as they waited for the curtain to part. It was as if somebody had hit the pause button on the remote control. These kids were tearing around the studio one minute and the next, consummate professionals.

Just before two o'clock, I offered a final glance down to Julia, sitting at the piano next to two of her fellow musicians—Libby with the violin and Trudy prepared with her guitar. All three appeared primed and ready for action. All I had to do now was begin the proceedings and start the show from behind the closed curtain.

I turned on my microphone, used my tongue to moisten my top lip, and then began speaking, using my deepest and most dramatic narrating voice...

"Building children's toys in the workshop of a greedy factory owner, far from here," I began, reciting from my script, "Cornelius the elf dreamed about what could be. No elf from his tiny town had ever been selected to attend Santa's Training School for Christmas Elves. Cornelius desperately wanted to be the first. This, then, is his story..."

Chapter Twenty-Eight

I had chronically underestimated how much sweets, ice cream, and popcorn the good folk of the Isle of Man could consume. Initially, when reviewing our stock cupboard and fridge in the upstairs studio at JAVA THE HUTT, I was worried I'd ordered far too much. However, our supply was utterly demolished by the time of our second show. And it wasn't just the refreshments table that'd been decimated. The additional books I asked Mark at WORDS AND SPACES to print off had also been snapped up by those attending the musical, in addition to some online sales as well.

Of course, this was a lovely problem on both counts because if the stock flew out, the much-needed cash would flow in the opposite direction just as quickly.

With our cupboard bare, I was duly dispatched to procure more refreshments from the wholesalers and additional books from the printers. Although once again, I'd likely be testing the boundaries of just how much the boot size and rear suspension of an ageing Nissan Micra could accommodate. I decided to start with the grocery supplies...

"Right. Now where to begin?" I said, guiding a shopping trolley with one hand and reading from my grocery list in the other. This place was enormous. From outside, it appeared as if it were just an unassuming warehouse in the middle of an unassuming industrial estate in Douglas. But once inside, this place was heaven for anybody who liked to consume food or drink beverages. A maze of shelving units stretched out, packed high with merchandise filling every available inch.

However, what was magical was the fact that everything on the shelves came in such large quantities. You didn't just buy a single *packet* of Haribo gummi sweets, for instance. Instead, you purchased a discounted box of *forty-eight* packets of Haribo gummies. As such, it was the place where the shops came to shop.

Wandering through the confectionary aisle, I could only imagine how much Evie would love it here. The hardest thing was making sure I didn't get carried away myself and fill my trolley up with more than I came for, such as the massive box of Galaxy chocolate bars I knew would feel right at home in my kitchen pantry.

"Steady yourself, lad," I quietly admonished myself, shifting my focus to the task at hand like the disciplined refreshments stallholder I was. But progress was delayed at the moment because of several people in front of me who also seemed tempted by the cornucopia of items they didn't really need, but nevertheless wanted. However, I was in no rush just now and happy to let my mind drift away to thoughts of what it might be like to win a 2-minute trolley dash competition around this place.

I slowly shuffled along, subconsciously tuning my ears into the radio playing on the overhead speakers. Until, that is, my attention was diverted by the sound of somebody humming an oddly familiar tune. I looked up from my shopping list, cocking my head as I tried to discern the humming's origin. At first, I thought it was the woman further up the aisle who I could see stocking up on packages of toilet rolls. But then I heard the humming again. I turned as I triangulated its source. There, a shop assistant was busily unloading a pallet of washing-up powder, taking care to ensure the assorted boxes were packed on the shelves in a uniform manner.

I remained where I was with my left ear directed towards him, trying to figure out where I'd heard that melody before and why it sounded so darned familiar. I thought it must be the theme tune to some cartoon I'd enjoyed as a kid, or maybe the jingle to a breakfast cereal commercial. But I couldn't quite put my finger on it. It was maddening.

And then it hit me. *That's our song*, I realised. I quickly reached for my mobile phone, covertly pressing the video record button. I was beaming from ear to ear, because what the shop assistant was humming was none other than a catchy number from our musical, one where Cornelius the elf struggles to build a child's tricycle under the scrutiny of the recruiters from Santa's training school.

As soon as I had heard the tune for the first time during rehearsals, I knew we had a winner with that one.

"Julia is going to love this," I muttered, stepping closer to better pick up the audio content. Oh, it's fair to say I was in my element by this provided distraction. I could even picture little Eric in my mind's eye, the talented child actor who played Cornelius, where Cornelius is trying to build that blasted bike with the pressure of securing a place at training school at stake. I think I may have even started humming along myself, caught up in the melody and consumed by overwhelming pride in the wonderful song Julia had created and admiration for our amazingly capable cast.

"Oi! What the hell are you doing?" an annoyed voice growled, tearing me away from my daydream.

It was the humming shelf stacker in front of me, only he wasn't humming any longer. Instead, he was looking over his shoulder, a large box of Daz detergent held frozen in mid-air.

"Pardon?" I asked, while becoming aware that my phone was now mere inches away from the irate fellow's nose as he turned to face me completely. I relaxed my arm, letting my hand gently drift down to my thigh, in hopes that it wouldn't be obvious what I had just been doing. But it was too late.

"Are you *videoing* me?" the man asked, guessing correctly.

I thought about denying it. But he'd seen me doing it. And I was the only one present who'd crept up behind him with their phone held out, directly invading his personal space around and about his neck and shoulder area. So there wasn't much I could say in my defence except to offer the truth.

"Yeah. Yeah, I am. Or, I was," I admitted. "You see, my girlfriend Julia wrote that tune you were humming," I explained. "And I just wanted to record you because I knew how thrilled it would make her. It's about Cornelius. Cornelius the elf. Remember...?"

The shop assistant smiled serenely, and I thought at first that everything was okay. But then he retrieved his walkie-talkie from his utility belt and positioned it in front of his lips, depressing the talk button. "Derek to base. Over," said Derek. "Can we have security to the washing-up powder aisle? Over."

The walkie-talkie crackled into life as an answer shortly came through. "Berthold's currently on a fag break," came the response. "Over."

Derek groaned, shaking his head before once again depressing the talk button. "Well, go and get him, Karen! We have a potential situation in the washing-up aisle!" he said. "Over."

❋ ❋ ❋

Fortunately, by the time Berthold finished replenishing his nicotine levels and attempted to leap into action, there wasn't any action to really leap into, as I had been able to successfully convince Derek that I wasn't some kind of nutter who went around videoing strangers for perverse kicks.

And as Derek explained—once we'd got to chatting—he had indeed been humming one of the tunes from our musical. Although he hadn't the pleasure of attending himself, his wife and young daughter saw it the previous evening and had thoroughly enjoyed themselves. So much so, in fact, that his daughter hadn't stopped singing the songs (the lyrics of which were helpfully printed out in the programmes we provided at the shows). Additionally, Derek conveyed his regret that he'd been unable to acquire more tickets for his daughter, who wished to attend again, only this time with her friends.

"Are you telling me it's sold out?" I asked him, completely flabbergasted. I knew that ticket sales had been going well, but I'd no idea all upcoming performances were sold out. As a courtesy for not having punched me in the face or calling the police, I promised Derek I would contact him if any tickets should become available.

Once I'd finished off my checklist and emptied the contents of my shopping trolley into my car, it became apparent there wasn't much room left for the books I still needed to collect. As such, I decided to swing back to the coffee shop to unload first. But before I headed off, I couldn't help trying to make Julia's day:

> Adam: Hey xx, I've just picked up supplies for the refreshments stand. You won't believe what tune one of the shop assistants was humming.

I attached the video I'd surreptitiously captured (which Derek, once I'd been found out, had fortunately never asked me to delete), and pressed the send button. As Julia was at school, I didn't expect an immediate response. However...

> Julia: Wow, I don't think I've ever seen that much Daz detergent in one place before. Anyway, what tune is it? I can't tell Xx

> Adam: Don't you have the volume on? Turn it up :-)

> Julia: Can't right now. Oh, super exciting news from Chloe, by the way. Was going to tell you later. But as you're here on the phone

> Adam: I'm all ears x

> Julia: She had somebody contact her from the Gaiety Theatre. They asked if we'd be interested in putting the show on over there next Christmas!!! Oh, must go just now. Talk later x

This was big news indeed. Whilst we were all eternally grateful for the use of Jack and Emma's upstairs studio and couldn't have done it without them, there were only so many people we could squeeze in up there. The Gaiety Theatre, on the other hand, was a different league altogether. As one of the finest venues in the UK and beyond, appearing at the Gaiety held a certain prestige. With over eight hundred seats, a successful run would also do wonders for TAPPIN' FEET'S coffers, I couldn't help thinking—including the potential for more of me and Evie's books being sold.

After tonight's show concluded, there were only four more performances remaining. I was beginning to feel I was in the middle of the most fantastic holiday I'd ever had, but part of me couldn't stop thinking that I would soon be packing my bag before returning home to reality. So this news about the Gaiety certainly perked me up. The prospect that we could be back, doing it all again, next Christmas in front of a packed-out theatre was mind-blowing.

I started the car, hearing my first Christmas song on the radio. Ordinarily, I'd grumble and immediately switch the station. However, I sat in the car with the engine idling this time, singing along to Chris Rea's seasonal favourite about him passing the time away while driving home for Christmas. And I couldn't help but enjoy an ironic laugh because this was Adam Catchpole here, the disliker of anything Christmas-related. Yet here I was now singing along to a yuletide classic as I considered how best to celebrate this cracking news about the Christmas-themed musical I helped create.

"Bloody bonkers," I said aloud, feeling a touch emotional at that moment. It wasn't lost on me that if I hadn't left my house on that one fateful day to go and buy replacement lasagne dishes, none of this would have ever come to pass. I wouldn't have smashed a stage set by falling into it, I'd likely have never heard about Chloe and her dance group, I wouldn't have met Julia or her daughter Evie, and I'd most probably still be alone in my study, sulking in my underpants and wondering why the whole world had it in for me.

Granted, I was still persistently short on cash and potentially facing eviction at present. However, strangely enough, because I had other positive things going on in my life to carry me through, I now felt more equipped to help mentally deal with the negatives.

"Jayzus, Adam," I said to myself, pushing in the clutch. "You're not just turning into that cheesy Christmas movie script. You're also starring in the sequel!"

✷ ✷ ✷

After a brief pitstop to feed Barry the cat and give him a cuddle lest he feel neglected, I headed over to the coffee shop. The next performance didn't start for another three hours or thereabouts, so I reckoned I still had loads of time to restock the refreshments stall before I popped out to secure an additional supply of books as I'd planned. There was also something quite enjoyable about being in the middle of a coffee shop's general hustle and bustle. Plus, Emma made an absolutely fabulous quiche, which I thought would save me from having to possibly cook something for my tea.

Soon enough, following several trips back and forth from my car, the refreshments station was amply provisioned once again. I worked up something of an appetite, and so I sat in the coffee shop waiting for my serving of quiche I'd ordered, along with a side of chocolate fudge cake for dessert.

"There you go," Jack said, placing a tray on my table. "Mind if I join you before the Christmas musical rush begins later on?"

"Of course, please do," I said, reaching for my generous portion of quiche Lorraine, which was so full of lovely Gruyère cheese and smoky bacon goodness. "You don't mind if I get stuck in?" I asked, before doing precisely that.

I'd only managed to stuff a couple of forkfuls into my gob when the rhythmic rumble of thunder disturbed my tranquillity. However, as it was a cloudless, crisp winter's day, I knew there must be some other plausible explanation. And looking up from my food, I saw that there was.

"Ehm, Jack...?" I said, amused to observe my companion and boss with his head in his hands and his eyes shut tight, snoring. "Jack, are you with us...?"

Jack was jarred into a semi-conscious state by the sound of my voice. "I'll be right there, Emma," he said, looking confused, like he didn't know where he was. "Wait, was I asleep or something?" he said, gathering his wits.

"Hmm, I think so, Jack."

In response, he took a generous slurp of the coffee he'd brought along with him to the table. "Wow, I guess the last few days have caught up to me," he said with a yawn. "Working from seven in the morning until eleven at night sure does take it out of you," he remarked, taking another gulp of his coffee.

I felt a wave of guilt wash over me. After all, I was the one who'd asked if we could host the Christmas musical here, never giving too much thought in advance to the additional hours Emma and Jack needed to invest by keeping the place open.

"Ah, I'm sorry, Jack. I imagine you'll be glad to see the back of the musical and get your life the way it was again?"

Jack removed his head from his hands, narrowing his eyes like I'd said something ridiculous. "What? I've had an absolute *ball* this week," he insisted, while stifling another yawn, which might have seemed a little contradictory.

"You have?" I asked, cutting off another hunk of quiche with my fork. "It's not been too much work?"

"It has, a bit, yeah. Still, when I first opened this place with my ex-girlfriend, back before Emma, the place was like a ghost town," Jack explained. "To the extent that when she buggered off and left me, I was only a couple of weeks away from having to close the place down. So to see the place *now*, packed with people enjoying themselves, is pretty darned terrific as far as I'm concerned."

I was relieved, because the last thing I wanted to do was to have taken advantage of Jack's good nature.

"And it's because of that fact that I actually wanted to talk with you," Jack added. "Extension!" he then blurted out.

I had no idea as to what this sudden verbal spasm could possibly indicate. I wondered if Jack had somehow developed a case of Tourette's. Alternatively, I wondered if Jack had perhaps dozed off again and was somehow talking in his sleep just now with his eyes held open. "Extension…?" I asked.

Jack nodded. "Yes, an extension," he responded. "The musical is meant to conclude soon, right?"

"That's correct."

"Well that's the thing, Adam. Every remaining performance is already sold out, and I don't know about you, but I must have been asked for tickets twenty or maybe thirty times today alone," Jack advised. "Soooo, I wondered if you all wanted to extend the show for a bit longer…?"

This offer took me entirely by surprise. My first reaction was to respond with an immediate, resounding yes. However, it wasn't really for me to decide. Rather, it was for Chloe, Julia, Evie, and all the others to ultimately choose.

"Wow, Jack, I can definitely ask everyone, but are you sure?" I answered. "I mean, you already look like you're running yourself ragged."

"Sure I'm sure. In business, you need to make hay while the sun shines, as they say. And with more people streaming in while your shows are performed, or stopping by to look for tickets for those shows, well, the increase in foot traffic through my front door only translates to more customers for my till," Jack replied. "So, yessir. The offer's there. And you're all most welcome."

I sure didn't need further convincing, because I thought it was a bloody marvellous idea. It all hinged on whether Chloe and Julia felt the same. "Let me have a word with the others, Jack. And I'll let you know later?"

Jack finished his coffee, and then stood up to attend to a waiting customer who'd appeared at the counter, with Jack seeming happy to stave off sleep for a good while longer by keeping himself busy. "Sounds good," he said. "And I imagine there will be a lot of happy campers if you do extend the run."

"I know Derek will be overjoyed, for starters," I said, referring to the humming shop assistant fellow I'd captured on video. Not that Jack would've had any clue who that was, of course.

"Leave it with me, and I'll get back to you as soon as possible," I added. "And pass on my gratitude and my thanks to Emma, Jack… Jack…?"

But Jack seemed to have dozed off again as he stood there, looking now like one of those animals able to sleep while they were standing up.

"Jack! Jack, are you asleep again…?"

Chapter Twenty-Nine

As we approached the moment we'd all been dreading—the final scheduled performance of *Santa's Training School for Christmas Elves – The Musical*—Chloe and Julia sat the gang down for a serious chat before things were to kick off, prior to the audience getting there yet. I watched on from the wings, scanning their little faces as they sat wide-eyed, wondering what was happening. It was the same for the senior group of elves, standing in a semi-circle behind the children with expressions of uncertainty hidden somewhere beneath their heavily applied stage makeup.

Chloe clapped her hands smartly together to preface her first remark. "You are all superstars!" she announced, a declaration that raised an immediate cheer from everyone gathered together in the upper-floor studio. "However, sadly, all good things must come to an end…" she added, this time with a bit of a sigh.

"*Booooo!*" came the collective response, followed by a moment of silence as the reality of Chloe's words sunk in. The journey was coming to a close. It was apparent just from the glum looks that the assembled actors felt the same sense of melancholy I'd experienced earlier in the week at the prospect of the musical drawing to its conclusion. We were like one big madcap family, practically living in each other's pockets for several hours daily. Along with the excitement at what we were doing, it was impossible as well not to get swept up by the shared sense of camaraderie.

For some, the experience could have been claustrophobic, with all of us sailing on the same small ship, so to speak. But for somebody who lived alone, this daily interaction was an absolute pleasure, and I adored every moment of it. And it was a sentiment the kids and the senior elves shared as well, if the somewhat despondent mood in the room was any barometer.

Chloe waited for the murmurings of discontent to settle down, offering a sympathetic smile to those who needed it.

"However," Chloe said, briefly flicking her eyes to Julia, standing beside her in a way that could only be described as conspiratorial. "What if... we extended the show *for another seven days...?*" she proposed, emphasising the last few words of her question for maximum impact. She allowed her query to float around the studio. But oddly, no one was answering her just yet. "Would you all like that...?" she asked, after she was only met with a haze of confused faces.

"Mummy?" Evie offered, with her hand raised in the front row. "Mummy, have you and Auntie Chloe been drinking wine in the afternoon again?" she asked—an enquiry which raised an immediate guffaw or two.

Chloe laughed off the suggestion, along with an embarrassed, slight reddening of her cheeks in response. "Not yet, Evie. Not yet. But soon..." she said. She then went on to reveal the details of Jack's suggestion and generous offer—to extend use of the studio for the purpose of an additional week's worth of performances if the cast were amenable to it.

For some in the group, this might have been a busy or perhaps hectic time of year in the run-up to Christmas. So Chloe made it clear that there was absolutely no pressure on anybody to commit more of their time if they didn't wish to. But if they were agreeable—and with their parents' kind permission, of course, where applicable—to putting on a handful more performances, then that's precisely what could happen. The show would go on.

There was an audible, incredulous gasp as the assortment of cast members looked at each other, with the younger of the group in particular squirming about like a swarm of ants had crept into their pants. "You're being serious?" Evie was first to ask, followed by a round of excited chatter from her mates.

Chloe smiled, giving the impression she wanted to squirm with excitement as well but was only just managing to restrain herself. "We're very serious," she insisted. "And that's not all..." she added, along with a strategic pause for dramatic effect. "You know how there's a Christmas show at the Gaiety Theatre each season? Well, guess which *super-talented* dance group has been asked if they should like to perform Santa's Training School for Christmas Elves next year!"

"Uhm... us...?" Evie, the group's unofficial spokesperson, put forward, not sounding entirely confident on the matter.

"Yes," Julia entered in. "Us!"

It took a moment or two before those in the group erupted with a burst of whooping and hollering at the prospect of both continuing this festive adventure for another week or so *and* performing at the Gaiety Theatre the following year. I don't mind admitting I was front and centre of the celebrations.

Much later that night, lying in bed wide awake and staring at the ceiling, I was still pumped with excitement as a result of just how thrilled everybody else had been. It must have been about two in the morning when I started reflecting on how much I'd missed out on by remaining holed up in my study for months at a time, barely seeing anybody or making contact with other living human beings. If I had still been like that, I'd have missed out on evenings like tonight.

During that earlier, more insular period of my life, I justified my solitary existence as a means to get a significant number of words typed up on whatever novel I might be working on at the time. But looking back, that wasn't the case, because often I stared aimlessly at a blank Microsoft Word page a lot of the time, reflecting on how rubbish my life had become. But now, since I'd stepped out of my comfort zone and got involved with extracurricular activities, not only did my writing levels *not* decrease, but I felt the overall quality of the content produced was of a superior standard to my previous writing. A point I was eager to further prove to myself when I commenced work on my next novel in the coming year.

Listening to the wind buffeting my bedroom window just now, I further reflected on how, not too terribly long ago, I was contemplating what would happen to me if I should jump off of a cliff (although I suspected I knew the outcome). Even the very thought of it made me shudder now. And I wasn't just thinking about the unpleasantness of bouncing off the rocks and plunging into the sea from a great height. Rather, it was because I was presently very happy with my lot for the first time in a long time. I had my family, of course, but I now had good friends around me as well, and I was excited about where the next stage of our adventure would take us. If I'd have hurled myself off a clifftop, I would have missed out on all of this. That awful idea made me grateful that my previous intrusive thoughts had remained merely thoughts.

Of course, there were still elements of my life over which I had minimal control. And I accepted that with an upbeat attitude rather than falling down a mineshaft of despair about it. I knew I'd struggle to get the public to buy more of my existing collection of books, for instance, without a sizeable advertising budget to work with. So, without that, I had shifted creative direction and started working in a new genre that would hopefully soon bear fruit.

One circumstance I couldn't influence so much, and the thing continuing to cause me the most anxiety, was the ongoing mortgage debacle. It was ever-present in my thoughts, always lingering there in the back of my mind. This was why I had reached out to Bethany at the bank and arranged a meeting in the morning to discuss the deteriorating situation. It was remarkable how attentive the bank was when you owed them money. Try to get somebody to return your call if you simply have a missing bank statement or want to amend a standing order, on the other hand, and it was a different matter altogether. You could be waiting weeks for a call back. I wasn't assigning blame for my current state of affairs, however. It was all my fault. Whether they ought to have lent so much money to a bloke with a varying, unpredictable income stream and minimal business acumen was a discussion for another day.

For months, I'd been worried about scraping enough money together to maintain a lifestyle I thought I wanted, dreading the arrival of my postman for fear of what correspondence he might deliver. Again, I couldn't assign blame there, as it wasn't his fault. And in fact I'd recently made every effort to help Paddy feel more welcome, making sure not to pull a face if he handed me something I didn't want such as another notice of arrears.

When I'd requested the appointment earlier in the previous day with Bethany, I had no idea what I wanted to accomplish with it other than to ask for a continuing stay of execution, as it were. But then, lying in bed wide awake at this current ungodly hour just now, it suddenly hit me in the face like a wet, slippery fish. Maybe a mackerel? Perhaps a salmon. I wasn't sure which.

Regardless, I realised what I wanted to achieve from my upcoming meeting with the bank. I finally figured it out. I knew what I needed to do.

❊ ❊ ❊

Descending the set of outdoor steps after exiting my bank, I had to resist the overwhelming urge to start dancing lest I fall arse over tit on the polished marble. When my shoes eventually made safe contact with the pavement at the bottom of the steps, I took a deep breath, feeling like the shackles had been removed. I could have quite happily kissed Bethany, but I suspected I may not have been welcomed back if I had given in to the temptation of doing so. Instead, I considered sending her flowers to show my appreciation and perhaps a complimentary feedback letter to her manager.

I looked up to the heavens, wondering if I'd need to utilise my brolly. As my Scottish friends would say, it was a grey, "dreich" day. But that didn't dampen my spirits in any way. Instead, I strutted through the main shopping street with assured confidence, much like John Travolta in the opening credits to *Saturday Night Fever*. I felt marvellous. The prospect of a lunch date with the lovely Julia further raised my mood. And after that, I had an enjoyable shift to look forward to, as I was driving a crowd from the Lonely Heart Attack Club to what I was informed was a goat yoga class.

I still wasn't sure if goat yoga was a genuine thing, or how one might possibly go about convincing a goat to perform yoga, or if it was actually even of any benefit to the poor creatures in some way. I suspected I was in for a bit of gentle teasing when I met up with the gang, all for being so gullible again as to fall for what they were telling me. But I didn't mind one single little bit, because life right now was good.

Julia was already sitting at a table by the window when I arrived before JAVA THE HUTT. I waved, catching her eye and blowing her an outsized kiss through the glass when she glanced up from her menu. Although the friendly-looking bloke offering me a fingertip wave from the adjacent table might suggest my gesture of affection may have wafted in the direction of the wrong person.

Once inside the coffee shop, the warm air of the café's heating soothed and caressed the chill from any exposed skin. "Heya," I said, leaning over to give Julia's cheek a large kiss after removing my coat, hoping this would serve to clear up any possible confusion with the welcoming, demonstrative chap at the nearby table. "I've not kept you, have I?"

"Not at all, but I've only got about twenty-five minutes before I need to return to the school," Julia advised.

"I can recommend the quiche," I said, tipping my head towards the serving counter.

"Perfect. Oh, and a Diet Coke would be tremendous."

"Coming right up, m'lady," I said before heading to the counter to place our order.

Jack, who was cheerful as ever, greeted me with a smart salute. "Let me guess. Quiche Lorraine again?"

"Times two, buddy. Plus Diet Coke," I said.

"Diet Cokes for you both?" Jack asked, pen poised, wanting to make sure he got it right.

"Yep. Trying to watch my figure," I said with a smile, patting the fine layer of whale blubber insulation on my belly.

"Gotcha," said Jack, jotting the order down on his notepad. "Go and sit yourself down, Adam. I'll have it brought over."

"Very kind. Much obliged."

"Well, you'll need to keep all of your strength for the goat yoga class, if you choose to participate," he joked with a friendly wink.

"Cheers," I said, even though I had no idea what he meant, still having no clue how anyone was supposed to coax a group of goats into performing yoga, though I suspected it wouldn't be easy.

Sitting down opposite Julia, I carried on about the whole goat yoga thing, asking if she knew what it was and if she could explain it to me at all. However, Julia gave me the most peculiar look.

"Adam!" she said, interrupting my babbling.

"Yeah?" I replied.

"You don't force goats into various yoga positions!"

"You don't? Then why do they call it—" I began to ask.

"The goats just stand on your *back*, and things like that," Julia advised, as if this should have been completely obvious to me. But before I could ask for clarification, she spoke again. "But anyway, never mind that. How'd you get on at the bank…?" she asked.

"Oh, the bank?" I said. "Yeah, good."

Julia stared at me. "Good? That's it?"

I laughed apologetically. "Sorry, I'm still imagining goat hooves digging into someone's back, and wondering why they'd want to do that. The people, I mean. Or the goats as well, now I'm thinking about it. It's really very—"

Julia clicked her fingers like a hypnotist bringing somebody out from a trance. "Adam! Concentrate!" she said. "So if your meeting with the bank was *good*, as you describe it, does that mean they're not going to kick you out onto the street?"

I briefly considered how I was going to put what I was thinking into words, fidgeting with the bottle of salt on the table for several moments. "Okay," I began, wondering if what I was about to say made any sense other than in my head. "Okay, do you know how I was driving around in an expensive Porsche that I couldn't afford to make the monthly payments on, insure, or for that matter fill with petrol?"

"I do. But?"

"And…" I continued, moving my hand to attend to the pepper shaker now. "And the moment I returned the Porsche, trading it in for my little beige Nissan Micra, I felt an immediate sense of relief."

"Relief because it was beige?" Julia asked, not really following along with my train of thought. But then she suddenly appeared horrified. "Wait, hang on. Are you saying the bank is repossessing your home?" she asked, loud enough for anyone sitting nearby to hear. "They *are* chucking you out on the street?"

At that moment, I was worried for Bethany's well-being, afraid Julia would march into her location to administer a severe tongue-lashing, or worse, on my behalf. "Yes. But no," I said. "It's more of a mutual decision rather than them kicking me out."

I explained things in more detail as those at the nearby tables did their best to pretend they weren't listening when I suspected they were. I revealed how I'd been open and honest with Bethany, admitting how I wasn't confident that I'd be able to catch up on my mortgage arrears anytime soon, if at all. And when you factored in the rising interest rates, this only further served to compound my financial woes. I then told Bethany I'd only purchased the house to satisfy my then-girlfriend's expanded ego, and joked that I hadn't stepped foot in some of the rooms for months.

And this wasn't so much of a joke, even, as there were two spare bedrooms in the home with en-suite bathrooms, for instance, in which I couldn't be certain if the plumbing still worked because I hadn't bothered to turn the handle on either of the faucets in ages. Having said that, it wasn't as if I didn't adore the home, because I did. The location of the place was wonderful, and you couldn't ask for better neighbours.

But the truth of the matter was that I couldn't really afford to live there. It was as simple as that. And to continue to do so would mean hiding from my postman on a regular basis and pretending to anyone on the outside looking in that all was well in the world of Adam Catchpole. When it wasn't. Financially speaking, at least. On the other hand, my mental health and general outlook were the best it'd been in months. I was happy. I just no longer wanted, nor needed, an oversized country pile where I couldn't even afford to put the bloody heating on.

Hearing this, Bethany got busy on her computer to calculate a redemption figure for my mortgage. Then, if I remained firm on the idea, I could stick my house on the market and settle what I owed to the bank. Hopefully, depending on the final sale price, I would have enough equity remaining to put an adequate deposit down on something more modest. Well, that was the plan at this current stage.

The minute she offered me a way of escaping a world of hiding from correspondence with red ink stamped on the front in bold, I knew that's precisely what I wanted. Like my Porsche, I no longer needed a status symbol that I couldn't afford, just to try and make me feel good about myself. I suppose I did for a time. But I was no longer that person. Because now, I was remotivated and optimistic about my writing.

In Julia and Evie, I also had two extraordinary ladies in my life. On top of that, I was having a lovely time helping out with a dance group. And on top of *that*, I now had a part-time job as well that I couldn't wait to attend to. After all, where else do you get to drive a group of absolute legends around a wonderful little island and spend your afternoon watching a goat trample all over them?

"You already look more relaxed, Adam," Julia said sympathetically, holding my hand after listening patiently to my explanation. "And if it means you're not constantly worrying about money all the time, then it can only be good, right?"

Gabby, the waitress, appeared with our lunch just as Jack had promised, placing it on the table. "Heya. Special delivery," she said cheerfully. "So, it's the first performance this evening of the show's extended run, yeah?" she asked by way of conversation.

"Sure is," I replied. "You coming?"

"I wouldn't miss it for the world," Gabby assured me. "I'm also bringing my sister and her kids," she informed us. "I couldn't get any tickets for them previously, despite knowing the owner of the place," she said with a laugh. "Well, cheers, then. I hope you both enjoy your quiche."

And we did. Enjoy the quiche, that is. Which was polished off in short order so that Julia could return to work on time. Not that I had the luxury of too much time, either, as I'd need to collect the minibus soon to fetch the troops and bring them to another goat yoga session. "Thank you," I said, gazing fondly at Julia from my spot across the table.

"What for? You're the one who paid for the lunch today," Julia pointed out.

"For being in my life," I advised. Which, on reflection, was probably one of the most romantic things that'd ever come out of my mouth.

Julia motioned as if she was going to place two fingers down her throat, threatening to regurgitate her lunch. But of course she was only teasing me. (Or at least I hoped so!)

"You're not a bad catch yourself, Adam Catchpole," she replied. "Ooh, you see what I did right there with the clever wordplay?" she asked. "Maybe *I'm* the one meant to be the author, rather than…"

I wasn't listening now, however. Not at the present moment. I absolutely wasn't trying to be rude, of course, but I had spotted an email notification on the screen of my phone. I hoped it was from Bethany, who advised me earlier that she would send a note with the redemption figure on my mortgage. Then I'd know roughly how much I had left to play with once the bank was repaid. I could then figure out if I'd be able to afford a nice little flat somewhere, or whether I'd soon be living in a tent on Douglas Beach.

"Apologies, Julia. Let me quickly see if this message is from the bank, and then I'll walk you back to your car, all right?" I said, rising from the table and slipping my jacket on while juggling my phone between my hands. Once the business of getting my jacket on was sorted, I pressed the email icon on my mobile and immediately recognised the sender's name. "Oh, my God!" I said, looking up from the screen. My knees felt wobbly, and my phone-wielding hand started to tremble.

"Adam...? It's not any bad news, is it?" Julia asked, looking very concerned. "Has the bank changed their mind? Or something else? Something worse...?"

"It's, erm... no, it's not an email from the bank," I replied weakly, opening up and then scrolling through the body of the message. "This is crazy..."

"Adam, what's the matter? *Adam*? Adam, you look like you've just seen a ghost."

"It's not a ghost, though pretty close to it," I said as I placed my phone inside my trouser pocket. "It's an email from an old friend of mine I've not heard from for over thirty years."

Julia appeared relieved that it wasn't notification about someone's sudden illness or death or being struck by a bus or some such thing. "Oh, well that's good, then, yeah? Who's it from?"

I was still reeling from the shock at seeing the particular name on the screen, so it took me a moment to respond.

"It's... it's a message from a friend from school who lived on the same street as us when we were both kids," I explained. "It's from Robert. It's from my old mate, Robert Bentham..."

Chapter Thirty

In what felt like little more than the blink of an eye, the second string of performances passed in no time at all. The cast and crew of *Santa's Training School for Christmas Elves* were understandably gutted when the curtain came down, one final time, on the extended run of shows. Yes, everybody was a bit downhearted. But as Chloe made a point to remind the group at the wrap party, "It's *not* the end! Because we'll all be back, performing this show at the Gaiety Theatre next Christmas, yes?"

It was the thought of coming back and doing it all again that effectively raised everyone's spirits. The journey wasn't over.

Although I couldn't help but notice that Jack Tate wasn't his usual self when I spoke with him over a glass of fizz.

"Well, I suppose it's because I've just really enjoyed having you lot around upstairs," he explained, when I questioned his glum expression.

I could completely understand where he was coming from, as the positive energy radiating from the performers was infectious. However, as I reminded him, it would be some time before Tappin' Feet HQ was habitable once more, so the generous offer to use his studio could continue for the foreseeable if he was prepared to endure putting up with all of us a bit more. A situation he said he was more than happy to accommodate for as long as required.

To thank Jack and Emma for being such gracious, lovely hosts, Chloe presented them with a photo of the cast, framed alongside a programme signed by the entire troupe. Now, I didn't take Jack for being the emotional type, but he was blubbing the moment he set eyes on the gift.

Similar to the initial run, the second release of tickets had been snapped up in no time, with some previous attendees even having returned to enjoy another performance. The healthy ticket sales had undoubtedly been helped along by the glowing review in the local newspaper, whose headline read: *"A festive musical extravaganza simply oozing with local talent and charm."*

While this wholly positive assessment was most gratefully received by all, there was also the small matter of the show's commerciality under review, as this was, after all, the reason for staging the production on short notice in the first place. As we knew from the beginning, the significant numbers appearing in the cast reduced the number of spectator seats available for purchase, as there were only so many warm bodies that could safely and legally be crammed into the upper-floor studio at one time. However, taking into account the revenue generated from ticket sales, plus the money earned from the refreshment stand, it was still an amount not to be sneezed at. Just over thirteen thousand pounds had been raised altogether, when all was said and done. Money that would flow directly into the TAPPIN' FEET headquarters rebuild costs.

Yes, there was still some way to go, financially speaking. But the collective efforts of all involved had taken a significant bite out of the total amount needed. And knowing Chloe Tappin as I now did, I understood she would likely never rest until her dance school was properly back in action. It was too important both to her and the community. She also had the benefit of knowing a small army of people were ready, willing, and able to volunteer their services as and when required, myself included.

One slight advantage of the show's ending—if there could be such an advantage to that, at least—was that I would have more open time in my diary. Accordingly, I started to think about what book I'd jump into next. Considering I'd ended up enjoying writing the book just submitted to my agent, the front-runner in my mind was to start working on its sequel. Although, I'd first need to wait for Milly to get back to me and let me know if she thought the first one was any good!

Away from musical and literary concerns, I'd also recently been along to meet with the estate agents. Considering that it was very near to Christmas at present, they suggested I ought to wait until early January before listing my property. But they had no doubt it wouldn't be on the market for too long before it was snatched up. Fortunately, several smaller properties on their books were ideal for me and, crucially, within range of my more modest budget. So I hopefully didn't need to go shopping for a new tent.

As it would likely be my last Christmas in my current house, I'd somehow offered to host Christmas dinner. It was a moment of madness fuelled by red wine that first planted the idea in my head. And before you knew it, I'd invited my sister and her family, my mum, Julia and Evie, Carol my neighbour, and Chloe.

For me, bangers and mash with gravy was regarded as a fine, gourmet meal in my kitchen. As such, by the time I'd put my empty wine bottle in the recycling bin the following morning after my bright idea, I was already starting to doubt my ability to serve up a three-course meal to nine people. Still, all wasn't lost because I had a culinary ace up my sleeve, somebody who was a dab hand around the kitchen and was more than happy to lend aid in ensuring I didn't poison my guests. And this was none other than Carol, my fantastic neighbour who I'd miss more than anything when my house eventually went on the market and sold.

All in all, I'd resigned myself to moving out of my home. Sure, I'd miss the place. But I certainly wouldn't miss the extortionate and eye-watering mortgage payments. I still hadn't got around to giving Barry the cat the news about our impending move. Being both an indoor and an outdoor cat, I knew he had quite an active social life in the area, so I wasn't entirely sure how he'd react to us upping sticks for pastures new. I felt confident that Barry was the adaptable sort, however, so I had no concerns that he'd settle in wherever we went and wouldn't struggle to make new friends.

And I was pleased to also have another friend in my life, as it should happen. Since my last visit to my dad's grave on his birthday, I'd been thinking a lot about Robert and my childhood. There was always a sense of melancholy in remembering these things previously, particularly during the run-up to Christmas. But lately I've been reflecting on the nicer memories, such as carefree summer afternoons out playing football or cycling with my mates, or other times where you couldn't wait to get home to get changed out of your school uniform and spend the remainder of your day out exploring or maybe building a base out of old wooden pallets and a tarpaulin "borrowed" from a local building site.

But as far as that fateful day in 1984, I had heard nothing about Robert since then. He never returned to our school, and seemed to just vanish off the face of the earth. In case my memory of events was sketchy, I'd recently asked my mum if she knew what had become of him. But like me, she too was none the wiser, aside from hearing some simple 'over the fence' gossip at the time.

Curious, I searched social media, hoping to locate him that way, but that avenue bore no fruit. With limited other options at my disposal, I Googled his name and eventually came across a website for a marine biological company in the south of England. It listed a Robert Bentham as working as one of their team, along with a headshot photo and his work contact details. I wasn't convinced it was the same person, as it had been many years since I'd seen him and of course no one looks the same as they did when they were a kid. But from what I could recall of his face, there might have been a vague similarity...?

Fast forward to two weeks later when I got a response, with an email from Robert dropping into my inbox. It was him. It was my old friend Robert Bentham, whom I'd not seen for close to thirty-five years.

We've since spoken a couple of times, which I found to be quite an emotional experience, though not an unpleasant one. Robert didn't go into too much detail about what happened to him back then, but from what he did say, he was taken away from his father and ended up having a happy and loving childhood with an adoptive family in the UK, plus reconnecting with his mum later on as well. He now had a son, he told me—a son who by all accounts was obsessed with all things Lego, just like we were as kids!

I was delighted for Robert. Pleased he'd made a success with his life after what was a pretty miserable start. He was thrilled when I suggested we meet up the next time I was over in the UK. I would have proposed a visit over here for him, but I suspected he may not be so keen on returning, even after the passage of years.

Reconnecting with Robert felt like I'd finally answered a question on my mind since I was a child. I was already looking forward to Christmas for the first time in I didn't know how long. And now, speaking with Robert as well was the icing on my yule log.

Chapter Thirty-One

Why did nobody ever inform me how much a Christmas turkey and the trimmings to feed nine people, plus me, would cost? I now felt guilty for all the times I'd eaten my own body weight in turkey and such at other people's homes.

I thought I was being organised, at least, in pre-ordering what I needed from the butchers with an agreed pick-up time on Christmas Eve afternoon, at which point I would take care of some of my other shopping as well. But... *Jayzus*, the town centre was bloody chaos. People were running about with a mixture of confusion and panic written on their faces and numerous plastic shopping bags weighing them down.

And talk about the season of goodwill. A frail old dear who must have been in her eighties shoulder-barged me out of the way when she thought I was heading towards the one last box of Christmas crackers in Marks & Spencer. It was a good thing I looked over my shoulder first, as I was just about to give the offending party a good tongue-lashing, and I wouldn't have liked trying to explain myself to store security as to why I was arguing with a blue-haired octogenarian.

And then, as I was stuck in a considerable queue at the toyshop while picking up a gift for Evie—a considerable queue that refused to advance—I started reverting to my old ways of thinking. *Bloody Christmas*, I grumbled.

This was fortunately just a blip, however. Because by the time I finally reached the front of the queue, I'd already reminded myself of how my life had changed for the better. Yes, it was busy in town, with everybody walking about with sharpened elbows. But I convinced myself to simply relax about the situation, even managing to ignore the toddler behind me who somehow thought it would be a marvellous idea to kick me repeatedly in the calf muscle. A few months ago, I might have considered kicking the little hellion back. But not now. I'd changed.

While the painful recollection of a particular Christmas from many years ago was still present, I could push it to the back of my mind. The reason for this was the arrival of more recent, enjoyable memories that served to dilute the pain and distress. Of course, I knew the pain from these older memories would never entirely go away. But I felt much better equipped to deal with them now. Even with the current toddler-based assault on the back of my legs to contend with.

Once I had the harried shop assistant's attention, I handed over a fifty-pound note to purchase a piece of moulded plastic that may or may not get played with once or twice before being consigned to the back of the wardrobe. But rather than reflect on whether it was possible I could be wasting my money, I chose to focus instead on the joy on little Evie's face that was sure to occur when I handed the gift-wrapped present to her.

I smiled at this realisation, for I had Carol's theory about "the sentiment" rattling around my cranium again. She was absolutely spot on. Some achieve "the sentiment" by watching cheesy Christmas films. Those weren't for me, really. So, as Carol had suggested at the time, I needed to get outside and do something selfless. And when I did, my life indeed had changed for the better. Although, replaying those last few words in my mind nearly made me gag, as it was the perfect, cheesy blurb to advertise one of those ridiculously cheesy films.

I planned on suggesting that Carol write a self-help book about the subject. Because if she could turn a miserable old introvert into the epitome of festive cheer in less than two months, then I reckoned she would be onto a winner. If only she knew of a talented author who could help her write it and share the royalties!

Well, I was the epitome of Christmas cheer right until I presented myself before the butcher and was handed the invoice for my turkey with assorted trimmings. At that moment, I felt like running home and attacking my Christmas tree with a chainsaw! Fortunately, I owned no such chainsaw.

✳ ✳ ✳

The glorious smell of a roasting turkey, in addition to the warming sensation of a malt whisky sliding down my throat, did wonders to restore my goodwill. As such, my Christmas tree was safe from harm and remained upright and intact.

When I was a child, I recall being given a slice of freshly cooked meat shortly before going to bed on Christmas Eve. There was just something wonderful about the scent of turkey wafting for hours through the house until it was done—and lingering afterwards, in fact. Sadly, on this occasion, the tantalising aroma wasn't gracing my own home because the bloody huge bird I bought earlier in the day wouldn't fit inside my oven! Thankfully, Carol and her significantly more spacious oven came to my rescue. And that's where I had the pleasure of spending the latter portion of my Christmas Eve, keeping my turkey company at Carol's house.

However, I couldn't quite put my finger on it, but Carol didn't seem her usual bubbly self. For a self-confessed Christmas-a-holic, I assumed she would be bounding around the house like Winnie-the-Pooh's friend Tigger. But Carol was subdued, appearing a bit down in the dumps, even, if I was interpreting her mood correctly. More like Eeyore than Tigger just now, it seemed to me.

"You're sure I'm not disturbing your evening?" I asked, worried I was intruding on her peace and quiet. And then I thought about her husband, who'd not long passed. Perhaps this was a difficult time of year for her, I wondered.

Carol waved away my concerns. "I'm good," she said. "After all, it's Christmas Eve, I've got my best festive jumper on, and I'm holding my finest crystal whisky glass. Even if it *is* empty…"

I didn't need asking twice to act as a barkeep. "Shall I top our glasses up?" I asked, rising from the sofa. "And I could crack open that box of chocolates I brought over as well?"

"Sounds like a plan," Carol agreed.

Once into the kitchen, I took a gander through the glass of the oven door, carefully inspecting the magnificent beast held captive inside. I didn't know exactly what I was hoping to accomplish by this, but it made me feel like I was doing my bit. "The turkey looks good! It's coming along splendidly!" I shouted to Carol, as I poured us both a generous measure from the bottle of twenty-year-old Glenfiddich in her kitchen.

"Smells good, too," Carol said, appearing in the kitchen behind me. "Another couple of hours, and it should be done."

"Oh, I would've brought this over to you," I said, handing Carol her drink. I wasn't sure why she'd followed me into the kitchen, and I was still troubled by her uncustomary, subdued demeanour. "You don't seem yourself today, Carol," I offered. "Feel free to tell me to keep my nose out of it if you want, but is everything okay?"

Carol swirled the honey-coloured liquid around her glass, looking like she wanted to say something but wasn't sure quite how to go about it. "Adam…" she said after a moment, still gazing down at her glass. "Adam, there's something I've been meaning to talk to you about. In fact, you've been on my mind constantly for the last couple of days…"

If she didn't appear so serious and earnest right now, I'd have thought Carol was leading up to the punchline of some sort of joke. "Erm… what? You have?" I asked.

Carol took a sip from her crystal glass. Then, with her eyes now fixed on mine, she whispered softly. "Adam, I like having you so close to me," she advised. "And a thought's occurred to me…"

At this point, I could feel my left eye start to twitch.

"Carol, I'm not… It's not that… I mean, you know that I'm fond of you, of course. But I don't…" I stammered. I then downed my whisky, all of it, in one go, before continuing. "Carol, you do know that I have a girlfriend, don't you? A girlfriend you'll be seeing at our Christmas dinner tomorrow…?"

Carol tilted her head slightly, staring at me hard, as if there was something seriously wrong with me. "Adam," she said.

"Yeah…?"

"You're an idiot!"

I had no idea what was going on at this point.

"Ehm… another whisky…?" I asked with a nervous laugh. "Oh wait, you're not ready for… I mean, that was me that just drank… Uhm, maybe I'll just pour myself an additional…"

"Adam, do you honestly think I was hitting on you just then?" Carol asked, incredulous. "I mean, *seriously*? I'm old enough to be your mum!"

I started squirming, shifting my weight from one foot to the other anxiously. I was never any good in these sorts of situations. Situations, that is, where I'm making an arse of myself.

"I, erm… Carol, I don't really know what I ought to be saying just now. Um… another drink? Oh, wait, you don't—"

"Adam, will you bloody relax? The thing I actually wanted to talk to you about was your *house*."

"Oh. Oh, right," I replied. "What about it?" I asked, doing my best to relax as instructed.

"Well, I wondered what you'd think if I considered *buying* it, is what," Carol revealed.

Carol then clarified what'd been on her mind, explaining how she had a chunk of money that was doing nothing but languishing in her bank account. (An excellent problem to have, I pointed out.) She described how she'd never been too interested in stocks and shares and that sort of thing, but was more comfortable putting money into bricks and mortar—something tangible—if she knew the area well. And as she lived across the road from my home, it's fair to say she was familiar with the area. However, she was reluctant to proceed because she hadn't wanted me to think she was somehow capitalising on my misfortune.

"Don't worry about that for a moment. Honestly, I'd rather my home went to a… well, to a good home," I assured her. "And I can think of nobody better than you to buy it."

"Thing is, if I did, I'd need a *tenant*…" Carol replied, raising an eyebrow in anticipation of my response. She didn't say anything else just yet, waiting first for her words to penetrate my brain.

"What? Do you mean *me*…?" I asked.

"If you'd like to, yes. That way, you'll have no rush to move out, or to panic about having to find another home somewhere else to purchase," Carol answered. "Plus, we can come up with an agreeable, manageable amount for rent that'll help you get financially back on your feet."

I was exceptionally fond of my house. I just couldn't afford the present mortgage. So this was an offer that was too good to be true. Only, miracle of miracles, it *was* true.

"Aww, Carol, that— that would be amazing. I'm gobsmacked. I don't even know how to thank you for this."

"I'd expect you to mow my lawn periodically, whenever it needs it," Carol immediately replied, evidently having given this some prior thought. I wasn't sure if she was joking or serious about this requirement, but I would absolutely have no problem mowing her lawn for the rest of my days if that's what she so desired!

I held out my hand. "It's a deal," I said. "Only…"

"Only?"

"If you take me, you take Barry the cat."

"Deal. I'd never break the partnership up," Carol replied, shaking my hand, which she didn't immediately release. Then, as she applied firm, increasing pressure, she menacingly stared me down. "Just earlier," she said, her eyes narrowing. "Just earlier when you were convinced I was hitting on you. Why didn't you *immediately* snatch me up? Are you implying that I'm not a catch?"

I offered an exaggerated gulp, once again unsure if Carol was joking. "Carol, if Julia and I ever break up, your name will be the first on my dance card," I promised her. "Now, can you please let go of my hand…? You're squeezing so tightly I think you might be in danger of breaking some phalanges."

❊ ❊ ❊

Since Stacey my ex left, I wasn't bothering with Christmas decorations until only recently. She hadn't been especially fussed about them either, back when we were together, but we had at least felt the collective pressure to do something, even if it was simply a garland hanging on the front door or an anaemic-looking tree visible through the living room window.

I could never get my head around the sort of people who would spend days covering every available surface of their house, garden, lawn, and driveway in flashing lightbulbs, only to have to spend the same amount of time taking it all back down again a few weeks later. All I could think about was the ginormous electricity bill to pay for a pointless display you couldn't even see when you were inside of the house. I mean, where was the logic in that?

But that was then. Because now I got it. I understood why folks risked life and limb to venture up their ladder to decorate their roofs each year and place additional strain on the National Grid.

Earlier in the week, I'd been over at Julia's house when I was dispatched to pick up some snacks for movie night. Accompanied on my walk to the shops by Evie, she insisted we take the scenic route so she could marvel at all the Christmas lights around the neighbourhood. Evie hardly spoke a word for somebody so often a chatterbox, instead captivated by the sparkling garden displays, flashing window fairy lights, and rooftops covered in strips of multicoloured bulbs. There was even one property where festive music was being pumped out through a speaker concealed in a fibreglass snowman. Only a few short months ago, I would have viewed this as a complete waste of time, money, and effort. In short, a load of bollocks. But seeing Evie's look of wonderment, I understood it.

The property owners probably weren't overly concerned about their electricity bill, or, for that matter, how much time it took to create their illuminated display. They did it to make others happy. They did it to selflessly inject some of the Christmas magic they'd experienced as children, and continued to experience as adults, so that the likes of Evie could appreciate it too.

Now, rather than look at these people as silly muppets, wasting their hard-earned cash for no good reason, I saw them for who they were—generous people who simply wanted to share that feeling of yuletide warmth and charm with their neighbours.

And that realisation was the reason I now had a six-foot plastic snowman with a sparkly carrot nose and flashing buttons on its chest, standing on guard duty in my front garden. Sadly, I had no budget to purchase any friends for him. Although, to be fair, I had left it late, as the shop shelves were all but bare apart from "Mister Freeze," as he'd been subsequently christened by Evie.

Not everybody was a fan of the snowman, however. Barry the cat wasn't sure about the new arrival, as the increasing number of scratch marks on Mister Freeze's plastic base would confirm. Not that I could blame ol' Baz, mind you. After all, for years he'd been in the company of a miserable, introverted sod for whom January couldn't come soon enough. But I'd try and work on him. And once he enjoyed a slice of my succulent turkey, I reckoned he'd also start to enjoy the festive period just as much as I was.

I'd been making shuttle runs across the street to Carol's house throughout Christmas morning. Not only was my oven not up to the task when I'd needed it most, but I realised I was painfully underprepared to host a meal for more than two people. Fortunately, Carol was the hospitable type who, unlike me, owned more than two dinner plates and two pieces of cutlery. Oh, and she owned a gravy boat. And wine glasses. And a festive table runner also. And, well, pretty much everything, as it should happen. She truly was a godsend. With her considerable help, I had both a turkey cooked to perfection and enough plates and such to feed all my guests.

By four o'clock that afternoon, the sumptuous feast had been effectively demolished. And with Carol's happy collusion, Mum was already on her second bottle of red. I suspected the pair would become good friends because they were getting on like a house on fire with a shared appreciation of the grape.

And after a few drinks, I knew what was coming: Mum and my sister Helen were in my ear telling me how wonderful Julia was, and how she was too good for me, really, and I was so lucky to have her. In the kitchen while warming the brandy sauce for pudding, they snuck in to say just how surprised and proud of me they were following the shame and horror of the viral video debacle several months ago. Ever supportive, my mum and my sis.

"Oh. Did I say I love the rubbish Christmas decorations?" Helen casually remarked, grazing on the cheeseboard once outside the kitchen again and moving over to the living room.

"Oi! They cost me a fortune from the pound shop!" I protested. "In fact, I think I'm now their best customer. They even offered me a gold loyalty card."

Helen looked worried that she had perhaps offended me. "No, I didn't mean it like that at all," she said. "It's just that they remind me of our house when we were kids," she advised, taking another admiring gander at my ceiling—a ceiling draped in gold and ruby-red foil garlands stretching from each of the four corners before meeting in the middle. "They make me smile."

I knew precisely what she meant. Although she was indeed correct—they were rubbish, and a nostalgic throwback to a time gone by. Any young person peering inside my house would likely think I'd gone mad or was stuck in a time warp because of my naff decorations. But I didn't mind. After all, they were simply intended to make people smile. So, mission accomplished, as far as I was concerned.

"Did I tell you how much I love my new earrings?" Julia said as I toured the room, topping up the champagne flutes I'd borrowed from an accommodating Carol.

"Hmm, yes, you may have mentioned it once or twice," I replied, gratefully accepting the puckered lips Julia thrust towards me. "I'm pleased you like them."

Julia then drew my attention to Evie, who was kneeling on the carpet near the Christmas tree. "And who knew you had your finger on the pulse of what to buy a five-year-old girl?" she remarked.

"Well, I figured you can't go wrong with a doll's house."

"Did you have one when you were a little boy, by any chance?" Julia teased. "Because that would be very cute if you did."

"No, but I may have played with my sister's a few times. But if you tell her, then..."

"My lips are sealed," Julia promised. But then, turning to face Helen at the other side of the room: "Helen! Wait until I tell you what I've just heard about your brother..."

Even though most of my guests claimed they were "absolutely stuffed" after the generous dinner we'd had, it didn't stop everyone from putting their hand up at the offer of Christmas pudding or the trifle that Mum had brought along. So, after another quick dart across the street to collect some pudding bowls from Carol's house, we all reconvened around the dinner table.

"I'd like to propose a toast before we all get stuck into dessert," I said, after checking that everyone's glasses were topped up—and with Evie's glass, along with my two nephews, Helen's boys, being filled with sparkling grape juice instead of wine. Except I wasn't sure what to offer up for a toast, really, because I hadn't thought it through that far in advance.

As I stood there, my mind drifted back to memories past. I remembered walking through Scatty Newbold's shop, intent on buying a Christmas tree. I thought about my dad insisting on making us drink a cup of tea on Christmas morning when all I wanted to do was kick the living room door open and rip open my presents. I wish that I'd been more patient with him, appreciating now that all he wanted was some quality, quiet time spent sitting together as a family. And finally, Robert Bentham jumped into my mind. But this wasn't an image of him cowering on the floor of his living room being threatened by his dad. Instead, I chose to think of him smiling and happy as we played together with my Lego pieces. A much more pleasant memory.

"Any chance...?" Paul, my sister's husband, interjected. "We're wasting away to nothing over here," he joked, patting his already expanded belly.

"Ah. Sorry," I said, snapping back to the present. "To Christmas and to absent friends," I announced, deciding to keep things short and sweet as I raised my glass.

"To Christmas and to absent friends," came the response, from all gathered.

"Ah!" I then said, before spoons could be deployed. "I also have a special announcement to make while I have your attention!"

I maybe shouldn't have just said that as I just did, as all eyes instantly turned to Julia, probably expecting me to share news of an impending marriage between the two of us, or perhaps expecting that Julia was in fact expecting, ready to welcome another child into her life in about nine months' time or thereabouts.

"Sorry to disappoint," I said with a chuckle, as I interpreted the expressions around the room. "But this announcement relates to the world of the written word," I clarified. "I have exciting news."

My sister immediately placed her two palms together in a sort of hopeful prayer. "You've heard back from your agent?"

I took a quick sip of my champagne before answering. "Yup, I did indeed! She emailed me, late yesterday," I said. "Who knew a literary agent worked on Christmas Eve?"

"And…?" Julia pressed. "Has she found a publisher for your new book?"

I nodded, raising my glass again. "She sure has. But not the one you're thinking of," I answered cryptically, getting the set of confused looks I'd been expecting. "You see, I actually sent my agent two books for consideration at the same time."

"Have you been drinking that brandy sauce before we started in on our champagne?" Julia asked. "*What* second book?"

I flashed a smile towards Evie. "Evie, I hope you don't mind," I said. "But I also took the liberty of sending my agent Milly a copy of Santa's Training School for Christmas Elves."

Evie suddenly tuned back into the adults' boring conversation, her ears perking right up. "Oh? Did she like it…?" she asked.

"Like it, Evie? She absolutely loved it! And so did the publisher she sent it to."

I explained to Evie and the rest of my guests that Milly had received interest from *multiple* publishers, as it should happen, from which my agent had the wonderful problem of having to select the most favourable offer. In practical terms, this meant the book Evie and I created would now be distributed by a major publisher and appear in bookshops all over the UK and beyond.

"You mean I'm going to be a famous author?" Evie asked. "Like the Harry Potter lady?"

"Oh, I should think so, Evie," I advised. Then, shifting my attention to Chloe, "It should also result in regular financial contributions to Tappin' Feet's bank account," I said.

Chloe looked lost for words, initially. "Adam, you don't need to do that," she told me.

"*Pfft*," I said. "Evie, do we need to do that?"

"Hell, yeah!"

Julia gave her daughter a meaningful glare. "Evie! Language!" she admonished.

"Hell… *yes*…?" Evie offered, revising her words, although obviously not in the way her mum had intended.

All Julia could do was shake her head and sigh, and after everyone was finished having a good laugh, Julia raised a finger to ask me a question. "So what about the initial book you submitted?"

"Yeah," Carol added in. "What about that first Christmas book you were so reluctantly writing? When's that going to be seen on the bookshelves?"

However, I didn't have quite the same positive news to share in that regard. At least not yet. "Millicent tells me she's still shopping it around," I advised. "But she's quietly confident it'll get snapped up by a publisher soon. Although…"

"Although?" Julia said, looking like she was about to throw her spoon at me for including too many pauses introduced for added dramatic effect. "Although, *what*?"

"Although… I didn't eventually write the reluctant Christmas novel I spoke about. Not precisely," I revealed. "Instead, I combined that with the other idea my agent had suggested, blending the two categories together."

I could see the cogs whirring inside Evie's mind as she thought back to recall our previous conversation. "Adam, does that mean you added in bits about spicy pepper and chilli powder to the book as well?" she asked, referring to when I mentioned to her about the other genre my agent told me was very popular, to which Evie had of course misunderstood.

"Uhm… Yeah. There *are* a lot of spicy bits in it," I admitted, and it wasn't exactly a lie. "And you know what? It turns out I'm pretty flippin' good at writing spicy stories."

I raised my glass again, looking slowly around the dinner table.

"Cheers, all! Here's to a most wonderful Christmas and a Happy New Year!"

The End

The author hopes you enjoyed this novel. If you did, he'd be honoured if you were kind enough to leave feedback on Amazon. You can view all of the author's other fine books (including the further exploits of the gang from The Lonely Heart Attack Club) and get in touch via his website:

www.authorjcwilliams.com

Printed in Great Britain
by Amazon

55144495R00158